He was ready to s   d
towards the town   rt
watering a new e   ot
yet. America was w........ ....re
he'd begin. He might, he thought, even choose to stay
when he'd destroyed everyone on his list. It had been a
long time since he'd lived a life in England: practically
a hundred years. It was certainly something to think
about. So much to think about. So much to plan. A
whole new life, in fact.

Also by Andrea Hart

A MIND TO KILL

and published by Corgi Books

THE RETURN

Andrea Hart

CORGI BOOKS

THE RETURN
A CORGI BOOK : 0 552 14623 4

First publication in Great Britain

PRINTING HISTORY
Corgi edition published 1999

Set in 10/12pt Sabon by Kestrel Data, Exeter, Devon.

Corgi Books are published by Transworld Publishers Ltd,
61–63 Uxbridge Road, London W5 5SA,
in Australia by Transworld Publishers,
c/o Random House Australia Pty Ltd,
20 Alfred Street, Milsons Point, NSW 2061,
in New Zealand by Transworld Publishers,
c/o Random House New Zealand,
18 Poland Road, Glenfield, Auckland
and in South Africa by Transworld Publishers Ltd,
c/o Random House (Pty) Ltd,
Endulini, 5a Jubilee Road, Parktown 2193.

Reproduced, printed and bound in Great Britain by
Cox & Wyman Ltd, Reading, Berks.

For Nicholas and Helen
with love.

Prologue

The name was unimportant, one of the few accidents of rebirth, but for this return it was Harold Taylor and he was a reincarnation. He also killed people.

Unlike others who believed themselves to have had previous lives, Taylor most definitely knew: doubly unique, he had total and perfect recall of each existence.

As Myron Nolan he'd taken Mafia tuition on New York's mob-controlled waterfront to make millions as a US Army quartermaster sergeant during and after the Second World War.

He'd discovered the advantages of a military existence – the ability to steal and to kill with impunity – serving as Patrick Arnold in the British Army in the First World War, which had also given him his first experience of a court-martial and on that occasion a firing squad that had reduced that life to his shortest ever.

Until the public recognition had been so cruelly – wrongly – taken from him, his favourite had been as Maurice Barkworth, a name still listed in the medical reference books of the late nineteenth century, for almost twenty years of which he'd been fêted as one of London's leading surgeons, specializing in the experimental treatment of the human eye.

He'd qualified as a doctor in America, where forty

years previously, as Luke Thomas, he'd travelled West on an early settlers' wagon train as far as the then Spanish-governed town of St Louis to establish the first of his several self-patronized brothels.

It had all begun as Paul Noakes, in the raucous, teeming St James's streets of eighteenth-century London. There, in the temple of his beloved shaman mystic, he'd literally abandoned himself, body and soul. And in exchange been taught the mantras and the blood sacrifices necessary to return from the afterlife. He hadn't, of course, believed it. Not then. Not until his death, when the flames in which his parents destroyed him had begun to melt his first body and he'd felt the agony and then the total, moment-of-death peace of meeting his mystic teacher on the threshold of the afterlife.

Do you want to live again?

Yes.

Water – cultivate – every existence with the blood of others.

That is my pledge.

And your guarantee of rebirth. Do not fail me and I will never fail you.

He enjoyed the killing, which he'd been encouraged to do. Offering the sacrifices, which the shaman, who called himself Tzu – 'master' – appointed him to perform: who'd taught him the ritual dismemberment, which none of the other reincarnation disciples could bring themselves to perform and who therefore respected him, because he could. It was almost as good as the sacrificial ceremonies themselves, having the respect of others.

He'd believed in reincarnation when he'd been reborn in America with the power of absolute recall, of course.

8

And from that time the sacrifices continued, his victims always those who'd offended or harmed him in his previous existence.

This latest time was going to be different, Taylor determined. He'd always remembered and he'd always learned, certainly. But always from the past, never exploring the possibilities of the future.

This return he would. He felt – he was sure – he could transmogrify. Was even more curious to see if he could bodily transfer, possess the presence and mind and soul of another living being, which Tzu had preached was possible. He could return so much more quickly if, at the very moment of death, he immediately possessed another living being. Transmogrify and possess. Both would be wonderful. Exciting.

It was time to start. He was ready.

Chapter One

London – his first home – was always the best, the place he most enjoyed. Every reincarnation was exhilarating but this time – here, where his life had begun centuries ago – he felt an extra excitement, an anticipation.

At that moment, standing amidst the vehicle swirl of a Piccadilly he'd first known as a muddied thoroughfare of hand-hauled and horse-drawn carts, the man this time with the name of Harold Taylor determined to make it particularly special. Not just as he had over the past two hundred years with every return. More. Much more.

Maybe, the most outrageously exciting thought of all, actually to let people – ordinary, stupid, one-life people – know. That would be incredible. Unprecedented. He would become famous. Infamous. Terrify everyone by what he was: what the specially chosen in the super-natural afterlife were capable of. With him, on this occasion Harold Taylor, twenty-five years old, of in-exhaustible private means, the most capable of all. The *super* supernatural.

He'd definitely do it all on this return! Plan it with the care with which he was planning the sacrificial killings of those who'd hurt him – got in his way – the last time and go through the whole paranormal spectrum. Good word, spectrum. An after-image. That's what he'd show

11

everyone. The most sensational after-image, beyond their simple conception. No, not inconceivable. Only inconceivable until he proved he could return from a previous life. Indestructible, no matter how hard the ordinary little people tried to defeat him, obliterate him. Beyond mortal harm. Beyond everything and everyone.

Now was *precisely* the time for everyone to know. To realize and to worship: the world an electronic global village, no-one, anywhere, separated by more than a television satellite or Internet website. Absolutely perfect.

Like the killings in America it had taken him more than a year patiently and unhurriedly to prepare, every victim in their appointed place on his death list, each about to die as and when he, the immortal judge, decided. And now here in England, the last two to be fitted into the orderly, infallible scheme. Just one more afternoon of surveillance, ensuring the bastard who probably deserved to die more than any of the others maintained the pattern he'd so far followed every day and it would all be ready.

Which left the morning for other things: for the reminiscences he'd until now postponed, single-minded in his priorities. For savouring the sights and sounds and smells and memories that went back more than two centuries, sights and sounds no longer here. Not that long since the last time, of course. Just over fifty years. But even in that short time there seemed so many changes. Nothing appeared the same. Everything better. Even the buildings that had been here then, which a lot of them had despite the blitz, looked different. Bigger. Cleaner.

Cleanliness – always so important, no matter who he returned as – was certainly a positive perception. The old buildings, the historic ones that had survived the bombing, had been soot blackened then, like the people who had hurried head bent and war weary among them. Now those same buildings were proudly scoured white and the people who still hurried did so proudly, heads high, confident.

The ethnocentricity was very different, too. Just before the invasion of Europe, the period of his last return, there had been Indians and Sikhs from the then existing Empire and the black cannon fodder from America but the coloured faces then had been in uniform, very few on the streets. Now they were everywhere, yellow and brown and black and every colour in between, in clothes of every style and hue, a polyglot society.

He'd never considered returning as anything but a Caucasian but with his mind so occupied by thoughts of experimentation and sensation-causing he abruptly wondered how difficult it would be to become part of another culture. Probably not difficult at all. There was always the growing up – or had been, so far – in a family of his choice to learn how to behave and adapt and to belong to the current period, even if his personality and perfect recollection of each previous existence remained unaffected and unaltered.

It might one day be an interesting extension to be Indian or black or native American. Or Chinese, as Tzu had been, with his secrets of ancient teachings and rituals, cast out by those who'd taught him, vilified as a black disciple for following the supposed evil instead of the supposed good. Or then again as an animal, as so many religions – the Hindu most devoutly of all – believed to be possible. Or a bird. To be a bird – descendant of another unbelievable creature, the dinosaur – would be truly fascinating, literally soaring above

13

the ordinary people upon whom figuratively he had only ever looked down. But it might not be possible to take the body of another animal and retain the human ability to reason and think. Maybe that would have to remain an unrealized fantasy.

Taylor's immediate destination was the end of an essential pilgrimage and he went directly to it, on the corner of Duke Street and Mason's Yard, although he knew from previous reincarnation visits that the temple – his shrine – wasn't there any longer. Hadn't been for almost two hundred years, since the terrified church authorities had held services of exorcism before physically urging the mob and the militia to raze it to the ground, burn the debris – particularly the symbols – and scatter the ashes, idiotically believing that would destroy its power. They'd been too late. They'd hanged and burned his teacher, not knowing that Tzu had grown tired of returning and already chosen the disciple who'd sworn the pledge. *Give yourself to me, in body, mind and soul and in return I'll grant life after life, mind upon mind. Take blood. Cause blood. Water every existence with the blood of others, of those that offend.* It had been a perfect life, over and over again, the best bargain he'd ever struck, one he'd never for a moment regretted. Nor would he, ever.

For a long time he remained where the temple had once stood, recalling the sacrificial services and how eagerly he'd done whatever was demanded of him. Most vividly of all he could remember the special prayers and incantations and that morning he silently recited them, renewing the promises that in turn enabled him to renew himself after every death.

He only moved when he became aware that by remaining so long in one place, head bowed, he'd

14

attracted the attention of people at a pavement café in Duke Street. Still he didn't hurry, meandering at his leisure through the streets of St James's. Not just the temple had gone. So, too, had the tenement in which he'd originally been born and so many of the landmarks he'd known in that first life.

The buildings seemed much bigger, the streets much wider. But he wasn't sure the atmosphere was better. He'd felt more at home in his true beginning, running the sewered, brazier-lit alleys among the stalls and the barrows, from the meanest selling sour meat to the best like that of Mr Mason who sold the candle-ends they said Mr Fortnum got from the Royal palaces by permission of King George himself.

Noisier then. More dangerous. Everyone grabbing, stealing, fighting to stay alive. Perhaps more at home but hardly safer. Despite his father's job – work that made the family rich, judged by the standards of the day – in these streets he'd cut a lot of purses, becoming expert with the knife, and bundled a lot of skirt-lifted whores – bunters, as they were called then – with money he stole, knee-trembling in the archways or more comfortably in the park that was still there, just ahead.

He walked nostalgically into it, able to find the exact spot, by the lake, where he'd started the terror. Carrie, she'd said her name was. Not a full-time bunter. Scullery maid earning an extra copper. Big tits that had come off clean as a whistle, much easier than the head, which he'd left eyeless – because an eye always had to be offered as a sacrifice to the unseen future – facing Buckingham House, not then the palace it later became for King George.

Taylor retraced his steps past St James's, the palace that had then existed, and up to where he'd killed the

15

others, one in the archway, the other in an alley which wasn't there any longer. What a panic he'd caused! Militia and the Watch on the streets, braziers on every corner for more light, men forming patrols, hullooing one to the other to make themselves braver, the news-sheets talking of a monster and the hand of the Devil himself, not knowing how close to the truth they were. *Water every existence with the blood of others.*

Taylor went out reluctantly onto Piccadilly, where that day's odyssey had begun, crossed it and got to Regent Street, his mind adjusting to another time, another life, another century. Cobbles on the main gaslit avenues that echoed under the horses' hooves and the wheels of the hansom cabs: child brothels – boys and girls – along Pall Mall: silk top hats and frock coats and dresses dusting the ground: the mourning queen, grieving for Albert: of being honoured – sought out for expert opinion – and of being lionized by society hostesses. The house was still there in Harley Street, the nameplate still that of a doctor. What would have become of the laboratory at the back, the basement dissecting room?

Reminded by the striking of an unseen clock, Taylor hailed a taxi, discarding the past on the ride to Waterloo station and then during the short journey to Richmond. He was still fifteen minutes early, getting into position in the side street with a view of the old man's shabby terraced house. The bench on which he sat, appearing to read the *Daily Mail*, had been vandalized and was uncomfortable with two slats missing.

His unsuspecting victim left his house precisely at twelve-thirty, as he had every day that Taylor had been watching, a hunch-shouldered, shuffling figure in a stained raincoat, despite warm spring sunshine. It took

16

him twenty minutes to get to the Almoner's Arms and half an hour to finish the pie and pickles, with two halves of bitter, before shuffling out again. On his way back he bought a *Daily Mirror* at the same newsagent's from which Taylor had earlier got his newspaper.

Taylor filled in the afternoon at the cinema by Richmond Bridge and was back in position fifteen minutes before the old man's Social Services carer arrived, promptly at seven-thirty. She left just as promptly at eight.

He was ready to start the killing, he knew, as he turned towards the town and the railway station: ready to start watering a new existence with blood. But not here, not yet. America was where most had to die, so that's where he'd begin. The old man could wait, until he was ready. He'd do it when he returned to England for the final but necessary stalking of the widow he first located a whole year earlier. He might, he thought, even choose to stay when he'd destroyed everyone on his list. It had been a long time since he'd lived a life in England: practically a hundred years. It was certainly something to think about. So much to think about. So much to plan. A whole new life, in fact.

Chapter Two

Beddows said, 'OK. Life's not fair. The other guy always gets the breaks.' He smiled.

Wesley Powell thought that sometimes Beddows tried just a tad too hard to be Harry-the-Hard-Ass, the headquarters animal who knew all the tricks of Washington survival. Why was he sneering? After the recent fuck-ups maybe he should take lessons. He said: 'Anyone outside recognized it as serial yet?'

Harry Beddows shook his head. 'Texas and Alabama are a long way apart. I hope they don't, for a while. Don't want the son-of-a-bitch trying to be a media star.'

'How did we make the connection?'

'Field offices in San Antonio and Birmingham independently filed reports here. Gal in Research and Records, Amy Halliday, made the computer match.'

'You told the field guys yet?'

'You're the case officer. Down to you.' The division chief hesitated. 'Be good for you to tuck this one away, Wes.'

'You telling me something I need to know?'

'Don't get paranoid.'

It was becoming difficult not to. They still hadn't got a killer for the kidnap case he'd co-ordinated and which had gone as cold as a polar bear's butt. And before that he'd screwed up on a militant group investigation, realizing the lead to their bomb factory too late to prevent six people, one a child, dying in a mall explosion in Des Moines. Powell suspected it was getting difficult for his former friend to keep covering his ass. The unprompted qualification surprised Powell. For the first time he acknowledged he did think of Harry Beddows as a *former* friend. There was still some kind of special relationship, certainly, but since Beddows had got the top job Powell had grown aware of a reserve, a barrier, separating them. It wasn't just professional. In San Diego they'd been a foursome, Beddows and Cathy, he and Ann. But since the divorce from Ann there weren't any more social situations: he couldn't remember the last time he'd been to the Beddowses home. Or even had a drink with Harry, after work.

Powell said, 'It gone to Quantico yet?' The FBI's criminal profiling Behavioral Science Unit was based at the Bureau's violent crime analysis centre at the Virginia training academy.

'This morning,' confirmed Beddows. 'Not a lot for them to work on yet.'

Powell picked up the two case folders. 'A twenty-six-year-old trucker with a twenty-one-year-old hooker and a sixty-six-year-old black ex-con. Why the hell choose them?'

Beddows said, 'You tell me.'

'I will,' said Powell, too casually.

'It's important that you do *exactly* that,' said Beddows, at once and very seriously. 'Keep very closely in touch. Learn to be a team player, not a one man band. That's not the way to get ahead.'

His ass *was* on the line, Powell recognized. And this

19

case had all the hallmarks of being a bastard. Life definitely wasn't fair.

Wesley Powell's first thought at Amy Halliday's entry was that they should have met somewhere other than in his office, somewhere neutral, which would have avoided any superior-to-subordinate difficulty. And was at once astonished at himself. He *was* superior, in grade, experience and authority. They were about to embark upon an investigation in which her participation would, at most, probably be little more than peripheral; her involvement was in recognition of her initial identification of the crimes for what they were. Each and all of which made his office the *only* place to have met. He remained curious at his initial reaction.

The woman certainly didn't act as if she felt subordinate. She came in quite confidently, her face relaxed but not smiling. It was she who offered her hand, a second before Powell.

Vaguely gesturing towards the case files on his desk he said, 'You did well, making the match.'

A smile came at last, although only fleetingly. 'The magic of computer science.'

'Which I don't understand. But surely computers are only as good as the people who operate them.' Amy Halliday was a stand-back-and-think-about girl, not someone about whom an immediate judgement could be made. The word, he supposed, was petite, although she was interestingly full busted beneath the severely practical business suit. The heavy, black-framed spectacles didn't overwhelm the small features, contributing rather than detracting from the studious attractiveness. Behind the glasses the eyes were deeply blue, almost black, and the bobbed hair was black, too. There was no jewellery – no rings at all – apart from a silver cross on a choker chain holding it high at her throat. She looked like the intimidating sort of girl who played chess well and was good at puzzles and quizzes. He hoped she was.

She adjusted her skirt, although without tugging at it, when she sat down and met his obvious examination with a direct stare of her own, allowing her eyes the slightest wander of returned assessment. She said, 'Could be a bastard. No obvious pattern.'

Powell only just avoided a frown at the sort of remark he expected from the professional profilers at Quantico rather than from a computer jockey in Research and Analysis. 'It'll come, maybe with the next killing.'

'You going to create a task force?'

The directness was unexpected in the watch-your-back artifice of Pennsylvania Avenue. She'd proved herself good at her job, he remembered: perhaps she regarded that as her strength. Harry Beddows was obviously impressed – as Powell himself was increasingly becoming – and Beddows wouldn't risk his own self-preservation with anyone he considered second rate. He said, 'That's the way it's done. Deciding where to establish it is going to be a problem, if he goes on striking as far apart as this.'

'My section head's made me available. With this much territory to cover you're going to need a lot of technological back-up . . .' The smile came again, as quickly as before. 'That's if you want me aboard, of course. You might have other people in mind.' She'd accessed his personnel file before the meeting – pulled his photograph up on her screen – but hadn't quite got the right impression. Crinkled hair that probably didn't need combing a lot, square featured with a tiny cleft in the chin, brown eyed; athletic body – broad shouldered,

21

narrow hipped – although the file didn't mention any sport. It was the attitude the photograph hadn't been able to catch, the eye-to-eye, what-you-see-is-what-you-get insouciance. No, not insouciance. That indicated a conceited casualness and she didn't imagine him uncaring, despite the recent screw-ups. Properly sure of himself, she corrected. In different times and in different circumstances it might have been interesting to find out a lot more about Wesley James Powell not included in his already closely studied personnel file. But now was very definitely not that time. She'd got the professional break she'd angled so hard for and she wasn't going to be distracted from that in any shape or form, even if that shape looked intriguing under the sports jacket and button-down Oxford.

Powell was asking himself questions. Was the self-assurance, bordering on conceit, genuine? Or forced, to impress him? Whichever, it was succeeding. 'I don't have anything – or anyone – in mind at the moment.'

'You'll need premises. Computer facilities and filing and record staff back-up. My discipline.'

Powell smiled wryly. 'Sounds like you've got it all worked out.'

'I have, as much as can be worked out at the moment.'

He found her honesty unsettling and knew a lot of word manipulators at Pennsylvania Avenue would, too. 'You're telling me I can't do without you?'

'That's the message,' she said. There was a hopefulness in her attitude. 'I really would like to be part of whatever team you put together.'

'Why don't we agree that you are?'

Her smile was dazzling. 'I was worried I came on too strongly.'

'It worked, didn't it?'

'I won't let you down. This is important to me.'

'I already got that impression. I think it's important to both of us.' Was that an admission he should have made to someone he didn't know? Amy Halliday was a disarming person, quite unlike anybody he'd ever encountered before in Research and Analysis.

She said, 'What do you want me to do, while you're away?'

'There's not much you *can* do, on what we've got at the moment.'

'You mind if I get everything that there is, in Texas and Alabama, sent up? There are templates I could start, for a proper database later.'

She certainly seemed in one hell of a rush. But wasn't that what they were supposed to be? 'Go ahead.'

The smile came again. 'Thank you. For everything.'

'Let's hope it works.'

'It will.'

Wesley Powell left a message on Ann's answering machine but she didn't return the call so he telephoned again. She answered on the second ring.

'I called before,' he complained.

'I've only just got in. I haven't had time to get back to you.' His former wife was a teacher at the Arlington school quite close to the Key Bridge.

'Is Beth there?'

'She's gone to a movie.'

'She's thirteen years old.'

'So's Jennifer, who's in her class. And Jennifer's sister is seventeen, OK?'

'What's the movie?'

There was a sigh, from the other end. 'Disney. You got something to say to me, Wes?'

No, he thought. Hadn't had, for years. Not ever. He'd never have married her if she hadn't been pregnant. Why she *had* become pregnant, he was sure. To get away from the three-kids-in-a-bed existence in the San Diego clapboard and the straying-hands father. Anyone would have done. It had just happened to be him. He said, 'I've got to go away. I don't know for how long. So I'll have to cancel Beth this weekend.'

'I'll tell her.'

'I wanted to tell her myself.'

'She should be back by eight.'

Which was too late for a thirteen-year-old with school the next day. 'I'll call.'

'Jim got let go.'

Shit! It hadn't been a long relationship, maybe six months with his ex-wife's new partner having to work away some of the time, but Powell had been hopeful. If Ann remarried it would save a chunk of alimony. 'I'm sorry. I thought he was a foreman. Secure.'

'There were four. He got unlucky.'

In between the three calls it took finally to reach his daughter Powell packed a case, cancelled deliveries and warned the janitor he was going out of town. When he finally got Beth he said, 'It's nine o'clock. Isn't that a bit late, honey?'

'We stopped for pizza,' said the child.

'Wasn't Mom worried?'

'Why should she be?'

There wasn't a lot he could do, Powell accepted. It wasn't enough to challenge the custody order and he could hardly have Beth staying with him, liable as he was to be sent to the other side of the country at a moment's notice, like now. He wished it was different. He didn't know anything about the man Ann was with now. Beth

24

was always noncommittal when he asked how things were between her and Ann and he'd become increasingly worried that the silence itself meant the situation wasn't good. 'How's school?'

'Geography's not so good.'

'Mom told you about the weekend?'

'Yeah.'

'I'm sorry.'

'Where you going?'

'Texas. Where's Texas?'

'Dad! I know where Texas is!'

'Maybe we can fix something longer than a weekend when I get back.'

'That would be cool.'

'Be good.'

'Sure.'

'I love you.'

'I love you, too.' Powell wasn't sure he told his daughter that enough. Or proved it.

It had been a first-time experiment for the man who was Harold Taylor and he'd never experienced such power in any previous life – been able to create such total, abject terror. It had been fantastic. The black bastard who'd actually killed him – the one whose retribution it had been the most important of all to realize – had virtually gone insane. So, too, had the needle-dicked trucker who hadn't been so tough at the end, pissing himself, begging for mercy, screaming he wasn't responsible for what his father had done. And the whore had been a good fuck, into the bargain.

But the very end had been the best. He'd never before changed his features in front of his victims, facially transmogrifying into the person he'd been when they'd caused him harm. He did it now, in front of the mirror, sniggering in self-admiration at the transformation of Harold Taylor into Myron Nolan and then back again to Harold Taylor: back and forth, back and forth, Harold into Myron, Myron into Harold. It *was* horrifying. Staggeringly, numbingly horrifying.

He reverted at last to his new face, gazing down at the list on the table in front of him. Still a lot to go, waiting, unsuspecting. He'd do the facial trick every time now, make them remember who he was before he slowly punished them, for what they'd done.

He was having a hell of a time. He sniggered again, at the word: having a hell of a time showing them what hell was like.

Chapter Three

Budd Maddox, the local San Antonio FBI agent, had been a contender for the American Olympic boxing team and still looked fit enough to qualify. He was waiting for Powell at the end of the disembarkation pier, a towering black so tall that Powell had physically to look upwards at the man. The crushing handshake came with the boondock resentment towards a higher-grade takeover by a headquarters honcho. Powell had known it – and probably shown it – himself when his rising-through-the-ranks territory had been invaded. He was prepared for it: headquarters thinking, don't offend the local guy. Still on the concourse Powell said, 'You were right. It is serial. There's been another. Birmingham, Alabama. So I'm co-ordinating.'

The huge man smiled down at him, the reserve perceptibly lessening. 'A national case, then?'

Powell smiled back at the other man's professional awareness of Washington knowing that he'd got a case right from the very beginning. And when they solved it, there'd be the public recognition from the major media exposure. If it turned out to be the first killing, Texas would have the right of trial and execution. 'And you rang the bell.'

'He wasn't killed in the city,' said Maddox. 'It's

27

county, not metro. Sheriff's name is Lindropp, Burt Lindropp.'

Caught by the tone of the other FBI man's voice Powell said, 'We got a problem?'

'Lindropp's enjoyed being on television and getting his name in the papers. I'm to tell you to call for an appointment. And Dr Jamieson, the medical examiner, says he'll make time.'

'Why's it always got to be like this between us and local agencies?' wondered Powell, irritably.

Instead of answering, Maddox said, 'I had someone named Amy Halliday on. Said she had your authority to have the complete files sent up?'

'That's right,' frowned Powell, curious at the other man's response.

'That's the problem,' admitted Maddox. 'I already sent virtually all that I've got.'

'Positive local obstruction?'

'That about sums it up,' said Maddox.

'Then we'd better see what we can do for ourselves.'

'They won't like it, we don't go to them first.'

'They don't get a choice.'

Outside the terminal the heat was like a heavy hand pressing down upon them. Some men were actually wearing cowboy hats and tooled boots. Powell took off his jacket and loosened his tie, the way he preferred to work anyway. In Texas a hip-holstered .44 Smith and Wesson wouldn't attract any attention except, perhaps, for its smallness compared to what everyone else owned. As they moved off Powell said, 'Talk me through it.'

'A real crazy,' said Maddox. 'Dead guy's named Gene Stanley Johnson. He and his sister worked the family trucking business set up by his father, about thirty years ago. He was twenty-six. Single. Girl's name was Billie

28

Jean Kesby. That's her real name, which was lucky. Charged under it three times in El Paso, for prostitution. When they were found both had been decapitated, each head arranged upright beside the body. His dick, also cut off, was in her mouth. Both her breasts had been amputated. Their eyes had been gouged out and a religious cross cut into their foreheads.'

'Jesus!' said Powell.

'He sure wasn't looking after his flock this day,' said Maddox. 'The Johnson business has five rigs, bigger than hell. Liquid gas. Barbara – that's the unmarried sister – ran the business side, Gene looked after the rigs and organized the truckers. Was one himself . . .' As he joined Highway 10 Maddox said: 'This was his route, on the 15th. Same every Wednesday, regular delivery to LA. He pulled into a truck stop, about three miles past the 290 junction, just short of Segovia . . . That's where Billie Jean was waiting—'

'Waiting?' broke in Powell.

'That's the way it looks.' He jerked his head towards the rear seat. 'Place is called Jilly Joe's. Got the owner's statement in the case there, you want to read it.'

'How much further past the stop were the bodies found?'

'No more than two miles.'

'We'll stop by on the way back, after looking at the scene. Who found them?'

'Another trucker who'd seen them both at Jilly Joe's. Name of Cummings, Sam Cummings.' Maddox slowed and said, 'Here's the stop.'

Heat was shimmering off the black top and the scrub and desert of the Edwards Plateau stretched away to the end of the world, edged at the very extreme by purple hazed mountains. The truck stop was all by itself on

29

the desert's edge, a rambling, single-storey clapboard surmounted by a sign that proclaimed JILLY JOE'S, and was encircled by red and gold lights that permanently chased themselves around the lettering. There didn't appear to be any outside perimeter and there were six enormous trucks and five cars that Powell could see, strewn haphazardly where drivers had simply braked to a halt. It seemed much closer than two miles when Maddox said, 'And here's where the bodies and the rig were found.'

It was the only spot in what seemed hundreds of miles in which there was an abrupt upthrust of rock that appeared to have pulled the ground up with it. There was an engulfing eruption of dust and sand as Maddox pulled off the metalled road. Maddox parked on the far side of the outcrop. The murder area was still marked out by stakes and yellow scene-of-crime tape, although several of the markers had fallen over and the tape flapped in the wind, as if trying to summon help. There was a wide, dark brown – almost black – patch baked into the lighter desert sand. Maddox said, 'Blood. That's where they were found.'

Closer, Powell could still see part of where the body positions had been taped out, side by side.

'The heads were there—' said the man, pointing to the left of the outlines. 'Gene's dick in her mouth . . . there weren't any eyes . . .'

'You mean they'd been taken out? Or pushed into their heads?'

'Dr Jamieson found the left ones way back in the heads. But not the right.'

'You find them anywhere here?'

'The bodies had been removed before I arrived. All the examinations completed.'

30

'What!' demanded Powell, outraged.

'That's the way it happened: all done before I could intervene.'

'What about the sheriff's people?'

'They haven't made their evidence available yet.'

It was worse than he'd imagined, decided Powell. 'Were the buzzards here, before the bodies were found? Desert animals?'

'No-one said.'

He hadn't asked, Powell decided. 'The eyes could have been taken as a souvenir. Serial killers collect mementoes. What else?'

'The crosses, like in a church, cut into both their foreheads. Right between their eyes.'

'What about clothes?'

'Naked. And with their arms and legs splayed out, like in a star shape. All their clothes were folded up, real neat.'

'On their backs or on their fronts?'

'On their backs. With their heads propped up beside.'

Powell gestured further along the just visible track that disappeared over the rise. 'Where's that lead to?'

'A broken-down shack, abandoned years ago. Just three walls standing now. Roof's fallen in.'

'Who owns it?'

Maddox brightened. 'According to the land registry the last owner was a desert bum, looking for gold where there isn't any. Ownership died with him.'

Powell walked a little way up the track towards the rise, then came back. 'You weren't able to carry out any proper scene-of-crime examination, right?'

'Whatever forensic there was had already been done. People gone.'

'Sheriff call you?'

'Highway Patrol.'

How the hell much longer was it going to take for local forces to accept the Bureau as an expert, specialized addition, not an enemy intruding into every investigation? 'What made Sam Cummings stop?'

'Johnson's truck was all silver. It wasn't quite hidden by these rocks, not like our car. Flashing in the sun like a beacon, apparently. He recognized it and decided to take a look. Says he guessed what they were doing and decided to have a piece himself.'

'He say anything about another vehicle?'

Maddox gave an embarrassed shrug. 'I haven't seen his full statement. Just a preliminary.'

Powell sighed, guessing the answer before asking the question. 'He followed Johnson along the track in his own rig?'

'Right.'

'When you got here, after the sheriff's people—'

'And the Highway Patrol,' broke in Maddox.

The other man was mounting a defence against future criticism, Powell knew. '. . . and the Highway Patrol, what about tyre tracks *beyond* where Johnson had stopped, going to or coming from the disused shack over the hill?'

'No-one said. It's not in any Highway Patrol reports.'

'Let's get back to Jilly Joe's, out of the sun,' said Powell, careless of the despair evident in his voice.

There were only three rigs and some cars strewn outside the stop and maybe ten men inside when they got back. It seemed very dark, in contrast to the white brightness outside, and they had to stop just inside the door to refocus. In the abrupt silence at the entry of two city-dressed strangers, even carrying their jackets, Tammy Wynette's 'Stand by Your Man' sounded harshly loud from the music selector. Maddox led the way across to where a black-waistcoated, black-aproned man stood behind a bar that ran half the length of one wall.

'Joe Hickley,' introduced the local man. 'Owns the place. Wes is down from Washington.'

'That important, eh?' Hickley was almost as broad as he was tall, a barrel of a man. There was no stetson but Powell guessed there would be cowboy boots. There was a long snake tattoo curled around the man's left arm and an insignia – an army or naval unit – on the other. There'd be a shotgun or a baseball bat beneath the bar and Hickley would probably be prepared to use either.

'Maybe,' said Powell. 'Could do with your help. Like to hear what happened that day.'

'I already told Budd all I can remember.' The man was talking to them loudly, enjoying the attention, at the same time moving professionally up and down the bar, dispensing drinks.

'Tell me again,' encouraged Powell.

Hickley smiled, extending both hands in front of him. 'That gal had tits out to here. Halter top, no bra. Jeans cut into shorts right up to her pussy. Every guy in the place had a permanent boner. Couldn't walk straight. She didn't have any pants on under those shorts.'

'She ever been in here before? Worked the place professionally?'

'Definitely not. Against the law.' Hickley poured himself a drink and said, 'You guys want something?'

'Miller Lite,' accepted Powell.

Maddox nodded for the same.

As Hickley poured, a faded, tired-looking woman with straggled hair emerged from the rear of the bar. The man said, 'About time. You take over the bar. I got business

33

to talk.'

'Fuck you,' said the woman, totally without feeling. She ignored Powell and Maddox, almost automatically starting to serve behind the bar.

'Jilly,' identified the owner.

Powell wondered how she came to have her name in front of the man's. Glad of the undivided attention, Powell said, 'So the girl was here before Johnson came in?'

'For a good half-hour.'

'Doing what, apart from giving everyone a boner?'

'At one of the window tables at first. Sat on one chair with her legs out on the other, showing her wares.'

'What time was this?'

'Eleven, eleven-thirty.'

'What'd she drink?'

'Wild Turkey.'

'At eleven-thirty in the morning!'

'I tell you, this was some piece.'

'So it's on offer?'

'Two guys go over, one after the other. Chester Payne, from town, and another guy I don't know at the time: turns out to be Sam Cummings. Start the business, how about drinking with me honey, that sort of thing. She blanks them. Chester, pissed off at her, says "What's the rules here?" and she says "There aren't any involving you. I'm waiting for someone . . ." '

'That's what she said! That she was waiting for someone?' Powell pounced.

'The precise words.'

'Then what?'

'Gene comes in.'

'You know him?'

'He's a regular, on the Wednesday LA run.'

34

'Let's wind back a little. From the time Johnson actually came in.'

'Before then, even,' insisted Hickley. 'She's on her second Wild Turkey, at the table. Suddenly she gets up and is at the bar, with the cheeks of the prettiest ass you've ever seen winking like little moons over the mountains, asking for a refill . . .'

'Johnson hadn't come in by then?'

'Immediately after, before I'd had time to serve her.'

'Where'd he park his rig?'

'Right out front.'

'So she saw him pull in?'

'Couldn't have missed him. That silver thing glowed in the sun like it was on fire.'

'Did he come on to her right away?'

The man shook his head. 'Left quite a distance between them at the bar . . .' Reminded, he gestured without asking to their beer. Both agents pushed their near-empty glasses forward. Powell put down $5 and left the change lying on the counter.

'We talked for a moment, Gene and me,' picked up the man. 'It was her who hit on him. Looks along the bar while we're talking and says, "Hi, how'ya doing?" Just like that. And he says he's doing just fine but a whole lot better since seeing her and she suggests they go back to her table. Which they do. And quicker'n a rattler with jack rabbit she's cosying up, rubbing her leg against his under the table and Gene's looking around as if it's all a dream, which for the rest of us it is and a damned wet one at that.'

'You get any feeling that he knew her?'

'Absolutely not,' insisted Hickley. 'This was the first but she went for him big time.'

Powell turned his back on the bar, to look out into the

parking area. Over his shoulder he said, 'They go back to the table she was at in the beginning?'

'The one right in the middle,' confirmed Hickley.

'From here you've got a pretty good view of the draw-in. How'd she get here?'

'I didn't see her arrive outside. First I seen her was when she came through the door.'

'What about buses?'

'There're Greyhounds but this isn't a stop.'

'From where you're standing now, looking out over the park, did you see any car follow Johnson and the girl after they left?'

'No,' said Hickley.

'You sure?'

'Mister!' said the man. 'I looked after that ass till it disappeared over the horizon!'

Powell moved away from the bar, orientating the place in his mind, going to the unoccupied table at which Billie Jean Kesby had waited, leaning forward on it to gauge the view she would have had. Without looking at the other FBI man he said, 'I've got the picture here. You want to call the medical examiner? Tell him we're on our way?'

Maddox said, 'What about the sheriff?'

'My priority, not his,' said Powell.

Maddox made the call from the car. As they drove Powell said, 'We got anything from the sheriff's department to make this a proper investigation?'

'No,' admitted Maddox. 'But everything Joe said back there I've already sent to Washington.'

'I'm going to bring in our own forensic team,' announced Powell. 'I want the disused shack taken apart, shingle by shingle. I want the cab of Johnson's rig stripped and examined for anything that might be in it or

36

on it or around it. I want personally to interview Sam Cummings, tomorrow. And Johnson's sister. And I want to go back through the history of the Johnson family from the time their ancestors first arrived in America and then, if possible, what the history was in whatever country they came from, before that. I want you to go up to El Paso, find out why Billie Jean had moved down here. What Vice here have on her. By tomorrow this time I'll have from the sheriff every report and scientific analysis that's been made, by everyone involved. And while we're about it, I want the driver of every Greyhound bus that came along this route, either way, from first light to midnight the day of the murder asked about anything they saw around where Johnson's rig was found, particularly any other vehicle. You think of anything to add to that?'

'No,' said Maddox, even quieter than before.

'You can start setting it up while I'm talking to Jamieson.'

Kingsley Jamieson was an extremely fat, red-faced man in protestingly tight clothes – his shirt front gaped, between button places – who smelt of scented pipe tobacco and whom Powell guessed only just managed to stop short of calling Budd Maddox 'boy' before the resident FBI man left to start on Powell's listed demands.

The man took a bottle and two glasses from the bottom drawer of his desk and said, 'You'd like a little sour mash? Helps against cholesterol.'

'No,' said Powell. 'I'd like to see the bodies and discuss your findings.'

The obese medical examiner frowned, disappointed. 'Later, then.'

The bodies of Gene Stanley Johnson and Billie Jean

37

Kesby were uniformly grey, from refrigeration and blood loss. The heads were bagged individually and on their respective trolleys. Johnson's penis had been removed from the woman's mouth and was bagged, beside the man. The woman's breasts were beside her. At Powell's request the medical examiner took the heads from the specimen bags. Both victims were blond. With stiff, offended formality Dr Jamieson said the bodies were of a male and female Caucasian. Both were well nourished, with no evidence whatsoever of any organic illness. Neither had there been any evidence of brain abnormality or disease, although both had suffered severe trauma to the eye sockets. The left eye of each victim had been in its socket, although burst and forced back almost to the optic nerve from violent pressure. The right eyes had been missing. The woman had been genitally disfigured, although not extensively. Cause of death in both cases was most likely a single puncture, directly into the heart, by a rounded instrument so thin, less than a quarter of an inch at its thickest, that the wounds had virtually sealed themselves and only been found after a minute, magnified examination of the upper torsos. There were no trunk injuries apart from to the neck and the genital areas.

'Have you sectioned the penis, for semen traces? And taken vaginal swabs?'

The fat doctor frowned, affronted, and Powell knew at once that he hadn't. Jamieson said, 'Why should I have done that?'

'If there had been sexual intercourse there would probably have been semen residue.'

'Johnson was naked when he was found! It's obvious there was sexual intercourse.'

'It isn't obvious at all,' challenged Powell. 'He's a

38

trucker with a long journey ahead of him who's picked up a whore in a truck stop. He wouldn't have got completely undressed to screw her. They wouldn't have neatly folded their clothes. It would have been a short time, just dropped his trousers . . .' Powell moved the sheet further off the bodies, bending close to the legs and arms. 'You examine the knees, forearms and hands for sand grazes . . . ?'

The examiner's condescension was going. 'No. Why?'

'Or their backs or buttocks?'

'No.'

'If they *had* done it outside his cab, either he on top of her or she on top of him, there'd have been sand grazes.'

'I could re-examine,' offered the doctor.

Powell didn't respond. Instead he bent over Johnson's body again, examining the ankles and wrists. 'Don't you think these are restraint bruises?'

'That's what I described them as in my report to the sheriff,' said Jamieson.

'What about fingernail debris? Any hair, skin, blood – sand again – where he tried to fight off an assailant?'

'No.'

Powell wasn't sure the man had even checked. 'What was there?'

'Sump oil. Indeterminate dirt. The nails were chipped but from neglect, not from resisting an assailant. Certainly no skin or hair. Nothing like that.'

The chest cavities had been entered from the side. There were no incisions around the heart wound, which really was extremely small, even under magnification, very close to Johnson's left nipple and just below where the girl's left breast would have been. Powell said, 'You haven't sectioned the entry wounds.'

'I followed them from my incision to the sides of the

39

chests.'

'I want the precise lines. Whether they are upward or downward or came more from the left or from the right. And whether they were clean or struck a rib.'

'Why?' demanded the man, truculently.

'To know if the killer was right or left handed. And how big or small he was. And where he stood when he was killing them . . .' He bent even closer over the chest wound, adjusting the magnification. 'What about the amputation of the penis and the breasts? Were they hacked off? Or could there be an element of medical knowledge?'

'The amputations were very clean.'

'And the necks?'

'Clean again. But there is some sawing.'

Powell straightened from the body, his back cramped. 'Thank you.'

'I'll carry out a second autopsy, to cover the points you've raised,' offered Jamieson.

'Don't bother,' dismissed Powell. 'I'm including a forensic pathologist in the team I'm bringing from Washington.'

Dr Jamieson's face blazed. 'I *am* a forensic pathologist, sir!'

'So I was led to believe,' said Powell.

Budd Maddox had obviously heard of the confrontation with the medical examiner when he telephoned Powell at the hotel but didn't try to discuss it and Powell said nothing, either. The meeting with Johnson's unmarried sister, Barbara, was fixed for nine the following morning. Sam Cummings was due from El Paso by midday. Greyhound had promised the names and addresses of all their drivers by then, too. The sheriff had called the local

Bureau office demanding to know why Powell hadn't contacted him yet.

He said, 'There's a lot of catching up to do, isn't there?'

'Too much,' said Powell. There was a danger of it being yet another fucked-up investigation, he thought. When he telephoned Washington Amy Halliday said she was assembling what was available but that she needed more. Powell said he knew that already.

He'd watched Marcus Carr and made his plans eight months earlier, so it was obviously necessary to check everything again and Harold Taylor was glad he did. It had been quite immaterial that the wife would have to die as well – he'd even been looking forward to a bigger audience for the facial change – but by following the old man that first day in Pittsburgh he'd discovered she was hospitalized after a heart attack and wouldn't be in the apartment after all. The shock of having her husband murdered would probably kill her now. The best thing, to put her out of her misery.

It wasn't a problem, having to reorganize everything: he'd made allowances for setbacks and this hardly qualified. He'd have it all rescheduled in a week. Would the connection have been made by then, between Texas and Alabama? He hoped so. He'd become quite determined to create a sensation. Killing Carr would probably cause one, all by itself. The three so far were low life. Carr was a retired army general and retired army generals didn't go around getting their heads and their dicks cut off.

Taylor stirred as Carr emerged from his apartment block, a diminutive man striding briskly upright, despite his age, and cautiously fell into step a good twenty yards behind. According to the newly established routine, now that there was no-one to fix his breakfast, Carr should stop at the hotel coffee shop four blocks down the street. It was the return timing that Taylor wanted to get firmly established.

Chapter Four

The Bureau pathologist from whom the only real progress came that day was a startlingly attractive black girl named Lucille Hooper in whom Powell almost at once detected a no-shit mindset so he didn't warn her of the attitude she'd encounter from Dr Kingsley Jamieson, confident she'd handle it well enough by herself. During the 7 a.m. conference he did, however, give the forensic group a general caution of the local resentment and when Barry Westmore, the forensic team leader, asked how bad it was, Powell said, 'As bad as it can get.'

'We starting from scratch?' demanded Westmore.

'Worse than that,' said Powell, conscious of Budd Maddox's discomfort, beside him in the San Antonio FBI office. 'I'm going to kick ass today but I'm not sure what good it'll do.'

Barbara Johnson was ten years older than her brother and looked it. She wore jeans and a check shirt and moccasins instead of boots. Her hair was strained back in a band and there was no make-up. There wasn't any obvious grief but then, Powell reflected, grief affected people in different ways.

It was more a man's than a woman's office, with no attempt to pretty it up with plants or pictures. Powell guessed the empty desk on the other side of the room from hers had belonged to Gene Johnson. It hadn't been tidied. The huge yard beyond the darkened glass windows, between the two hangar-sized storage sheds, was deserted: the rig Johnson had been driving was still in the police pound – at that moment, Powell hoped, being swarmed over by the Washington scientists he'd just finished briefing.

Barbara Johnson cut off his hopefully sympathetic apologies for bothering her by saying, 'Why don't you just get on with it by telling me what you want?' The Texas accent was very pronounced.

'You close to your brother?'

'I thought so.'

'You talked to each other? Confided?'

'To a point.' She lighted a cigarette with a Zippo she held almost awkwardly by its case top. Her fingers were stained brown by nicotine.

'He talk to you about girlfriends?'

'There was no-one regular.'

'He talk about anyone recently? A blonde?'

'I know about the hooker in Jilly Joe's. And no, he didn't.'

'She told people there she was waiting for someone. And made a play for him the moment he walked in.'

'He was a good-looking guy. If he knew her he didn't say anything to me about it.'

'Would he have done?'

'If she was a hooker, you mean? Maybe not. It wouldn't have meant much, would it? Just a fuck.'

Beside him Maddox stirred. A woman in a man's world, thought Powell. She hadn't cursed to shock. It was the way she talked. 'He was supposed to be driving a rig? Working?'

44

The woman allowed herself a tight smile. 'Drivers get rest breaks. It doesn't take long to get laid.'

Powell wondered how she knew. He got the impression she was a willing spinster, as least as far as the opposite sex was concerned. 'Joe Hickley says Gene always stopped by on a westerly run?'

'I don't know why but he did. I think it's a pretty shitty place, but he liked it.'

'Everyone know he always stopped?'

She shrugged. 'I guess. It wasn't any secret.'

'You ever lost a rig? Had it hijacked? Or had a cargo stolen?'

'Never,' said Barbara, the pride obvious. 'All our drivers have CB, as well as mobile phones. Some carry weapons. Gene did.'

Jesus! thought Powell. He hadn't heard anything about a weapon. Or a mobile phone. 'What sort of weapon?'

'Colt Python. Big bastard. Three fifty-seven Magnum. He was good with it. He liked guns. Had several but the Python was the one he always travelled with.'

The right of every American to bear arms, thought Powell, bitterly, paraphrasing the creed that the Rifle Association always misquoted. 'He carry it on his person? Or keep it in the cab?'

The woman regarded him warily, nervous of state line firearm infringements. 'He had a holding clip fitted, in the glovebox. Carried it there. Locked, of course. And he had a licence, for all of them.'

'What about the phone and the CB, when he stopped? He take the phone with him or call in and say he'd be out of touch for a while?'

'Sometimes. Not always.'

'What about the 15th?'

'He didn't call in after leaving that day.'

'You hear anything from anyone here – or get the impression yourself – that you were being watched?'

The woman shook her head. 'Nothing. And we're careful. Our cargoes are valuable.'

Powell said, 'I'd like to get some family history, Gene's most of all. If Budd could call by your place, at your convenience, and go through things when you've had the chance to think about it?'

She shrugged again. 'Not sure how I can help you. We didn't go in for that family history, early settler shit. From what I know Dad's family was originally Scandinavian. Lived first in Galveston, before the flood. After that they moved up here. Grandparents died before Gene and I were born. Dad served in the Second World War but not Korea. Went overseas, in some military police unit: there's pictures of him in uniform, in Germany, places like that. He set the trucking business up around 1957.'

'That's the sort of stuff I want,' encouraged Powell.

Gene Johnson's desk was a hamster's nest of paper scraps and telephone notes without name-identified numbers, all of which they bagged, each to be contacted. There was an address book with names against numbers in a top right-hand drawer which they added to the collection. Another drawer held a selection of *Hustler* magazines, as well as other pornography, in addition to *Soldier* magazines. There was a half-empty bottle of Jim Beam in a bottom drawer, with four unwashed glasses, and in another an almost full box of .38 shells.

The state of the dead man's office desk was scant rehearsal an hour later for the condition of the dead man's apartment, the door to which was still blocked by criss-crossed police No Entry tape secured by the sheriff's seal, which Powell broke to Maddox's protest that Lindropp wasn't going to like it and Powell's insistence that he couldn't give a fuck.

The outside surroundings were an exquisitely preserved example of Spanish and adobe architecture and the inside was a refuse tip. It stank, of stale air. The dishwasher gaped open like an over-filled mouth with dirty crockery and glasses that overflowed into the kitchen sink. There were more unwashed plates on the kitchen table and several glasses, empty beer bottles and another half-empty bottle of Jim Beam in the main room in which clothes, shirts and shorts, were discarded over sagged although comparatively new furniture. The bed was unmade. There was a .45 Smith and Wesson automatic, with a full clip of 9mm shells, in the bedside drawer, alongside a pack of coloured condoms. There were two membership cards and some match packs which the local FBI man identified to be from topless bars and massage parlours. There were a lot more *Hustler* magazines and four pornographic videos beneath the bedroom VCR machine. One was *Debbie Does Dallas*. There were two different female voices on the answering machine, both asking Johnson to call them back, and Maddox made a note to get the incoming numbers from the telephone company. There was an unlocked gun safe in a bedroom closet, containing a pump action shotgun and a .44 Magnum Colt Anaconda pistol, both loaded. In a bureau drawer there was $350 in a money clip and an expired membership card of the National Rifle Association. Scrawled on a cocktail napkin from the Red Rattler lounge was 'Annie, $150.'

After half an hour Powell said, 'We're wasting our time. There's nothing here that's going to help.' Was he doing just that, wasting his time on established routine?

Serial killings usually had patterns, but in the killings themselves, not a routine that identified the perpetrators. Which made what he was doing now largely pointless. But after so many mistakes, one after the other, he couldn't afford *not* to do it, he told himself. And his intuition, an antenna upon which he frequently although privately relied, was telling him these were different serial murders. The distance between Texas and Alabama was the most obvious: multiple slayings were usually in a tightly limited radius, which the killer knew and in which he felt safe.

'Let's hope Sam Cummings will help.'

'Let's hope something will,' agreed Powell.

Cummings was a thin, leering-faced man of thirty whose halitosis challenged his body odour. Being involved in an FBI investigation into an horrific double murder was obviously the biggest event in his stunted life and he entered the San Antonio office clearly well rehearsed, in demeanour and attitude. Powell wished the trucker had bathed as thoroughly. He patiently endured a near-gynaecological lecture on Billie Jean Kesby's attributes to get to the trucker's rejecting encounter, demanding at once, 'What did she say to you?'

' "I'm OK. I'm waiting." '

'They the actual words?'

'The very ones.'

'Did she mention Gene Johnson by name?'

'No. But from how she moved when he came in it was obviously him.'

'You knew him, before then?'

'No.'

'How close were you when you hit on her? As close as you and I are?' Powell was facing the man across

Maddox's desk, about five feet between them, and was getting both the bad breath and the sweat.

'Much closer. Put my foot up on the chair that she had hers on and kinda leaned forward, nice and personal.'

'It was coming up to noon, the hottest part of the day. She'd just walked in from the desert. So how did she smell? Hot? What?'

'Sweeter than a rose in June.'

'You mean of perfume? Or that she didn't smell of sweat?'

'Perfume. Heavy. Nice.'

'No sweat at all?'

'Absolutely not.'

So there had to have been a car, somewhere. 'You saw her walk in?'

'You bet your life I did.'

'You see how she arrived outside? A vehicle?'

'Nope.'

'So how'd she get there?'

'Another trucker maybe? I don't know.'

'When Gene came in and saw her did he give any sign of recognition? Or did he just look because she was hardly dressed?'

'I don't think he knew her.'

'How long after they left did you leave?'

The sly smile was immediate. 'Maybe half an hour.'

'You see any cars leave from outside, in between the time they left and you left?'

'No.'

'You expect to see the two of them again?'

'Nope. I just drove along thinking what a lucky bastard he was. I settled down, got the air cool, tuned the radio. Not really thinking about anything. Then after about fifteen minutes I see the flash. Don't understand it

49

at first and then I realize it's the sun, off a stainless steel rig . . .' The leer came. 'Thought they were doing the business.'

'Which *was* their business. Why'd you stop?'

The smirk stayed. 'You didn't see this bunny. There was more than enough to go round, believe me.'

'You didn't think either would object?'

'Rule of the road, as far as a trucker's concerned.'

'So what did you find?'

For the first time the macho slipped and Cummings became completely serious. 'Couldn't see anything at first. They should have heard me coming, but I gave the horn a little toot, just in case. Still nothing. So I stopped, waited. Didn't want to spoil a guy's fun. Then I saw it . . .' The man stopped, swallowing, all swagger gone. '. . . I thought it was rocks, from the outcrop. Then I saw it was fucking heads, two of them, with his dick in her mouth. Without any eyes. Then I leaned across the cab and saw the bodies, spread out like they were . . .'

'You're still in the cab?'

'You bet your fucking life I'm still in the cab and the first thing I do is that I lock it. Then I get out my gun – I carry a .38 ACP Colt – and after that I get on the phone to every 911 and emergency number I can think of ringing . . .'

'You didn't at any time get out of the cab?'

'Are you kidding! There's the heads of a guy and a girl I've seen drinking and cosying up less than an hour ago staring up at me from the desert, except they haven't got eyes any more. And you're asking me if I got out to take a look! Come on!'

'How long before the police – sheriff's people and the Highway Patrol – arrived?'

'Longest fucking time of my life! Forty-five minutes at least.'

'So for forty-five minutes you sat in your cab, looking at what was in front of you?'

'And almost shitting myself.' Cummings actually shuddered.

'While you were sitting there you never saw anyone – anything – apart from the bodies?'

'No, sir.'

'Could you see around Johnson's rig, further up the track?'

'Kind of.'

'Did you look along it?'

'Sure I did. I didn't know from which way they might come at me, did I?'

'Did you see any track marks, in the sand, beyond Johnson's truck? Going on up over the rise?'

Cummings thought for several moments. 'No.'

'No tyre treads?'

'No.'

'Or footprints?'

'No.'

'Do you think you would have?'

There was another hesitation. 'I think so. I mean I was really looking!'

'You see any tyre marks or footprints leading away from Johnson's rig, back towards the highway?'

'No.'

'What about buzzards? Prairie animals? Anything come around the bodies?'

'No.'

'You got out when the police arrived?'

'Highway Patrol first. Yeah, then I got out.'

'Did you see any tyre marks or footprints then?'

'The sheriff's men arrived almost immediately after. A lot of guys walking about. And I wasn't looking any more. I knew I was safe.'

No-one else was looking, either, thought Powell: not properly. 'Did you see anyone go up to the top of the rise, to see what was on the other side?'

'Someone may have done. I didn't see. You seen what they did to Gene?'

'Yes.'

'Jesus. Fucking maniac.'

'Yes,' agreed Powell. 'Whoever did it is certainly that.'

Lucille Hooper didn't finish her autopsies until the afternoon and declared her findings, knowing their importance, even before sitting down.

'Billie Jean had sex. But not with Gene!'

Powell said, 'How can you be sure? You can't get a DNA match between the bodies that quickly.'

'We got all the time in the world,' said the medical examiner. 'And all the vaginal semen, too. The penis isn't reliable for semen residue after intercourse. The urethra is the place. It was clean. We need a DNA comparison, of course. But I think our killer banged a willing Billie Jean while Gene had to look on, with handcuffs not just around his wrists but around his ankles, too. He was naked then – there are sand burns on his knees and there was sand beneath his finger and toenails. And not just his shoulders and back were sunburned but the soles of his feet, too, where he'd been forced to kneel. The way I see it, he got completely undressed, let himself be cuffed for something kinky she was suggesting, then got himself forced down into a squatted, kneeling position with both sets of cuffs tied together somehow . . .'

'Billie Jean was part of it?'

'The lure, certainly. To get Gene out into the country. Her usefulness ended there.'

It fitted the picture he was building, Powell decided, as she continued. In both Johnson and the girl there was evidence of long term gonorrhoea which did not appear to have been treated and Powell thought: so much for Jamieson's insistence that neither had suffered any medical condition. Jamieson hadn't mentioned the abortion indications that Lucille found in Billie Jean, either. Although the one eye that had been recovered had burst, under intensive magnifications she'd discovered the injuries had been inflicted by an elliptically shaped hard object, not a finger the nail of which, at such force, would have cut as well as indented the globe. An instrument had been used to remove the right eyes, around the sockets of which there was extensive leverage damage. The forehead crosses had definitely been incised, not scratched. She'd subjected the minuscule chest wounds to the same degree of ultra-magnification that she'd used upon the left eyes and detected perfectly rounded discolorations to the skin around the wound, consistent with the murder weapon being driven in to its hilt. That made the shaft of the murder weapon a quarter of an inch at its widest diameter and exactly four inches long, measured from where the tip stopped in the heart.

Lucille was sure both had been dead before the heads, penis and breasts had been removed. The entry wound went from right to left, establishing the killer as left handed, and in a downwards direction, which meant the killer was either taller or had stood over them. She had experimented by putting the heads back onto the torsos and was satisfied that to remove them the killer had stood behind the corpse, which had been propped in an upright position and further straightened by the head being held by the hair or chin for the cutting instrument to be drawn backwards, starting at the front right – also showing the killer to be left handed – and going through to the back. This had resulted in saw-like injuries, although the edge of the weapon had not been serrated. The relative jaggedness of the amputation had been caused by the awkwardness with which the bodies had to be held. The heads had been amputated by the cutting instrument passing cleanly between the third and fourth cervical vertebra and facet joints. The cuts that had removed the penis and the breasts had been extremely clean, like that into the forehead. The ultra-magnification had detected sand adhering to the knees and buttocks and there was also sand in the hair at the back of the girl's head, although both heads had been found upright, with the necks embedded in the sand and supported by twigs broken from desert driftwood. There were injuries to the scalps, at the back, where pieces of wood had been forced into them to provide support, as well as a substantial amount of sand in coagulated blood at the necks, at the point where they had been severed. There were no marks on the wrists or ankles of the woman to indicate that she had been tied or restrained.

Powell nodded. 'So the sequence was that they were killed by the wound directly into the heart, stripped, propped up and then mutilated, in that order?'

'Yes.'

'What about the amount of blood? The ground is heavily stained.'

Lucille smiled. 'Careful. They were dead before the heads came off. The heart – the pump – had stopped. There wouldn't have been a gush. There'd have been a lot, certainly. The ground staining was *after* they were laid out, in that star shape.'

'How close would the killer have been, behind Johnson?'

'Touching. Probably the support, to keep the body upright.'

'So he'd be bloodstained?'

'Oh yes,' Lucille quickly agreed. 'And heavily, that close. He'd have been pulling the blood in upon himself. And I see where you're coming from. How does a bloodstained person get away from a murder scene that exposed without being seen? One answer would be totally to strip off.' She paused. 'And don't forget it was the killer, not Gene, who had sex with the girl. He'd have reason to be undressed.'

'We can positively identify him from his semen DNA when we get him?'

'Absolutely.'

Powell smiled. 'You've done brilliantly.'

'That's my job,' she said, smiling back.

He stayed smiling. 'How did you get on with Dr Jamieson?'

She regarded him seriously. 'You know what the son-of-a-bitch called me?'

'What?'

'Girl!'

'What did you call him?'

'Boy. He didn't seem to like it.'

The day went progressively downhill after Powell's meeting with Lucille Hooper. A heat-exhausted, sun-reddened Barry Westmore returned from the desert to announce that after so long they were wasting their time and would have to rely on whatever Powell managed to

55

get from the sheriff. They'd virtually dismantled the abandoned, collapsing shack and collected as much of its interior as they thought might produce something, for shipment back to Washington. They'd stripped the seating and lining from the cab of Johnson's rig, also to go back to their specialized laboratories. Westmore openly and irrationally challenged Powell's insistence that they forensically sweep Johnson's apartment, and flushed with angry embarrassment when Powell mildly pointed out that if they managed a DNA match of anything identifiable as Billie Jean's from the rig with anything in the apartment it would establish a prior association between Johnson and the girl.

'It isn't any good, my people trying to work like this,' protested Westmore. 'We need to be on a crime scene as soon as it's discovered.'

'It didn't become serial before Alabama,' reminded Powell. 'You'll be there soon enough the next time.'

Burt Lindropp was what was known as a good ole boy. There was the regulation cowboy hat and boots and ironically the silvered pistol high on the man's left hip was a .357 Magnum Colt Python. It appeared polished to match the sheriff's star beneath which it hung. He would, Powell knew, be a friend of every person it was politically and personally important to know in the county and beyond. The moment the soft handshake ended Powell decided that beneath the fat, affable, courteous exterior was a man with the temperament of a rattlesnake with an amphetamine habit.

'Seems the rules weren't quite followed here, son.'

'What rules?'

'Made it quite clear to your boy that I wanted my people around when you looked through Gene's apartment. Now I hear you been there already. Broke my seal, even. That's discourteous, sir. Downright discourteous.'

'I didn't have time.'

'People are kinda polite around here, sir. They make time, particularly when I ask them to.'

'If you're offended, then I'm sorry. But that's not what I'm here to talk about.'

'I *am* offended, son. And getting more so.'

'It wouldn't be difficult for me to become offended, either, sheriff. But I don't think that would help what we're both supposed to be interested in: finding a maniac killer. So why don't we start behaving like adults and less like something out of a Tennessee Williams play.' Fuck the man and the Washington lore about not offending the locals, thought Powell. He wished he'd eaten lunch. And slept better the previous night. He wondered if Lindropp knew who Tennessee Williams was.

Red pinpricks began to form upon Lindropp's already flushed cheeks. 'I'm not accustomed to being talked to like this, son. And we don't need any of your smart young scientific boys coming in from the big city, telling us how to run our investigation. Which, in this case, is running along pretty nicely.'

Powell wished the man would make his mind up whether to call him sir or son. 'I really am glad to hear that. Because I don't think the local FBI office here has been properly included, as it should be.'

'Don't consider it something we can't handle ourselves, without any outside interference. All pretty straightforward, to me. Gene's a good boy. Little headstrong, maybe. No real harm. Met a willing gal, made a mistake. A tragedy.'

'Killed by someone passing through, is that what you think the evidence points to?'

'Something like that. A drifter. Happens a lot.'

'I don't think it does,' said Powell. 'So I'd greatly appreciate my office getting all your evidence files. Today. I want to know what happened to the Colt Python that Gene always had clipped inside the glove box of his cab. I want to know whether Gene was robbed, after being killed. And what it was that was taken, obviously, so we can circulate pawnshops, places like that, as well as the letters and the bank statements. The bank statements might show unusual payments or withdrawals, which I'm sure you've followed up. And I want everything that was in Billie Jean Kesby's purse and a list of all the jewellery that was recovered. You do understand, don't you, that this is now a federal case? Taken out of your hands.'

Lindropp's face was now scarlet. 'You're talking as if we've got a crime wave on our hands here.'

'It's become one. There's been an identical murder in Alabama. We're talking serial killings. But when we get whoever did it, Texas will have right of trial. Which will be a national affair and every aspect of your investigation will come under courtroom scrutiny.'

The man's mouth actually hung slightly open. 'You serious?'

'Totally serious. You will make everything available to the FBI office here, won't you?'

'Yes, sir.'

'Today.'

'Yes, sir.'

'There!' said Powell, rising. 'We got along real fine in the end, didn't we?'

* * *

The more he thought about it the more Harold Taylor wanted an audience. To know – to see and to feel – the sensation he could cause, not just in those fleeting last moments, before he killed those who had to die, but for much longer. For people who would go on living to realize who he was, what he was. To marvel. He'd have followers, disciples. Become a messiah. He couldn't understand why it hadn't occurred to him before. So much time lost. Wasted. Then again, maybe not. The world was a global village, he remembered. Now was exactly the right time. Perfect. But how? All he had to do was work out a way. He knew he could do it: he could do anything he wanted. There were still those who had to die, of course. No reason yet to stop doing that. Never a reason to stop doing that.

He was glad he'd chosen to live, for the moment at least, close to Washington, DC. It was a grand city, properly impressive, the avenues made for marching legions. And convenient, for most of the people he had to kill. Conveniently within striking distance, he thought, amusing himself with the choice of words.

Chapter Five

As the division chief Harry Beddows had every right –
and the unquestionable authority – to establish an
incident room in the FBI's Washington headquarters. But
Powell was irritated that Beddows hadn't discussed it
until he'd called from San Antonio airport on his way to
Alabama. When he'd protested Beddows had dismissively talked of team work, but during the flight Powell
decided a more accurate although clumsier definition
was apparently active participation without culpable
responsibility. An arrest would be Harry Beddows's
success, a failure down to Wesley James Powell, wrongly
chosen – already doubted – team leader. Washington
fucking politics. But he wasn't in Washington. He was in
Birmingham, Alabama, his future seemingly hanging by
a thread. Even more annoying was that Amy Halliday
hadn't said anything about the formation of a task
force involving herself, clerks and the returning forensic
group.

The Birmingham investigation appeared to be im-
peccable, the co-operation between City Homicide and
the Bureau faultless.

The body of Jethro Morrison, a recidivist criminal
who had spent thirty-one of his sixty-six years behind
bars, had been found in Lane Park, close to the botanical

gardens, displayed and mutilated in an identical way to those of Gene Johnson and Billie Jean Kesby in the Texas desert. Unlike Johnson, fibres from his shirt, in which there had been a minuscule slit, had been found in the wound, indicating the victim had been dressed when he was stabbed, although naked and spreadeagled when found, his clothes neatly folded beside him. His pockets had contained five rocks of crack cocaine and there had been $2,400 in small-denomination notes, none larger than $20. The local medical examiner had established that at the time of his death Morrison was suffering from ulcers and the considerable damage to the nasal membrane indicated substantial and long term cocaine abuse. Both eyes had been destroyed but only the left found, forced into the severed head. Death had been caused by the same sort of narrow-bladed knife. There was no restraint bruising to the wrists or ankles.

The rest of the forensic routine had been just as immaculate. Birmingham homocide squad had alerted Charles Andrews within thirty minutes of themselves being summoned to the murder scene, for the local FBI man to be present throughout the scientific examination of the park area. Which had found nothing. The one potential witness, Michael Gaynor, had been led to the body by the frantic barking of his dog.

The dead man's son, also named Jethro, headed one of the city's three major organized crime families. Local drugs squad listed the father as a deliverer and collector. Andrews said, 'Junior thinks it's a territory thing. Told us to go fuck ourselves. That they'd handle it their way. We're expecting a war.'

The dossier between them on Andrews's desk in the local FBI office off Main Street was almost six inches high and Andrews had confirmed that it had been sent to

Amy Halliday on their way in from the city airport. With so little for him to do, Powell thought with luck he'd be able to get back to Washington by the following day. He said, 'You tell the son about Texas?'

'Didn't know how you wanted to handle it,' said Andrews. He was a neatly unobtrusive, bespectacled man whom it was difficult to imagine had killed someone, which Powell knew Andrews had: a serial rapist he'd trapped with a thirteen-year-old victim in a New York tenement. The rapist had fired four shots at Andrews, all of which had missed, and was turning the gun on to the child when Andrews fired back, just once.

'The old man had quite a rap sheet,' said Powell, tapping the file in front of him. As well as convictions for larceny, grand theft auto, armed robbery and drug dealing there were two separate murder investigations which had failed through lack of evidence.

'A saint, compared to the son,' said Andrews. 'Local Public Enemy Number One.'

'I think we'll stop the war before it starts: see Gaynor later,' decided Powell.

The legend over the door described it as the Hillside Sports and Social Club. It was close to the railroad station and the only reasonably maintained property in a decaying terrace of houses so dilapidated they looked like animals, gradually lying down to die. Cardboard and packing crate planking filled more windows than glass, and the street and an empty lot immediately alongside were littered with cars being leisurely stripped of wheels and fittings. Their entry was met with an even greater silence than at Jilly Joe's.

It was bare-board basic, a lot of round tables, three pool tables, all occupied, a bar to the right and an annexe at the far end formed by a slated partition that came halfway across the room. It was dominated by a single but larger round table, at which three men sat looking out into the main room, lords of all they surveyed. The music was monotonous rap, like rain on a tin roof.

'That's Jethro Junior at the back table. The guy in the middle, wearing the dress,' identified Andrews.

Jethro Morrison Jnr was young – twenty-nine, Powell knew, from the police file – and big, more than a head taller than the two men either side of him, even sitting. His hair was cut extremely short and a tightly clipped beard fringed his jawline. Powell was unsure if the man was wearing a collarless shirt or a full caftan. It was yellow and shone like silk. There was a gold choker beneath, a heavy gold watch, the face surrounded by diamonds, and three diamond rings, one on his left hand, two on his right. As they walked the length of the room men began easing themselves into the partitioned-off area until Jethro Jnr gave a hand movement, as if shooing away bothersome insects. He said something and everyone around him laughed, dutifully. From a group outside the club Powell had seen two men hurry in ahead of them, so Morrison had known of their approach: could have left through any of the four doors behind him or even tried to impede their entry, if he'd chosen to do so. He'd obviously decided instead upon a cabaret, with them as the star act. There were four more men protectively behind Jethro Jnr, as well as the two at the table, by the time Powell and Andrews reached the man. As they did so the gang leader said, 'I don't recall your ringing for an appointment' and there was another obedient round of laughter.

'Let's not fuck about,' said Powell, heavy with conde-scension. He pulled out a chair directly opposite the gang leader and sat down. The local FBI agent did the same. There was noise behind them of people crowding the entrance from the larger room.

Jethro Jnr said, 'You're in nigger country now, honky. You gotta show respect.'

'I told you not to fuck about,' repeated Powell. 'I want to find who killed your father. This time around anything else doesn't interest me. OK?'

Jethro Jnr nodded in Andrews's direction. 'I told him it wasn't nothing to do with you people. That he wasn't to worry himself about it.'

Powell very obviously and slowly lifted the briefcase he'd carried into the bar onto the table and equally unhurriedly took out photographs. Without speaking Powell dealt out the scene-of-crime photographs of Gene Johnson and Billie Jean Kesby. Initially – very briefly – the man feigned uninterest, then bent over them.

'Where's this?' he said.

'Texas. Five days before the same thing happened to your father.'

'Who was he?'

'A trucker.'

'The chick?'

'A hooker.'

'Why'd it happen?'

'It's serial. Nothing to do with any other gang, here in Birmingham.'

'So there's no cause for war,' came in Andrews.

'Why my daddy?'

'I don't know,' said Powell. 'I want you to help me find out.'

'Me, help you! Feds!'

There was a snicker from the assembled audience but Powell knew the other man's cabaret was falling flat.

'It's the only chance you've got of finding out who cut your father up.'

The gangster winced before he could stop himself, turning the expression into a frown. 'You mean it, about not being interested in anything else?'

'Yes.'

'You got the authority to say that?'

'Yes.' Harry Beddows would probably have his ass.

There was a long pause, the man staring very directly at Powell. At one stage he made another shooing-off gesture and there was a scuff of people moving back into the main part of the club. Powell didn't look around and was glad Andrews didn't, either. Finally the black man said, 'You jiving me?'

'You've seen the pictures. You saw what happened to your father. We're your chance to get even.'

There was another long pause. Jethro Jnr said, 'OK,' but doubtfully.

'You see your father, the day he died?'

'Saw him every day.'

'The night it happened?'

The man nodded. 'He left here around six, I guess. No later than six-thirty. Said he had a little business. Had a few customers. Made him feel independent.'

'You know who his customers were?'

'Old guys.'

'Names?'

There was a shrug. 'Some.'

Powell gestured vaguely around the room. 'Any here?'

'Maybe.'

'Your father was found at nine-thirty. I need to fill in the time from his leaving here until then.'

'Same deal we've got?'

'Same deal.' Powell was conscious of his colleague shifting beside him.

Morrison nodded to the man at his left, who got up immediately and went out into the bar. Jethro Jnr said to Powell, 'Leroy and my daddy go way back.'

'Leroy?' queried Andrews.

'Leroy Goodfellow,' said the gang leader.

The name sounded genuine enough to check out in records, acknowledged Powell, grateful for the local man's question. Jethro Jnr looked over Powell's shoulder at the shuffling approach. Again Powell didn't turn.

Leroy Goodfellow was a wizened, slightly hunched man with completely white hair. He remained standing until Jethro Jnr nodded permission to sit and stayed looking more at the man in the caftan than at Powell. The gang leader said, 'You're cool, Leroy. Amnesty. Tell the man whatever he asks. OK?'

'Whatever you say, Jethro.'

'I say it's OK.' Morrison nodded, as if giving permission for Powell to begin.

Powell said, 'How long did you know Jethro Senior?'

'Since we were kids. Always run together.'

'Do time together?'

'Some.'

Something else that could be confirmed in Records. 'When was the first time?'

'Really kids.' There was a nostalgia in the singsong voice.

'Eighteen? Nineteen?'

'End of the Second World War. All nigger units. Brothers together. More comfortable than being on the streets here, 1944, '45. Lot of deals to work up. Army rations. Cigarettes and petrol and a lot of people to buy:

66

white guys as well as niggers, despite segregation . . .' He laughed. 'We get picked up, Jethro and me. Pull five years apiece almost here on our doorstep. Military stockade just outside Florence. We're pissed, right. Then you know what. Our unit gets sent overseas, all the Brothers get put in the front for the honkies to hide behind. They get 70 per cent casualties in some final push or other. And we're here at home, warm and safe, working the prison almost as well as we worked the streets outside . . .'

The locally based agent shifted again, impatiently. Powell said, 'Afterwards you and Jethro stayed together?'

'Both local boys. Good to have someone you can trust your life with, on a long stretch. That was how close me and Jethro was. Watched out for each other.'

Permanent losers, thought Powell. 'And when Jethro Senior's luck changed, he looked after you?'

'Yes, sir!'

'Tell us about the night of the murder,' cut in Andrews. 'You with Jethro Senior here?'

The old man shook his head. 'Met in a bar up on Wilmington. Always did. Every Monday, regular. Jethro and me.'

'What time?'

'Quarter of seven. Around then. I was there first. Wanted to be there when Jethro arrived.'

'Why?' demanded Powell.

Goodfellow looked warily at the young black man, who nodded. Goodfellow said, 'Little business. I'd kinda found some watches. Some jewellery. Good stuff.'

Andrews shifted once more, uncomfortably. Powell came forward in his seat. 'He take it off you?' No watch

– apart from the one the man had been wearing – or jewellery had been found on the body.

'Agreed to. I reckoned it was worth three or four grand. He said he wasn't carrying that much. That he needed a second opinion. So we arranged to meet the following day.'

'What happened to the watches and the jewellery?' demanded Andrews.

'We're not inquiring about that,' said Powell, quickly. 'You talked business, made an arrangement. Then what happened?'

Leroy Goodfellow again looked for guidance to Morrison, who was smiling at Powell's intervention. At the younger man's further nod Goodfellow said, 'Jethro gave me a little stuff.'

'Crack or cocaine?'

'Cocaine.'

'He have any crack?' asked Powell, testing.

'I asked him for a rock but he said he didn't have any to spare.'

'So he was going to see someone else?'

'He was anxious to get away, sure.'

'He say who?'

'Just someone from the old days.'

Powell came forward again, urgently. 'Who!'

'Didn't say.'

'What did you think he meant by it?'

'I know what he meant.'

'Leroy, you're not making things clear!'

'He said Florence,' protested Goodfellow, indignantly. 'Someone from the old days in the stockade.'

'Someone you'd have known, being in there with him!' seized Powell. 'He *must* have said a name.'

Leroy Goodfellow shook his head, still indignant.

'Said he'd bring him along the next night as a surprise, when we discussed the jewellery and stuff. That we'd have a reunion.'

Charles Andrews managed to contain himself until they got into the car, after a promise from Jethro Morrison Jnr to call if he discovered anyone else who had been with his father on the night of his death. Andrews didn't fire the ignition. Instead he twisted in his seat and said, 'Jesus fucking Christ! Have you got *any* idea what you've just done! Two weeks ago a quarter of a million's worth of watches and jewellery was stolen from a bonded Customs warehouse in Mobile. And you've just given Jethro Morrison Jnr a fucking amnesty for the heist! And you know what I think? I think some of the fucking jewellery he was wearing was part of it. They're laughing themselves silly back in there.'

'We stopped a turf war in which innocent bystanders might have got hurt. Killed even,' said Powell, mildly. 'And we got a lead.'

'A lead! You believe that bullshit? You just got conned, about the jewellery. That's all. What if it's even half true? The old man pulled five years and served every one of them. How many cons you think he met in that time?'

'I don't know,' admitted Powell. 'But we're going to track down every one of them who's still alive, even if it is a waste of time.' If he'd made a mistake it had been a bad one.

Michael Gaynor was a wisp-haired, quickly blinking, timid man who worked as an assistant in the bookshop and souvenir outlet at Arlington, the slave-built, pre-Civil War house that was Birmingham's chief tourist attraction. He came nervously into the Bureau office, declined coffee or tea – anything to drink at all – and sat constantly moving one hand over the other as he talked, as if he had in some way become dirtied by finding the headless body. He unfailingly referred to Jethro Morrison as 'that poor man'.

'You told the police you saw someone else in the park, before you found the body?' urged Powell.

'A man,' said Gaynor. 'Not particularly tall. Slightly built.'

'Age?'

'I'd say about thirty.'

'Black man or white man?'

'White.'

'Hair?'

'Dark.'

'Long or short?'

The man made a cupping gesture with both hands, around his head. 'Long. Covered his ears. But very neat.'

'What sort of face?'

'Small features.'

'Glasses?'

'No.'

'What colour were the eyes?'

'It was too dark to see.'

'How was he dressed?'

'Dark clothes. Dark trousers and a windbreaker. Sweater underneath.'

'So you saw him quite clearly?'

'Clear enough. There's like a street lamp, where the paths intersect.'

'Clear enough to see if he was bloodstained?' asked Andrews.

70

'I would have thought so. He wasn't, though.' Gaynor shuddered at the prospect.

Hopefully Powell said, 'It sounds like you really looked hard at him?'

'It's a park. I'm a careful person.'

'What was a careful person doing in the park at night?'

'My dog's a Dobermann. People don't mess with Dobermanns.'

'This man, did he look at you?' said Andrews.

'Kind of. Half and half.'

'Anything that made you feel he tried to avoid being seen? Did he turn away, anything like that?' persisted the local Bureau man.

'No.'

With growing belief Powell said, 'He speak to you?'

'No.'

'You speak to him?'

There was a barely perceptible pause. 'No.'

'People don't mess with Dobermanns,' echoed Powell. 'He show any nervousness, like changing direction when he saw you had a dog?'

'No.'

'Do you think you could recognize him again?' asked Andrews.

The man shook his head, doubtfully. 'I'm not sure.'

'What about the way he walked? Fast, as if he was trying to get away from something?'

'No.'

'Was he carrying anything?'

'Not actually carrying. He had a shoulder bag, like a satchel. The strap was on his shoulder.'

'Did it seem heavy, like he had to hold himself to support it?'

'No. But he had his hand inside it.'

'How do you mean?'

'I could see his other hand, opposite the bag. But not the one on that side, although his arm was straight down by his side. I guessed he had his hand inside.'

'You really did pay a lot of attention to this man, didn't you?' pressed Powell, surer now.

'Not really.'

'A Dobermann's an active dog, isn't it?'

The man smiled, fleetingly. 'They're great dogs. Loyal.'

'You exercise him every night?'

'Always.'

'Always in the park?'

'I clear up after him.'

'Mr Gaynor, I'm really not interested whether you clear up after your dog or not,' said Powell, patiently. 'I want you very clearly to understand what I am saying: all I'm concerned with is the murder of Jethro Morrison and how you might be able to help me solve it. Nothing else. Not how or where you exercise your dog. People you might meet doing that.'

There was a pause. 'I think I understand.'

'So you go to the park most nights?'

'Yes.'

'You have friends there? Other people who walk their dogs, like you do?'

'I see people sometimes.'

'As well as walking your dog, did you go to see anyone in the park that night?' came in Andrews.

'No.'

'Did you see anyone you knew?'

'No.'

72

'Did you say anything to the man you passed, just before you found the body?' asked Powell.

'I may have done.'

'What?'

'I may have said "Good evening." Something like that.'

'What did he say back?' demanded Andrews.

'Nothing.'

'But he looked at you, so you could see him quite clearly?'

'Only for a moment.'

'Do you see your friends – other people walking their dogs – anywhere in Lane Park?'

'By the hothouses of the botanical gardens.'

'I want you to do something for me, Mr Gaynor,' said Powell. 'Tomorrow I'm going to get a lot of photographs, which I want you to look through. Pick out any you think might be the man you saw. And I'd appreciate it if you could give me the names of some of your friends who are regularly in the park, who might have seen him as well as you. And I want you to work with an artist. See if you can get an impression of the man you saw that night. You think you can do all that for me?'

'The papers say the poor man was a gangster.'

'He was.'

'I don't want to get involved with gangsters.'

'They won't hurt you. They want the murderer found as much as we do.'

'I'm not sure,' said the man.

'Just come back tomorrow and look at the pictures,' said Powell. It would be easy enough to persuade him to co-operate with a drawing: the mistake would be in crowding him.

73

'He's gay,' declared Andrews, re-entering the office after arranging transport for the nervous man.

'You're going to make a great detective,' said Powell. 'Let's get from Birmingham Vice all the mugshots of any male who's been arrested or charged with lewd behaviour, anything whatsoever homosexual. Male hookers, too.'

Following the rules of investigation, thought Powell, remembering his Texas doubts. And as he did so, as if on cue, Andrews said, 'Routine doesn't trap serial killers.'

Powell said, 'You got a better idea we'll go with it.'

'I'll get the mugshots from Vice,' said Andrews.

In his Pittsburgh hotel room Harold Taylor felt the beginning of the sexual excitement that always came when he was close to a killing. He wouldn't have a whore this time. Try not to, at least. But he'd make the murder last: string it out for as long as he could. That might even be better than sex. Try at least. See what it was like.

Marcus Carr personally answered the telephone, which Taylor expected him to, having followed the old man into his apartment block thirty minutes earlier.

'The Pentagon? What about?' demanded the man, irritably.

'Records, sir. We really are sorry to trouble you.'

'It's not convenient. My wife's unwell. Hospitalized.'

'It won't take longer than half an hour. I was going to suggest around ten-thirty tomorrow morning?'

There was a pause. 'I can give you half an hour. No more.'

'That will be fine, sir. We really are most grateful.'

Chapter Six

'Taylor, sir. I called yesterday, from the Pentagon.' He'd allowed the retired general ten minutes after following him back from the hotel coffee shop.

'Third floor, 36.' It was peremptory, dismissively curt, from a man who'd only ever known command.

The door release buzzed. It was an expansive lobby, with a lot of glass and well tended, large-leafed plants in wood chip pots, a couch daring anyone to sit upon it. Almost as clean as he kept the rented house outside Washington, although it would be difficult for anywhere to be as clean as that. Hated dirt. Any disorder. He checked the elevator indicator, to ensure no-one was descending, before standing in front of the reflecting mirror. Ears first, smaller, flatter. Eyebrows heavier, then the eyes, more pouched, older, against the higher cheekbones, the skin lined, older too. Grey haired. Myron Nolan appeared. Magnificent. Terrifying. He wanted an audience! *Had* to have an audience. He reverted to his reborn identity, stretching his face like someone awakening from a deep sleep. He giggled, seeing the joke. That's what he always did, woke up from a deep sleep.

The elevator was as reflectively clean as the outside mirrors, more spotless glass, the metal rails burnished.

He emerged at the third floor onto deep pile carpet, unmarked cream. It was a nice place to live in. There was another giggle. And to die in.

Carr opened the door immediately, staring out imperiously, the attitude of expected respect ingrained. 'What kept you?'

'Elevator was slow, sir.'

For a man well into his eighties the face was surprisingly unlined. It creased now, into a frown. 'Not usually.'

'It seemed to be today.'

Carr at last stood aside. 'Half an hour, that's all.'

'I hope Mrs Carr is recovering well.' The apartment was immaculate, the carpet pure white. Not for much longer, he thought. Through the panoramic window, to the right, it was just possible to see the Point State Park, which still didn't seem a good enough reason for living there. After a week he'd decided he didn't like Pittsburgh.

'Thank you,' said Carr, curtly, the barest response. 'What's your rank?'

'Civilian employee, sir. Records, like I said.' Carr was much shorter than he remembered – hadn't there been a height requirement in the Army? – a rather ordinary, tiny man without a uniform. He was wearing a white polo shirt, green check slacks and white loafers.

'Sit there,' ordered the man, isolating a chair. 'What's this about records?' He spoke looking at the shoulder satchel, taking a seat that put him slightly higher.

Little-man inferiority, Taylor recognized. 'It goes back a long way, sir: 1949.' He'd stretch it out, make it last as long as possible.

'In Germany then. Control Commissioner.'

'That's the period I'm looking at. You were a colonel?'

76

'That's right.' Carr shifted, impatiently. 'What, precisely, is it you want to know?'

'Do you remember a quartermaster sergeant named Myron Nolan?'

The smooth face creased again. 'I don't think so. Should I?'

'I'm sure you could if I reminded you.' Not the face yet. Too soon.

'That's impertinent!'

And it's going to get worse. 'There was a court-martial. You were the president. Involved death and injuries to some children.'

The frown of forgetfulness went but Carr's face remained stiff at what he considered insubordination. 'I said your attitude is impertinent.'

This was good! 'Was he?'

'What!'

'Myron Nolan. Did you think he was impertinent?'

'Who's your commanding officer?'

'Difficult to say. Don't think I can help you there.'

'Give me your direct line number. I want to speak to someone in authority there!'

'Just hear me out about Myron Nolan?' He let the pause last almost too long. 'Please.' When the man didn't respond, Taylor said, 'You do remember the man now – the name – don't you?'

'He killed those children. Sold contaminated drugs on the black market. A lot died. Others were maimed. A bastard.'

'Penicillin and streptomycin. It was actually thirty who died. Fifteen were crippled.'

'Jailed for life, for manslaughter,' said Carr, in further recollection. 'I wanted execution but the Judge Advocate said it was legally impossible on the charge.'

'He did die. Murdered in military detention in 1951.'

'Pity it took so long. Bastard.' The irritation momentarily slipped, in his remembered outrage, quickly to return. 'I'm waiting for your department number.'

They were only a few feet apart, six, maybe eight, and the apartment lounge was very light in the bright morning sun. Taylor still leaned forward, narrowing the gap, not wanting the old man to miss anything. He did it as he had in the lobby downstairs, ears, eyes, sagged skin, instant ageing. Carr blinked, then squeezed his eyes closed longer, tighter, someone imagining an aberration, an optical spasm.

'Recognize me? Look hard. Remember? It's me. Myron Nolan. Back from the dead.'

Carr's expression was close to a smile, beginning as a snigger of disbelief but strangling into a whimper, terror clogging his throat. 'I don't . . . what . . . ?'

'I can come back. Always come back. Always punish.'

'I don't think I'm well . . . please . . . help . . .'

'No help, Marcus, No respect, no mercy, no help.'

'No, please . . . I'm not seeing . . . my eyes . . .'

'You're going to die, old man. Be cut up. Little dick. Little eyes. Little pieces.' It was fantastic. Orgasmic. Better than a woman. Far better than a woman, no matter how good she was. He let the previous face go, brought it back, Nolan, Taylor, Nolan, Taylor.

Carr had recoiled into his chair and was trying to push himself even further away, scrambling feet churning the carpet. His eyes bulged and a fat tongue, bleeding where he'd bitten it, protruded. There were no words, just a sound, the mewing of a trapped animal, unable to escape.

Too quick. It had all happened too quick. Carr hadn't lost his reason yet: started gibbering. Taylor reached into the satchel, bringing out the ice pick, holding it up between them. 'This is what I'm going to do it with. Direct into your heart: a moment of exquisite agony.'

The whimpering old man tried to move, more instinctive than intentional, falling to one side to get out of his seat, but Taylor was ready, catching Carr easily with his right hand to twist him back, exposing his chest fully for the thrust from his left. Carr looked down, watching the point go into him. As quickly the head came up and he managed: 'But—?' and then the pain came and he screamed, just once, and died.

Taylor stood back, letting the body fall to the floor. Some general: hadn't even tried to fight. Wouldn't have mattered – he was too old, too small – but he should have fought. Tried something. Coward. Desk jockey soldier. Known a lot of them during the war. Been one himself but at least got through the supplies he was responsible for: enough for the poor bastards at the front and enough for him, safely out of range, to make everything worthwhile.

It was an afterthought – one that pleased him – to keep the Myron Nolan face. Poetic justice. Unhurriedly, almost casually, he undressed, stacking his clothes carefully a long way from where he intended to operate. It took him longer to strip the still warm body, neatly folding each article as he removed it. He was careful to put them clear, too, although there wouldn't be any splashing. He knew what he was doing: had done it a lot.

He took the scalpels and the specimen jar, laying everything out as neatly as he'd insisted his theatre should be in the last half of the previous century. He punctured the left eye first, with a single downward thrust, but took care with the extraction of the right, immersing it in the preserving fluid in the specimen jar.

It was a little dick and there was hardly any blood when it was severed but a lot more, which there usually was, when the head was amputated. The last act was to incise the cross.

He laid the body out, positioning the pieces, before guessing at the bedroom from which the bathroom ran, *en suite*, and got it right first time. He hummed when he showered, a wordless tune, thinking how much more civilized it was cleaning himself properly like this than it had been in the desert and in the park, from the canister. Too much blood from the trucker and the whore had dried on him, stiffening his skin. He shuddered at the physical memory.

Dry but still naked he returned to the lounge, finally replacing Carr's clothing beside the body, ensuring that each piece was in perfect alignment with that beneath it.

'I'm afraid General Carr won't be able to visit his wife today,' he said to the efficient ward receptionist who immediately answered the telephone.

'Is there a problem?' she asked at once.

'He's come down with a cold. His doctor doesn't think it would be fair for him to bring it into the hospital.'

'Quite right.'

'It might be a couple of days.' It wasn't enough just to die. He had to rot.

'I'll tell Mrs Carr.'

'How is she?'

'No improvement, I'm afraid. Can I tell her who called?'

'Someone the general knew a long time ago. She wouldn't recognize the name.'

The janitor, who was doing something to the wood chips around the plants, looked up enquiringly as Taylor emerged from the elevator. 'Morning?'

'Morning.' In the reflection he realized he still had the Myron Nolan face.

'Visiting?'

'Someone I knew a long time ago.'

The man looked at the satchel containing the scalpels and the souvenir eye. 'Mind me asking who?'

Shit! 'General Carr. Enquiring about his wife.'

The janitor relaxed. 'Not at all well, I hear.'

'Getting better, though.'

'That's good to hear. Have a nice day.'

'I already have.' As he walked away Taylor, who was Myron Nolan, obediently recited the mantra and the Tzu creed, *water every existence with the blood of others.*

Chapter Seven

Wesley Powell felt like the host of a party at which everyone else had arrived before him. They might have started without him – almost had done – but he'd catch up by the end of this first examination, he determined. If his FBI career was on the slide he'd end it on his terms, not through internal political manoeuvring.

The incident room had been created from a small, side-officed conference room on the sixth floor of the Bureau building. Filing cabinets had been assembled along the entire corridor wall, at right angles to which a battery of screen-flickering computers was installed. On the opposite side of the room evidence boards designated by name to each victim had been erected on easels and upon them were displayed scene-of-crime photographs, maps, diagrams and Michael Gaynor's artist impression of the man he'd encountered in Lane Park. In front of them stood two female file clerks, one almost glandularly fat, the other contrastingly thin. Both smiled hesitantly at Powell, who nodded back. Both were middle aged and seemed totally unmoved by the horrific photographic collage they had made.

The oval conference table that dominated the room was already set for the meeting, red-covered, alphabetically indexed dossiers prepared in front of six places.

Harry Beddows gestured Powell towards the top of the table, a man bestowing an honour, and took the seat that put him directly to Powell's right. Geoffrey Sloane, the forensic psychologist profiler assigned from Quantico, was to Powell's immediate left. He remained expressionless on Powell's arrival, although they knew each other. Amy Halliday faced Lucille Hooper, next to whom sat forensic scientist Barry Westmore. Both girls smiled towards Powell, who nodded back but didn't smile.

Beddows patted the file before him, sweeping his arm around the room and announced, 'We're in good shape, up and running, and it's down to Amy. I'd like personally to thank her. What she's done is remarkable.'

'From what little's available, it's certainly damned impressive,' agreed Sloane. He had a thick, phlegmy voice.

The dark-haired girl smiled again, looking towards Powell. He said, 'So what *have* we got?'

'Amy's created the master file and computer programs,' said Beddows. 'Let's have the outline from her.'

'Billie Jean Kesby was well known to El Paso vice,' began Amy, at once. 'Able to steer Maddox to some friends, clubs she worked out of. Story is that she met a guy asked her to go on a trip with him, to San Antonio . . .'

'Description?' demanded Powell.

She shook her head. 'None of the other girls saw him, apparently. Billie Jean used to advertise, in local sex mags—'

'She have an answering service?' broke in Powell, again.

'Machine,' confirmed Amy. 'Maddox has the tape. It's on its way.'

'We can get voiceprints but they're only useful *after* we make an arrest, as confirmation of an identity,' said the head of the forensic team. Westmore was a small, intense man who blinked a lot behind thick-lensed, rimless spectacles.

Amy indicated Gaynor's recollection of the man he had seen in the park. 'Even though Billie Jean's friends say they never saw the guy she went on the trip with we're wiring that to Maddox, to have it run by them just in case. If necessary I can work from that drawing to create three-dimensional computer graphics . . .' She coughed and Beddows edged the water carafe along the table towards her. She smiled, gratefully, and went on: 'I've accessed military justice records. There was a Leroy Goodfellow in a temporary army stockade in Florence, Alabama, from late 1944. Same time as Jethro Morrison, as Goodfellow says. Jointly sentenced for the theft of army materiel, each given five years, served a total of nearly nine, additional sentencing for being involved in a prison riot and assaulting a guard. Broke both the guy's legs.'

'A con who tells the truth: very rare,' said Sloane.

Powell had worked with Sloane on the flawed militant group investigation and had been warned by Beddows that the psychologist had filed a complaining memorandum direct to the Director absolving himself from culpability after the mall bombing. At Beddows's insistence Powell had written an answering, rebutting defence – Sloane's assessment was that the bomber had been a loner, without any organizational back-up – but remained unsure whether that hadn't drawn more attention to the screwed-up episode than it had alleviated blame. The psychologist affected pipes with bowls fashioned into animal heads but played with them constantly, like worry beads, more often than he smoked them. Today's shape, revolving through his fingers, was a horse's head.

'He overlooked the extra sentencing,' Powell pointed out. 'And he had nothing to lose by telling me what he did.' And everything to gain if the old man and Jethro Jnr had worked a scam over the jewel robbery, he thought.

Amy turned towards the pathologist and said, 'The murder wounds are unusual . . .' and then stopped, invitingly.

There was a hesitation before Lucille said, 'I'm betting on an ice pick as the murder weapon. The dimensions would fit. But the amputations are surprisingly clean. Could even be a proper medical scalpel. I'd have thought it impossible for someone without an element of medical knowledge to have decapitated three people – three people who were already dead and had to be man-handled into a cutting position – and to have emerged each time between the third and fourth cervical vertebrae and the facet joints without bone damage. But the cutting edge did, every time. Without touching a bone on either side.'

'It could well be someone who's worked in medicine. Hospital orderly, Medicorps, a doctor even,' came in Sloane.

'And it's a man, even if it isn't the same guy that Gaynor saw in the park,' picked up Lucille. 'The semen DNA definitely isn't that of Gene Johnson, so it's got to be that of the man who had sex with Billie Jean before he killed her and Johnson. And he's young, not much older than mid-twenties. There was a high sperm count. We get him we can convict him.'

'And he's very dark haired,' came in Westmore. 'We

85

recovered quite a lot of hair from the dismantled cab of Johnson's rig. Hair DNA matches that of the semen. I'm pretty sure I've got his fingerprints, too. We lifted Johnson's and Billie Jean's. There was a third set, particularly around the glove box from which the gun was taken.'

'You getting any sort of picture from this?' Powell asked the psychologist.

'Some,' said Sloane. 'He's definitely young, strong. Have to be to move around the 196-pound dead body of Gene Johnson. A complete sociopath, violently schizophrenic. We know he's capable of normal sexual intercourse but he probably gets more sadistic satisfaction from inflicting pain, although it's usually important for the victim to be alive when that pain is caused, to heighten the sensation of absolute power. Obviously some vivisection knowledge, although we shouldn't tie ourselves in too tightly on it being medical. Could be a butcher, veterinary, work in a slaughterhouse. The neatness with which the clothes are folded and left at the scene indicates a strong obsessional streak in the insanity. Cleanliness will be important to him: I'm surprised, considering the bloodstaining there would have been, that he chose to kill outside, in a desert and a park where he couldn't clean himself at once. The cross in the forehead has religious connotations. But not a belief: an anti-belief. That's why the head is cut off. The cross is the religion and God, the decapitation is killing God. The removing of one eye is the usual serial killer souvenir syndrome. There's no shortage of money: he's easily able to go from one side of the country to the other, so we're not looking for a bum or a drifter.'

'Pretty much classic serial killer scenario, apart

perhaps from the savagery of the mutilations and the religious overtones?' queried Beddows.

'That's what I think the evidence shows so far,' agreed the forensic psychologist.

'I don't,' disputed Powell. Thank God he had more than just his intuition, he thought.

There was a stir around the table. Tight-faced, Sloane said, 'You know something the rest of us don't?'

'No,' said Powell. 'Serial killing is random, right? Sociopaths striking at random?'

'Usually,' said Sloane, refusing to commit himself outright.

'Gene Johnson was a horny guy. Seems to have spent all his time involved in or hunting sex when he wasn't driving his rig. Our killer knew that: had checked Johnson out, watched for some time. That isn't random. Our killer went all the way to El Paso to get a hooker Johnson didn't already know, someone who wouldn't tip Johnson off for money that she'd been paid to pick him up in a truck stop the killer knew, from surveillance, Johnson stopped at every Wednesday. When he made contact with Jethro Morrison, our man convinces him it was someone he knew more than forty years ago, during Morrison's first prison sentence. Which the killer also knew to be in Florence, which was only a temporary jail. Morrison served a total of thirty-one years in various penitentiaries. Why specify where he first did time? That isn't random. These are different killings. Planned. Prepared for.'

A stir went around the table again. When no-one else responded Westmore said, 'They're valid points.'

Stubbornly Sloane said, 'We've only got Leroy Good-fellow's word, about Florence.'

'A con who tells the truth: very rare,' echoed Powell.

'This is the first time we've examined what we've got,' came in Beddows. 'We can't be specific, this early.'

'That's exactly my point,' insisted Powell.

'Which I think we've all taken,' said Beddows.

'What there isn't any dispute about is that we've got a homicidal maniac on the loose, wandering from one side of America to the other. So what about going public, warning people?' Powell spoke directly to the division chief, putting the onus for a decision on the man.

Amy said, 'I could do the three-dimensional computer graphic from the artist's drawing in two or three hours, to issue to television along with any media release.'

Beddows shifted, uncomfortably. 'There's always the danger of shaking other crazies out of the trees. Copycat stuff. Or creating a challenge to the guy himself. We go public and the public are going to expect an arrest and start asking questions when we don't quickly make one.'

'Like they are when he kills again and it becomes obvious we knew the risk but *didn't* issue a warning,' persisted Powell.

'I feel we should think about it a little more,' said Beddows.

By which the man meant waiting until he'd got a decision from the Director, Powell guessed. Insistently he said, 'I don't think we should wait long.'

Powell didn't consider he'd caught up by the end of the meeting but decided against extending it by further suggestions, which he was surprised no-one else made. When it broke up, Beddows followed him into the temporary side cubicle, only just stopping at the last moment instead of taking Powell's chair, as task force leader, behind the desk. Instead the man perched awkwardly on the desk edge.

Beddows said, 'I thought that was useful.'

'For a first meeting,' qualified Powell. 'You intend all along to include me in it, Harry?'

Beddows frowned. 'What are you getting at?'

'It was already fixed. What if I hadn't been ready to come back from Birmingham?'

'Director wants movement on this,' said Beddows. 'It was only preliminary, going through the motions. I'm not marginalizing you.'

'That's good to hear.'

'But there is something.'

'What?'

'There's been a complaint, from San Antonio,' declared the division chief. 'Sheriff and the medical examiner.'

'The sheriff was obstructive and the pathologist incompetent,' said Powell. 'It's not important.'

'It might be,' said Beddows. 'Maybe you should get your own memo on file.'

'Harry, I'm busy. Internal affairs or the Director want an explanation, I'll give it to them when they ask. I'm not going to spend my time defending myself against things that don't need a defence. It's not going to be a problem for you.'

'It was you I was thinking it might be a problem for.'

Bullshit, thought Powell. 'Trust me.'

He'd just finished fully reading Amy Halliday's immaculately prepared dossiers when she came through the door, knocking as she entered. She said at once, 'You pissed off at me?'

'No.'

'Got the impression you were.'

Powell shook his head, embarrassed now at his earlier

attitude. If there had been any lack of consideration – insufficient consultation – it was hardly her fault. He'd come close to being immature. 'I'm not.'

'In that case why don't we lunch and talk about the things we didn't cover at this morning's meeting, which maybe we should have done?'

She had every reason for her confidence, he thought, regarding her quizzically. 'If it was that obvious why didn't you raise it?'

'Like I said, I had the feeling I'd already upset you. So I held back to follow your lead.'

They went to the New Old Ebbitt opposite the Treasury building because it was a convenient walk from Pennsylvania Avenue but there was half an hour's wait at the bar for a table. Amy joined him with martini – gin, straight up with a twist – but refused a second. At least two men of whom Powell was aware made their admiration obvious but Amy did not appear to notice. Her hair was perfectly bobbed and he was conscious of only the barest of make-up. He didn't think the suit could be silk, but it had a sheen and there was an optical illusion where it folded, changing the dark green to grey. She didn't seem as petite as she had at their first meeting.

It wasn't until they'd got their table and ordered – scrod for him, Caesar salad for her, with a Napa Valley Chardonnay – that Amy said, 'I agree with you. This isn't normal serial . . .' She grimaced, pulling down the corners of her mouth. 'OK, I know I've got no right or training to challenge a qualified forensic psychologist but since I've been in Analysis I've compiled eight serial killing profile histories. I know the difference between serial routines and serial patterns. These don't fit.'

'So you know what I want?' said Powell, testing.

'The common denominator. I've asked Maddox to

hurry the Johnson family background and I've pulled everything I can from Records on Jethro Morrison. Trouble with Morrison is that so much of his sheet isn't on computer database. What's on paper I'll transfer to disc. And I'll go ahead and make the graphic of the artist's drawing, list Gaynor's physical description alongside. We'll have to go public some time. When we do, we'll be ready.'

'That impression might be a picture of a man Gaynor wanted to meet, rather than the one he did,' warned Powell.

She shrugged. 'It's all we've got, at the moment. Any other ideas?'

'I wish I had just one.'

'You want any changes to the incident room?'

'You set it up?'

She nodded.

'Why didn't you tell me?'

'You *are* pissed off with me!'

'I thought you might have said.' Powell was uncomfortable, embarrassed at himself.

'I thought Harry told you. It was his idea: his place.'

'It's not important.'

'It is,' she argued. 'The most important thing is that you and I don't fall out. Have any misunderstandings.'

'We won't,' promised Powell.

Beth was in when he called and said she hadn't decided what she wanted to do that Saturday but that she would, by the time he picked her up. It was only when he replaced the receiver that he realized he'd forgotten to buy Beth anything in either San Antonio or Birmingham. He really didn't like being a part-time father.

91

Chapter Eight

Powell detoured back across the 14th Street Bridge from his Crystal City apartment to a florist he knew in the Washington Hotel complex to buy the cactus. The salesperson, with a promising southern accent, immediately disappointed him by not having anything unique to Texas so he bought one with a single red flower, like a protruding tongue, that she assured him grew in every desert she'd ever heard of, including those in Texas. He dumped the identifying DC wrapper in an outside trash can and continued on the north side of the river to cross the Key Bridge into Arlington.

Jim Pope opened the door. The sweatshirt was stained and he hadn't shaved. It didn't look or smell as if he'd showered, either. He said, 'Hi' without interest and stood aside for Powell to enter the apartment. Ann was in the kitchen annexe, in a crumpled housecoat. She wasn't wearing any make-up although her blond hair was tidy because of how short it was cut. The colour was growing out at the roots, though. Ann didn't smile. She shouted: 'Beth! Dad's here.' To Powell she said, 'You want coffee?'

'No thanks.'

'We didn't expect you for another hour.'

'I want a full day, after last weekend. I have to bring her back early.'

The woman looked at the cactus. 'How was Texas?'

'Hot.' Powell held out the plant. 'I brought this back for Beth.'

'I didn't think it was for me.'

As Pope came into the room behind him Powell said, 'How's it going? Any luck?' Pope was a slob, he decided, suddenly. It wasn't right for his daughter to live with the man.

'Construction business is dead,' complained Pope.

Powell wished Beth would hurry. 'Maybe it will pick up.'

'And maybe I'll win the Virginia State lottery and live happily ever after with the fairies,' said Ann. Over her shoulder, more loudly, she shouted: 'Beth, come on! Your dad's waiting.'

The girl came hesitantly from her bedroom, the smile matching her uncertainty. The sweatshirt and jeans were freshly washed and so was the girl. The perfume experiment was too heavy. He guessed she'd spent a lot of time getting the ponytail as perfect as it was. He wouldn't draw attention to it by asking how much longer she had to wear the teeth retainer. It was the sort of thing he should know anyway. He said, 'You look terrific.' He held out the cactus. 'Brought this back for you from Texas.'

The child took it, smiling again. 'I've seen them here.'

'They grow all over,' said Powell, caught out.

Beth kissed him and said 'Thanks,' then carried it back into her bedroom.

When she emerged again Powell said, 'I have to bring you back by five, honey. It's a running case. Sorry.'

'That's OK,' shrugged the child.

93

'That OK with you?' he asked his ex-wife.

She shrugged, too. 'You're not taking me to Paris as a surprise, are you, Jim?'

The man didn't reply, slumping instead in front of the television. Cartoons were showing, *Tom and Jerry*. He seemed engrossed. The apartment, Powell saw, was an even bigger mess than it had seemed from the doorway. Ann had trapped him into marriage to stop living like this, he thought. To his daughter he said, 'Let's go.'

In the car Beth said, 'What's the case?'

This wasn't the sort of conversation he wanted. 'Murder,' he said, shortly.

'Tell me about it.'

'We're not talking about murder on our day together. We're not talking about murder, period.'

'Why not?'

'Because I don't want to. What would you like to do? We could go on the river maybe. Or to the Smithsonian. That's a great natural history building, isn't it?'

'Disney Dad!'

'What?'

'That's what divorced fathers are called. I saw it on television. Disney Dads because it's always a problem knowing what to do with their kids on visitation days. So they always go to Disney.'

'Well we can't because there isn't one here. So what do you want to do?'

'You really want to know?'

'I really want to know.'

'Go home to your place. Just hang out. Eat lunch there.'

'I got nothing in the refrigerator.'

'We could stop at a market,' the child pointed out, logically. 'That's where people buy stuff.'

Which was what they did. They bought burgers and hot dogs and buns and Dr Pepper's and Häagen-Dazs and on their way to Crystal City Beth declared it was really fun and she was having the best time. Powell decided he was, too. Back at the apartment he lied and said he hadn't let her win at junior Scrabble and at lunchtime Beth insisted on grilling the meat, which she did perfectly. She laid the table just as well. He had determined against asking but as they ate Beth said, 'Mom and Jim are fighting.'

'People do.'

'They do all the time. I wish they wouldn't.'

'What do they fight about?'

'Jim not having a job, mostly. Mom says he isn't trying.'

'How is he with you?' asked Powell.

She shrugged. 'OK.'

'You and he ever fight?'

'We don't talk much. Which is fine.'

'It'll be all right, between him and Mom,' said Powell, not knowing what else to say.

'Could I stay with you some time?'

He stopped eating. 'You know you can. Any time . . .' He hesitated. 'It's difficult, just now. Obviously. But when it's all over maybe I could fix it so we could spend a whole lot more time together.'

Her face opened, into a smile. 'You really mean that!'

'I promise.'

'You're promising a lot, Dad.'

'And I mean it all.'

Beth demanded to clear the table and Powell called the FBI Watch Room while she did so. The duty officer said there hadn't been any traffic on the Texas or Alabama murders. In the afternoon they found an old movie on

95

television. They watched with Beth curled up, her head against his chest, and Powell fell asleep. It was Beth who woke him. 'It's four-thirty, Dad. You wanted to take me back by five.'

'Thanks.'

'You snore.'

'I'm sorry.'

'You did mean it, about you and me, didn't you? Being together more?'

'I told you, it's a promise.'

Nothing had been done to clean or tidy Ann's apartment when they got back. Pope was still unshaven, unshowered and in the same stained sweatshirt, four bottles through a six pack, slumped in front of the television: the only improvement was a Judy Garland classic instead of Tom and Jerry. Ann's sweatsuit wasn't fresh either, although it wasn't stained. She hadn't made up and was flush faced and Powell guessed he and Beth had interrupted another dispute. He guessed Beth thought the same. Within minutes – seconds – of entering the apartment she'd retreated within herself, formally thanking him for a wonderful day before disappearing into her bedroom saying that she had homework to do. Pope continued to ignore him and Ann seemed anxious for him to leave, so he did.

How much better would it be for Beth if he got out of headquarters? Unanswerable question. His recollection was of working longer hours – spending more time away from home – in every field office in which he'd worked than he did now in Washington.

Which was past history, not a reflection that was going to help him sort out his current problem. Even as an agent-in-charge, able to depute, he couldn't imagine how it would be possible for a thirteen-year-old girl permanently to live with him. He wasn't sure, at that precise moment, how he could properly fulfil the promise that he and Beth would be together more. But he would find a way. He had to. He didn't like – want – Beth living in the sort of environment he thought existed with Ann and her lover.

Amy Halliday was in the incident room, in the centre of her computer bank. She looked around, smiling, at his entry, said 'Hi', and went back at once to her screens. Michael Gaynor's impression of the hurrying man occupied the first. Then, in order, came graphics of Gene Johnson, Billie Jean Kesby and Jethro Morrison. Without looking around again Amy said, 'I know we've got pictures of all three but I can make the graphic three dimensional. Look!'

The features of all three slowly rotated from left profile to full face to then left profile. The impression was of their being alive.

Amy said, 'I think that has more impact on a television screen.'

'I think you're right.' Powell paused. 'I didn't expect to find you here.'

'Thought I'd look in, see if there was anything. While I was here I decided to do this.'

'I've kept in touch with the Watch Room, during the day,' said Powell, unsure why he felt the need to justify himself.

'I've checked Despatch: Billie Jean's answer tape hasn't arrived,' said Amy. 'When we go public it might be worthwhile posting something on the Internet. We've got a home page.'

'Let's keep it in mind. You eat lunch?'

'A sandwich.'

'If you haven't any other plans, you want to take pot luck somewhere in Georgetown?'

'I don't have any other plans.'

It was hardly pot luck because Powell liked the French café opposite the Four Seasons Hotel and being early they didn't have difficulty without a reservation. Amy joined him with a martini again but before she tried it she said, 'We setting out to make a habit of this?'

She'd recognize bullshit without needing a farmyard, he decided. 'You know what they say about there being no such thing as a free lunch: or in this case, dinner?'

'I've heard it said.'

'We have, as another expression goes, been thrown together. And as you said, we don't want any misunderstandings. At the moment I don't know where the hell you're coming from. I think it's time I found out.'

She sipped her drink, solemn faced. 'Too pushy, eh?'

'You tell me.'

'It's quite simple. More than anything else I want to become an FBI agent. I know it's not the usual route, but Research and Analysis was the only thing advertised. And there are precedents for internal transfer. I know because I checked. More than twenty, in fact: five from my own department. And I've got all the necessary academic qualifications, college degree, stuff like that. I know because I checked that, too.' She finished in a rush, breathless.

'And you want to start at the top?' smiled Powell.

'No,' she said, seriously. 'I just want to *start*. I impressed Harry Beddows by making the connection between Texas and Alabama. It was a chance. Why shouldn't I try to run with it? Look good on a transfer CV, don't you think?'

'You and Harry . . .' Powell began, not sure how to

finish. He knew of at least two affairs Beddows had had, when they'd worked together in San Diego. There were probably more.

'No, he's not fucking me,' she said, bluntly.

'That wasn't how I was going to put the question.'

'It was what you would have meant. Something it's even more important for you to believe is that I'm not putting myself in competition with you and I'm not going to try to score off you and I never will . . .' She allowed another brief smile. 'I don't actually think I'd get far, if I tried. I know how good I am at what I *do* do – and that I'm far too pushy and that I too often frighten people off – but I know just as well what my limitations are: that I've got a long way to go, even if I hide it well.' She finished her drink. 'There! Have I earned my dinner?'

'You're getting there,' said Powell. She was either the best con artist or the most unusually ingenuous woman he'd ever encountered. At the moment he was going for ingenuous. 'What about Amy Halliday the woman?'

She didn't smile and for a moment Powell thought he'd pushed too hard. Then she said: 'Only child. Dad worked in Silicon Valley, so we lived in San Francisco. Majored in Sociology at Berkeley. Got fascinated by crime, so my career was decided upon. Mom and Dad died together, which was lucky because they were too dependent upon each other to ever be apart, in a car crash, two years ago. I worked in San Francisco PD in records, saw the Bureau ad and here I am.'

Still too much like a CV, which wasn't what he'd wanted to hear. To ask further *would* be pushing too hard.

After they'd ordered, she said, 'I know that the deal is

that you're paying for this meal, but don't I get to learn a little, too, about Wesley James Powell?'

Powell supposed it was fair exchange but initially he was reluctant, starting out as generally as possible by admitting he'd applied to the Bureau because he couldn't think of anything else to do after leaving college and because his encouraging father had been an agent in the days – 'awesome days, by the decree of the Lord God himself' – of J. Edgar Hoover. He later decided his attitude must have reflected his problems of the last few months, because Amy picked up on it immediately.

'You're a good law officer.'

'Let me guess: you checked my case record!' It hadn't been a difficult guess: she'd known his full name.

'I'm too determined to make a mistake about a team leader.'

He looked at her curiously. 'You mean you would have passed on this – even though you got the chance by making the connection – if you hadn't had confidence in who was heading the investigation?'

'I'd have given it a lot more thought than I did.'

'I guess there's some flattery mixed in there somewhere,' he said. 'Thanks.'

'More practicality than flattery.'

'The success rate hasn't been so good just lately.'

'A bad run, one after the other. It happens.'

He still didn't know her well enough to talk about Beddows's heavy innuendoes. Or about how much his attitude was being affected by his far too belated concern about Beth. There was a break while they ordered. As the waiter left, he said, 'Maybe my luck's changed, having a researcher as career anxious as you. You're not going to miss anything, are you?'

'I might, if we're not a complete team.'

'I think we're going to be.'

She was silent for several moments, picking at the duck she'd ordered. 'As we're baring our souls, I guess we might as well get something else out of the way.'

Powell waited, curiously.

'I know you're divorced, although I don't know if you've got a current relationship.'

When was it going to stop! 'Accessing internal personnel files is prohibited: I actually think it's illegal.' He was aware there wasn't the rebuke, outrage even, there should have been in his voice.

'No misunderstandings, remember?' she said, impatiently. 'I don't have any personal situation. And I'm not looking for one. So by being a complete team I mean a complete *professional* team. Nothing more. Nothing else.' For the first and only time there was an uncertainty in her attitude.

'You believe me if I say I'm not looking for anything other than professional, either?' Considering his disappointment at what she'd just said, he decided he'd sounded quite convincing.

'I could try.'

'Try.'

'Watch me!' she said, turning the word.

Although his intention to create a sensation hadn't diminished – if anything it had increased, although he still hadn't decided how he would achieve it – the anonymity of the Washington suburbs perfectly suited Harold Taylor. He considered the isolated clapboard house he'd rented at Belmont, between Fredericksburg and Charlottesville, to be in an uninhabited no man's land, the residents closest to him almost a quarter of a mile away and having no more interest in him than he

101

had in them, although he amused himself by thinking that one day they'd queue up to lie about how well they'd known him and what sort of man he was.

He'd fitted the basement up first, creating the false wall to hide the safe and the specimen refrigerator and the things he carried in his satchel bag and the minimal laboratory equipment he'd acquired on this return, although he virtually accepted that the belief he'd once held – become moderately famous for, in early nineteenth century London – was a false premiss. Certainly there'd been no evidence in the retained eyes of Gene Johnson or Billie Jean Kesby or Jethro Morrison and he straightened now from the microscope examination of the orb he'd taken from Marcus Carr, positive its retina held no image of him as the last person the retired general had seen, at the moment of death.

He carefully replaced the latest eye in its preserving bottle before he returned it to the refrigerator and stacked the microscope and his testing equipment alongside. It was difficult because when he'd built the shelves he hadn't made allowance for anything extra, like Gene Johnson's handgun. It looked jumbled and it offended him: he couldn't understand now why he'd taken it. He removed the gun from the shelf, worked the safe combination and put it there, smiling in satisfaction at the neat improvement.

Time for England, he decided: England and a shambling, incontinent old man and the elderly widow who had unknowingly inherited the fault of her husband. Maybe, too, for a woman or two. There was, after all, no hurry. But first a visit that had greater priority than all that.

James Durham was on the murder list: the next intended victim when he returned from London. But

James Durham was the paymaster. And before he died he had to pay over the final $500,000 of the money he'd stolen. He'd been given ample warning, to convert what was necessary.

The retribution always had to be absolute.

Chapter Nine

It was unfortunate, although inevitable, that this particular pleasure had to end. He'd enjoyed terrorizing James Durham for as long as he had, having his own performing animal to jump and bark – do any trick demanded – whenever he'd snapped his fingers. But it couldn't be helped. There would, at least, be a final confrontation after this one. Durham would really know it was going to end then. The control – the total life or death power – would be phenomenal when he changed his face, finally to let the man know that for all the time he'd believed he'd been handing over blackmail money he had in fact been repaying Myron Nolan every cent that he'd embezzled all those years ago. It would literally be justice being seen to be done, through fear-frozen eyes.

The anticipatory fear was obvious in Durham's voice even before Myron Nolan's reincarnation identified himself. 'You!'

'I gave you three months.'

'I'd hoped you might have fallen under a bus. Or caught cancer.'

Harold Taylor intruded a long pause. 'What makes you think you can talk to me like that?'

'I can talk to you how I goddamned please.'

Taylor frowned, irritated at the unexpected bravado. He was glad now he'd decided upon the payment the way he had. 'Apologize.'

'Go to hell.'

In different circumstances the truism of the remark might have been amusing. 'You're irritating me. And you can't afford to irritate me. I said apologize. So apologize.'

There was silence from the other end. Taylor didn't break it. At last Durham said, his voice strained, 'I'm sorry.'

'And "I promise not to say anything like that again".'

'I promise not to say anything like that again.'

'Ever.'

'Ever.'

'That's better. I'm outside. I'm coming up.'

'It's not—'

'It can't ever be inconvenient when I come. You haven't got anyone there, have you? I've been watching the apartment for three hours.' He had, from the comfort of the Waldorf-Astoria, which was almost directly opposite Durham's apartment on New York's Park Avenue. He was calling from one of the public phones in the hotel lobby.

'No.'

'And if you've got an appointment, cancel it. I come first. Always. That's the rule, isn't it, James?'

There was another silence.

'James?'

'Yes.' The voice was subdued, the man beaten.

'You tell the concierge you're having the visitor he'll know, from before. Mr Barkworth.' It was a nostalgic reminiscence sometimes to use the name of his last full reincarnation in London, as an early nineteenth-century

105

surgeon in the vanguard of medical scientific development, particularly in the new-found discipline of ophthalmology. It was also the false name in which he'd banked the family inheritance from this existence, close to $1 million he hadn't needed to touch for a long time, not since putting the squeeze on James Durham. It was ironic that it was because of what Durham had done that he now kept his own money so well hidden, in a numbered account in the Cayman Islands.

'It's not the same man. He's changed.'

'Tell him Barkworth. That he needn't bother with ID.'

The lobby of Durham's apartment block was not as clean as Marcus Carr's had been. There was still a lot of glass but with a man behind the desk, watching him come in, he couldn't amuse himself as he had in Pittsburgh. The concierge was a black, so tall and thin that his uniform badly fitted, too big at the shoulders but too short in the arms.

'Mr Durham is expecting me.'

'Mr Barkworth?'

'That's right.'

'He called down. You mind signing in, sir?'

Taylor hesitated, not expecting the demand. There was no reason to protest. At least the lobbyman hadn't asked for documentation, which he didn't have. The elevator smelt of stale tobacco and there were stubs in the ashtray. Taylor wrinkled his nose in disgust. After the facile but unexpected defiance on the telephone he anticipated something further, perhaps the stupidity of keeping him waiting in the corridor, but the apartment door opened at once.

Taylor knew Durham to be eighty-three and although there was no physical likeness – Durham was a large, broad-shouldered man against Marcus Carr's rotund smallness – there was a similarity in their apparent good health. The brownness of Durham's face – since his retirement from the law firm he'd founded he'd spent a lot of time at his fishing cabin in the Catskills – was heightened by his very full, although totally white hair and he was clear eyed and clear skinned.

Taylor walked in, uninvited, and went directly to the drinks tray, pouring himself Scotch from a decanter. It was important to impose himself absolutely after the telephone nonsense. Durham stood watching, blank faced.

Taylor said, 'Well?'

'I've got it.'

'Of course you've got it. You stole it.'

'I've got it together in cash.'

'That's what I gave you three months to do. That was very generous of me.'

'This is the last. You said this would be the last!'

'You're a millionaire, several times over. Why should you worry?'

The elderly man's face twisted. 'So you're going to want more. Blackmailers always do.'

'You should know. You're the criminal lawyer. And the criminal. You know it from both sides, James. Just like I know how your entire life – all those millions – was built on stealing from Myron Nolan, before and after he was murdered.'

'You said you'd bring the documents this time,' said the old man, plaintively.

Theatrically Taylor snapped his fingers, as if in sudden recollection. 'Would you believe it! Slipped my mind. Means I'll have to bring them another time.' This charade was the best part of the torture. There had

107

been documentary evidence, statements from the banks they'd hidden from the military police investigators and to which he'd given Durham access, with power of attorney, when he'd trusted the lawyer: statements he'd got independently when he'd stopped trusting him, showing Durham's consistent looting. But they'd all been returned to Durham by prison authorities unaware of their significance, after his death as Myron Nolan, as part of the estate for which the lawyer was responsible. And which he had gone on plundering.

Durham extended his arms, palms upwards. 'God how I'd like to kill you, with my own bare hands.'

'Murder as well as larceny and embezzlement! Who would have believed it of such a well-known, upstanding citizen of this fine city?' Abruptly Taylor changed the tone. 'What you'd like to do and what you're going to do are a very long way apart, James. You're going to go on doing exactly what I tell you, as and when I choose to tell you. And the moment – the very moment – that you imagine some independence like you imagined this morning on the telephone you stop and think for a moment how everything you built up – your practice and your reputation and your respect – would crumble if I took what I know to the police. Never forget that's the choice you've got.'

'You're never going to let me, are you?'

'No, never . . .' He paused, smiling at the joke he'd try to remember to tell Durham next time: 'not for as long as you live. Now you go to that great big safe set into the closet floor and get me the money you've had three months to get together.'

The lawyer returned so quickly that Taylor guessed he'd already had the cash ready, out of the safe. It was divided between two large, equally filled, brown envelopes. The lawyer offered them to Taylor and said, 'Four hundred thousand.'

Taylor took it, shaking his head, savouring the surprise he'd intended even before Durham's insolence. 'Price has gone up,' he declared.

'What!' Durham's face fell.

'I've made some more calculations. Three months ago I thought $400,000 would repay everything you stole from Myron Nolan. But it won't, will it? The actual figure, to clear the slate, is $500,000 . . .'

'That's not true!'

'You know it is. Like I know it is because I've got the documentation, remember? Means you owe another $100,000.'

'But I haven't . . .' started the lawyer, desperately.

'And I also think you should be fined for the way you behaved on the telephone,' stopped Taylor. 'Always got to pay for your sins. Wasn't that the principle in all those cases that made you famous?'

He wasn't sure whether the visible tremors going through the other man were fury or despair. 'I don't have $100,000 in cash in the apartment. Don't be ridiculous!'

'On this occasion, I'll take a cheque. You can tell your bank, before I leave, that it's to be paid by special clearance.'

'They won't take instructions by telephone.'

'Yes they will, from someone like you: a respected, well-known customer. Come on now! I've got a lot to do.'

Durham's mouth opened and closed, but no words came, and Taylor decided the shaking was fury. When the man finally spoke, the one word – 'bastard' – only just croaked out.

'You trying to get another fine here, James?'

Leaden footed, Durham crossed the room to a bureau in the corner, took out a cheque and for a moment stood forlornly with it in his hand, staring down at the floor.

'I said come on! T-A-Y-L-O-R. And get a hold on that anger. I don't want any query on the signature.' He stood over Durham while he wrote and remained close to the man while he talked to his Wall Street bank, wanting to hear everything the high deposits manager said from the other end. He also needed the name of the man, Howard Drew, through whom the arrangement was being made.

When Durham replaced the receiver he said, 'There! See how everyone does what they're told when they're told by a rich man. How you do everything you're told when I tell you!'

'Get out,' said the lawyer, although quietly, drained of any remaining anger. 'Please, just get out.'

Taylor caught a shuttle back to Washington with ample time to get to the Connecticut Avenue bank in which he'd opened an account and rented a safe deposit box within two days of his decision to make the city his base. His banker was a girl of about thirty whom he'd briefly considered trying to date, a milk-fed blonde with exciting-looking ties, named Thelma Jones. She raised her eyebrows at the size of the cheque and said the stock market must be doing well and Taylor, who'd described himself as a freelance broker on his bank application details, said it was if you knew what you were doing. He gave her Howard Drew's name to contact in New York and the special clearance arrangement was confirmed with one telephone call. That transaction completed, he went to the safe deposit division and retrieved his box, emptying most of the contents of the brown envelopes

110

into it. He allowed himself $75,000 for the trip to London and bought his first-class ticket in cash, for a flight on the following day.

By the time Taylor returned to his no man's land house to pack, Thelma Jones had spoken at length with her department head, who agreed with her that they had to obey the law.

And in New York James Durham was still numbed with despairing disbelief at the inconceivable mistake that he, a criminal lawyer of all people, had made. There wasn't any escape. He could possibly argue statute of limitations: negotiate a deal. How long would it be before they came for him? All he could do was wait.

Taylor's flight left Dulles airport promptly at 11 a.m. At noon, after complaints about the smell from other residents, the Pittsburgh janitor used his pass-key to enter Marcus Carr's apartment to find the putrefying body of the retired army general. The janitor vomited.

Chapter Ten

Matt Hirst, head of the FBI's Pittsburgh office, was waiting for them in the corridor, driven out by the smell along with four or five local police officers. Two of the local men were very slowly taping off the corridor, determined to keep a job outside. Hirst was a stocky, red-haired man whose freckles were even more pronounced against a face turned chalk white by what was inside the apartment. He was already protectively suited. He said, 'I've never seen anything like it. Never.'

Lucille Hooper, who, like the rest of the FBI group except Powell, had put on her forensic protection in the corridor, said, 'This is how I become the most popular person on the Task Force' and held out a jar of strongly mentholated balm. She already had a heavy smear beneath her nose. Everyone copied her, even Geoffrey Sloane.

Marcus Carr's body was displayed in exactly the same position as the other victims. Decomposition was already well advanced. More flies remained than swarmed up at the disturbance of their combined entry. The grotesqueness of the body was heightened by the fact that the face sockets were filled with maggots, making it appear that Carr was white eyed. The forensic team distributed themselves according to their functions. Powell, just minutes behind, went from room to room, keeping out of their way, before returning to Hirst. He said, 'How much do we know about Marcus Carr?'

'Retired army general. Quiet. Well liked. Lived in this block for fifteen years. Wife had a long history of heart problems, so they needed to be near the hospital . . .'

'Where's she now?'

'*In* hospital. According to the janitor she had a heart attack three weeks ago. I called, while I was waiting for you. She's been in a coma for the past three days. She's going to die . . .' Hirst paused. 'Janitor says he hadn't seen the general for about a week but that there was a guy, a stranger he hadn't seen before, who visited around that time.'

Barney Zeto's basement office was crowded, with three extra people in it, but it was better than trying to talk to the janitor in the corridor with the pervading smell. Powell took it at the other man's speed, needing the background anyway, listening to Zeto's account of a childless 'army gentleman, wonderful wife' too independent to have a maid ('Mrs Carr's upbringing, I supposed. She was German: they'd met in Berlin just after the war, when it was hard there') who'd remembered him at Christmas and took an interest in other people's kids, a man who'd actually used his influence ('lotta respect locally, the general') as a college governor to get Zeto's nephew a football scholarship.

'Tell me about the man you saw,' prompted Powell, at last.

'You think he could be the man who did that up there?'

'Until I find him and he convinces me he's not,' said Powell. 'He definitely told you he'd been to see General Carr?'

Zeto nodded. 'I'm responsible for the security in this place . . .' The man swallowed, realizing how badly he'd failed. 'So when I see him come out of the elevator, carrying this bag, I decide—'

'What bag?' interrupted Powell, urgently.

Zeto made a vague shape, with his hands. 'Big, briefcase-type thing. With a strap.'

Gaynor's description, recognized Powell. Just as he'd recognized the military significance of an army stockade in Alabama. It was coming! 'How'd this case work? You mean the handle was a strap? Or that it had a strap that went over the shoulder?'

'Strap that went over the shoulder.'

'You thought this stranger might have something in there he'd stolen, from someone in the apartments?'

'At first,' agreed the man. 'That's why I stopped him. Got to talking.'

'You ask to look inside?'

'Was going to, until he mentioned General Carr. If he was a friend of General Carr's he had to be all right, hadn't he?'

It would have been cruel to give the obvious answer. Powell said, 'I want you to really concentrate . . .' He nodded sideways. 'Matt here will come back tomorrow, go through what you tell us, in case you remember something more. But for now I want you to describe this man to me. Everything about him that you can. It's very important. OK?'

'OK,' said Zeto. 'Odd.'

Powell hadn't intended to interrupt – prompt at all – but he couldn't risk any wrong directions. 'What do you mean, odd?'

'He seemed young, bodily. Slim, no gut. Walked easily, young-like, know what I mean?'

114

'Kind of,' said Powell, cautiously. 'So what was odd?'

'His face. His face didn't fit his body. It was an old face, pouchy. Bags under his eyes, lot of wrinkles.'

Powell had a stomach drop of disappointment, changing his original intention. 'Let's forget the face, for a moment. Describe him bodily.'

'Slightly built, average height.'

'Bodily, how old would you have said?'

'Thirty, tops.'

He'd definitely prompt, Powell decided. 'Black hair?'

'Kinda mousy. Lotta grey at the sides.'

It *didn't* fit Gaynor's description! The man Gaynor had wanted to encounter rather than the man he had, Powell remembered. 'Long or short?'

'Crew cut.'

Shit! thought Powell. 'What kind of clothes?'

'Dark trousers – but trousers, not jeans – and a windbreaker. And a sweater.'

Back where he'd started, with a vague comparison to Gaynor's impression. Abruptly, annoyed with himself for not thinking of it earlier, Powell said, 'This block got CCTV?'

'I've already checked,' came in Hirst. 'Loop's wiped every four days. I've retrieved the film, for enhancing, but I think we're too late.'

Why the hell wasn't life just very occasionally fair? thought Powell. There was silence for several moments, no-one sure how to continue. Powell remembered something Zeto had told them earlier. 'You described the general as a man of routine?'

'His army training, I guess.'

'He have any regular places he used to go that you know about, where he might have met this man you saw?'

The janitor shook his head. 'Not without Mrs Carr, until she got taken into hospital this time. They were inseparable. Celebrated their golden wedding here.'

Powell thought immediately and intuitively that there was something there. But what? 'Until she got taken into hospital,' he echoed. 'You mean he began doing something regular *after*?'

'No,' dismissed the man. 'Nothing like that. Used to go out to eat more often, breakfast, dinner sometimes. But that's all. Just local, places he could walk to. The Hilton a coupla blocks up. More convenient than doing it himself, I guess. It was Mrs Carr who wouldn't have help: did everything for them. He was kinda lost without her.' He paused. 'Now it's Mrs Carr who's lost him.'

Powell's intuitive feeling was that he'd missed something but he knew that whatever it was – if, indeed, it was anything at all – he'd have to wait for it to become more obvious than a simple impression. He said, 'I'm going to have a drawing sent from Washington, which Matt here will show you. I want you to look at it very carefully. Tell us if you think it could be the man you saw. And in between I want you to think of anything else you can about General and Mrs Carr – and the man – and write it down so you'll remember, when Matt comes. OK?'

The man nodded. 'The management come to you, ask you if you think I didn't do right not checking the guy out more thoroughly, you going to say I screwed up?'

'No,' said Powell. 'I'll tell them you couldn't have done anything more at the time and that you've helped us a great deal.'

'I appreciate that.'

In the elevator on their way back up to the sixth floor

116

Hirst said, 'If you've got a suspect picture, there's been more?'

'Two cases. Three people dead,' said Powell. 'We're not going public on it yet.'

'That a good idea?' queried Hirst.

'No,' agreed Powell. 'Just the way it's being played.'

'Zeto's description anything like that you've got from the others?' asked the local agent.

It came to Powell as he was about to leave the elevator. He stepped out but remained standing directly outside in the corridor.

'What?' demanded Hirst.

It was not intuition after all, simply being a competent cop, but thank God the possibility had occurred to him. 'This block's on a main highway. Carr went along it every day since his wife got ill, certainly for breakfast, according to the janitor. Check all the stores – check everything – for a CCTV. If there's a bank it'll be more than a four-day loop. Maybe at the Hilton, too, which we know he went to.'

'You think he was stalked?' said Hirst.

'I think we need to check all we can, to find out.'

'It looks like a denominator,' agreed Amy. 'But where's the military link to Johnson?'

'That's what you had to stay behind in Washington to research,' said Powell. He'd left the murder scene early for the local Bureau office to pass on to Amy what he considered relevant and to get Gaynor's impression wired to show to the janitor.

'Everything's arrived: Maddox's stuff, Morrison's records and Billie Jean's answer tape.'

'Anything?'

'Wes!'

117

'Sorry. Getting too used to Wonder Woman.'

'You staying down?'

'Tonight, certainly.'

'You think the janitor's is a positive sighting?'

'More positive than Gaynor's but there's some wide disparities.'

'The man Gaynor wanted to meet,' she remembered.

'I already thought of that. We won't issue it – or your graphics – until we've got it sorted out,' Powell decided.

'Harry Beddows says for you to call.'

'Tell him I will, when I've had the assessment meeting.'

There turned out to be very little to assess, when the rest of the Task Force assembled an hour later.

Barry Westmore had found fingerprints in the apartment bathroom that matched those from Johnson's cab. From the Carrs' bath and from a towel discarded in a laundry basket they'd recovered black head and pubic hair the forensic scientist expected to make a DNA match under analysis with the black hair also lifted from the Texas cab. Lucille Hooper apologized in advance for how imprecise she would be, hampered by the advanced decomposition of the body. That decomposition, as well as Carr maintaining low central heating, had kept the body warm, making it impossible to estimate the time of death to within a twenty-four-hour period, although she didn't think any longer than a week, which fitted Zeto's lobby encounter. There was a little of the eye remaining in the left socket, nothing in the right. The finger extremities had been eaten away, which made it difficult to establish under-nail debris. Geoffrey Sloane insisted it fitted a predictable pattern and that the killer's having showered afterwards, as well as the neatly folded clothes, confirmed the obsession with cleanliness and tidiness.

'We've got a military denominator,' suggested Powell.

'Too tenuous,' rejected the psychologist.

'But worth checking?'

'If there's anything to check.'

'There was no forced entry. And no external evidence in the apartment of a struggle,' Barry Westmore pointed out. 'He either convinced Carr that he knew him. Or had a reason to be let in.'

'As he did with Jethro Morrison,' reminded Powell. 'And why's he so careless? Having tricked his way into his victim's confidence he doesn't take any precautions, leaves fingerprints, forensic evidence, everywhere. And why does a man so obsessed with cleanliness screw a hooker without a condom, risking infection?'

'We've got a serial killer, pure and simple,' said Dr Sloane. 'Doesn't think – worry – like an ordinary person or an ordinary criminal. Some things don't fit but nothing ever does, not perfectly. Nothing here changes my profile. I think we should go public and start issuing it.'

'I agree with—' began Powell but stopped at Matt Hirst's flushed entry. He had several film canisters under his arm.

'What?' demanded Powell.

Hirst shook his head, bemused. 'It doesn't make sense. There's a man with two different faces.'

It was as good, as satisfying, as every return to England had been. It really would be good to live out this existence here. At once came the contradiction. What about the other intention, which excited him far more: causing a sensation? He still hadn't thought of a way to

119

achieve that. More important than deciding where finally to settle this time. He was aroused. Easy to satisfy that, the way he usually did. Water every new existence with blood. Fresh blood, he decided. Not that of someone on the list. He needed a woman.

Chapter Eleven

He was shaking with fury, almost beyond control, which he never became. Always in total command, in charge. He shouldn't have let her live. She didn't deserve to live. Should have been shown her mistake – the last thing she'd have seen on this earth – for laughing at him. *Him!* Laughing at *him*! No-one could laugh at him. Be allowed to think they were superior. Maybe he would kill her. Not now. Before he returned to America, to finish the list. A final, parting gesture. Knew where she operated from. What she looked like. Bitch. Whoring, cock-sucking bitch. Not give her any mercy. Not kill her, before setting out the sacrifice. Cut her tits off first. Let her know why he was doing it. Teach her. He'd refused before, when the room had been too filthy. But none of them had laughed at him before, sneering he couldn't do it: grateful for getting the money they'd agreed and the tip, without having to do anything. Could have fucked her brains out: would do, before he killed her. Not just laughed at him. Badly lied to him about the room. Promised it would be clean, with a bath, even though he'd warned her. It had been disgusting, verminous: torn sheets thick with semen, blood, dirt. Unbelievably disgusting.

'Whereabouts in Park Lane?' demanded the driver of

the taxi who'd brought him from King's Cross.

Harold Taylor concentrated for the first time, seeing the Dorchester ahead. 'Here's fine.'

He hesitated on the pavement, knowing the direction he wanted but momentarily undecided. He felt he needed to be washed, cleansed, in surroundings if not by water. He liked the predominant whiteness of the Dorchester's cocktail bar, the ambience of fresh-smelling people in polished surroundings although the smell of cigarettes and cigars was distasteful. He chose the bar and was careful to sit with his satchel wedged between his feet, where he could constantly feel it, to be sure it wasn't stolen. He supervised the mixing of the martini, wanting to taste the harshness of the gin, which he did, so he ordered a second. He recognized as a professional the blonde at the end of the bar who was waiting and half smiled but she was high class and would have a maid, which wasn't convenient. It was unfortunate, because everything – she most of all – would be clean. Always needed it to be rough – street whores – to get an erection but was always terrified of catching something. He considered a third drink and decided against it, leaving without again looking at the girl.

Shepherd Market was very busy, which was how he liked it, the restaurants crowded, people spilling out of the pubs into the narrow streets and alleys. There were a lot of girls to choose from and he chose carefully, wanting one who appeared to be working alone, without a pimp. He was on the point of approaching one when he saw the obvious eye contact between her and a man in a parked Jaguar, about ten yards away. Four others were unacceptable, because they were smoking. He decided upon the redhead.

'Hello.'

122

'Hello.' The smile was quick, professional.

'You working?' Good teeth, big tits.

'Sure. You're American?'

'That's right. What are we talking about?'

'What are *you* talking about? You got special toys in that bag?'

'Maybe. That a problem?'

'No. But it'll be extra.'

'That's OK. What are we starting at?'

The assessment was quick, professional again. 'A hundred: anything kinky extra, depends what it is.' She couldn't quite keep from her voice the hope that she hadn't pitched too high.

'Sounds good. A hotel?'

'You'll have to pay for the room, of course.'

'How much?'

Emboldened she said, 'Fifty.'

'Is it clean? It must be clean, with a bath.'

'Bath will be £25 extra.'

'That's OK.'

'I'll do whatever you want,' promised the girl, setting off past the cinema. 'We'll have a really good time.'

'I know we will.'

'My name's Beryl.'

'Harold.'

There was a vacant taxi coming up Curzon Street and Beryl hailed it with a flail of arms. He missed the address she gave, so as they sat he said, 'Where we going?'

'The Grand.'

'You're sure it's clean.'

'As a whistle. My dad's name was Harold. What part of America you from?'

'All over.'

123

'Here on holiday?'

'Business.'

'How long for?'

'As long as it takes.'

'Might see you again, then? I've got a number you can call.'

'Let's see what it's like tonight.'

'You won't be disappointed, I promise.'

'You got any toys with you?' he asked, looking at her shoulder bag.

'A dildo and some nipple clamps,' she said. 'What have you got?'

'Wait and see,' he said.

'You going to surprise me?'

'Probably.'

'Almost here now,' said the girl, as the taxi turned down the Bayswater Road. 'You'd better give me the money for the room. And for the taxi.'

He gave her two £50 notes and one £10. The hallway was shadowed and dark but didn't hide Beryl sliding one of the £50 notes into her pocket. The night clerk only looked at the whore. On their way to the room, in stronger light, he saw how brightly red her hair was dyed, badly clashing with the different red of her dress. From the mangy state of it the animal from which her fur jacket had been made could only have died from old age. Beryl was very slightly cross eyed.

'Nice room, isn't it?' she said, proprietorially, when she let them in.

'Lovely.' If Beryl had been his first choice that night he'd have paid her off in the hope of finding somewhere better. The curtains were threadbare and a hole was trodden in the centre of a carpet dotted with cigarette burns. The mirror of the dressing table that was the only furniture apart from the bed was whorled with verdigris stains. But there was a bath that he'd need to wash clean before he used it and when he pulled the covering back he saw that the bedsheets, so thin they were opaque, hadn't been used before.

Beryl said, 'You want to fuck without a condom, it's an extra £50.'

'I don't think so.'

'A hundred then.'

As she took the money he saw her fingernails were badly bitten.

'What do you want to do?'

'Let me undress you.'

She raised her arms, wriggling her hips, as he lifted the dress over her head and lay back on the bed in what she imagined to be a provocative pose, easing her body this way and that for him to remove the bra, pants, suspender belt and stockings. She lay with her hands above her head, bringing her breasts up, as he undressed.

'Like what you see?'

'Very much.' Her breasts were full, the nipples big.

The girl whimpered, pretending to enjoy them being kneaded. 'You want to put the clamps on?'

'Yes.'

She groaned more loudly when he did and said, 'Mercy, mercy', play-acting.

'Go down on me,' he said.

She did hungrily, another part of the act, head pumping back and forth.

He had to do it, let her see. He'd come when she did. 'Look up at me, so you can see my face.'

She stopped working on him, crouched between his

straddled legs, her mouth still open. 'What are you doing?'

'Can't you see?'

'Your face! What's happening to your face!'

'Isn't that clever?'

'Don't. I don't like it. Please. It's not nice.'

'You know what you've seen?'

She didn't reply. She was crawling backwards, down the bed.

'You've seen something that no-one else in the world has ever seen. That no-one else in the world would believe . . .' He was quicker than her when she ran, getting to the door first, blocking her. 'You haven't got any clothes on.'

'You're one of them funny buggers! I should have known.' She went back to the bed, snatching up her underwear and starting to get into it. He saw that her hands were trembling.

'You believe in ghosts, Beryl? People being able to come back from the dead? Be reincarnated?'

From her handbag she unexpectedly snatched a bone-handled cut-throat razor, flicking it open to expose the blade. It wavered in her shaking hand. It looked very dirty and he grimaced.

'This is a fucking razor! And I know how to use it. Get out of the fucking way or I'll slash whichever face you want to pull.'

'You might be reincarnated one day, Beryl. You won't be able to remember this life, though. Not many people can. Some, but not very many.' He went towards her as she opened her mouth to scream.

'We've got more powerful photo-enhancing equipment in Washington, but this should be good enough,' said

Barry Westmore. 'But at the moment it beats the hell out of me.'

Westmore, his photographic specialist Murray Anderson, Powell and intermittently Matt Hirst had spent four hours at the Pittsburgh police laboratory, carrying out every examination Anderson devised, magnifying until the picture disintegrated on the screen every millimetre of the CCTV footage of two identically dressed men, one young from several sightings on the Hilton hotel security video, always close to an easily recognizable Marcus Carr, the other old from a single shot, dated against the day Barney Zeto encountered the stranger in the apartment block lobby. Both carried shoulder satchels. Anderson's first action was to enlarge both and print off freeze frames. The photograph of the young man was remarkably similar to Michael Gaynor's impression of the man he'd seen in Lane Park. When Hirst returned with it to the apartment block the janitor denied ever seeing the young man in the artist's drawing or in the freeze frame. He'd positively identified the elder as the man he'd confronted in the lobby.

'Father and son?' suggested Powell. 'Some kooky guys dress identically like that.'

Westmore pointed to the two largest freeze frames that had been lifted and were now pinned on boards. 'We've got to run them by physiognomy people back in Washington: get the precise measurements and make graphics to overlay one face on to the other but look! There's not a single matching facial characteristic. They're two totally different people.'

'The heights compare,' said Anderson. 'So do the shoulder widths.'

'A disguise mask!' suggested Hirst. 'One of those things that pull right over your head. I've seen them at parties, gorillas, stuff like that. The neck goes right down inside your shirt collar!'

Westmore pointed to the blow-up again. 'And the gap between the mouth and eyes of the mask and those of the person underneath is as wide as a cavern. That's no mask. That's a real face.'

Lucille Hooper had worked in another part of the building, carrying out her detailed autopsy in the police mortuary. All four men turned as she came into the room behind them. She said, 'Seems like an appropriate entry.'

'Why?' asked Powell.

'Picked up a message at the desk to call the incident room, so I did. Media have got the serial connection. Harry Beddows is going ape.'

'I left messages! Told Amy!' Beddows shouted down the phone.

'And she told me,' said Powell. 'I haven't had time. Things have been breaking here. And for Christ's sake stop yelling.'

'What things?'

'We think we've got a picture of the killer. But there are two different faces.'

There was a long silence from the other end. 'What the hell are you talking about?'

'That's our problem and what I've been busy on. I don't know what I'm talking about. It's on security video and it doesn't make an ounce of sense.'

'What are we going to tell the media? They're screaming for a release.'

'We don't tell them anything about this,' warned Powell. 'We do and we're never going to be able to get the lid back on the box. How'd the media get it?'

'You didn't know Pittsburgh PD made a release.'

'Saying it was serial?' demanded Powell.

'No. Just the Carr killing. Some smart-assed AP desk man recognized the similarity with the Birmingham killing which their Birmingham stringer had filed earlier. Ran a cuttings check and came up with Texas. Your sheriff's the star of the moment: talking about rituals. AP wire is running a monster serial killer piece, no-one safe in their beds. Public Affairs say to let them know if you want a media person down there.'

'No,' said Powell, shortly.

'They also want something to say, in a release. We're running behind here.'

'It's obviously the same killer and there is an element of ritual, in the forehead crosses. I think there is a connection between the victims, except for the hooker, but Geoffrey Sloane's against me. By now Amy should have some background about the victims.'

There was another silence. Then Beddows said, 'Nothing more than that? I can't say we've got a positive sighting?'

'You do and you'll obstruct my investigation. And I won't carry the can.'

The silence was even longer. 'That a threat?'

'You know I couldn't afford to.'

'We've got to say something!'

'A positive line of inquiry.'

'We try something as shitty as that the media will eat us alive.'

'We try anything more and they'll spit the pieces out and us with it,' said Powell.

Two hours later, in his Park Avenue apartment, James Durham sat watching the main NBC evening news, his third Scotch clutched in his hand, undrunk, forgotten.

He knew the names of all three men, although the father, not the son, in Texas. And felt hollowed out, not understanding. All he understood was that everything was over. Everything crumbling around him. He began to cry.

Chapter Twelve

'How the fuck can one human being do something like that to another?' demanded the detective sergeant, Anthony Bennett.

'Poor little cow,' agreed Malcolm Townsend.

Both detectives were standing just inside the door, giving all the space to the forensic squad in front of them. Townsend said, 'What do we know?'

'Name's Beryl Simpkins,' said Bennett. 'Professional tom. Worked Shepherd Market. Arrived last night with a man around eleven. Paid for all night. Clerk found her this morning.'

'We got him?'

'Waiting downstairs. He's shaken up.'

'Who wouldn't be, finding this before breakfast?'

Townsend was a large man, the muscles of an amateur league rugby player in danger of going to fat. He was on the promotional fast track, already a chief superintendent at thirty-eight. Bennett, by comparison a thin, studious-looking man, was just as ambitious, determined to make inspector by swimming as closely as he could in Townsend's wake, the suckerfish to the shark. He hadn't been sure how much mileage there'd be in the killing of a whore until he'd seen the body. The injuries and mutilations guaranteed some headlines, although it would be important to catch the bastard quickly, before he killed again.

He said, 'Guy that did this is a nutter, real Jack the Ripper.'

'We'll issue a very full press statement, to warn the girls,' decided Townsend. 'And liaise with Vice. Get the word put out we want to talk to any tom who's recently had a kinky client, likes to inflict pain, maybe he hurt himself . . .' He hesitated. 'You're right: he's got to be a nutter. Get some people to check psychiatric hospitals for any escapes or recent releases of sexual deviants. Try Broadmoor yourself.' To the forensic squad he called, 'Anything hopeful?'

'He had a bath, I'd guess after he did it,' said a balding, protectively dressed scientist, from the bath-room door. He held up a linen strip. 'Towel's wet, with some black hair adhering. More hair in the bath, too. And there's enough fingerprints, all sorts, to fill a book. This is a busy place, doesn't get properly cleaned all that often.'

Before his superior could state the obvious Anthony Bennett said, 'When they're all printed up I'll run them through Records.'

'Let's see what the clerk can remember,' suggested Townsend.

Keith Mason, a small, timid man who twitched rather than blinked, was sitting on the very edge of an upright chair behind his desk in the office, which had already been handed over to the day manager. Before either detective could speak Mason said haltingly, 'The company want me to tell you that this is a respectable hotel and that they're devastated that anything like this could have happened.'

Townsend leaned slightly towards the man and said,

'And I want you to tell the company that *I* know this is a pay-by-the-hour knocking shop, which doesn't interest me as long as I get all the co-operation I want. If I don't I'll get the Vice Squad to prosecute and close you down . . .' He paused, smiling. 'We understand each other now?'

'Yes,' said the night manager, meekly.

Townsend said, 'Good. Now tell us all about it.'

'I don't know anything,' said the man at once. He stuttered.

'You'd be surprised,' said Townsend, soothingly. 'What hours do you work, as night clerk?'

'Ten to ten.'

'Beryl a regular?'

The man nodded. 'Already been here twice last night, before the last time.'

'They pay in advance, right?' came in Anthony Bennett.

The man nodded again.

'How much?' demanded the sergeant.

'Fifty pounds. And she had a £50 note. I remember that. I only took a few last night.'

'Where is it?' demanded Townsend.

Instead of replying Keith Mason went to a safe in the corner of the office, turned the combination and took out ten separate £50 notes. Bennett took them, recording each number before dropping them by their corners into a glassine evidence bag and gave the man a receipt.

'What time did Beryl arrive, the last time?' coaxed Townsend, after the night manager sat down again.

'Just before eleven.'

'You were alone at the desk.'

'Yes.'

133

'Was it busy or were Beryl and the man the only people in the foyer?'

'A couple had just gone upstairs. And two more couples were coming in at the same time: I could see them paying off taxis outside. But for about three or four minutes it was just Beryl and her client.'

'People like Beryl and her client don't register, do they?' said Anthony Bennett.

'No.'

Townsend looked meaningfully at the subdued manager. 'So you had three or four minutes to look at the man with Beryl?'

'That's not the way,' said Mason. 'Men are often embarrassed with prostitutes so you don't look at them. This man stayed some way from the desk, where the foyer is shadowed. It's like that on purpose, for the same reason.'

'Describe what you can about the man,' urged Bennett. 'Take your time. Don't miss anything out, even if you don't think it important.'

Arranging his recollection, Keith Mason didn't speak at once. Then he said: 'White man. Young. Mid-twenties. Dark hair. Quite slim—'

'Slim or definitely thin?' broke in the sergeant.

'Slim. Fatter than me. About the same height as me, though. Dark suit and tie, with a white shirt. No topcoat. And a satchel. Black.'

'Satchel!' seized Townsend.

'With a strap, for his shoulder. They carry them sometimes. Sex aids.'

'What about his face?' said Bennett.

'I really didn't look.'

'Beard?'

'No. I would have noticed that.'

134

'Moustache?'

'I don't think so.'

'What about his nose? Big? Small?'

'I really didn't look,' repeated the man.

'They speak to each other, so you could hear his voice? Any accent?' picked up Townsend.

'Beryl spoke to him. Said it was all fixed up. He didn't say anything.'

'Do you think you could work with a police artist? Make a picture?'

Mason shook his head yet again. 'I honestly didn't see enough to do that.'

'What about if you saw him again? Do you think you'd recognize him?'

'I don't think so.'

Townsend sighed. 'You didn't see him leave?'

Mason shifted, uncomfortably. 'No.'

'How many doors are there?'

'Five, including the front. A fire door at the side and the back and two back doors.'

'Can you get to them without passing the front desk, where you were?'

'I lock the front door at three. Then I check the others, which all lock from the inside. The release bar on the side fire exit was up, where it had been opened.'

As Bennett hurried back upstairs to fetch a fingerprint officer Townsend said, 'You've really been very helpful.'

'Well?' demanded Townsend, in the car returning to New Scotland Yard.

'Going to be a bastard,' judged Bennett.

'Beryl got any kids?'

'Not according to her police record.'

'That's something, at least. Poor cow.'

*   *   *

135

There was the sound of slow movement from beyond the door and then the clatter of a failed first effort to slip the catch. It went down the second time but he had to push from the outside to help it open. Samuel Hargreaves was still slight but bowed after so many years, head forward over his chest, barely supported by a weakened neck. That should make it easier than usual, thought Harold Taylor. The old man had rheumy eyes and there was beer on his breath. He said, 'Sorry about the delay. And the door. My hands.' He held up fingers gnarled and twisted from arthritis.

'Mr Hargreaves? Samuel Hargreaves?'

'That's right. You're the American lawyer?'

'That's it. Can I come in?'

The man shuffled backwards and supported himself against the wall to turn. The house stank, of dust and urine and cooked fish. He led the way into a kitchen, where the smell of fish was strongest. There was some simmering on the stove. Two cats, entwined in the same basket, looked up uninterestedly but then immediately rose, backs arched. Hargreaves said, 'Bill and Ben. Good companions, cats. Don't seem to like you, though. Do you want some tea?'

'No, thank you,' Taylor said. His stomach was churning at the stink. He wished he'd known about the cats.

The man collapsed into a sagged, blanket-covered chair in front of an unlit grate. The cats were stiff legged beside him. 'Surprised to hear from you. You said a legacy? How much? Who's it from?'

'We've got to establish you're the right Samuel Hargreaves first.'

'What do you want to know?'

'In the late Forties, early Fifties, you were in the British Army?'

'National Service,' said the man. He looked down at his pets. 'Be quiet! Sit down!'

'What unit?'

'Medical Corps.'

'Where?'

'Catterick, first.'

'Then where?'

'Berlin.'

'What sort of work did you do in the Medical Corps in Berlin?'

'Pharmacy. Stores. Can't remember anyone from then likely to leave me any money. I really am sorry about Bill and Ben. Can't understand it. Not normally like this.'

The animals were making Harold Taylor extremely uneasy. 'You handle a lot of medicines in Berlin?'

'That was my job.'

He couldn't stay in the house much longer; couldn't prolong it as he'd intended. This was foul. Obscene. 'Penicillin? Streptomycin from time to time?'

'Course I did. What's this got to do with . . .' began the old man and then looked up with his weak eyes to the face that was transforming in front of him.

'Remember me, you bastard?' demanded the man now with Myron Nolan's face.

Hargreaves moaned, eyes rolling upwards in a faint, and pitched forward from his chair, scattering the cats. As he did so his bowels collapsed, adding to the stench.

Amy Halliday managed to intercept the FBI Task Force as they were about to board the Bureau plane to Washington. She told Powell, 'You were right about the link. It's Florence.' He listened for a further ten minutes and decided to fly direct to Birmingham. 'Tell Charlie Andrews I want another meeting with Jethro Jnr.'

'Beddows has scheduled a conference that the Director is going to chair.'

'Tell him it has to be postponed.'

'How about *asking*?'

'Tell him,' insisted Powell.

Chapter Thirteen

The FBI pilot kept the plane's engines idling, stopping only long enough for Powell to disembark. Barry Westmore promised the results of the scientific tests and examinations he needed later that day. Powell said by then he'd be back in Washington.

Charles Andrews was waiting at the airport, a car ready on a part of the terminal feed road upon which parking was prohibited. He said, 'Jethro Jnr first, then Gaynor. I thought we could call by the Arlington house instead of calling Gaynor in, for what you say you want?'

'It'll only take a minute,' agreed Powell.

'Jethro Jnr said it was right you made an appointment this time. He's put the word out on the street that he's got an amnesty for every crime going back to the death of Jesus, and Birmingham PD are pissed about it. I haven't told them you're coming back. And Harry Beddows wants to speak to you a.s.a.p.' He nodded to the car phone. 'You want to do it from here?'

'No,' said Powell. Instead he told Andrews about Pittsburgh and what Amy Halliday had discovered wading through records.

Andrews said, 'How do you explain that?'

'I can't,' said Powell. 'I'm hoping Leroy can.'

'Shit, look at that!' exclaimed Andrews.

There was an expectant crowd in the debris-strewn lot around the Hillside Sports and Social Club and as they got out of Andrews's car there was a camera flash and television lights flared on.

Charles Andrews said, 'Jethro Jnr's fifteen minutes of fame.'

Powell managed to get halfway along the gauntlet before a microphone appeared in front of him.

'. . . breakthrough in these serial killings that's brought you back here today?' finished a voice that Powell hadn't heard begin.

'All information has to come from Bureau Public Affairs in Washington, DC,' said Powell firmly, forcing his way on.

'Is an arrest imminent?' demanded the unseen questioner but Powell shouldered his way inside without replying.

There wasn't a spare seat and there was hardly any room left to stand inside the huge main room. The hubbub that greeted them died almost at once. The only comfortably clear area was at the far end, beyond the slated partition. Jethro Morrison Jnr sat smiling a gold-toothed smile from his round table. The caftan was azure blue, worn with a Muslim cap. The links in the three-strand gold necklace were so wide it made the sort of breastplate featured on Egyptian tomb walls. He was flanked by the same two unnamed attendants, with Leroy Goodfellow to his left. The crowd parted into another processional avenue and as he got closer Powell saw there was a waiting bottle of Mount Gay rum. Behind him Powell heard Charles Andrews say, 'Holy shit of angels!'

Someone in the crowd heard too and said 'Hallelujah',

and there was a snigger of laughter from a small group. From the brightness Powell knew the local television cameraman had followed them into the club.

'Welcome, Brother!' greeted Jethro Jnr, ringmaster to the circus, loud enough for the remark to be picked up by the camera's boom mike. 'Sit. Take a taste.'

The two FBI men sat. Well rehearsed, another gold-draped man poured drinks for everyone around the table. Leroy Goodfellow was suffering a cocaine cold and from his sniffed fidgeting Powell guessed he'd just contributed to his malady. Powell and Andrews took the offered glasses. Jethro Jnr lifted his hand as if in benediction and the chatter behind them quietened. The cameraman and the reporter came into the annexe. Able to focus beyond the light for the first time Powell saw that both men were black. So was the stills photographer.

Jethro Jnr raised his glass and said, 'To the defeat of crime.'

There was a ripple of sycophantic laughter from the main room. Powell said, 'I'll drink to that' and did. Charles Andrews didn't.

Jethro Jnr said, 'Us Brothers gonna show you the way again?'

Andrews shifted uncomfortably.

Powell said, 'I hope so.' His glass was attentatively refilled.

'Mutual co-operation, niggers helping honky law, honky law helping niggers. Don't that sound the best?' The man spoke looking more to the cameras than towards Powell. There was a giggle from the room. The resident Bureau agent shifted again.

Powell brought his glass up. 'Here's to a perfect world.'

141

Jethro Jnr hesitated, face briefly clouding, then drank. 'What can we do for you this time, Brother?'

'Better than last,' said Powell. 'And without an audience. Just Leroy.'

The stiffening of the gang leader's face lasted longer the second time. He said, 'You're a guest in my house. I ain't got nothing we all can't hear.'

Powell tapped his briefcase. 'I brought the photographs of your daddy, just in case you forgot what happened to him.'

Jethro Jnr, with a bully's recognition of an unafraid opponent, dropped the badinage. 'How close are you to getting who did my daddy?'

The cameraman zoomed in tightly as Powell said, 'Getting closer all the time. At the moment you're holding things up.'

'Want Jethro with me,' said Leroy Goodfellow, urgently.

'Fine by me,' accepted Powell at once, nodding to Andrews. 'You and Jethro, he and I.'

'Hey, man . . . !' began the television reporter.

'No!' said Powell. At once, smiling, he said, 'You don't want that, do you, Jethro? You want your daddy's killer caught, right?'

'My house, my rules,' announced the mobster, seizing Powell's offered escape. 'Things to talk about in private.' He was rising when he finished, leading the way through the central door of the rear five into a lavishly furnished office. He hurried to the commanding, buttonback chair behind an equally imposing desk. Powell, Charles Andrews and Leroy Goodfellow took seats fronting it. The walls were papered with photographs of people the dead man's son clearly considered famous. He was featured in all of them. The only one Powell recognized was Muhammad Ali. There was a bar to the right but Jethro Jnr didn't offer drinks.

He said, 'You mean that, about being as close as that to who did it?'

Powell said, 'I could be but Leroy's got to tell me what I want to know.'

'What's the deal?' demanded the gang leader.

'No move on anything you tell me today, Leroy,' said Powell. '*Anything*. You understand?'

'Don't know what you want,' said the old man uncertainly. The excitement of the cocaine hit was fading.

'You answer straight – honest – whatever it is. You won't incriminate yourself. You're cool. OK?'

'Tell the man,' ordered Jethro Jnr.

Goodfellow looked doubtfully between Morrison and Powell and then shrugged.

'Tell me about Florence,' demanded Powell.

'Told you,' said Goodfellow. 'Me and Jethro pulled five apiece, heisting war materiel. Saved our asses.'

'And you got extra time you didn't tell me about, all for things you and Jethro did running a gang inside,' said Powell accusingly.

The old man shrugged again. 'Happens. Not a problem.'

'Worked the prison as well as you did the streets, that right?' prompted Charles Andrews.

'Sweet as a pussy's cherry.'

'How many?' asked Powell, glad Andrews had joined in the questioning. 'Just you and Jethro? Or a gang of you?'

'Maybe eight, nine guys,' said the old man.

'Names?' said Andrews.

143

Goodfellow shook his head. 'Long time ago. Not sure any more.'

After the way she'd so far proved herself, Amy could probably get the names from records in minutes, Powell thought. 'Jethro the boss?'

'Good organizer, Jethro. Got respect.'

'What happened if Jethro didn't get respect?' came in Andrews.

Goodfellow grinned brightly towards the dead man's son. 'It sure as hell got taught.'

The gangster smiled back, proudly.

'Who's the muscle: you? Or the others?'

'Jethro didn't need no help.'

'But he sold muscle, right. His and yours and everyone else's in the team.'

'Useful thing, muscle, when you're in the can.'

'Who was the customer?'

Goodfellow hesitated until there was an encouraging gesture from Jethro Jnr.

'White guy,' mumbled Leroy Goodfellow. 'Lifer. Big operator.'

'He run your landing, in Florence?' suggested Andrews.

'Ran the whole fucking prison!' said Goodfellow, still with open admiration after so long. 'Always a load of money: and I mean a load. Buy what he wanted.'

'He buy guards as well as your muscle?' pressed Andrews.

Goodfellow nodded.

'Tell us how it worked,' said Powell.

'He could get anything you wanted,' said Goodfellow. 'Booze, cigarettes. Feelgood stuff . . .' The man sniffed, as if to indicate what he meant. 'Any sort of food. Hookers, sometimes. Certainly for himself. Had regulars. Horny mother.'

'How do you know all this?' queried Andrews. 'We're talking segregation time, even in jail?'

Goodfellow looked wary. 'Segregation didn't matter none to this guy.'

'But it would have mattered to you,' challenged Powell. 'You couldn't have gone into any white part of the prison.'

'Could if he said so.'

'Did he?' said Andrews.

'Sometimes.'

'So you worked for him?' said Powell, hoping the name he'd got from Amy would come from Goodfellow unprompted, although it hardly mattered because he was totally sure now.

'Lot of bad guys in prison,' said Goodfellow seriously, totally unaware of the irony.

No-one else thought it amusing, either. Andrews said, 'Jethro and you and the others kept him safe? So he saw to it that you had the run of the prison: go where you liked?'

'Sweet life,' recalled the old man, nostalgically. He looked towards the other black man. 'You got a little touch for me, Jethro? I'm awful dry, all this talking.'

The man crossed to the bar and returned with a fresh bottle of Mount Gay and four glasses, nodding an invitation to Powell and Andrews. Neither accepted this time. Deciding he couldn't wait any longer, Powell said, 'What's this guy's name had all this influence?'

'Myron Nolan.'

It *was* the name Amy had pulled from Records. Powell said, 'If he was paying a lot of people off he must have had money? *Very* big money?'

'Fucking fortune,' agreed Goodfellow. 'Main reason we had to look after him. Keep the bankroll safe.'

145

'How'd he make it? Get it into the prison?' asked Charles Andrews.

'Don't know how he made it before he was sentenced. Financed the rackets inside. Money made money. Had a lawyer visit regular. Myron used to pay off the visiting day guards, for him and the lawyer to meet by themselves, in the guards' office sometimes. Do what they liked. That's how it worked with the hookers, too.'

'What was the lawyer's name?'

'Never knew. Never ever saw him. Just knew it happened. None of our business.'

'This is important, Leroy, so I want you to think carefully about it,' cautioned Powell. 'Was Myron Nolan ever visited by family? Or someone like a special friend?'

Goodfellow shook his head, helping himself to more rum. 'Can't ever remember him talking about kin. Or of him being visited by anyone apart from the lawyer. And the hookers, of course.'

'Tell me about Myron Nolan,' demanded Powell. 'What sort of guy was he? Big? Small? Mean guy? That sort of stuff.'

'Didn't take no shit, from no-one. Didn't need no muscle on a one-to-one. Just needed back-up against another team.'

'Hard man as well as rich?'

'Always. Never knew it no other way.'

'He have other people working for him, besides you and Jethro and your team?'

'Bought his own cell. Had two white dudes clean for him. Fags. Not that he was that way. Horny, like I said, but for pussy. But fags are particular, right? Neat and tidy. Myron's cell always had to be neat and tidy, like him.'

'Like him?'

146

'Florence was a stockade, right? Temporary. You got a shower once a week, if you were lucky. Myron got his every day. His own stall, separate from everyone else. Anyone try to use it, doubt if they would have walked again. No-one ever tried. Never knew a guy shower so much.'

'You say there were eight or nine others, so with you and Jethro that made about ten guys?' said Andrews.

'That's about it,' said Goodfellow, needing to rub his nose with his hand as well as sniff. He took a third drink, enjoying his moment of notoriety.

'Quite a team,' said Powell, taking his direction from the other FBI man. 'Guess Myron attracted a lot of jealousy, all that business, all that money?'

'You're damn right,' said the old man, guilelessly. 'That man, he had a fucking empire, like General Motors.'

'So who'd he deal with, when he wanted something done? All of you individually? Or just one of you? Who's the muscle closest to him?'

'Guess that had to be Jethro. Jethro was kind of in charge.'

'Jethro kill him alone or did you help?' asked Powell, quietly.

'By him—' started Goodfellow, abruptly stopping at Jethro Jnr's shout.

'Hey now . . . !' began the son but Powell said, 'Cut the crap. Cameras are outside. All past, all over, a long time ago.' Going back to the old man Powell said, 'Now I want you to try again, Leroy. I'm going to tell you why it's important and I want you to think really hard, harder than you did a little while back. If someone in Nolan's family knew it was Jethro who killed him, even though it was never proved in the investigation

147

afterwards, they could have killed Jethro in Lane Park, even though it all happened a long time ago. So. Did any family or friend – anyone at all apart from the lawyer and hookers – visit Myron Nolan in the Florence stockade?'

Goodfellow allowed some deep thinking time. Then he said, 'No, sir. I don't believe no-one ever did.'

'How much did Jethro get, when he killed Myron Nolan?'

'I don't—'

'You do and it's not going beyond this room.' Powell stopped him curtly. 'I can't catch who killed Junior's daddy here, you don't tell me.'

' 'bout five grand.'

Powell guessed at ten. He wouldn't need to trace any others of the gang. 'What about the rackets?'

Goodfellow sniffed a reluctant admission. 'Didn't have the outside contact, like Myron had. No supply. Kinda broke up.'

Powell lifted his briefcase on to the desk and stood over it, carefully making his selection in the order he wanted. He offered Goodfellow the Pittsburgh Hilton video freeze frame of the young man following Marcus Carr. 'You ever seen this man before? Take your time.'

Leroy Goodfellow squinted at the print. 'No, sir.'

'You sure? Absolutely sure?'

'Positive.'

Powell took out the picture of the older, identically dressed man recorded on the camera virtually outside the Carr apartment block. 'How about this man?'

Goodfellow's face opened into a smile, which at once became an expression of uncertainty. 'That's Myron. But I don't understand . . .'

'No,' agreed Powell. 'Neither do I.'

148

It didn't improve when they stopped at the slave-built tourist attraction on their way to the airport. Michael Gaynor frowned at the picture just identified as that of Myron Nolan and insisted he'd never seen the man before.

When he saw the younger man's photograph Gaynor said, 'Oh yes. That could very easily be him. Why are they both dressed the same?'

'One of the many questions I don't have answers to,' admitted Powell.

Powell had cut short his Birmingham airport argument with Beddows by claiming that his plane was about to leave – which it hadn't been – hoping for time at Pennsylvania Avenue to talk through a lot of things with Amy and Barry Westmore. He'd phoned both from Birmingham, too, giving a precise arrival time so they'd be waiting.

Both were, in his side office off the incident room, but Powell had overlooked the security system throughout the FBI headquarters building, in which access and movement are governed by electronically controlled gates recognizing a person's individual ID tag inserted into a slot. The tag also identifies the holder and instantly plots where he is in the building.

Powell was only just able to hear what both had to say – and tell them about his encounters with Leroy Good-fellow and Michael Gaynor – and was looking at the photograph Amy had obtained from Army Records when the division chief stormed in.

'What the hell's going on!' Beddows yelled. He was puce-faced with anger, a vein pumping in his forehead. He ignored Amy and the forensic scientist.

'I wish I could tell you,' said Powell, mildly. The

149

Birmingham detour would shortly be shown to be justified and he was curious at Beddows's over-reaction.

'No-one keeps the Director waiting! *No-one.*'

You poor, politically driven bastard, thought Powell, although totally without sympathy. 'You'd rather have the Director and the Bureau – everyone, including you and the division you're in charge of – made to look ridiculous?' He realized, surprised at himself, that he was enjoying having Amy Halliday as audience to the row.

Beddows faltered. 'How?'

'By talking about a dead man coming back to life after almost fifty years.'

For the first time Beddows looked at the other two in the office. He shook his head, bemused. 'What's going on? What's he talking about?'

'We've got a situation none of us can understand or explain,' said Barry Westmore. 'And if we don't it *is* going to make us all look ridiculous. I don't believe in ghosts but I believe, like Wes says, that we've got evidence of a man coming back to life.'

Powell was looking at the division chief intently, believing he could analyse the visible change in the attitude of a man he'd once known so well. Beddows's anger instantly evaporated. In its place was emerging an awareness that so far he was uninvolved in the absurdity of what he was being told by two supposedly sane men, one a practical scientist. Testingly Powell said, 'You want to tell the Director that? Or shall we?'

'He's waiting,' said Beddows.

'I need Amy and Barry with me: their input,' said Powell. 'There hasn't been time for a composite analysis.'

Clarence Gale was a tall, thin, dried-out man who'd

served fifteen years as a judge on the New York bench, been a friend of the new President's family for ten years longer than that and hoped for the attorney-generalship when the man was elected to office. He'd been so disappointed when he hadn't got it that he'd considered refusing the alternative Bureau stewardship, but only briefly, because Clarence Gale had ambition of elephantine proportions and had decided the FBI was an excellent stepping stone to a political career. To that end he had become the most publicity conscious, media available Director since J. Edgar Hoover, whose reputation he was determined to outdo. Gale's boast was that he was sufficiently politically astute to gauge wind change, not just on Capitol Hill but around the corridors of the White House even before it wafted into the Oval Office. And it was politically astute to be personally briefed and ready to respond either to Congress or the President on an otherwise unimportant serial killing now that the latest victim was a general that newspapers and television were calling, with some justification, a hero of the Second, Korean and Vietnam wars and who had finished an outstanding military career as a deputy Joint Chief at the Pentagon.

With four people, three of them carrying folders and documents, Gale assembled in his conference room rather than in the adjoining office, which would have been too small. Before they sat, Beddows began apologizing profusely for the postponement; Gale impatiently cut him short by saying he hoped the delay was worthwhile. Beddows, his distancing strategy decided upon, said he hoped so, too.

'Perhaps Special Agent Powell can help us decide?' Beddows finished, accusingly.

'I'm not sure that I can,' said Powell, unconcerned by

the buck-passing because what Amy and Westmore had to add made everything even more inexplicable. He gave his résumé out of sequence, because the mystery only truly began with Marcus Carr. With the headquarters state-of-the-art equipment Westmore had succeeded in even greater enlargements of the two men on the Pittsburgh videos and he presented these to Beddows and Gale, as he talked. Gale listened judge-like, expressionless. By comparison Beddows sat, face twisted and frowning, unwittingly doing a bad job of concealing his total lack of comprehension.

'Michael Gaynor thinks the younger is the man he saw in the park the night Jethro Morrison was killed,' said Powell. 'Leroy Goodfellow immediately identified the older man as Myron Nolan, who was murdered in a military stockade in Florence, Alabama, in April 1951 . . .'

There'd been no time for rehearsal and Powell hoped Amy remembered when he turned invitingly to her. She did.

'He was serving life there,' she picked up, immediately. 'He'd been sentenced by a military tribunal of the Four Power Commission in Berlin, in August 1949. He'd been transferred to the Control Commission at the end of the war. He originally arrived in Berlin as part of the American Third Army, in which he'd been a quartermaster sergeant . . .' She hesitated. 'These army records, which I only today got from military archives in Adelphi, Maryland, aren't complete. There are some gaps, which I hope to fill but can't guarantee: they're obviously not on any computer database. From what I have been able to get of the trial transcript Myron Nolan was a major black marketeer. Leading up to what became the Russian blockade of Berlin there was an enormous black market, in everything. Even drugs and medical equipment. Nolan sold contaminated penicillin and streptomycin to a German paediatric clinic. There was a near-epidemic of polio and a high incidence of tuberculosis at the time. Thirty children died. Fifteen of the polio sufferers were permanently crippled . . .' She hesitated again, going into her folder. '. . . As I said, the trial records are incomplete. But there are two things . . .' Along the table she slid an army regulation photograph and a right and left profile and full-face arrest picture and another ageing evidence picture. 'The photographs are the official ones, taken in 1949, of Myron Nolan. And those are his fingerprints, taken at the same time . . .' Amy turned, gratefully, to Westmore.

'The military tribunal photographs identically match that taken by the video camera close to General Marcus Carr's apartment in Pittsburgh fifteen days ago,' responded the scientist. 'We've subjected all the video freeze frames of both men to every sort and type of photographic comparison known to us, scientifically. Every physiognomy specialist we have here is satisfied – prepared to swear in court – that the faces are those of two different men. Just as every other specialist believes the two bodies are the same . . .' Westmore got up and went round to the top of the table where the Director sat with the video stills set out in front of him. 'Here,' he said, pointing between the two sets. 'That ring they're wearing on the pinkie of their left hands is identical. And look. There's sufficient of the dial showing beneath the cuff in both sets to see that the wristwatch is the same. Every body measurement is identical, to a fraction of an inch. Only the faces are different.'

'A disguise mask,' blurted Harry Beddows.

'We've positively eliminated that,' dismissed

153

Westmore, still standing at the Director's shoulder. 'And I haven't yet got to the strangest part of all.' He went quickly back to his separate folder, selecting a series of fresh photographs before returning to where the Director sat. 'These are prints taken from the cab of Gene Johnson, the Texas victim. And these are from the bathroom and living room of General Carr's apartment . . .' He placed them side by side and then pulled into a comparable position the prints from the fifty-year-old Berlin court-martial records. 'They perfectly match – in fact they *are* – the fingerprints of Myron Nolan . . .'

'. . . who was stabbed to death in Florence, Alabama, on 6 April 1951,' Powell reminded them, resuming the narrative. 'At that time Jethro Morrison was serving a sentence for the theft of war materiel. He was the boss of a protection gang Nolan employed to keep him safe: he was King Rat of the jail, running all the rackets. Nolan's murder was one of two that could never be proved against Morrison, through lack of evidence. This morning Goodfellow admitted Morrison did it, for Nolan's $5,000 bankroll—'

'This is absurd: doesn't make any logical sense,' protested Beddows before Powell, in turn, cut him off.

'Marcus Carr, then a lieutenant-colonel, was the chairman of the military tribunal that imposed the life sentence on Nolan. Gene Johnson was the son of Major Patrick Johnson, an investigator attached to the US Army Provost Marshal's office. He made the case against Nolan.'

There was stunned, uncomprehending silence. Clarence Gale said, 'Dead men don't come back from the grave.'

154

'There's scientific evidence that Myron Nolan has,' said Powell.

'Absurd,' repeated Beddows. 'Totally absurd.'

None liked to be beaten – to have to admit total bewilderment – and the conference continued uneasily, everyone ill at ease. It was Amy who broached the suggestion of the supernatural, although it wasn't the word she used. She talked of 'something unknown, strange', to be immediately confronted by Clarence Gale and Barry Westmore's insistence that there had to be a logical explanation. Beddows at once saw the signpost and followed the Director, suggesting everything would become clear when an omission or oversight in the analysis was realized. Westmore replied, indignantly, that there was no fault with any analysis and Powell said he looked forward to getting Beddows's assessment the following day, after the division chief had independently studied the case files. There was a virtual repetition of the Pittsburgh photo laboratory discussion that extended to cosmetic surgery face change until Westmore said that while it was technically possible synthetically to copy fingerprints it had never, to his knowledge, been achieved successfully outside the lab and that those in Johnson's cab and the Carr apartment were unquestionably genuine. And there was no evidence of plastic surgery.

'One thing's obvious,' said Gale. 'We can't risk going public until we do understand. We *would* be ridiculed.'

'Facts are facts,' protested Westmore, mildly.

'And they remain limited to the five of us in this room until I order otherwise,' said Gale. It wasn't going to do his Washington career any good whatsoever if the merest whisper of this cockamamy story leaked out before he had a complete handle on it.

'One of those facts is that all three victims, in some way or another, are provably linked to Myron Nolan's imprisonment.' Powell looked to Amy. 'You got the names of others?'

'Some, not all,' she said at once. 'Like I said, the records aren't complete. After fifty years I don't know how many are still alive, how many dead. Obviously I won't stop looking.'

Powell went back to the Director, glad to be able to bypass Beddows. 'Shouldn't we consider the security of any who are still alive?'

It was a decision the man – a trained judge who liked incontrovertible evidence making incontrovertible sense – didn't want to make. Avoiding it, Gale said, 'Let's find names and locations.'

That evening Powell received two telephone calls at his Crystal City apartment, directly after watching the main evening news, horrified at how he'd appeared.

Beth said excitedly, 'I just saw you on television, with a man they said was a gangster. You looked terrific. Some of my friends saw you, too!'

Amy said, 'I thought you looked just like Eliot Ness.'

'He was untouchable,' Powell pointed out. 'I thought I looked like someone in the pocket of a big time gang leader.'

'That too,' she agreed, unhelpfully. There was a pause. 'No luck with names and addresses. I'm going home.'

'See you in the morning,' Powell said. It wasn't until he'd replaced the receiver that he wondered if she hadn't expected him to say something different. At once he remembered Amy Halliday's insistence on no personal relationships, and wondered why the doubt had occurred to him after he had assured her he felt the same way. Perhaps it was because he didn't feel that way any more: he didn't think he ever had.

Chapter Fourteen

Nothing was as he remembered it, which was hardly surprising after more than half a century, but he was still disappointed. The last time he'd been through Surrey and Sussex and Hampshire it had been difficult to find a blade of grass in the churned landscape left by the tanks and the armour and transporters and the troops already invading Normandy to make it safe for him to follow to pursue the unbelievable opportunities of war. Now, apart from some small towns he mostly thought ugly, the countryside was green and placid, cows grazing as they were supposed to according to postcards, and in two villages through which he drove church bells were ringing.

He stopped at the second, close to Cuckfield, to buy newspapers and because the pub looked inviting, but that was disappointing too, thatched and red brick outside, light-fluttering fruit machines and canned Muzak inside. He considered driving on but he wanted to read about himself and his left hand was still sore from where the bitch had caught him with her razor before he'd got it away from her – the same hand that the fucking cats had scratched – and importantly the place was clean, actually smelling of polish and disinfectant.

He took a half-pint of what the barman assured him to be their strongest beer and settled in the corner seat furthest from the bar, to read. The feeling, he supposed, was pride. He hadn't made every front page – just most of the tabloids – but the headlines were big on the inside pages: words like monster and Dracula and even, predictably, Jack the Ripper, although he didn't like the quote from the unnamed police spokesman describing him as a homicidal maniac. He was curious at the police insistence that there were some important clues. The British media coverage was much more hysterical than that in America. But then, he reflected, England was a much smaller country. And America was far more accustomed to multiple killings. It was only the fact that Carr had been a general that had finally got the story into the *New York Times* and the *Washington Post* on the day he'd left.

He put the newspapers aside, feeling fresh disappointment as well as pride. Good, but not the sensation he wanted. Too small: at a distance. No-one in the bar was looking at him, terrified of him, in awe of him. The interest was too casual, a barmaid and one man gazing right through him as if he didn't exist. That had to change: change dramatically.

He'd positioned himself as far away as possible from the fruit machines, and the Muzak wasn't as intrusive as he'd first thought so he decided upon another drink and at the bar impulsively chose a ploughman's lunch after learning what it was from the man who was served ahead of him.

Disappointing or not, he was still glad he'd allowed himself the nostalgic detour. He felt relaxed after the two killings, in no hurry. First he'd followed the most direct route to find the widow of Major Walter Hibbs.

According to the map that came with the hire car the hamlet, just outside Midhurst, would be about thirty miles away: an hour and a half's drive. Midhurst would be the place in which to base himself while he checked out the Hibbs house after more than a year, to make sure everything was as he remembered: that his preparation for this killing remained as foolproof as the others before it.

A sprightly busybody of a woman, he recalled, chairperson of this, chairperson of that, well-born if fading British gentility taking its natural place of command in the scheme of things, following in the footsteps of her bastard, bristle-moustached husband.

Taylor guessed it would take two days, to be sure. But it could no longer if necessary. As long as it took: all the time in the world, this and every other world. His decision after the first visit was to do it in the evening. Wait for her to return busily home from whatever parish function she'd been performing, make the rehearsed, seemingly half-awkward approach ('my father was stationed around here during the war: think he might even have known your husband. The name is Hibbs, isn't it?') to gain her confidence and then take the very necessary satisfaction, chip chop, chip chop.

His mind still upon the detour he'd allowed himself, Taylor suddenly wondered about extending it. He still had retribution to exact in America, so he couldn't finally decide about settling there or back here in England. Again, no hurry. But why not cross to France, as he'd done as Myron Nolan in 1944: take the route he'd taken behind Patton's army, through the same towns, maybe even into Belgium? It would be different there now, like it was different here now. No more eager amateurs willing to do whatever he wanted, two at a time, three at a time, for nylons or coffee or butter. Anything. Hi, Joe, whadya know. Got a present for me, Joe? You got a present for me I got a present for you, Joe. He smiled at the reminiscence. Definitely an idea. Another experiment, another new experience.

It didn't take Taylor as long as he'd expected to get to Midhurst and there was a vacancy at the first hotel he tried, a beamed lopsided place in the main street proud of its coaching inn history prominently displayed in the reception area. He insisted upon inspecting the room before taking it and agreed that he needed a reservation that night for dinner.

It was still only four o'clock when he approached the tiny village known as Lower Norwood, although not marked as such on his map. He recognized the needle tip of the church spire first, thrusting up from the hills in which it was folded, and then the top field, with its curious cows, of the main farm. Abruptly, at the top of the hill, it was laid out before him, as if for approval: the faraway church, the required pub with a swing and a roundabout for children in the rear garden, and the combined post office and general store. Several of the houses were thatched, none of the roofs new, one badly in need of replacing. Mantua House, the Hibbses home, was grey stone and slate roofed, at the far end, close to the church and set back more than any of the others in larger grounds dominated by huge firs, their bottom branches so low they swept the ground like skirts.

To Taylor's left there was a long draw-in, for the twice a day bus. He parked there and momentarily considered taking his satchel before deciding against it, instead locking it securely in the boot with his souvenirs of the killings so far. The cows lost interest and went back to their grass. Whatever new experience he sought in the future, he wouldn't return as a cow, he decided. Why not as a female, though, he thought, caught by the idea. Something else to think about. Forget cows. Wouldn't come back as a bull, either. A man putting a tractor away in an open-sided farm building examined him, briefly, but quickly had to concentrate on what he was doing. Two women outside the post office stopped their intense conversation at his approach. One smiled and said 'Good evening.' Taylor said 'Good evening' back. Quite different from the lunchtime pub: not a lot of strangers came here. What about this pub, coming up on his left? Would it be open? Couldn't remember, from his last visit. Used it once – no fruit machines or canned music – but at lunchtime again, never this late. It would be the obvious gathering place at night. English tradition. Not the sort of place Mrs Hibbs would go to, though. Not a pub. Below her status. She'd take sherry. Maybe with a dry biscuit. Not for much longer.

Mantua House seemed different. He wasn't immediately able to decide how. Bedraggled came to mind, which wasn't the right word but just as quickly he changed his mind. It was *exactly* the right word. The last time he'd seen it the house – the creeper and the climbing flowers and the lawn-skirting trees – had been immaculate: freshly washed windows glinting, the garden and its plants trained and orderly. It wasn't any longer. Now bedraggled tiredness was on the point of becoming positive neglect and the untidiness offended him. He stopped at the gate, gazing anxiously up the weed-dotted drive towards the silent house. Anger took over from the anxiety. Surely the old bitch hadn't died! Surely he wasn't going to have to start all over again, find children: he'd be totally cheated if there were no

162

surviving relatives. It had happened, in the past. More than once. Couldn't stand that – hated that happening. The whole point of exacting retribution was that he always refused to be cheated.

'Can I help you?'

Taylor physically jumped at the question, unable to tell where the voice came from. Then a woman moved into view from behind the privet hedge to his left, pruning shears in hands encased in grimed gardening gloves. It was difficult to guess her age. She could have been anything between thirty and fifty, as bedraggled as the house, in shapeless, mud-smeared trousers, wellington boots and darned sweater. There wasn't any grey in what he could see of the auburn hair sprouting beneath a rim-curled man's trilby hat, so maybe she was closer to thirty. Her face was scrubbed clean of make-up, shining with perspiration. There was a smear of dirt along the side of her nose.

'I was just admiring the house. Georgian, isn't it?' he said, knowing it was.

'I thought you might have been a PG. Didn't want to greet you like this if you were. That's why we insist on advance reservations.' The voice was soft, educated.

'What's a PG?'

'Paying guest. Recognized you as American, even before you spoke.' She looked at him, expectantly.

Falling back upon his prepared story, Taylor said, 'I'm staying in Midhurst. Nostalgic trip. My father was briefly stationed here during the war, just before the invasion. He often talked about it.'

She smiled. Her teeth were very even. 'My father was a soldier. He fought, too.'

'Was?' probed Taylor, hopefully.

163

'He died, ten years ago. Only Mother left now. And she's not well. Suffered a stroke, six months ago.'

'I'm sorry,' he said, dutifully. Not as bad as he'd feared. Two for the price of one, without any effort. A bonus, in fact. If the old bitch was here, that is. 'Must be difficult, running a guest house and caring for a sick mother?'

'There's a nurse who comes in. Mother's really no trouble. It's a tragedy. She was such an active person before it happened. Ran the village.'

Taylor was glad that they were separated by the gate. She'd smell of sweat. He wondered what she would have done for a bar of soap or a pair of nylons in 1944. She had big tits, under that filthy sweater. 'I would have thought it was still too much, trying to handle the garden, as well.'

'George – he's the gardener – does most of it but he's been ill, too. Things have got a bit behind. I'm trying to do what I can to help.'

'Pity I didn't know about you before I booked in at Midhurst.'

'Should have read the local guidebook first,' she said, smiling again. She looked back along the hedge, to the unseen pruning that still had to be done.

He'd have to come back to discover their routines, make sure he wasn't surprised by the unexpected arrival of the nurse. 'I'm going to stay around for a few days, try to find some of the places my father talked about. Maybe I'll see you again. What *is* there to see, around this particular village?'

'The church is old. Norman. There are some wonderful walks, across the downs, to some of the other villages. You like walking?'

He made a doubtful expression. 'Can't honestly say

I've done a great deal.' Not in this lifetime or the two that preceded it, he thought.

'There's the guidebook in the village shop,' she said, pointing over his shoulder. 'That'll tell you all there is.'

'You've been very kind,' he said. 'Good luck with your gardening.'

She smiled ruefully. 'I hate it! I get so filthy!'

He stopped at the shop and bought the local guide, intrigued by her parting remark. Maybe she would have done a lot for a bar of soap.

There was no dispute about jurisdiction or demands from the Regional Crime Squad to become involved or to co-ordinate, because they didn't want to be stuck with it either. Detective Chief Superintendent Henry Basildon, Richmond's most senior investigator and as such directly responsible to Surrey's Chief Constable, wished there had been. He would have been very happy – delighted, even – to have dumped the murder and mutilation of Samuel Hargreaves into anyone else's lap but his own, just as Detective Chief Superintendent Malcolm Townsend would have liked solving the murder and mutilation of a twenty-nine-year-old Shepherd Market whore named Beryl Simpkins to be anyone's responsibility but his.

As it was, Surrey's Chief Constable talked personally with London's Metropolitan Police Commissioner, who agreed that a joint investigation, headed equally by two such experienced officers, was the most practical, cost-effective and efficient way to handle atrocities dominating every newspaper, radio and television channel. Having two forces involved made it easier for both police chiefs to apportion blame if the killing continued.

Basildon, who'd hoped the Mets would take it, vehemently said, 'It's going to be a fucking albatross around our neck! A right bastard.'

Townsend, who'd hoped it would become Richmond's job, equally emphatically said, 'Madmen! They're the absolute worst.'

The mentally deranged, particularly those unable to stop themselves committing horrific crimes attracting the hysterical publicity that these ones already were, did nothing to further or enhance a policeman's career. There was no logical way to anticipate – and therefore to prevent – the next outrage. When it happened, which it inevitably would, it would stoke even greater sensation and with that sensation would come demands for the ordinary, law-abiding public to be protected. And when they made an arrest, usually more by chance than by deduction, the invariable plea was insanity or diminished responsibility. That left the whole thing to fizzle out like a damp squib, with no shining light, credit or recognition, which for people with ambition, which Basildon had in equal measure to Townsend, made the whole episode a waste of time.

The men had liked each other from the outset, each well aware the other knew every score backwards and that there wasn't going to be any need for explanations. Christopher Pennington, who was Basildon's support officer, felt the same way about Anthony Bennett. Townsend's aide was satisfied, too, although he'd tempered his initial enthusiasm about the benefits of the Bayswater murder. All four men wore single-breasted, waistcoated pinstripes that every professional villain recognized from fifty paces as the undesignated uniform of don't-fuck-with-us detectives who'd heard every alibi and even invented a few themselves. They were confident men.

166

They'd met at the Yard to compare dossiers and because it was convenient for the taxi driver who'd come forward that day to say he'd picked up Beryl Simpkins and her third client. As an unnecessary reminder Christopher Pennington said, 'I've never known a case where there's been so much evidence in such a short time.'

'I wish it led somewhere,' complained his superior.

In the thirty-six hours since the discovery of Hargreaves's body by his morning carer, AB group blood from the Bayswater hotel had been matched with droplets lifted close to the cats' basket in Hargreaves's living room. That was already undergoing DNA comparison, together with the black head and pubic hair found in both bathrooms and the semen and pubic hair from Beryl Simpkins's mouth. Already fingerprints from both bathrooms and from one of the £50 notes from the hotel safe had been matched, although nothing had so far shown on fingerprint records in England, Europol or Interpol. For that reason they weren't hopeful when they got the genetic string of an identity from Britain's DNA bank of recorded sex offenders.

'Imagine anyone doing that to a cat,' protested Pennington. 'Decapitating them and taking their eyes out like that!'

Both Townsend and Bennett, neither of whom knew that Pennington's wife exhibited short-tailed Siamese, looked surprised.

'Hargreaves was probably pissed off losing his head, too,' said Basildon, impatiently. 'We absolutely sure about the psychiatric hospitals?'

'Total blank. Nothing that fits,' insisted Bennett.

Pennington nodded in agreement.

'There can't be a connection between a £30-for-thirty-minutes slag and a shitty old-age pensioner, surely?' mused Townsend.

'We're running all the antecedents we can find, on both of them,' assured Pennington. 'Absolutely nothing so far.'

They stopped at a knock on the door and the police artist escorted the taxi driver back into the room. Paul Stanswell was a fat, mottle-faced man whose hair receded to the middle of his head. The respectability of a suit, shirt and tie was spoiled by the two-toned red and white trainers. The detectives knew that Stanswell had dressed for his own self-orchestrated arrival press conference, posing for pictures, television and press interviews after telephoning the Press Association to announce the time he would be getting to New Scotland Yard. He sat now with his hands cupped across a sagging belly, a man sure of his sudden importance.

Stanswell's drawing was of a lightly built, young-faced man with slightly protruding eyes and dark hair cut short at the crown but worn comparatively long at the back. There was no facial hair. It was a dark suit, with a muted tie against a white shirt. Down the side of the impression the artist had printed the physical description.

Townsend said, 'You sure that's him?'

'Stake my life on it.'

'The hotel clerk said he carried a satchel on his shoulder?' reminded Townsend. 'Thought it might contain sex aids.'

'Don't remember a satchel.'

'You'd recognize him again?' asked Bennett.

'Guarantee it.'

'You knew Beryl?' said Townsend.

'Picked her up a few times. That's why I recognized

168

her when I saw her picture in the paper.'

'You run a lot of toms and their clients to hotels?' asked Basildon, the questioning prepared.

'I drive a cab. Customers flag me down.'

'Paul!' sighed Townsend. 'Answer the fucking questions properly. We're in a hurry.'

'I've run a few around,' conceded the man, deflated.

'Since it's happened, you heard anything about girls getting customers rougher than usual? Real kinky?' asked Townsend.

The driver shook his head. 'I know the word's out, but no.'

'You hear, you call me right away, OK?' said Townsend.

'You betcha life on it,' promised Stanswell.

'It's other people's lives we're worried about,' said Pennington.

After the man left the four detectives considered the drawing in silence for several minutes. Basildon said, 'I've seen better.'

'And worse,' said Townsend. 'It's all we've got that's new so I think we should issue it, keep the publicity going. You never know.'

The artist's impression, together with the pavement interview with Paul Stanswell, was the second item on that night's television news. Harold Taylor watched in the lounge of the Midhurst hotel, sipping brandy to help digest an uninteresting dinner. The resemblance was too vague – his eyes certainly didn't protrude – and the item was too brief to be of any real concern but it would obviously be carried in the following morning's newspapers, enabling much closer and more detailed study. And he'd thought a lot during the meal, contemplating something new.

'I hope I'm not ringing too late,' he apologized, when she answered the telephone. 'We met this afternoon when you were pruning the hedge.'

'I don't go to bed early.'

'I'm not particularly happy where I am. I wondered if I might book in with you tomorrow?'

'Of course.' She sounded pleased. 'You haven't asked how much.'

'How much?'

'How about £40?'

The hope reminded him of how Beryl had named her price in Shepherd Market. 'Forty pounds is fine. You were wearing gardening gloves this afternoon?'

'I don't understand.'

'Miss? Or Mrs?'

'Janet,' said the woman. 'Janet Hibbs. Miss.'

'Maurice,' he supplied, deciding upon his favourite previous reincarnation, which he often did when he was enjoying himself. 'Maurice Barkworth.'

He apologized to the hotel receptionist for having to cut short his stay and spent some further time getting her to list the best restaurants roughly within a twenty-mile radius. For that she accepted the £5 tip. He really was going to enjoy himself, Taylor decided.

'For fuck's sake, Wes!' protested Harry Beddows. 'Jethro Morrison Jnr has been cruising Birmingham for days, boasting about an FBI amnesty and giving the local PD the stiff middle finger! And then you pose on television drinking rum and being called Brother by the son-of-a-bitch!'

'I was set up,' accepted Powell. 'First there is no general amnesty. Secondly I needed information in a

170

hurry, I needed Junior's co-operation to get it and I didn't have time to argue about the cameras. If I'd tried, he would have thrown us out – *on* camera – and on balance I think we came out better the way I did it.'

'The Birmingham Commissioner has complained to the Director,' disclosed Beddows. 'Word is that the local congressmen are going to get in on the act, as well. It's always open season on the Bureau, you know that.'

'I got what I wanted, when I wanted it,' insisted Powell.

'At a cost.'

'Worth it,' persisted Powell.

'I don't think so.'

'You don't think so? Or the Director doesn't think so?' demanded Powell, in open challenge. It had already been a frustrating day: Amy had made no progress in locating other likely victims and no-one had been able to come up with an acceptable suggestion for anything that had happened.

'It's the same,' said Beddows. He paused. 'We're wide apart, aren't we?'

'Seems that way.'

'That saddens me.'

Powell shrugged, disbelieving the man. 'Things change. I guess I'm sorry, too.'

'After what happened before and these complaints now – especially if we get some smart-ass congressman wanting home state headlines – I'm not going to be able to save you if this case doesn't come out 101 per cent right.'

'I don't expect you to.'

'Just wanted you to know.'

'And now I do.'

In New York John Price, the agent in charge of the FBI's Manhattan office, said, 'I agree, Mr Durham. I think there are a lot of things my superiors in Washington would like to talk to you about.'

Chapter Fifteen

It was Powell's conscious decision to go to New York to meet James Durham on the lawyer's territory, on the man's own terms, rather than have him come to theirs in Washington. They didn't have enough – have *anything* – to bring Durham to them, so at the moment it was co-operation, not coercion time.

In the brief time available before the meeting towards which Powell was flying with an FBI attorney, Amy Halliday had discovered that James Durham was a retired criminal lawyer with a lifetime's record of success, ability and respect on the New York circuit, the well earned holder during that time of every prestigious honorary office and position not just at state but on two occasions at federal level.

Additionally John Price, who was old and experienced enough to know the difference between shit and gold, judged Durham to be a frightened man who knew something important enough for it to be well worth an hour's flight to find out what.

'Impressive guy,' assessed Brett Hordle, next to him on the shuttle, handing back what Amy had assembled. 'American Bar Association *maxima cum laude*. I'm awed.'

'If I wasn't, I wouldn't be going myself to see him,'

said Powell, who didn't get the impression that Hordle was awed about anything. 'As of this morning we've had fifty-five calls from people positive they know who our serial killer is. Two say it's aliens, collecting samples of earthly beings.'

'The Director doesn't like immunity deals,' announced Hordle. 'We think there's a need here, I want us to discuss it first. No knee-jerk stuff, OK?'

Powell turned towards the other man. 'No, I'm not sure it is OK. This is my case. If I think it's worthwhile I'll go for it.'

'Those aren't my instructions.'

'How many immunities have you negotiated?'

'Enough.'

'How many with lawyers with Durham's track record?'

'What are you saying?'

'I'm saying that we might only get one chance and I'm not going to risk blowing it seeking an adjournment. We're into an investigation here, not a trial or an arraignment. I lead, you follow.' The pause was intentional. 'OK?'

'I think I may have to talk with Washington before we meet Durham.'

'I think that may be a good idea,' said Powell. When the fuck was something going to go easy! Just easier would be enough.

'I despise crooked lawyers: they're the worst,' announced Hordle. The FBI lawyer was a neatly dressed, meticulous man who'd marked his place as he read with a silver pencil. Sometimes he'd made notes with it on a yellow legal pad.

Powell sighed. 'That's our job, dealing with crooks. And sometimes that really is what we do. We *deal*, for the greater good. Durham came to us with something to offer. I want to know what that is. And I'm going to find out.'

'He didn't come to us voluntarily,' cautioned the other man, with legal pedantry. 'He got caught and told the DEA he wouldn't talk to them without talking to us at the same time. We don't even know how a drug enforcement agency is involved. This isn't a one-shot meeting.'

'The DEA is a situation that needs resolving,' agreed Powell, impatiently. Along with several others, he thought. The Alabama senator had given lengthy complaining *New York Times* and local newspaper and television interviews about apparent FBI association with known criminals, and the *Washington Post* had that morning run a critical leading article. It would be good to have something – *anything* – that made sense, and infighting between government agencies helped no-one except a wandering serial killer.

'It's essential we have an agreed strategy, before we meet Durham,' insisted the lawyer.

'We going to play it softly, softly, until I give an indication otherwise,' ruled Powell. 'I need a friendly witness, not a hostile one. We need a break, a big one. There's things about this that don't have any logic, any sense.'

'How desperate are we?'

'As desperate as it gets,' said Powell. Was he talking professionally or personally? As far as he was concerned the two were indivisible.

Powell had refused Price's offer to meet them, choosing the quicker 53rd Street helicopter service. At the Bureau office Price said, 'He's dirty, obviously. Too clever to give me anything but this is a no-shit guy. Good front, but he's flaky: the ice rattles a lot in his drink.'

'What's he given?' demanded Hordle.

'Only that he may know something that could help in the murder of General Marcus Carr. But won't go any further than that until he meets a senior FBI representative as well as a Bureau lawyer with authority to accord legally binding undertakings.' The Manhattan agent was a man past his prime sliding into carelessness. He was balding and dishevelled in yesterday's shirt, the seat of his pants shining from wear. The lapels of his jacket were oddly curling in on themselves, the pockets sagged by the weight of hidden mysteries.

'You tell him it's an offence to withhold information material to a federal murder investigation?' demanded Hordle.

Powell shifted uneasily. John Price looked at the lawyer with something close to astonishment. He said, 'Sir, I was talking to a man with close to forty years' experience of the American criminal system, state and federal. And I was trying to get a steer to what he had to offer us. No, I didn't remind him of the law. I figured he knew that pretty much as it was.'

'Softly, softly until I decide otherwise,' reminded Powell. 'Everyone clear on that?'

'I have to see the law is properly observed here,' persisted Brett Hordle.

'And I have to find a serial killer as of this moment causing the Bureau a lot of heat,' said Powell. 'I want this taken as far as it will go – as far as *I* say it will go – before resorting to pressure and legal arguments. If that means bending the rules, I'll bend the rules. And take all the responsibility for doing so.'

'You try anything clever and Durham refuses to co-operate in court, where's your prosecution?' challenged the FBI lawyer.

'We get our killer, we've already got enough forensic to put him away for a million years,' said Powell. 'All we need is where to look. We get that, I don't give a damn about Durham or what he did.' He looked at Price. 'What's the Drug Enforcement Administration got?'

'Just the required notification from a Washington bank, under the 1970 Act, of a large deposit in favour of a new customer.' He offered a Photostat of a cheque for $100,000 made out by James Durham to a Harold Taylor against a Washington bank. The holder's address on it was Belmont, Virginia.

'They seen him yet?'

'He refused. Said he'd only talk to us. And mentioned General Carr.'

'The DEA want involvement?'

'I work closely with them sometimes,' disclosed Price. 'I said if there was any drug involvement, I'd bring them in straight away.'

'Let's go and find out,' said Powell.

James Durham *was* flaky but doing his best to disguise it, apart from the size of the midday whisky. The ice really was rattling, very slightly. Everyone refused the lawyer's offer to join him. Durham was an indulgently large man who perfectly fitted the opulence of his Park Avenue apartment. In normal circumstances Powell guessed the lawyer would have the condescension of a very self-satisfied man: even now there were touches of it in the way he was offering seats and accepting introductions after the drinks refusal, trying to give the impression of a man in control of his surroundings and the people in it. His concentration was upon Brett Hordle, one lawyer trying to establish the mettle of another.

177

Formality, with the necessary reminder of the seriousness, Powell decided. He said, 'I am the agent investigating the murder of General Carr, which is linked to two other killings. I understand you have information that is material to that investigation?'

Durham sipped his drink to cover the nervous swallow. 'I think I have. But I want legal understanding between us.'

Brett Hordle shifted, but before the man could speak Powell said, 'What understandings?'

'I am in no way legally or criminally involved in these murders,' insisted Durham, quickly.

Powell remained silent, willing the other men with him not to speak, either. Durham gulped at his drink.

'I want that accepted, agreed, at the outset,' the man added.

'It's very difficult to accept or agree anything,' said Powell. 'We're here at your invitation, Mr Durham. Why should we imagine you're in some way involved in a multiple homicide?'

Durham clattered his empty glass on to the table beside him. 'I can possibly save the lives of others,' he announced. 'In return I want your legal guarantee that I will not be called or named in any subsequent prosecution. Nor will I be enjoined in any subsequent prosecution concerning these killings or on any other matters.'

'That's a very sweeping immunity,' said Hordle, getting in ahead of Powell.

'With every reason for your agreeing,' said Durham. 'You're hunting a killer who has to be stopped.'

'You know others he intends to kill?' pressed Powell.

'I think I might. I didn't, at first. Now I think I do.'

178

'Is the killer Harold Taylor, to whom you made out the cheque for $100,000?'

Durham looked towards the whiskey decanter. 'I don't know that he's the killer. I think he is involved.'

'And by association with him, you fear you could be considered an accomplice?' said Hordle.

Durham shook his head, although in refusal, not denial. 'Do I have a deal?'

'How many other victims do you think you might know?' asked Powell.

'Possibly three.'

Any one of whom Harold Taylor or an accomplice could be stalking as they talked. 'You've got your deal,' announced Powell.

Hordle began: 'From a legal point of view I really do think—' but Powell said: 'And from a commonsense point of view I think we need to prevent more killings, if it's at all possible. So we will.'

Durham swallowed, smiling uncertainly, looking at the other lawyer and then at the man's briefcase. 'You have an exculpation agreement?'

'Yes,' said the younger lawyer, reluctantly.

Durham insisted it should be Powell who witnessed the signatures. He finally poured another whiskey before settling back in his seat. 'It's probably best to start at the very beginning,' he said. 'In late 1949 I was engaged to act for an inmate of a military prison in Alabama jailed for life by a military tribunal in Germany. His name was Myron Nolan . . .'

As they let Durham talk Powell recognized how good a courtroom advocate the man must have been. Durham's confidence – condescension, even – returned with the non-prosecution agreement and he talked with

179

a lawyer's precision, every fact ready, the chronology in timed and dated order. And he'd been extremely clever, Powell further acknowledged. Durham had been more worried about a long-ago embezzlement than about more easily defensible inveiglement in a murder conspiracy. But if the man was right – and Powell didn't have the slightest doubt that he was – Durham had a different cause for concern about that, one that he didn't yet appear to have considered.

The moment Durham stopped, Powell said, 'An address! You must know how to contact this man Taylor. Have a phone number? Something?'

'No,' said Durham. 'He would just arrive, from nowhere. It was . . .' He stopped, uncertainly. 'His way of humiliating me, I suppose.'

'The first time was eighteen months ago?'

'Yes.'

'How?'

'Literally rang on the door. Said at once it was about Myron Nolan: about his estate.'

'Money from which you'd appropriated?' intruded Brett Hordle, brutally, annoyed at how easily the man had got his immunity.

'I went through every legal formality after Myron Nolan's death,' insisted Durham, his defence prepared. 'I advertised for living relatives and had inquiry agents search all available records.'

'Before which, having been feloniously gained, that estate should have been surrendered to the court that originally sentenced him,' suggested Hordle.

'Let's concentrate upon the present,' said Powell firmly. 'Who did Taylor say he was, when he came to you? Did he claim to be a relative of Nolan's?'

Durham shook his head. 'He refused to say *who* he

was. Just that he knew all about Myron Nolan's affairs – which he did, he knew *everything* – and that there was an undeclared estate of around $1 million.'

'Which he blackmailed you into giving him with the threat of exposing you for having kept it?' persisted Hordle.

Durham swallowed and nodded.

'Tell us about the other people you think are in danger,' said Powell.

'That was what he also wanted,' Durham hurried on, glad of the escape. 'He said he needed the names and addresses of everyone who'd been involved in his trial, in Germany: that he expected me to have the original depositions from which to start.'

'Did you have them?' came in John Price.

Durham shook his head. 'Not all. Only some. He made me hire inquiry agents again: give them what I had, to make searches. Legally I am the person who had them all located. Now three are dead.'

'Who are the others, apart from Gene Johnson, Jethro Morrison and General Carr?' demanded Powell.

Instead of answering immediately, Durham went to the bureau in the corner of the room and returned with a single sheet of paper. 'The man who unsuccessfully defended Nolan is named John Tibbett. He lives in Tucson. The prosecutor, Alan Onslow, is dying of cancer in a vets' hospital in Little Rock. The widow of another member of the court-martial panel, David Arnoldson, lives just outside Chicago.'

'What reason did Taylor give, for wanting them?' asked Powell.

'He didn't,' said Durham. 'Just that he wanted to find them and I could help—' Seeing the look on Brett Hordle's face, Durham added, 'I didn't have a choice! I

181

made a mistake, a long time ago when I was too young and too hungry. I was being made to pay for it!'

'You believe this is the full list?' asked John Price.

'He said there were more, that he was finding himself.'

'And you're absolutely positive you haven't any idea where Taylor lives?'

'None.'

Finally, almost reluctantly, Powell took the freeze frame pictures from his briefcase. He offered the print of the younger man first. Durham looked briefly at it, frowning. 'That's Taylor. So you knew about him all along?'

'Not really,' said Powell, handing the second photograph to the elderly man.

'That's . . .' started Durham, then looked up, bewildered. 'When was this taken?'

'Fifteen days ago,' said Powell.

Durham looked between the FBI agent and the photograph, vaguely smiling, his head shaking slowly. 'No,' he said, brittle voiced. 'No, that can't be. That's Myron Nolan. And Myron Nolan's dead. Murdered, in prison.'

'You sure about that: sure beyond any doubt?' pressed Powell, wanting an answer that would make sense of it all.

'Of course I'm sure,' insisted the retired lawyer, indignantly. 'I was the person who had to identify the body. I saw him lying dead, in the prison mortuary. You're mistaken about the photograph. You've got to be.'

'We're not,' said Powell, just as insistent.

'How . . .' said Durham uncertainly, his voice trailing.

'We don't know,' admitted Powell.

Durham looked back yet again at the photograph, then at the list that John Price had taken from him. 'Are you going to put them under protection?'

'Yes,' said Powell. 'And you, too.'

'Yes,' said Durham. 'I want that. That's essential.'

'I think so too,' agreed Powell.

'You can't be right, you know,' said the old man. 'It's a mistake . . . there's an explanation.'

'We can't find one,' said Powell.

None of them spoke going down in the elevator with James Durham. At the lobby the lawyer identified the Maurice Barkworth signature in the visitors' log Taylor had used for his most recent blackmail visit and Powell seized the entire book as an FBI exhibit from the startled desk clerk. Durham remained by the entry desk, watching them leave. Outside, on Park Avenue, John Price smiled expectantly and said, 'What's the story about someone who's supposed to have been dead for fifty years?'

'There isn't one,' said Powell. 'Not one that I yet know, anyway.'

At that moment, three and a half thousand miles away, Taylor smiled at Janet Hibbs in the bedroom to which she'd shown him and said, 'This is very nice. I'm glad I changed.'

'Good,' said Janet. 'Now let me show you the rest of the house. You don't mind meeting Mother, do you?'

'I'd like that,' he said. The transformation in Janet Hibbs was almost as surprising as anything he could manage himself. She wore tweeds and a sweater and was positively beautiful. Best of all she was clean, wonderfully perfumed and clean. This was going to be *so* good.

Chapter Sixteen

Edith Hibbs had a scrawny neck he could scarcely wait to cut into and the left side of her face had collapsed, pulling her mouth slightly open. She tilted vaguely to the left in the wheelchair that had been positioned in the window bay so that she could look out over the garden without being directly in the sun, which was flooding the room with brightness. Her eyes were closed when they entered but opened at once when Janet coughed, a pre-arranged signal. Awake and in conscious control the facial effect of the stroke was less obvious and she straightened in the chair, embarrassed by her frailty.

'Our guest, Mother,' announced Janet.

'It's good that you could come,' said the old lady.

There was only the suggestion of a slur from the twisted mouth. She'd hate having to surrender her house to strangers for money, Taylor guessed: prefer the charade that they really were guests. He briefly accepted the bony hand, glad that close that she didn't smell of piss, as he'd expected, and went into a charade of his own, saying how lucky he felt that they could take him into such a delightful house where he was sure he was going to be very comfortable. He didn't know how long he was staying but he hoped as long as possible in such a beautiful part of the country, far prettier than his father had made it sound recounting his time here, during the war. That prompted her reminiscences, which it was intended to do, and he dutifully studied the photographs the old woman insisted her daughter take from the piano top and side table of the man he remembered so well, actually dressed then as he was in the pictures in stiff, bemedalled uniform and cross-strapped leather, snapping high-voiced remarks across a courtroom table. *Despicable . . . charge should have been murder . . . inadequate penalty . . . despicable . . .*

He instantly recognized Janet's cue to leave, following her out into the deceptively wide and long corridor that bisected the house from front to back. It *was* a delightful house, better and cleaner than the hotel he'd just left.

Janet said, 'That was extremely kind of you, sparing the time. She misses people.'

'I enjoyed meeting her.' He had, he decided. Actually enjoyed acting out a part with the stupid old fool, like he was acting out a part now, making daughter as well as mother like him. Not a problem. Never had been: always a way with people, ingratiating himself and all the time laughing at their gullibility. Could he make Janet *really* like him before he killed them both? Impress her sufficiently to trust him, absolutely and totally: seduce her, even? He'd never done that: wasn't sure he knew how. He'd always paid for women, not needing them in any other way. Not needing – not himself trusting – anybody. He didn't need Janet, of course. What he wanted was the experience – something else new – of behaving like an ordinary, mundane person. He'd try: genuinely try. Test her. Her choice, without her knowing it. If she responded, she'd live a little longer. If

185

she didn't, he'd kill her that much quicker. Her chance to live or die. Life's lottery.

'It's her busy day. Hospital physiotherapy.'

'You taking her?' he asked, seeing the opening.

The woman shook her head. 'She gets collected. A special vehicle, to accommodate the wheelchair.'

'More gardening?'

She smiled at his question. 'I really don't know what I'm doing. I just go along with the shears cutting off bits that stick out and make the hedges look untidy.'

'Take the afternoon off, then. Show me one of the walks across the downs.' As he spoke Taylor felt the oddest sensation, one he didn't recognise. Surely it wasn't uncertainty: the thought of being rejected! Her fault if he was. Careful, Big Tits Janet.

For a moment she stood in the hallway regarding him curiously. Then she said, 'It would be good to get out for a while. I've hardly left the house since Mother became ill.'

'It's fixed, then?'

'Yes. And thank you.'

'What time?'

'Mother leaves at two.'

'And so shall we.'

He half considered transferring the satchel from the car boot to his upstairs room but decided against it. Safer where it was. A local woman came in to clean, Janet had said. Didn't want her looking at things she shouldn't see: an evil eye for an evil eye. Janet had nice eyes. Blue. Have one soon.

At the gate he hesitated, undecided. The village was very quiet, asleep in the sun. She'd expect him to look at the church; might even be watching. Norman, he remembered. He'd have some fun inside. Amuse himself.

186

He walked easily, unhurriedly. As he passed the Bold Forester he was aware of a man at the window, watching him. He smiled and the man smiled in return. The lych-gate was stiff, creaking open, and so was the church door, which groaned in protest. Inside it was unexpectedly cold and smelt of damp and dust: motes swirled in the sun shafts, coming through the stained glass. Flowers were dying around the altar, casting their petals, making a mess. He scattered them even more, tempted to desecrate the place further, pissing on it perhaps or heaping it with the dog shit he'd seen on the churchyard path. But that would mean handling it, which was unthinkable. And there was the man in the pub window who'd watched him going into the church. He wouldn't do anything, he decided. Tantalizing though it was – he ached to do something – he would vandalize nothing. Better – more satisfying in the long run – to go on performing his own private charade, the charming-to-everyone tourist. Then he saw the commemorative plaque to Major Walter Hibbs, MC, DSO. He spat on it, watching the spittle dribble down across the marble.

'They're going to suffer,' he said aloud. 'Suffer a lot.' He knew how he'd do it. Like he'd killed Johnson and the hooker, only much better. Tie the old bitch in her wheelchair and make her watch while he fucked the daughter: make Janet do everything to him – things they probably didn't know about – and then kill her and do the cutting. Tell the old woman while he was doing that why it was happening – what her husband had done to him, to deserve the revenge – and how he was going to do the same to her. Do the face change, too. Mustn't forget that. Do that to Janet, while she was still alive. While he was raping her.

Taylor found the Hibbs tomb in the graveyard, a large rectangular mausoleum with a metal gated entrance to steps leading down to a vault sealed by an aged wooden door. The memorial plaque to Hibbs was the same as that inside the church but alongside was another recording the death eight years earlier of Dr Timothy John Hibbs, aged twenty-five. Taylor spat on both and said, aloud again, 'Soon going to be quite crowded in there', and laughed.

There were three men in farm overalls at the bar of the Bold Forester and another man drinking alone at a table. The man who'd earlier watched him through the window was behind the bar. The farm workers stopped talking at Taylor's entry. The landlord, a red-faced, easily smiling man, nodded and beamed. You're looking at the man who's going to create the biggest sensation of your lives, thought Taylor. He said 'Good morning' generally, and got a chorus of replies.

Again he asked for the strongest beer and carried it to a table facing the other solitary drinker. The man was reading the *Daily Mirror*, holding it so that Taylor could see the artist's impression of the man supposed to be him occupying half the front page. Before leaving Midhurst Taylor had gone through all the morning newspapers, studying the drawing and reading Paul Stanswell's version of their encounter.

There were also several photographs of the taxi driver talking to the media outside New Scotland Yard. Taylor didn't recognize Stanswell from his journey in the man's cab and decided Stanswell wouldn't recognize him again, either. In the drawing both the eyes and the ears were too prominent and the hair had been made to appear receding, which it wasn't. The height was also miscalculated, making him a good two inches too tall. As

Taylor watched, the man finished what he was reading, closed the newspaper and put it face up on the table, so the sketch was directly in front of him. Suddenly conscious of Taylor's attention, he stared back. There was no identification. Taylor smiled. So did the man.

Taylor lunched on excellent home-cooked ham and salad and drank two more beers, the last at the bar after the farm workers left. The landlord introduced himself as George Potter and Taylor agreed he was an American visiting the village for a few days.

'Staying at the Hibbses house,' said the man, without having to be told. 'My missus helps out there.'

'I'll try not to make too much mess.'

'Our Vera's used to mess, keeping this place clean as well.'

'She does it well.' And was going to have to do a lot more than usual in a few days' time.

Edith Hibbs's wheelchair was being hydraulically lifted into the specially adapted hospital van as Taylor walked back up the drive. He stood aside, for it to pass. Janet was at the door of the house. She'd changed into jeans and walking shoes.

He looked down at himself and said, 'Am I all right like this?'

'You're fine. It's a designated public footpath. Not rough. I just thought jeans were better for me.'

Wouldn't stop me screwing you if I felt like it, he thought. Would he be able to get her to do it willingly? That would be different, making her like him that much. Probably too much to expect. Didn't want to frighten her. Be ordered out of the house. He said, 'I've been to the church. It's very pretty.'

'It is, isn't it?' She fell into step with him walking down the drive.

189

'Who was Timothy?'

'My elder brother. After he qualified he went to Africa with Medicins sans Frontières. Picked up a disease they said had something to do with monkeys. There wasn't any treatment.' She went through it quickly, wanting to get it out of the way.

'I'm sorry if it hurt, my asking.'

'We were very close. I miss him.' At the church she hesitated. 'We could have brought flowers from the garden.'

'Tomorrow.' She'd be putting flowers on her own grave!

She smiled. 'All right. Tomorrow.'

The path was signposted. At a stile she accepted his hand unhesitatingly. The jeans showed how tight her ass was. Have that, before he killed her. Have all of her. He liked her soft-fingered touch. Make her use those fingers and that full mouth, thinking there was a chance for her mother to live if she did everything he told her. She'd expect some personal history from him, he supposed. He had five previous existences to choose from, one himself as a doctor in early nineteenth-century London. How would she react to his attempts on that particular return to prove that the retina of murder victims retained the image of their attacker, which was why they always had to be destroyed? Better to invent. Or rather, half invent. There was still more money to come from Durham and when the retribution was over he'd thought of playing the stock markets, use it all as risk capital. That was the sort of thing that might impress her. Which was, after all, the game he was playing.

She did seem impressed, more so than he expected, the family's financial difficulties obvious in the quickness

190

with which she suggested, badly disguising it as a light-hearted remark, that perhaps he could recommend some good but safe investments for her and her mother. He went along with that, promising to study the English market and making up anecdotes of high-risk deals, allowing the modestly unspoken impression that he usually gained more than he lost.

There were quite long periods when they didn't speak at all, Janet seemingly quite comfortable with silence, which he picked up on quickly enough to avoid appearing uncertain by constantly talking. After that realization he let the conversation move at her pace and was glad he did. It was Janet who created the opportunity, asking if he was making the European trip alone or maybe being joined by someone ('all alone and unattached: actually ended a relationship just before I left Washington. Sensible girl found a much more reliable guy') and in return Janet volunteered that she'd just been let down by discovering that someone she'd formed an association with was already married.

'Which made coming to look after Mummy something of a welcome escape, although hardly a good career move. He was the commissioning director of an advertising agency with which I'd just got some freelance graphic design work. Nobody warned me of the full job description.'

They had cream teas in the next village, Graffham, and walked back with even longer periods of comfortable silence. They got to the house fifteen minutes before Edith Hibbs.

Janet said, 'I enjoyed that.'

'Maybe we could do it again before I leave?'

'I think I'd enjoy that, too,' she said, looking directly at him.

'It's a date,' he said, wondering if it would turn out to be one.

Day became night with their scarcely being aware of it, certainly not Powell whose absolute concentration was getting into place all he considered necessary. From the Manhattan office he faxed Amy everything relevant from the meeting with Durham, using it as a prompt when he briefed Harry Beddows, who had returned to await the search warrant after supervising the outside surveillance on Harold Taylor's deserted house. Beddows at once agreed the protection for Durham and the three other potential victims and to the build-up of the incident room staffing by withdrawing John Price from New York and Matt Hirst from Pittsburgh.

On the return shuttle Brett Hordle said, 'This is pretty crazy, isn't it?'

'Lot of things don't make sense,' agreed Powell.

'The old guy's got to be a relative of Myron Nolan's that no-one knew about, the younger one his son. How about that?'

'He'd have to be an identical twin. Nolan was thirty-five when he got murdered and that was forty-eight years ago. The man in the freeze frame picture isn't eighty-three years old. And according to Westmore's experts, there's no evidence of plastic surgery.'

'What's your theory?'

'I don't have one. Just more questions than answers.'

'Spooky,' said the lawyer.

'Yes,' accepted Powell. Suddenly it didn't seem ridiculous to use a word like that, although of course it was. He called Beddows on the public in-flight telephone just before landing at the renamed Reagan airport, relieved to find him still at Pennsylvania Avenue and further relieved that the search warrant wasn't expected for another hour, which gave him time to get to the house before it was executed. Beddows appeared to realize it, too.

'I'll still come,' insisted the division chief.

It was almost a petulant gesture, Powell thought. The entry would still be under his authority, as the deputed agent in charge of the investigation. Emphasizing it, Powell said, 'I want this very low key: strictly limited to surveillance and technicians.' Wasn't he being just as petulant; more so, even?

'We get the son-of-a-bitch and the heat's off.'

'We lose him and we double it. We don't know what's inside yet.'

There was a silence. 'It's ten o'clock. I told Public Affairs there might be something, so there'd be a spokesman available,' admitted the division chief.

'Your total responsibility, Harry. I run into a circus, you're the ringmaster. And I don't want to go on discussing this on an open line.'

To avoid a detour Powell asked the lawyer to take Durham's apartment visitors' book to the Bureau for scientific analysis. Renting a car at the airport, he quickly gained the beltway in the light evening traffic. He found Belmont easily and parked three streets away from the address provided by the DEA. As he approached he isolated a window-darkened surveillance van at the nearest intersection, giving the watchers a front and right-side view of the silent house, and a car much further along the street, which would cover the left side. There would, he knew, be a car in the road running along the back, although from what he could see of the house there seemed to be a solid rear fence. There was no car in the driveway, nor lights in any of the windows.

Powell approached the surveillance van from the blind side of the house, softly identifying himself at the nearside passenger door at the same time as tapping upon it.

There was a delay in the opening and the observer said, 'Shit, you frightened the hell out of me.' He leaned forward, to make it easier for Powell to get in. There were four other men, in addition to the driver and his observer. One was earphoned and in front of the electronic equipment that covered one entire side wall and another was hunched close to the rear window at infrared night viewing equipment, mounted on a tripod. The other two were sitting on jump seats, doing nothing.

The radio operator turned at his entry and said, 'Harry's on his way, with the warrant. Said to expect him.'

Nodding towards the equipment Powell said, 'You got any sensors against the windows for inside movement?'

'Waiting for the warrant.'

'Telephone taps?'

'Authorized by the same warrant.'

The driver said, 'There's no-one in that house. Guarantee it.'

'What about media?' asked Powell. 'You seen any television vans, stuff like that?'

'Christ, no!' said the radio man. 'You want that!'

'Absolutely not,' said Powell. 'Just hoping that nothing's leaked.'

The observer said, 'You going to go through that house properly you're going to need a lot of light. Which will warn him if he comes back while you're doing it. How you going to handle it?'

He was accepted as the control officer, Powell recognized at once. 'We'll wear earpieces, connected to you. Anything suspicious – anything at all – you intercept. Maximum caution: wear vests. He uses a knife, maybe several, but he's also probably got a magnum he stole from the first victim.'

'Here comes Harry and the entry unit,' announced the man at the window.

It was another unmarked van. It cruised past, not stopping until it was beyond any view from the house. Powell said, 'Tell them I'm coming across.'

The inside layout was electronically identical to the vehicle Powell had just left, but all the men in the back apart from the operator were already kitted in SWAT team all-in-ones. Powell was glad the bulletproof vests covered the FBI initials on their backs. Their equipment belts carried mace and stun grenades, as well as 9mm magnums. Each man had an equipment sack at his feet. Powell accepted the offered earpiece from the radio operator. The overalled unit leader said, 'Better let us check it out for entry, see there aren't any traps before you come in.'

The group quickly and surprisingly quietly left through the rear door.

Powell said, 'What happened with Public Affairs?'

'Stood them down,' said Harry Beddows.

'That's good. He's not in the house.'

'You think he's moved on?'

'We'll know that when we get inside.'

'Checked with the realtor,' disclosed Beddows. 'Taylor's taken the lease for a year.'

Powell's earpiece hissed and crackled. A voice said,

'It's safe. Come on in. It's sure as hell odd.'

The entry unit had done their best to set the drapes but the house was very obviously occupied, and as he approached Powell knew that if Taylor came back while they were inside it was practically inevitable they'd lose him. Powell stopped just inside, searching for the word and deciding it was sterile. Each piece of furniture appeared to have been arranged in a pattern. There was not a single indentation in any seat or cushion and in the kitchen the search was slowed by pots and jars and cans having to be replaced exactly as they were found, always in neat lines according to their size, always with the labels facing out. There was nothing half opened or in cans in the refrigerator. There were some clothes – two jackets, some underwear, socks and shirts and two pairs of shoes – in closets and drawers of the pristine bedroom with its rigidly made bed. All were neatly folded and arranged, once more according to size.

One of the SWAT team said from the kitchen, 'Will you look at this!'

When Powell arrived he saw strips of paper kitchen towel snowed across the floor.

The searcher said, 'It's all around the windows and door edges. Every gap and crack is plugged, sealing the place.'

Powell said, 'I think Geoff Sloane should see this.'

'The bastard's left some stuff. He's coming back,' said Beddows.

'From wherever he's gone to kill someone else,' completed Powell.

It was an hour before the shout came from the basement. When they got there the team leader was training a strobe light behind the broken-down false wall so that what was hidden behind would be brightly illuminated.

Four eyes, in specimen jars, gazed back glassily at them.

'He's definitely coming back,' said Powell. 'He didn't take his souvenirs.'

Chapter Seventeen

Wesley Powell managed three hours' sleep and wished he hadn't bothered. He'd felt more alert – more awake – when he'd got to Crystal City at three-thirty that morning than he did now. When he arrived at Pennsylvania Avenue just after seven Amy Halliday was already there, her machines on. She looked crisp, fresh and well rested, although she'd still been there at midnight, when they'd last spoken by telephone.

She smiled and said, 'Hello, stranger.'

'Certainly seems that long,' he agreed.

She gestured towards the computer bank. 'I'll have everything new on file in four hours.

'You're going to knock yourself out.'

'I'm fine,' she insisted, getting up from her station with a clipboard in her hand. 'No more possible victims' names or addresses: Army Records are a total mess. Those we do know are all under protection, according to the overnight messages from the local Bureau offices. Matt Hirst and John Price have arrived: both at the Marriott. I've moved two more filing clerks in, by the way. And I've gone through this morning's wire service round-ups of the papers and television. We're getting hit pretty badly, for holding back on any worth-while release . . .' She hesitated, looking grave. 'What the hell's it all about, Wes?'

He shook his head, helplessly. 'There's got to *be* an answer but I don't have it.'

'It's creep—' she tried.

'I know.' He stopped her. 'Let's not go down that route.'

'He's going to kill again, isn't he?'

'He probably already has. And all we can do is sit and wait for the body to be found.'

'Can I ask you a personal question?'

'Of course.'

'Hirst or Price taking over the incident room?'

A very vested interest, he thought. 'It's already being extremely well organized. I've got other things for them to do.'

He started on that the moment he got into his side office, reaching both agents before they left their hotel. He told John Price to go direct to Taylor's bank for every available record and sent Hirst to the realtor for the reference letters with which Taylor had secured the lease. As he replaced the receiver Mark Lipton, the head of Public Affairs, came on the internal line asking what in the name of Christ was happening and warning that if they didn't come out with something substantial soon ('like right now!') the media were going to roast the Bureau on a slow spit: imagining pressure, the man said that as soon as he finished speaking to Powell he was going to get on to the Director's secretariat to ask Clarence Gale to give a press conference. Powell ruined the man's threat by saying that any statement whatso-ever would only be made upon Gale's personal approval anyway.

'What makes these serial killings so different from the rest?' demanded the man.

'Ask the Director.'

'You forgotten a man can make a reputation for himself co-operating with the media on something like this?' enticed Lipton.

'That's exactly what I haven't forgotten,' Powell assured him, unhelpfully.

The announcement of a full briefing conference, to be chaired at noon by the Director himself, came from Harry Beddows.

'He wants answers,' declared the division chief. He perched himself on the edge of the desk again and Powell felt crowded. He said, 'Don't we all?'

'You heard from Public Affairs?'

'Fifteen minutes ago. Lipton himself.' Who'd clearly also spoken to Beddows, he accepted.

'He tell you what he's being asked?'

'What we're all asking each other, I guess. Without any answers.'

Beddows shook his head at the glibness. 'Who's the team leader? This could start going badly wrong for you, Wes.'

Responsibility avoidance time, Powell recognized. 'The buck's got to stop somewhere, isn't that what the little guy once said?'

'You want to be taken off the case, I'll do what I can to help.'

Powell regarded the other man in astonishment. 'You ever hear of a request like that being made before, from anyone who stayed on in the Bureau longer than the next hour!'

Beddows shrugged, colouring slightly. 'I got the feeling you're not 100 per cent into this. Lipton kind of agreed.

Said you just kept referring him to the Director.'

So a cabal was being assembled. All right, Powell thought, you want to play dirty pool, you son-of-a-bitch, you better be careful your knuckles don't get broken. He guessed he'd be identified in print by midday. It gave him an idea. Two, in fact.

Not having enough people on the first occasion, Clarence Gale's personal conference room was almost overcrowded on the second. Gale settled himself authoritatively, lacking only his robes, at the head of the table and Beddows took the chair to the right by unquestionable rank. Powell faced him. Amy, still flushed from Powell's unexpected decision to include her, was next to him, showing no nervousness as she distributed the updated dossiers she knew so well. Gale had shown no surprise at Amy's introduction but Harry Beddows, responsible for summoning everyone else, had frowned curiously at Powell's insistence.

To Powell the tall, desiccated Director said at once, 'You got a sensible explanation yet?'

'Not for everything,' admitted Powell cautiously. 'Some ideas maybe, when we've talked it through. Durham is adamant Myron Nolan's dead: that he identified the body before burial at Florence, in April 1951 . . . But there can't be any doubt now these are vengeance killings associated with the man . . .'

'And there's another tie-in,' offered Barry Westmore. 'Graphology are positive the signature in the entry log to Durham's apartment in the name of Maurice Barkworth is the same handwriting as Myron Nolan, on the military tribunal records. No question of forgery.'

'So he's definitely *not* dead?' sighed the Director.

'It wasn't Myron Nolan whom Durham met that day,'

Powell reminded them. 'I can't explain the handwriting. I can't explain the face on the freeze frame, seemingly the same age as Nolan was when he died. Or the fingerprints . . .' He was conscious of Harry Beddows smiling slightly from across the table. 'But what about this? Nolan was King Rat of the Florence jail. Ran it. Whatever he wanted, he got. Including hookers. If he could get women in and out, he could get a man in to fill a coffin and satisfy the prison personnel who actually weren't on the take, which can't have been very many from what Leroy Goodfellow says. All Myron Nolan would have needed was Durham finding someone no-one would miss and getting him into the stockade, to which Durham apparently came and went as he pleased, meeting Nolan in the comfort of warders' offices. And then for Durham to go through the formality of supposedly identifying the body and signing the forms and he's home free. And we know Durham is a crook, would have done it for money: even, for enough, arrange murder.'

'That theory's got more holes than Swiss cheese,' Beddows attacked at once. 'Durham admits stealing from Nolan. He wouldn't – couldn't – have done that if Nolan were on the outside. Jethro Morrison would have had to be paid off: had a hold over them for ever. And why would Nolan – or a family we haven't yet discovered – wait forty-eight years to start hitting his victims!'

'I offered it as an idea,' said Powell defensively. 'Give me a better one.'

'Give me evidence I can understand and I will,' said the division chief.

'There any benefit in getting the body exhumed?' wondered Matt Hirst.

'We could get DNA from hair and bone but we don't

have a surviving tissue source from Nolan to make a comparison,' Barry Westmore rejected the idea.

'What would it prove if it matched the samples we've picked up from the murder scenes so far?' persisted Hirst.

'That the body was Nolan's and that our killer is a member of his family,' said the forensic scientist. 'If it were identical, then the face on the freeze frame is an identical lookalike twin brother: that's the only way scientifically you get a perfect DNA match from two separate people. It wouldn't explain the ageless face, the fingerprints or the handwriting, though.'

'I still prefer it to people returning from the dead,' said Clarence Gale. 'We'll get the body up.'

'Shouldn't we go back to Durham on the idea of the body in Nolan's grave being that of someone else?' said Amy.

Beddows frowned sharply at her intrusion. 'We've already demolished that idea.'

'I don't think we have, not entirely,' said the Director. 'We've got people literally by his side. Let's hit him with conspiracy to murder, see how he jumps. What about the house? Neighbours?'

'Mr Invisible, according to neighbours,' quickly replied Beddows, safe with basic investigatory procedure. 'Haven't yet located any regular delivery people. Lot of evidence that he'll return. A fly settles, we know about it. We got people permanently inside, outside surveillance on every approach street. Telephone tapped. We're getting telephone records, incoming and outgoing, for the four months he's been there.'

Powell waited for the other man to complete his contribution. Then he said, 'I found the inside of the house curious. Not a single proper letter or document of any sort. Just a couple of circulars with postmarks ending five days after Carr died . . .'

'I've never seen a house like it, in any crime investigation,' confirmed Westmore. 'I only managed to lift three sets of prints throughout the entire building, all his. Not a single hair from the bed or around the bath. That's virtually impossible: the place *is* sterilized. Even the window cracks stuffed with paper to keep dirt out.'

'Perfectly fits the psychosis and the profile, although I've got to admit I've never encountered one to such a degree,' said Geoffrey Sloane, who'd arrived for the conference direct from his examination of the Belmont house. 'A nest is a total misnomer, but that's what it is, his nest. Where he personally lives. It's got to be perfect. Think of the neatness with which he displays the bodies and leaves their clothes. He's revulsed by the blood he gets covered in. Can't wait to clean himself. Why, in fact, he kills so neatly. He's limiting to the utmost his getting dirtied by what happens when he starts dismembering.'

'Why doesn't he bother about fingerprints at the murder scene?' challenged John Price.

'He's reduced the crime scenes to obscene filth. He's too impatient to get out, once he's cleaned himself. He's also supremely arrogant. Believes he's invulnerable. Beyond detection.'

There was a brief silence, as everyone digested the analysis. It was Matt Hirst who filled it.

'The two references he provided, to get the place, are both forgeries,' he announced. 'One was a credit assurance, from the bank that reported the deposit – he obviously stole some letterheads during a visit – who say they never wrote it. The other was from the National Gallery of Art, where he claimed to be employed as a restorer. They've never heard of him. We got a man there now, showing the younger freeze frame picture, just in case anyone recognizes him.'

'Everything we're discussing is covered in the dossiers I've supplied,' said Amy quickly. 'In addition I'm computer checking Social Security against the names of Harold Taylor, Maurice Barkworth and Myron Nolan. I'm also running a trace through all the credit card companies, in all three names. Credit agencies, too. And I'm promised Pentagon records of officers of contemporary rank with General Carr who served in Berlin in 1949, both in the Army and as part of the Four Power Commission. If I cross-reference them with Army Records at Adelphi we might be able to fill in some of the missing tribunal panel who could be at risk.'

Slow down, thought Powell. Gale seemed impressed.

'The bank are stalling,' said John Price. 'Say they complied with the Banking Act by reporting the deposit but we're going to need a court order for any account details. They let slip, though, that there's a safe deposit facility in Taylor's name.'

Gale turned to him but before the Director could speak Powell said, 'I've already spoken to Brett Hordle, who came to New York with me and is fully up to date. He doesn't think he can get anything until after the weekend: it'll have to be a private application in front of a judge.'

'Tell him I want the name of the judge. I'll speak direct, say I want it by tomorrow, at the latest,' said Gale. To Price he added: 'Tell whoever you're dealing with at the bank not to go away for the weekend.' He looked around the table. 'Anyone got any more points?'

'There's the media,' said Powell, who'd been waiting for the opportunity, aware of Clarence Gale's publicity pursuit. 'Harry's been talking about it to Mark Lipton, haven't you, Harry?' Payback time, Powell thought.

'No!' Beddows contradicted, off balance and momentarily confused. 'I mean it was just a general conversation. I didn't give any instructions.'

'I thought he complained about my insisting that any release had to be approved first by the Director. Wasn't that what you told me?'

'He's concerned about the attacks. So am I. I've left it to be discussed here, now.' Beddows was only just managing to keep the irritation from his face and voice.

'I'm concerned too,' said Gale. 'We need to get a handle on this right away. Get it right.'

'Didn't you think of inviting him, when you convened the meeting?' persisted Powell.

'Like you, I felt it should be fully discussed with the Director first,' said Beddows.

'Concerned as you rightly are, you must have thought about it?' pursued Powell. 'You think the Director should personally give a press conference?'

Gale looked sternly sideways. 'What personal press conference!'

'Mark Lipton's suggestion,' said Powell, hoping he'd pitched the ingenuousness properly. 'He talked to me about it before speaking to Harry, so I assumed it had been passed on for approval.' He attempted an innocent smile. 'Why don't I stop trying to second-guess and leave Harry to tell us what he's come up with?'

Stiffly Beddows said, 'I've already made it clear I think we should take guidance from the Director.'

'Lipton didn't have any thoughts either?'

'No!' snapped Beddows.

Hopefully stressing the positive contrast, Powell said,

'We can't make any disclosure about the names, freeze frame photographs or Belmont: he'll run if we go public on any of that. And he won't go anywhere near New York if he suspects we know about Durham. And until there's something more, his coming back here or hitting on Durham again are our best two chances – our *only* two chances – of getting him.'

'Which yet again leaves us with nothing,' sneered Beddows.

'To which the Director shouldn't be exposed,' Powell seized his chance. 'It leaves us with the truth. We're totally baffled and we don't understand it. We say so. We appeal for anyone who might in the past have known any of the three victims – which might, in fact, get us to other potential victims we don't yet have – and talk about one of the cleverest multiple killers we've ever confronted . . .' He stopped, looking to the forensic psychologist. 'All serial killers are control freaks, in some way or another, right?'

'Right,' agreed Geoffrey Sloane, curiously.

'If he believes he's controlling us, the FBI, you think that might tempt him into a challenge?'

Sloane smiled. 'That could work. That really could work!'

'The Bureau never admits it's beaten,' protested Beddows, coming in too late on Gale's media awareness. 'That's totally the wrong public message.'

Risking all, Powell said, 'Then until now the Bureau's been stupid not using the ploy. And it's not a message to the public. It's a message – a challenge – to an over-confident killer.'

As always, Clarence Gale's expression was impenetrable. Beddows was shaking his head, in open rejection. The psychologist still smiled, although doubtfully. The uncertainty was more obvious from everyone else. He wouldn't rush to finish, Powell decided. He was sure he could turn whatever was said into his planned denouement.

Predictably the attack came from Beddows, as Powell hoped it would. The division chief said, 'We're already being accused in the media of not knowing what we're doing. Now you're actually suggesting we agree that they're right!' He hesitated, with an imagined denouement of his own. 'That could end up with demands for the Director to be dismissed. Resign.'

'Didn't you tell me that Public Affairs were being asked for the name of the agent-in-charge?' asked Powell.

Beddows swallowed, gazing alertly across the table. 'Yes?'

'Then why don't we give it to them?' said Powell. 'Make it obvious that I'm the one who's beaten. That way the attacks are deflected from the Bureau and the Director, to me. And Harold Taylor's got a person he thinks he can control – manipulate.'

'That's a curious strategy,' said Gale, at once recognizing its necessary element of personal protection.

He was almost there, Powell decided. 'Only as far as the general public is concerned. I retain your total confidence, don't I, Mr Director?'

'Absolutely,' said Gale at once.

'And when we get Taylor I'm confident you'll make it quite clear that the whole thing was the subterfuge it is, to trap a killer.'

Gale smiled, halting the head movement towards Beddows. Instead he said to Geoffrey Sloane, 'What do you think?'

'I haven't heard anything better,' said the psychologist.

'Like I said, it could work. And Wes being identified certainly gives Taylor a target.'

'We'll do it,' decided Clarence Gale.

Powell's name was released in time for the early evening news. So was a photograph. The newscast also included the fact that the two previous investigations he'd led had ended badly. He hadn't expected Beddows to do that. Maybe it wasn't such a good idea after all. He certainly hadn't enjoyed playing the sycophant: he'd never make a team player, according to the Washington rules.

'Did I screw up?' demanded Amy.

'Close.'

'Your idea needed more support.'

'Beddows is too big for you to confront.' It had been Powell's suggestion they come to the conveniently close round bar at the Willard, to get her away from Pennsylvania Avenue.

'Gale was right about your strategy to confront him. It's certainly curious,' she said. 'It couldn't have been like this when you guys worked together?'

'It wasn't. Things change.'

'Why?'

'You know something? Once – just once – I'd like to be asked a question I knew the answer to.'

'Try this. Why did you insist on my being there today?'

'Who else in that room totally – from front to back – knew *every* detail in those case dossiers, apart from you? I didn't want any more questions I didn't know the answer to.'

She looked at him curiously. 'That all?'

'Didn't hurt to make an impression, did it?'

She hesitated. 'Then you should have told me before we went in. I might have kept quiet.'

'Gale went along with you. So you got away with it. And now he knows your face.'

'And everybody in America knows yours, after today's media release. And we've already agreed there's going to be another killing before we can stop Taylor. Maybe not even then. The public opinion pressure gets too much, you quite sure Gale will go on supporting you? Things change: your words.'

'It's a risk,' admitted Powell.

'Means I'm working for both our careers now.'

'Each dependent upon the other.'

'I'm happy with that,' she said, lightly but holding him in the direct look he'd come to recognize. 'And thanks for including me: letting the Director know what I look like. That was very generous of you.'

Was this an invitation for him to go beyond their agreed professional level? She'd made herself too indispensable – she genuinely was the only person who had the minutiae at her fingertips – for him to chance trying to find out. 'All part of the service.'

Beth said, 'I saw the newscast. Guys were saying you were incompetent.'

'As bad as that?' He was glad it had been Beth who answered the telephone. He hadn't wanted to talk to Ann.

'Dad, I'm serious!'

'So am I. Serious about tomorrow.'

'Mom thought you might have to cancel.'

'I won't, it I can possibly help it. I just might be a little late. Any plans?'

'What we did last Saturday.'

210

*   *   *

The time difference made it 4 a.m. in England, which Harold Taylor saw at once when the ambulance lights woke him, coming up the drive. The old lady was already being manoeuvred from her wheelchair into the vehicle, the hurriedly dressed Janet clambering in behind her.

'Do you want me to follow you?' he asked. Shit! They were being taken away from him: taken to somewhere he couldn't play the game he was enjoying! He burned with anger.

'I'll stay with her in hospital until I find out what's wrong.'

'I'll come in first thing, so you won't be stuck without a car. If you want me earlier, call.'

Janet smiled, through her concern. 'I always seem to be thanking you for something, don't I?'

Chapter Eighteen

He was too angry, fury literally shaking through him, even to think of returning to bed. For a long time all he could do was stump around the house, wanting movement, wanting to destroy. He actually considered it, smashing everything that was breakable before torching the place, watching it burn to the ground: wipe them out. Wrong way, he reminded himself, regaining control. That wouldn't *be* wiping them out. They'd still be alive. Shouldn't have let himself react like this. He was *always* in control, manipulating everyone else. Couldn't be helped, if the old bitch died. That was always allowed for. He still had Janet to play his new game with – intentionally delaying the killing – to make the pleasure last.

Needed to do something, though: punish them in some way. What? Invade their privacy: handle – fondle – their intimate things, learn their secrets. Taylor smiled, pleased with the idea. That was the way to control people. Know everything about them.

He was offended by the untidiness of the emergency there had been in Edith Hibbs's bedroom, the bed covering cast back, the heavy wardrobe door hanging open. The clothes inside smelt of mothballs and age. Nothing exciting inside: nothing he wasn't supposed to see. He was glad the commode didn't stink of her use. The smaller closets and two separate chests of drawers were better. A lot of underwear, most of it silk, long-legged knickers and chemises and stiff-boned corsets that would have encased her from breast to buttock, like armour. He sniffed them, particularly the knickers, wondering about the sort of souvenir he hadn't taken before. Not the old woman's. If it was anyone's it would be Janet's. Something to think about.

Taylor found the trove at the bottom of a built-in closet, box upon box of letters and albums as well as loose photographs and diaries, virtually the life history of Major and Mrs Walter Hibbs.

Taylor worked methodically, properly, taking each box from its storage place and assembling its chronology from the dated letters and diaries inside, starting in the order that Edith Hibbs had begun, from her wedding to the stern-faced bastard who even when he was young – nineteen, according to the marriage certificate he found – affected that ridiculous moustache. Everything about the two of them was ridiculous, he decided, reading steadily. At first the stupid bitch wrote as if she were talking to a real person. *Dear diary, I am so happy. Dear diary, I am so glad I saved myself for marriage. Dear diary, Walter is so wonderful: I am so proud. Dear diary, I pray that God will keep him safe.*

The drivel went on and on: about her fear of pregnancy and her joy of having a boy (*my angel, my most adorable baby*) to continue the family name and then of becoming pregnant with Janet (*it's happened again: why is God so good?*). She'd called Janet beautiful and he decided Janet was, even as a child, never gawky or awkward, definitely far more attractive in a dated photograph when she was nineteen than her mother had

213

been in her wedding portrait at that age.

The entries got longer – more detailed – with Edith Hibbs's maturity. The proud-parent university graduation photographs of begowned and mortarboarded Timothy and Janet each went with two entire page entries, as did Timothy's qualification as a doctor and his decision to volunteer for relief work in Africa. Timothy's illness had been remarkably quick, only three weeks. *Dear God, don't take him. How can he save if he is not saved himself? Not Timothy. Not my brilliant, wonderful Timothy. I cannot stop believing, but I will never understand.*

Whenever she had responded to a letter from her husband, during the war and when he was stationed abroad in its immediate aftermath, Edith had made a diary note, which made it easy for Taylor to read in their proper order Walter Hibbs's letters to her. As he did so he decided reports were a better description than letters. There was a complete lack of personal emotion or affection – my dear wife, your respectful husband – and Taylor sneeringly wondered how the man had succeeded in coupling with the woman on the two occasions it would have taken to make her pregnant. Perhaps the gardener had seeded more than his flowerbeds.

The smile, at his own joke, abruptly froze on Taylor's face and for several moments he sat holding the next letter in front of him in disbelief. It was him! The motherfucker was actually writing about him!

. . . as a man trained – qualified – for no other life I know I should not be surprised or sickened by the obscenity of war but I have recently become involved in a legal matter that is beyond belief. It would, of course, be wrong for me to give you any details – and so appalling is the case that I still would not, even if it were

possible – but suffice to say that there are evil, despicable men who actually see war and its effect as something to profit from. I believe such men are worse than animals and should be eradicated. Were it possible to recommend the death sentence in this case, in which sick waifs died or were crippled, then I would surely advocate it. It is insufficient for me to know that this inhuman monster is being removed from any civilized society for the rest of his unnecessary life . . .

He didn't need the name, to be sure! Didn't need anything more than the childlike upright script and groping attempt at outrage. It was orgasmic – something close to ecstasy – to know how much he'd affected the fucker. The words and phrases registered as he read the letter again and again. Beyond belief . . . appalling . . . evil, despicable . . . worse than animals and should be eradicated . . . inhuman monster.

'All of that,' Taylor said aloud. 'All and more. It would be beyond your belief what I am going to do to your precious daughter. I *am* an inhuman monster and everyone is going to know, very soon. Know more than they think they do already.'

It had never been this good. Never. He'd take the letter, of course. It would be the best souvenir imaginable, something to savour and enjoy, every day. If there had been a God to believe in, Taylor would have literally prayed for the old woman to recover quickly, to be returned home, knowing instantly, totally, what he would do. He'd tell them! With the old woman bound in her wheelchair and Janet naked and helpless – he supposed he'd have to restrain her, too – he would read out the letter, stressing the good parts, and then identify himself. That's me, an inhuman monster beyond belief. Change his face, to prove it. Find another phrase, from

215

all the crap the old woman had written: the diaries and letters were littered with insistences on how lucky she was. He'd quote her own diary words back at her, about how lucky he considered himself to be. He located a reference almost at once, actually describing Janet's birth – which made it fitting for her death. Satisfied, he reassembled everything and packed the boxes away precisely as he'd found them.

Carrying his two souvenirs, he moved on to Janet's adjoining bedroom, in as much disarray as a result of Janet's hurried departure as that of her mother's. She'd been wearing jeans and a sweater, he remembered. There was no discarded nightwear. So she slept naked. Just four dresses and a suit in the wardrobe. The pants and bra, three matching La Perla sets, were skimpy and interesting, the pants little more than thongs. The bras were 36, D cup. He really was going to enjoy himself. He'd take pants, as a memento: a special memory. The white pair. In her panic Janet had left her handbag as well a briefcase. The only letter in the briefcase was from a bank, giving her a month to reduce her overdraft to the agreed £2,000 limit: two weeks had already gone. Her diary was merely an appointments record, blank for the preceding month. The wallet in her handbag held £10, a Visa credit card and a photograph of a fair-haired, smiling man he recognized from his earlier search next door to be her dead brother. There was also a metalled strip of birth control pills, two containers already empty. No risk of her becoming pregnant ever again, he thought.

He accepted that with Janet only being there temporarily he couldn't expect to find any real secrets and he was so pleased by what he had already discovered that he wasn't interested in searching much further. He went cursorily through what had clearly once been Walter Hibbs's study desk. Taylor guessed some of the bottom drawer rubbish – pens, a tattered address book, a military manual and some programmes of military tattoos at Aldershot – had been put there by the man. The upper drawers were cleaner and held evidence of Edith Hibbs's village work, before her stroke: minutes of Women's Institute events and church council meetings. There was a letter, dated two months earlier, from her Midhurst bank asking for a revaluation of the house on which her overdraft had been secured. Unless the valuation showed a substantial increase on the previous one, of two years earlier, the manager doubted he would be able to agree the requested increase.

Janet Hibbs telephoned just after nine. 'It's a blood clot, in her left leg. But it can be dispersed by thinning her blood with warfarin. She'll have to stay in for observation for a day or two, that's all.'

'And then she'll be able to come back here?'

'If she responds,' said Janet. 'That's wonderful news, isn't it?'

'Wonderful,' he agreed. 'Would you like me to come to collect you?'

'I left in such a hurry I didn't even take a handbag, with money for a taxi.'

'It would cost far too much anyway.' And you've only got £10 in your wallet, he thought.

To prepare himself for her reminding him of his promise to give her stock market advice – determined to overlook nothing in his pursuit – he bought all the newspapers but didn't turn at once to the financial pages. First he went through the general news sections for the continued coverage of the murders of Beryl Simpkins and Samuel

217

Hargreaves. Only two, both tabloids, re-used the taxi driver's impression and that was reduced to extend only across two columns, making more ludicrous than yesterday any possibility of his being recognized. An unnamed Scotland Yard spokesman was quoted as saying they were intensifying their inquiries, which he knew to be police-speak for their having made no progress whatsoever.

It was Taylor's suggestion he wind the passenger seat fully back for her to rest on the return journey, which she did although protesting all she needed was a bath and that he was being far too considerate.

Both the landlord's wife and the arthritically slow gardener had arrived by the time they got back and Taylor didn't remain with Janet while she repeated the hospital's prognosis that her mother would be home in two days, reflecting as he entered the house that now he had an actual date. He'd kill them that first night. He would have tired of the game – and of them – by then. He'd have to think seriously whether to go to France or directly back to America, afterwards. There were still people to deal with in the United States. Maybe it would be better to finish the business and then come back to enjoy a proper vacation, without distraction.

Janet appeared totally recovered after bathing and washing her hair. He liked the cleanliness. She was immediately concerned he hadn't bothered to make his own breakfast but agreed it was too late by then and that she wasn't really hungry, either.

'The ham was good at the pub yesterday. And we did intend laying some flowers on the family grave,' he reminded her. 'Why don't we tidy everything up there, have a snack on the way back . . . ?' He was proud of the pause. '. . . Unless, that is, you'd rather help the gardener.'

'You're supposed to be on holiday!'

'Vacations are times to relax, do exactly what you want, how you want. Which I'm doing. I also didn't plan anything for today until I heard how your mother was. If it had been bad instead of good you might have needed someone.' It was embarrassing listening to himself!

'I'm going to miss you when you go.'

'I haven't gone yet.'

It was Taylor's suggestion to take a bucket and cleaning things and after clearing twigs and leaves from the vault's pebbled surround they cleaned the memorial plaques. There was a dried snail's path marking the previous day's spittle. Afterwards they went into the church and he stood back while she knelt and prayed, mentally planning what he would make her do on her knees very soon. No spit mark remained on the marbled wall memorial to Major Hibbs. Taylor was disappointed.

They encountered the vicar on their way out. Jeremy Vine was an urgent, prematurely balding young man who responded to the introduction as if he already knew Taylor, and betrayed the village's intelligence service by asking Janet about her mother without having to be told of the night's drama. The young man was glad it wasn't serious and promised to call as soon as the old lady returned home. Taylor wondered how much more hair the man would lose if he was the one to discover the bodies. Probably all of it.

Both he and Janet had ham, and today there was no-one reading a newspaper with his image on the front page. The same three farm workers greeted him like an old friend and all joined the landlord in hoping Janet's mother would be home soon. Vera Potter returned from cleaning the house while they ate and there was a whispered, smiling exchange of which they were clearly the object among the group at the bar. I hope I do, thought Taylor, mentally joining in the obvious conversation: I'm certainly going to try.

'You visiting your mother this afternoon?' he asked.

'Of course. I must check the petrol in the car.'

'With your mother safely in hospital you don't need to stay around the house, do you?'

'No?' she said, curiously.

'Why don't I run you in? I asked around, when I arrived in Midhurst: got some restaurant recommendations. I could pick you up when you leave the hospital and we could have dinner somewhere?'

'I . . .' started Janet but stopped.

'What?'

'I get breathless, moving too fast.' She smiled.

She was making the move! Encouraging, not offended. 'They write songs about lonely people.' What crap! 'Sorry. I'm not trying to take advantage of what you told me yesterday.'

'I didn't think you were.'

He had to keep the flirtation going. 'We're causing quite a lot of interest among the local population.'

'I know.'

'You mind?'

'Couldn't care less. What about you?'

'It's amusing giving them something to talk about.' And he'd scarcely started yet.

He chose a beamed and thatched restaurant at a place called Woolbeding – driving there to make the reservation to fill in his afternoon – because of the

220

hopeful significance of the name. Janet emerged from the hospital precisely at their arranged time. She'd heard of the restaurant but not been there and was clearly delighted to be going. Her mother thought the flowers he'd insisted upon buying were beautiful and Taylor nodded to the gift-wrapped package on the back seat and said, 'Chocolates, for tomorrow. I found a cute shop, while I was waiting. The woman said they were Belgian.'

'You're totally spoiling us!' protested Janet.

'Spoiling people gives me pleasure,' said Taylor, amused at the ambiguity she couldn't understand, and she stayed smiling with him.

They were early and studied the menu in the garden, in an abour by a noisily busy stream shallow enough to see darting fish against its bed. He lightly ignored her protests to order champagne, although only a half-bottle, carefully treading the line between over-impressing and overwhelming. Still tiptoeing, but wanting to relax her as much as possible to win this part of his game, he kept the fish course Chablis to a half-bottle but ordered a heavy Pomerol to go with their duck and urged brandy at the end.

Taylor consciously relaxed, intrigued by the novelty of an unknown social situation. It was surprisingly easy to turn remarks and stories deprecatingly against himself, making her laugh a lot. He remained constantly alert to give way when Janet talked, which she did easily and openly. She admitted she hadn't properly established herself as a graphic artist ('certainly not successfully enough to be freelance') and wondered if she ever would and if there would be an end to their financial difficulties. That led naturally to the previous day's investment conversation, to which he responded smoothly with

everything he'd memorized from the morning's newspapers he'd pored over while she was bathing.

'*Could* you recommend something?'

'I could certainly try.'

'We can't afford to lose any money.'

'We could go for blue chip: guaranteed government
stock, although the return is limited,' he improvised.

'Maybe you won't have time,' she said. 'You haven't
said how long you're staying.'

'I haven't decided myself yet. I'm in no hurry.'

'I don't think I've ever met anyone like you before. I
feel . . .' She hunched her shoulders, searching for the
words. '. . . Like I've known you for ages.' There was
another pause. 'Even that's not what I properly want to
say . . .'

More crap, he recognized. Holding her look he said, 'I
don't think you have to. But I think that I might be
feeling the same way.'

There was a long silence.

She said, 'Shall we go home?'

'Yes,' he said.

They didn't talk at all on the way back, nor when they
first entered the house. In the hallway they stood for
several moments looking at each other before he put out
his hand, which she took. If it hadn't been so important
to him he'd have been screaming with laughter: it was
hilarious!

There was a vague gesture towards the drawing room.
'I think there's some brandy . . . ?'

'I don't want anything else. Do you?' He mustn't
laugh! Ruin everything.

'No.'

'Let's go to bed then, shall we?'

'Yes.'

He let her ascend slightly ahead of him, watching the sway of her ass. Not tonight. Not unless she made the move. Didn't want to frighten her. Everything had to come at her invitation, on her terms. Fuck her without a condom, though. She'd be clean. First time he'd been properly sure. Never sure of those during the war – both wars – who'd done it for food or clothes. If they were as quick to open their amateur legs and sucking mouths to him they'd have been as eager to dozens of others. And Janet wouldn't expect him to wear anything. She carried that metalled strip in her handbag.

She went directly to his room, turning to face him again. Kiss her! She'd expect him to kiss her! Couldn't remember kissing anyone. Ever. Whores didn't kiss: thought a tongue, not a cock, was an obscene invasion of their bodies. Janet came to him, leading, because he was hesitant in his uncertainty. He didn't like it. It was filthy – disgusting – putting his tongue in her mouth, having hers in his. Had to do it. Do it and not gag. Whores were right.

He pulled away, feeling for the buttons of her blouse and she felt for him, undressing him and they let things lie where they fell. Her breasts were spectacular, the perfect size, dropping just very slightly when he un-clipped the bra, her pubic puff the perfect wedge, a pointing arrow directing him where to go.

It was Janet who led him to the bed, lying to receive him. She pulled his head to her, to be kissed again, and he closed his eyes against the nausea of it. He hurriedly pulled away, mouthing her nipples, and she moved to make it easier, feeling for him.

It was only when he felt her fingers – those soft fingers that he'd wanted so much – upon his penis that he realized how flaccid he was, limp and unresponsive. He

223

put his hands between her wet legs, ready for him, but still nothing happened and in his desperation he gouged into her, making her wince.

'Sorry,' he said. 'So sorry . . . not right . . . didn't mean to . . .'

'It's all right,' she said, easing herself further across the bed, for them to lie side by side, stroking his cheek, kissing his cheek. 'It doesn't have to happen first time . . . doesn't mean anything. We're both tired. Let's sleep. Both of us go to sleep.'

But he didn't. He stayed awake, furious again. Her fault. It had to be her fault. Couldn't be his. Wanted to kill her now, for doing this. Wouldn't, though. Better control than this morning. Important he wait for the old woman. Both had to know more pain than they'd ever imagined possible. Just forty-eight hours. Do it all then. That's when he'd fuck her. Fuck her until she screamed for mercy. She was going to scream a lot for what she'd just done. Never stop screaming. Being sorry.

Wesley Powell got in to the incident room early, to check and deal with everything quickly so that he could pick Beth up as closely as possible to his normal collection time. Although it was Saturday he was surprised that Amy wasn't already there. Or that she still hadn't arrived an hour later.

224

Chapter Nineteen

There was nothing to take the investigation substantially forward. The very full overnight report from the Manhattan office on James Durham's reaction to the murder complicity accusation seemed convincingly to destroy an already flawed theory. The lawyer had reminded the local FBI team that as he was legally still Myron Nolan's executor he had the right to oppose the intended exhumation – but that he would, in fact, support it – and unprompted offered to take a polygraph test on condition that the questions were entirely restricted to the murder and his identification of the body and in no way infringed upon the crimes for which he had immunity.

The telephone records of the Belmont house merely acted as further confirmation that Harold Taylor was the killer. There were two outgoing calls to James Durham's New York apartment, one to a Delta flight reservation desk that fitted their estimate of Taylor's arrival in El Paso, to pick up Billie Jean Kesby on his way to San Antonio, and another to Amtrac train reservations which coincided with the murder in Pittsburgh of General Marcus Carr.

There were also calls to a local taxi firm which had already been checked out. All journeys were to Reagan airport, connecting not only to the El Paso flight but convenient to the New York shuttle the days they knew Taylor to have been in New York, pressuring James Durham. The drivers were being traced that day to be shown the video freeze frames to establish if only one man – and which man that was – had been the customer.

There had been no reply to Amy Halliday's Social Security search or credit card checks and the judge's hearing to determine the Bureau's legal access to Taylor's bank records and safe deposit box was not scheduled until later that day.

'A lot of time for Beth,' suggested John Price. The New York bureau chief, divorced and unattached, had volunteered to be the weekend watchman.

'Let me know the result of the court application, the moment you get it,' said Powell. 'If I'm not at the apartment I'll be on the mobile phone.'

'Sure.'

'And I'll come back direct from taking Beth home. Be here around six, I guess.'

'Amy coming in today?'

'Expected her by now,' said Powell. It was just after ten. 'Guess she's got the right to a little free time. She's practically moved her bed in since all this started.'

'Dedicated gal,' agreed the other man.

He was taking a career chance, Powell acknowledged, heading back over the river towards Virginia. It was not essential for him personally to be present at the bank application: it was entirely technical, a legal plea to be made in camera upon evidence that he was not required personally to present. He still should have been there; would have been expected to be there, not just by Harry Beddows but by the Director, too. So why wasn't he? Because he deserved a little free time, too: free time with a kid he didn't already spend enough with and who was due much more. Much more of everything, not just time. He'd already given the Bureau three hours that morning, would give them whatever was necessary that evening and probably most of tomorrow. And he had no idea if he'd be able to make next Saturday at all. The attempted self-justification didn't really work.

Ann answered the door, looking much better than she had the last time he'd seen her. She'd had her hair done, blonding back the regrowing roots, and he thought it had been cut, too. She was made up and crisp in white sweater and slacks. She smiled and said 'Hi!' and as he followed her into the living room added: 'What time do you think you'll be back?'

'It's got to be by five. I'm taking time off, as it is.'

Her shout to Beth wasn't as strident as it had been before. Then she said to him: 'You're getting a lot of shit.'

'Goes with the job.'

'Case going as bad as television says it is?'

'We need a break.' He wondered where Jim Pope was. Maybe he'd found a job.

Beth came hurrying from her bedroom, already wearing her backpack, kissed him and said at once, 'I don't think you're no good. I think you're terrific .'

Momentarily the remark confused him. Then Powell said, 'Thanks for the vote of confidence.' To Ann he said: 'Five OK?'

'Not before. I might be going out. May be a good idea to call, before you leave your place.'

What was he going to do if something broke? A problem to be confronted when it arose. In the car he said they'd have to stay around the apartment all day, because he was on call, and Beth reminded him that was exactly what she'd wanted to do.

On the way they stopped at the same market as before and shopped for burgers, buns, hot dogs, Häagen-Dazs and Dr Pepper's. It was Beth's idea to get a Coors six pack. The beer Jim Pope had always seemed to be clutching, Powell remembered. The moment they resumed the journey Beth said, 'Can't I stay until seven, like always?'

'I'm on duty.'

'I've brought my homework!' protested the child, jabbing her thumb towards the backpack on the rear seat. 'I could do it with you.'

'You still can,' said Powell. 'Today it's got to be five.'

'What about next week?'

'We'll have to see how the case goes. Maybe.'

'Promise!'

'I can't promise. But I'll try.'

'Jim's gone,' the child announced, abruptly.

'Gone where?' asked Powell, stupidly.

'Left Mom. Walked out.'

Powell frowned briefly across the car. 'You mean for good?'

'I guess so. That's what mom said.'

Why hadn't Ann said anything? 'Mom upset?'

'Kind of, for a few days. She's all right now.'

'How'd you feel about it?'

Beth shrugged. 'He wasn't my dad. Just someone who stayed over.'

It all seemed remarkably casual, thought Powell, as he carried the groceries into the kitchen. Beth unpacked while he stacked away.

'Some guys at school say you're not any good at the job.'

'Don't let it worry you,' said Powell.

'I don't,' she said, unconvincingly.

'I'll prove them wrong,' he insisted, wondering about the conviction in his own voice.

'You really get all those cases wrong, like they said on television?'

'Only two, before this. And I haven't got this one wrong. I just haven't caught the guy yet,' said Powell. 'I can't be right all the time.'

'I always thought you were.'

'Just most of the time.'

It was Beth who determinedly changed the subject, walking back into the main room. 'I want to make lunch again, like last time.'

'That's the only reason I invited you, to cook and slave for me. How's school?'

'OK,' said Beth dismissively, with a nose-wrinkling grin that exposed her tooth brace.

'So how's it really going?' he said, not smiling back.

'Mom went to a PTA meeting the other night. They said I lacked concentration.'

Why hadn't Ann told him about that, too? 'What's your grade average?'

'Can I have a drink?'

'Help yourself.'

At the refrigerator she called out, 'You want a beer?'

'No thanks,' he called back.

She returned with a Dr Pepper's, the ringtop already popped.

He said, 'There are glasses. You don't have to drink from the can.'

'This is the way we do it.'

'You didn't answer me, about grades.'

'Cs.'

229

'What about Bs? Or As?'

'Sometimes. Not As. Bs.'

'How about Ds?'

'Dad!'

'Don't want you lying down on the job, honey.'

'I'm not, Dad. Honest. I'm trying but it's not easy.'

'What about Mom? Doesn't she help?'

'She's always got too much of her own stuff to do. And she says she teaches younger kids than me. That it wouldn't help.'

Jesus! thought Powell. He'd take that up with Ann when he delivered Beth back. He also remembered that this was supposed to be a visitation, not an interrogation. 'You get problems, why don't you call me?'

'You seem pretty busy most of the time, dad.'

'Never too busy for you.'

'OK,' she said, unconvincingly again. 'Can I watch TV?'

'What about the work you brought?'

'Later.'

'Television's off at midday.'

'Sit with me.'

Powell did and Beth immediately snuggled into his side, shrugging his arm around her. With the remote control in both hands she danced the Saturday morning channels, settling for *The Simpsons*. When it and the cartoon that followed finished Beth got up unasked, telling him to set the table while she made lunch. He did so with a beer he didn't want, drinking it because it had been Beth's idea to buy them.

While they ate Beth said, 'Last Sunday we went to Uncle Harry and Aunty Cath's for a barbecue, just like when we lived in San Diego.'

'You remember then?'

230

'Course I do,' said the child, indignantly. 'I was almost ten, wasn't I?'

Powell calculated that she would have been. There seemed to be a lot that Ann hadn't told him. Difficult though things were between them he'd have expected Harry Beddows to mention it, too. 'You go there often?'

Now Beth made a calculation, frowning. 'Not for a few months. Aunty Cath said it was a pity it couldn't be like it was before, all of us together.'

Powell held back from asking but didn't have to. Beth went on: 'Mom said it was one of those things.'

'It's good of them, to have you over.'

'We had steak. I don't like steak unless it's hamburger, like this. The pecan pie was good.'

Powell called the incident room while Beth cleared the table. There had been nothing new since he'd left, John Price said, but Mark Lipton had been on from the Public Affairs office, asking about a press release and had called him a stupid bastard when he'd suggested they say their inquiries were continuing. There were two television and three newspaper requests to interview Powell and he'd told the Public Affairs chief he'd have to discuss that personally with Powell. He was surprised Lipton hadn't called Powell at home. Harry Beddows had telephoned, asking for him. So had Amy, saying she'd be in later.

'I'll try to get back a little earlier,' said Powell, uncomfortably.

'I've got your number,' Price reminded him.

'I've had some quality time with Beth.' Had he? he asked himself.

'Up to you,' agreed the other man.

Beth's homework was geography and computer theory, which she admitted to be her two worst subjects.

231

He was in the middle of the geography project when the telephone's ring jarred into the room.

Amy said, 'I think I've got something. I need to talk to you.'

'I'll be in right away.'

'I'm at home. Can I come to you there?'

'What is it?'

'I think I know where he is. And that he's killed again. Twice.'

Powell thought Amy was right, within minutes of scanning the computer print-out she carried into the apartment, along with an encased laptop. When he looked up he realized Amy was doing her best to distract Beth, actually sitting beside her at the table and apparently studying the geography textbook.

'How?' he demanded.

'I didn't want to go into the Internet from an identifiable Bureau location, so I logged on from home. Surfed through some news pages and came up with those English reports. The methodology is surely too much of a coincidence?'

'Unless it's copycat, from our cases getting media play in England,' said Powell. 'But if it had I would have expected something from London by now.'

'What I did is unauthorized. That's why I wanted to see you away from the Bureau.'

'What you did was brilliant . . .' He looked at Beth. 'Afraid I've got to go back to the office, honey.'

'Dad!'

'You could start things from here, while we're on our way.' Amy smiled sideways at Beth. 'And while you're doing that we could do a little more of this project.'

232

He agreed with that, too.

Amy and Beth remained in the main room while Powell phoned from the bedroom extension. He told Price to call the English-based Bureau agent into the embassy immediately and to fax complete summaries of all their killings to the FBI office there, while the man was coming from wherever he was spending the weekend. Powell wanted from the man far greater detail of the two English murders than was available on the Net and also the names of the British detectives heading the investigations, to be able to talk directly to them. He insisted that no information whatsoever should be given to Mark Lipton and as he spoke wondered about telling Beddows or the Director, deciding against it until he knew more.

John Price said, 'We lost our man to the British?'

'I don't care who gets him,' said Powell. 'I just want him got.'

He tried Ann's number but got her answering machine and left a message for her to call back, either at the apartment or on his mobile. When he returned to the living room he saw Amy had her laptop on, with Beth at the keyboard, working – sometimes laughing – excitedly to the guidance. It occurred to him that his daughter didn't seem to laugh a lot.

He said, 'Now I really have to go, Beth. And I don't know what time I'll get back. You want to wait here, for Mom to collect you, or let me take you back on my way into Washington?'

'I've got a key. I guess I'll go home.'

'I'll see you at the Bureau,' said Amy, closing down her machine. To Beth she said: 'You did very well. Six months from now you'll be surfing the Internet and talking to Australia.'

On their way back to Arlington Beth said, 'I think Amy's amazing!'

'So do I,' said Powell, his mind on her Internet discovery.

Beth swivelled in her seat. 'You guys an item?'

Powell laughed outright. 'She's someone I work with. And who today did something pretty impressive.'

'It would be great if you two got together. You and Mom aren't going to, are you?'

'I guess not. And thank you for approving. Maybe we should tell Amy?'

'I won't tell Mom about her.'

'There's no reason at all why you shouldn't.'

'I know. But I won't.'

'I'll see you up,' said Powell, when they got to the apartment block.

'That's OK.'

'I'd like to.'

As they rode up in the elevator Beth said, 'Could we see Amy next week? We finished my computer homework: she made it fun.'

'I'll see if she's busy,' promised Powell. He would enjoy spending time with her as much as Beth would, he admitted to himself.

Beth hurried into the apartment ahead of him, abruptly stopping at the end of the corridor. Beyond, in the living room, Harry Beddows sat barefoot, his shirt undone almost to the waist. Ann wore only a T-shirt that ended just below her crotch.

He didn't sleep and just before dawn he was aware of Janet getting as quietly as she could out of bed to return to her own room. The only way he could think of

234

escaping the embarrassment was to kill her and he couldn't do that, not yet. So what was he going to do! He didn't know, he accepted. Which meant he wasn't in control and it wasn't possible for him not to be in total charge of everything.

Chapter Twenty

Beth said her friend Ann Marie only lived a block away and that she always went there by herself, so Powell let her go alone. For several minutes after the door closed behind her the three of them remained silent. Beddows buttoned his shirt. Powell enjoyed the man knowing how ridiculous – vulnerable – he looked. Ann too. Love – sex at least – gone sour, he thought. It wasn't much compensation for how long they'd both made him look ridiculous.

He said: 'Ever since San Diego?'

'It just happened,' shrugged Ann.

'No it didn't,' said Powell. 'I got sent out of town an awful lot when you were in charge there, didn't I, Harry? Wasn't that my reputation, the most travelled man in the office?'

'We tried to end it with my transfer here,' said Beddows.

'Was there ever the supply teacher – what was his name, Max? – that you wanted to come here to get away from?' demanded Powell.

'He was part of trying to end it,' said Ann.

'Rather than trying to make a go of it with me?'

'I didn't want to make another go of it with you!' she said, viciously. 'We were a mistake. Beth was a mistake.

236

I should have had an abortion; never married you in the first place.'

'You want me to say we're sorry, OK, we're sorry,' said Beddows. To Ann he hissed: 'Why the hell didn't you answer the call, like I told you!'

Powell wanted physically to hit her for what she said about Beth, actually twitched forward towards her before stopping himself. Ridicule – ridicule and something else he'd already decided to do – would hurt more. 'What, exactly, are you sorry for, Harry? Fucking up my marriage? Or really treating me like an asshole, manipulating my transfer here to Washington to help save the marriage so that you and Ann could go on screwing each other? Or what you've been trying to do since I've got involved in this case, and probably the unsuccessful ones before – stacking the deck against me with the Director, to get me transferred way out somewhere in the boonies, along with all the other mentally retarded? You sorry about all of those things or maybe just one or two?'

Ann said, 'Let us know when you've finished. Didn't you hear you didn't have a marriage to save?'

'You'll know when I've finished,' promised Powell. 'But not until I know what a cunt you've both made out of me. I need to know what I've got to recover from. What about Jim Pope?'

'We tried again to break it off,' said Beddows, quietly. 'I gave it one more try with Cathy. Ann and I agreed not to see each other; didn't for almost six months.'

'So Pope was just a fuck, while you waited! Why didn't you become a hooker, Ann? You like it that much – which I don't remember your doing – you should have made a proper business out of it.'

'We were both trying, for Cathy's sake,' said the

237

woman. 'What the hell's it got to do with you any-way!'

For a moment Powell had difficulty in forming the words. 'To do with you and me, nothing. You're right. We're finished. We never even started. But for months that motherfucker sitting there has been screwing me much harder than he's been screwing you. That's what it's got to do with me. And—'

'That's not true . . .' tried Beddows but Powell refused to hear him.

'You know fucking well it's true. Ann I can under-stand. Once a whore, always a whore. But doing – or trying to do – what you have professionally been trying to do to me is unbelievable.'

'Don't call Ann a whore,' Beddows protested, al-though weakly. 'We're going to get married. I've told Cathy. As soon as we're divorced Ann and I are going to get married. That's it. All of it.'

'No it's not,' Powell contradicted him again. 'We haven't talked about Beth yet. Beth isn't – wasn't – a mistake, not as far as I'm concerned. And she's very much to do with me. I want her. You can have the visitation rights you're entitled to, Ann, although I could probably successfully object even to that now we know you're not interested. But Beth is coming to live with me—'

'Don't be ridiculous!' said Ann. 'How can you look after a child?'

'I don't know but I will,' insisted Powell. 'I'll take her from you legally. There's two ways I can do that. We can do it by agreement and in private, just us and the lawyers. Or you can oppose me, in a custody court. If we go that route I'll have my lawyers apply for a public hearing. What do you think, Harry? You think the

238

Bureau would like to hear how you used your appointment as head of division to break up an agent's marriage and get your mistress from one side of the country to the other? And how that mistress, just a first-grade teacher but still a teacher, can't be bothered to help her daughter with school work; calls her a mistake that should have been aborted? It's not like the days of J. Edgar Hoover but I heard somewhere the Bureau still has a moral code. You know what? I bet a dollar to your dime you'd end up looking the asshole both of you must have laughed at my being, all this time. Think on it . . .'

'We don't need to think on it,' said Beddows.

Powell held up a warning, contemptuous finger. 'I still haven't finished. You try one more smart-assed move against me in the Bureau – get in my way, annoy me just once – I'll file an official complaint not just internally but in public civil court. From now on you're going to head the division with *my* permission and you're going to hate every goddamned moment of it. I wouldn't be at all surprised if you quit.'

He tried to clear his mind – to compartmentalize the anger and the humiliation – on his way into Washington but he was only partially successful.

The humiliation was the stronger feeling. They really must have laughed, derided him, for so long. But not any longer. From now on everything – their personal life and Harry Beddows's professional existence – *was* by his permission. How long would it be before he withdrew it?

Everything was smoothly in motion by the time he arrived at the incident room. The FBI agent attached to the London embassy, Jeri Lobonski, had been at home, only thirty minutes from Grosvenor Square, and was already in his office. He'd faxed five different newspaper accounts, received details of the American killings to pass on to the British, and was waiting for the investigating officers from New Scotland Yard and Richmond to contact him to authorize their getting in return the official scientific and factual evidence of the murders of Beryl Simpkins and Samuel Hargreaves for comparison. Jeri Lobonski had been promised callbacks within an hour. John Price had been given the same timing for Harold Taylor's bank records which the court had ordered to be opened to the Bureau, as well as granting legal permission to open the safe deposit box. That, however, wouldn't be possible until after the weekend because the vault was sealed by a time lock.

'And I know we're right,' declared Amy. 'I'm cutting a lot of corners. Hacking. But I've found a Harold Taylor on a Delta flight from JFK to London's Heathrow three days before the English hooker got murdered.'

'That's good,' said Powell.

She frowned at his reaction. 'So we know the name he's travelling under.'

'Yes.'

'You all right?'

'Sure.'

The doubt remained on her face. 'Beth OK?'

'It's personal. I'm sorry. You're fantastic.'

'I'm sorry, too,' she said at once.

Price said, 'You want me to call Harry, at home? He said this morning that I should get hold of him if anything broke.'

'I'll tell the Director, when we're sure,' said Powell.

He was, more quickly than he expected. Among the Scotland Yard material that began arriving within thirty minutes – along with the names of Chief Superintendents Malcolm Townsend and Henry Basildon – was the killer's DNA string obtained from the hair and blood in the Bayswater hotel and Richmond house. They perfectly overlaid those from the American crime scenes when Amy put them on her screen. So did the fingerprints.

Townsend and Basildon had already established both matches when Powell made the conference call to London.

'There's a lot about your stuff we don't understand,' protested Townsend, at once.

'There's a lot we don't understand ourselves,' agreed Powell. 'The only thing that's important at the moment is that five days ago he killed Samuel Hargreaves, so your killings are the most recent.'

'You believe he's still here?' said Basildon.

'I believe we've got to work on that assumption. I'd like—' Powell abruptly stopped, remembering it had just become a joint international investigation involving diplomacy – personal as well as political – and competing jurisdiction. He went on: 'I would suggest you alert your air and sea ports to the name Maurice Barkworth, as well as Harold Taylor.' As an afterthought, he added, 'Maybe Myron Nolan, too.'

'Already being done,' said Townsend, which was a lie. The conference call was being relayed into his Scotland Yard office on speakers, for both support officers to hear. Townsend nodded to Anthony Bennett, who immediately went into his adjoining office to contact Immigration.

'The Berlin trial of Myron Nolan is the key,' advised Powell. 'The connection, whatever it is, will be somewhere in Samuel Hargreaves's history.'

Basildon said, 'You going to issue a press release about this?'

'No,' said Powell, quickly. 'I want him caught, not on

the run. He's totally insane, has already killed six people and isn't going to stop.'

'We need to agree a working relationship,' insisted Malcolm Townsend.

'You already have everything we've got here. And you'll get whatever else we find,' Powell assured him. 'Total reciprocity.'

'That's the way we'd like to operate, too,' said Townsend.

'Absolutely,' confirmed Basildon.

'You got all my contact numbers?' pressed Powell.

'Right in front of me,' said Townsend.

'Speak to you tomorrow, if not before.'

'We'll be waiting.'

After the disconnection Townsend said, 'You know what we've got here after all, Henry? We've got the best career opportunity we're ever likely to get.'

'If we get the collar,' qualified Basildon.

'We get the collar and the glory is ours,' stated Townsend. 'If it fucks up it's America's fault. We can't lose, either way.'

'Just that he's in the United Kingdom?' pressed Clarence Gale.

'*Believed* to be in the United Kingdom,' cautioned Powell.

'No idea where?'

'We only made the connection three hours ago, sir. We've already exchanged all the relevant information and I've spoken personally to the detectives in charge.'

'Who *did* make the connection, the Brits or us?'

'Amy. By computer.'

'Useful to have on the team.'

'Indispensable.'

'I'll have to brief State,' said the Director. 'And the Attorney-General. All sorts of side issues now.'

'We still haven't arrested him.'

'You think you should go to London?'

'He could already be back here.'

'We'll keep it in mind. London intend making a release?'

'I've asked them not to. Same reasons apply there as they do here.'

'I think that's a hell of a risk. We got no control over the way they work, what they might do. And there's nothing to stop some journalist making the same connection Amy did. We'd really look dumb – you particularly – if it appeared we were following instead of leading.'

'Let's just keep it wrapped a little longer,' urged Powell, alert to his chance.

'No more than twenty-four hours, before we discuss it again. It *is* international now. I won't have the Bureau looking like the bag carrier, especially when we're not.'

Ann answered the telephone.

'What have you told her?' He should have stayed there, waited until Beth got back!

'The truth.'

'How did she take it?'

'I told her you wanted her to live with you. She's excited. Wants to know when.'

'You bitch!'

'That's what you said, Wes. I heard you.'

'Let me speak to her!'

He heard the phone slammed down, then feet running. 'Dad!'

243

'I mean it, Beth. On my life, it's a promise I'm going to keep. As soon as I get this case out of the way I'll take leave and we'll organize it.'

'I thought from Mom it was going to be right away!'

While Beth still had to live with Ann he couldn't make any situation worse between them. 'Mom made a mistake. Just hang in there, honey. It won't be long.'

'A to-die-for promise?'

'A to-die-for promise. Is Harry still there?'

'I love you, Daddy.'

'And I love you, Beth.' Powell replaced the telephone without asking to speak to Harry Beddows.

Taylor waited until he heard Janet moving about before he went downstairs himself. He was, of course, totally under control but unsure how it was going to be when he confronted her. If only he could kill her now instead of having to face her! As he went towards the kitchen he heard her humming, in tune with the radio.

She turned at his entry and said, 'Morning, darling.'

Darling! It was as if they had fucked and she'd enjoyed it. 'Morning.'

'Juice and coffee's ready. What else?'

'Nothing, thank you.' He had to say something! 'About last night . . .'

'Last night was wonderful, all of it.' She crossed to him, putting her outstretched hands on his shoulders. 'Stop apologizing for something you don't have to apologize for. You'll get a complex about it.'

The bitch was patronizing him, laughing inwardly. But she'd shown him the way. 'I probably already have.'

'We'll get it right.'

'I think I'm falling in love with you,' he forced himself to say.

'I think the feeling's mutual.'

It was even harder to force himself to kiss her.

Chapter Twenty-one

'So where do we go from here?' smiled Janet.

A new amusement, Taylor recognized: building up her every expectation, letting her imagine her life was going to be turned upside down – and wasn't it, literally! – but most of all that she was safe, with someone who wanted her. 'Guess there's a lot to talk about.'

He'd carried lounging chairs into the garden for them to lie side by side, but separated by a table for the breakfast coffee that Janet brought out behind him. Both had been aware of Vera Potter's smirking arrival, as he'd set up the chairs.

'The problem's knowing where to start.'

'I could stay on a little longer but eventually I've got to go back,' he said. She shouldn't think everything was perfect.

'I know. And of course I can't leave Mother.'

You're not going to have to, he thought: you're both going to leave together. 'I suppose it'll give us time to make our minds up.'

'Don't we need to be together to decide that?'

Hope building time: up and down on the see-saw. 'I'm lucky, moneywise. I can come back a lot.' Now she'd think their financial worries were over, too.

'I know it's manageable; lots of people have to be

apart. It's just not what I want. I'm coming to like being spoiled too much.' She turned to him, smiling. 'Wasn't I the one talking about everything moving too fast, yesterday?'

'Something like that. You going to tell your mother?'

'Do you mind if I do?'

'Of course not.'

'She'll be *so* pleased. She worries about my still not having anyone. She was married at nineteen.'

I know, thought Taylor. It would be good to build up the old bitch's hopes, too, before they really found out what was going to happen. 'Make it the good news to come home to.'

Janet looked at her watch. 'Which reminds me. Time to call the hospital.'

'Yes,' he agreed at once: her homecoming was the only uncertainty. 'It's important to know she'll be back tomorrow . . . to know that she's better, I mean.'

Alone, Taylor closed his eyes, relaxing. It was time to make other positive plans. If she was released, she'd be brought home during the day, the afternoon most likely. As part of this new game, allowing them to imagine their lives were changing for the better, he'd let them settle. Kill them in the early evening. He could shower and be away by seven. Away to where? Portsmouth was probably the nearest ferry port to the continent. He could be there in an hour, return the car to the Hertz office there. Needed to check if there was a night ferry but he was sure there would be. Or he could abandon the idea of France and Belgium. There was the choice of two airports, Heathrow or Gatwick. Reach either in two hours, Gatwick probably less. Vera Potter didn't arrive until ten in the morning, sometimes later if it took her longer to get the pub ready. By which time he could be

247

wherever he wanted. Sensible to have used the Barkworth name, at the hotel and around the village. The only association with his current identity was the hire car, for which he'd had to use a driving licence, and he'd always been careful to park it out of sight at the rear of the house, although even in such a small, gossipy village it was unlikely anyone would have noted the registration. All the police would have was a colour and there had to be a million dark blue Ford Escorts. He heard Janet returning and opened his eyes.

'Everything's fine,' she announced. 'Being released tomorrow unless anything happens in the meantime.'

'Wonderful!' said Taylor, swinging his legs around to sit on the lounger. 'What time?'

'Depends on the availability of an ambulance, but some time in the afternoon.'

'Her wheelchair folds up, doesn't it? If there's a problem we could collect her in my car: put the chair in the trunk. Then no-one will be disappointed.'

Standing over him she reached out, stroking his face, her crotch at the level of his face. 'I really don't want to lose having you around.'

He nuzzled forward, burying his head in the join of her legs, sure he could smell her perfumed pussy through the thin cotton of her skirt. He could do it now. He knew he could. Fuck her brains out. He licked out, against the fabric, so she could feel his tongue and she put her hand on his head, pulling him into her.

She said, 'We can't. Mrs Potter's still here.'

'A curse on Mrs Potter.'

'Let's hope it's not on me.'

He pulled away as she lowered herself on to the sunbed opposite. 'What?'

'It's around my time of the month.'

No! She was cheating him again! He'd make her give him head but that wasn't the same. He wanted to fuck her, rape her in front of her mother and he couldn't do that if there was blood. That would be obscene, disgusting. She was going to have to suffer so much. He said, 'We don't have to make love to *be* in love, do we? And it was me with the problem last night, wasn't it?'

The church bells tolled, briefly, and Janet said, 'The first call. I want to go to church this morning. I've got such a lot to be grateful for, to give thanks.'

She'd expect him to go with her. The thought of being enclosed with a lot of sweat-stinking farmers and their labourers revulsed him. 'I know I have too, but there's something else I want to do.'

'What?' she said, disappointed.

'It's a secret.' There had to be shops open in Midhurst on a Sunday. It wasn't important what sort: virtually anything would provide the excuse. 'What are we going to do for lunch?'

'Eat here, I thought. I hadn't really thought about it.'

'I'll be back by twelve.'

He was luckier than he'd expected, a good omen. There was an antiques fair in Midhurst, with three jewellery stalls and he paid £200 to an impressed woman in gypsy skirt and blouse for an intricate necklace of blue crystals on a gold filigree chain that came complete with an 1851 provenance and an appropriately aged felt-lined case. She willingly changed an additional £10 into coin and from a public kiosk in the High Street he checked Portsmouth ferry and Gatwick and Heathrow airport departures. Either would be convenient but he decided to return direct to America, from Gatwick. There were vacancies on an American Airlines flight at 2300 to JFK and he made a first-class booking on his open return ticket. On his way back to the car he found a wine shop and bought Beaujolais and Chablis and champagne. Remembering the distance he intended travelling the following night, he stopped at a garage to fill the Ford until petrol came to within an inch of the cap. There was an extensive shop adjoining the garage and he spent some time examining the various ropes available, finally choosing a 2mm-thick cord. He doubted their screams would be heard, because the house was set so far back from the road, but as a precaution he also picked up some thick masking tape. The pumps had been self-service so he bought perfumed wipes to clean his hands of petrol.

He got to the house before the end of church and by the time Janet returned he'd made the salad, quick-chilled the Chablis and set the lunch on a parasoled table close to one of the branch-skirted firs.

He laughed more loudly than he intended when Janet shook her head and said, 'I just can't believe this. I'm in heaven!'

You would be soon, if there was such a place, Taylor thought. He produced the necklace in the middle of lunch, sliding the scarred box wordlessly across the slated table towards her. Janet looked at it, also not speaking. She didn't reach out for it, either.

'With my love,' he said.

'This really is beginning to frighten me.'

'Don't let it.'

'If this place had a dungeon I'd lock you away in it, so I wouldn't lose you.'

'If you did that I couldn't spoil you.'

At last, hesitantly, Janet reached out for the faded case, making a slight whimpering sound when she opened it and saw the necklace inside. 'Darling! It's beautiful!'

'I didn't know your size, for a ring. And a ring would have been a commitment and when you get to know me better you might decide I'm a monster,' he said, amusing himself.

'Put it on for me!' she demanded, coming excitedly around the table.

As he did so Janet said, 'Everything's too quick – too new – but there's one thing I'm absolutely sure about. That's that you're not a monster.' Her eyes filled and then overflowed and she sniffed and scrubbed at her nose and face with her hand. 'Shit, I haven't got a handkerchief!'

'Too soon to be so definite,' he said, handing her his. He'd have to remember to throw it away.

'I *know*!' She turned and he steeled himself to kiss her as open mouthed as she kissed him.

He'd be glad – relieved – when he didn't have to do that any more. 'How was the service?'

'It would have been better with you there.'

'Next week.' The congregation would be saying different, special prayers then.

'You staying until next Sunday!'

'Don't you want me to?' he said, with mock offence.

'Oh yes, darling. Please, yes.'

'I'd get to know your mother better. She might not accept me.'

'That's my choice. Only mine.'

'I keep telling you, you might change your mind.'

'Do something for me?' asked Janet, urgently. 'Come *into* the hospital this afternoon. Be with me when I tell Mother.'

There'd be smells. Germs. 'She might not like me seeing her in bed.'

251

'She wouldn't mind. Please, darling! Please!'

'If you want me to.' He was becoming tired of this game. He was having to make too many concessions.

'Got it!'

There were only the two of them left in the incident room and Powell had been half dozing. He jerked awake at Amy's triumphant shout. It was ten minutes short of the 4 a.m. deadline he'd imposed upon her finishing. 'What?'

'I've broken the law, from a traceable Bureau location.'

'What?' he repeated, impatiently.

'He's got a bank-issued Visa card. I've hacked into the mainframe and got the number!'

'I thought you'd checked credit card companies, already.'

'It's newly issued. Hasn't been used. And the stupid fucking Army split Samuel Hargreaves's testimony from the Myron Nolan archive. Gave it a separate file. Hargreaves was the British Army pharmacy asistant who sold the bad drugs to Nolan. Did an immunity deal, just like Durham. Became chief prosecution witness at the Berlin hearing.'

'I'm personally going to see you get the transfer,' declared Powell.

Amy made no reaction to the implied praise or to the promise. She said, 'Hargreaves didn't get any sympathy from the tribunal. Got the hardest time from a Major Walter Hibbs. Who was a British member of the court-martial: the clinic where the kids died was in the British sector.'

Chapter Twenty-two

The operation shifted perfectly into gear, Malcolm Townsend and Henry Basildon compatibly driving, each confident of more than sufficient personal reward to be shared between them, with enough left over for their supporting inspectors, if they got it right. Which made getting it right the only consideration. Their support officers agreed. It created an absolutely committed control team.

By eight-thirty that Sunday morning Townsend had alerted the Metropolitan Police Commissioner and Basildon his Chief Constable – interrupted on the way to their respective golf clubs – and two hours later all ten Surrey detectives summoned by Basildon arrived at the conveniently centralized joint incident room at New Scotland Yard. The matching ten Yard officers were already waiting. Three were women. By then the publicity-conscious Paul Stanswell had been personally traced by Bennett to confirm without doubt that the younger of the video pictures was that of the man he'd carried with Beryl Simpkins – although he failed to recognize the older man – and been convinced that the Hackney Carriage licence for his taxi would be permanently withdrawn if he told the press. The timid hotel night manager, Keith Mason, hadn't been able to tell Pennington if either man had been Beryl's customer.

At eleven the two chief superintendents stood side by side before their assembled squad to share the briefing.

The different faces from the videos – already enlarged and pinned on display boards – had initially to be ignored: the Americans didn't understand them and neither did they. Nor the fingerprints of a man supposedly dead. Total concentration had to be upon what they did know, which was a lot.

They knew Harold Taylor, who sometimes used the alias Maurice Barkworth, had arrived at Heathrow airport three days before Beryl Simpkins died. They had Stanswell's positive identification. The fingerprints and DNA from their two murder scenes matched the FBI's irrefutable forensic evidence against Taylor for four identical killings, three of the victims involved in a military tribunal in Berlin in 1949 at which Samuel Hargreaves had been the chief prosecution witness against Myron Nolan, which almost squared the circle. The missing element was a British major, Walter Hibbs, who had served on that tribunal as a representative of the Four Power Control Commission. Their greatest advantage was having the number of a Visa credit card issued by Taylor's Washington bank, although he was believed to be travelling with a substantial sum of money. Almost as important was Washington's belief that the man had no idea how much they knew about him and wouldn't suspect a British hunt.

'We believe it, too,' said Townsend, when it was his turn to speak. 'It's going to stay that way. Which means no-one whispers a word to any friends in Fleet Street. I'll make a necklace from the bollocks of anyone I find leaking and that includes you, girls.'

It wasn't intended as a joke and no-one laughed.

'A disadvantage is that today's Sunday,' picked up Basildon. 'If Hibbs is still alive, we've got to keep him that way. But we haven't any idea where, in all of England, he lives; if he's still alive, even. Which hardly matters because Taylor hits relatives, too. And we can't get into the Ministry of Defence archives until tomorrow. I don't know what records, if any, there might be to trace Hibbs, but the Imperial War Museum, which is open, is the only idea we can come up with for today. Anyone any better suggestion?'

'Hibbs's regiment, if we know it,' said a London detective in the front row.

'We don't,' said Basildon, at once. 'And don't trust the rank, either. He'd be a regular soldier, on a military tribunal of this importance. He'd have been promoted, since 1949.'

'Telephone books?' said one of the women.

'The name's too common, without at least a region or county in England,' said Basildon.

Townsend said, 'We've posted an immigration red alert in the name of Barkworth as well as Taylor and Myron Nolan at all the Channel ports and at all airports. We want every – and we mean *every* – airport in Britain, not just Heathrow and Gatwick, checked for departures in the last three days and for any reservations in the coming weeks. Ferry ports are a weakness. Britain abandoned exit passport checks last year, although Immigration is still supposed but don't always examine those of non-EC nationals. If he gets aboard a ferry, we've lost him.'

'Which brings us to something you've all got to understand,' insisted Basildon. 'If Harold Taylor is still in England, we're not going to lose him. Any questions?'

'What if we don't get him?' asked someone at the back of the room.

'Rodgers, isn't it?' asked Basildon, recognizing one of his own men.

'Yes, sir.'

'You don't want to know the answer to that question, Rodgers.'

The combined squad was the best that Townsend and Basildon knew and their support officers could recommend and they were divided into teams with matching care, usually split equally between Surrey and Metropolitan officers. Because it was their equipment and facilities, all the technical staff were Yard employees.

As the teams dispersed to their assigned functions Basildon said, 'It seemed as if we had a lot, until we spelled it out. Now I'm not so sure.'

'You think of anything else?'

Basildon shook his head. 'Just a feeling that he's out there somewhere.'

It was the threatened Rodgers who jerked up in triumph from a desk halfway down the room, an hour later. He shouted: 'Taylor's booked on an American Airlines flight out of Gatwick, eleven o'clock tomorrow night!'

'*Yes!*' said Pennington, matching the enthusiasm. 'We've got him!'

More soberly Townsend said, 'It also means he's got Hibbs. Or the family.'

The old lady was dressed and in her wheelchair beside the hospital bed, a crocheted shawl around her legs. Her head was forward on her chest but came up as they approached. She frowned when she saw Taylor.

'A visitor you didn't expect,' Janet greeted her mother, stooping to kiss her.

Edith Hibbs straightened further, shrugging a cardigan around her, straightening the shawl. Taylor offered the chocolates Janet had insisted he carry in and said, pointlessly, 'For you.'

There was a wavering smile. She said 'Thank you', and looked curiously at her daughter.

Janet said, 'We've come to tell you something. A surprise: a marvellous surprise.'

'For us all,' he said. He wanted to reach out to touch the scrawny throat where he was going to make the incision. The ward was extremely clean and the odour was of disinfectant but he still sat further away from the woman than Janet, on the edge of the bed. He liked the conformity of the tucked-in sheets and blanket.

The bewildered look remained.

Janet said, 'We've come to like each other, Mummy. Like each other very much.'

'I'm not going back to America as soon as I planned,' he said, playing his part. 'And I'll be coming back very regularly. As often as I can.'

The lined face opened, into a hesitant smile. 'But that's . . .'

'I know,' said Janet. 'I can't believe it either.'

'Nor me,' he said. 'I hope you're as excited about it as we are.'

'I am! Of course I am. But it's so quick. I know nothing . . .'

'What would you like to know?' he asked, words mentally rehearsed during the drive from the house.

'Everything. I mean . . . ?'

In the beginning it was easier to tell the truth, because in this life he had been reborn, in Lowell, the only son of one of Massachusetts's leading architects whose wife's health had never properly recovered from the difficulties of his birth and who had died when he was only five. His father had never remarried although the man had screwed the housekeeper, always in the missionary position and usually on Wednesdays and Saturdays because he'd regularly watched them through the hole he'd bored from the adjoining box room, although he didn't recount that to Edith Hibbs. His father's supposed wartime experiences in West Sussex were all fantasy – the man hadn't volunteered – but it was true again that as the only son he'd been left wealthy from investments and insurance and the sale of the family house: his father had been a miserly man, as well as a hypocrite. His lies resumed with the invented years studying business economics at Harvard, because he'd never bothered with university, preferring to initiate and then pursue the torture of James Durham and locate the participants in the tribunal, like Hargreaves and Hibbs himself, two whom Durham couldn't find. Throughout, Janet listened as intently as her mother, believing she was learning for the first time about the man she stupidly believed loved her.

'You can't be sure, not yet,' insisted the old lady.

'We're not going to rush into anything,' promised Janet. 'We haven't really accepted it ourselves yet.'

I don't need to believe it at all, thought Taylor. 'There's no hurry, about anything. That's one of the troubles about my country. It seems there are more divorces than there are marriages.'

'I must get better. I *will* get better,' determined the old woman, abruptly. 'I've lost so much I *refuse* not to see my daughter be happy.'

You'll see a lot more than you expect a great deal

sooner. He said: 'That's how we want it to be. How it *will* be, the three of us all together.'

When they arrived, Janet had confirmed her mother's release for the following day, arranging too at Taylor's urging that they would personally collect her the next afternoon.

'Are you always this considerate?' asked the old woman.

'Always,' insisted Janet, before Taylor could speak.

'I think you're a very unusual young man,' she said.

'So do I,' smiled Janet.

You'll see, he thought. The second night's restaurant was one Janet had been to before, in Hoyle, and the meal – goose, with red cabbage – was better than the previous one. She lapsed into even longer silences than before on their way home, almost irritably insisting there was nothing wrong but at first he didn't recognize it, too preoccupied with his own uncertainly, knowing none of the lust he'd felt that morning in the garden. It was only when they got into the hallway, looking at each other again, that Janet said, 'I'm sorry, my darling. It *has* happened.'

Again she'd cheated him, he thought at once, his own doubts forgotten. She was unclean, filthy. But she'd expect him to share the same bed. 'Me last night, you tonight. We're doomed.'

'I'm sorry,' she repeated.

'It's no more important to me tonight than it was to you last night. One of those things. Do you hurt?'

'No. I've always been lucky like that. We can still sleep together . . . if you don't mind, that is.'

No! he thought. 'Of course I want to,' he said.

Of all the things he'd had to force himself to do since

259

this had begun the most difficult was to reach out and hold her to him, physically to feel her leaking body against his when she got into his bed, beside him. But as he did so he realized, astonished, that he had become aroused, prodding into her and that she could feel it, too.

'I'm sorry,' he said. The bitch! He could have done it! Fucked her blind, like he'd planned.

'There is a way,' she said, quietly. 'That is, if you want . . .'

'Yes,' he said. 'I'd like that. If it doesn't offend you . . . ?'

'No,' she said, sliding down beside him. 'I like it.'

Wesley Powell had again managed only three hours' sleep but today there was too much adrenalin for any tiredness. Nor was he depressed by the ferocity of the personal attacks upon him in the *New York* and *Los Angeles Times* and the *Washington Post*'s Sunday editions, and on all three television majors, all of which, in varying ways, demanded his replacement.

He'd fully staffed the incident room but hadn't expected Clarence Gale to be there in the early hours of a Sunday and was surprised at the summons. He was surprised, too, at Harry Beddows already being in the Director's office, although he supposed he shouldn't have been. Beddows nodded, for the Director's benefit. Powell ignored him.

'The British absolutely sure about tonight's flight?' demanded Gale, at once.

'Positive,' said Powell. 'I've spoken twice already to their guys, Townsend and Basildon. The panic is to get to Hibbs or his family, if one or all of them aren't already dead.'

'Whether they find Hibbs or not, they're sure to get Taylor when he arrives at the airport?'

'According to my last conversation with Townsend they've already formed a task force with the local police. He claims the airport's sealed. The danger is they'll overkill and Taylor will recognize something's going on.'

'And they'll lose him?'

'Townsend says it won't happen.'

'We could get there ourselves by Concorde!' said the Director, enthusiastically.

'Townsend says the British Home Secretary was talking to the Attorney-General, reminding us of jurisdiction.'

'A warning?' queried Gale.

'Absolutely.'

'There'd be no risk of losing him if they let him get on the aircraft. He'd be trapped then. We could meet it with a SWAT team.'

'They won't let him walk away,' insisted Beddows, speaking for the first time. 'He's killed two people there: more if he's found Hibbs. No force – no country – knowingly lets a multiple murderer go, no matter how much more certain an arrest is elsewhere.'

'You see the papers and television this morning?' Gale demanded, of Powell.

'Some. Heard about the rest.'

'It's our case,' insisted the Director. 'The British wouldn't have got near him without us. I'm going to talk today – now – myself to the Attorney-General. And to the Secretary of State. I take your point, Harry, about *in situ* jurisdication, but I want everything done to get him back, to face our courts. I want our guy . . . ?'

'Jeri Lobonski,' supplied Powell.

'I want Lobonski at the airport. As soon as the British detain Taylor we'll make a full media release. Ensure Lipton at Public Affairs is fully briefed, ready. The emphasis is that it's our success, understood?'

'Understood,' accepted Powell.

'And I want you and the girl . . . ?' again he paused, inviting.

'Amy Halliday.'

'You and Amy Halliday given every credit. In fact, after you've given Lipton everything he needs tell him to come here, talk to me. You've done well, Wes. Damned well. People are going to know it.'

The tight-faced Beddows wheeled upon Powell in the corridor when he considered they were far enough away from the Director's office. 'Motherfucker!'

'Damn!' exclaimed Powell, mockingly theatrical. 'I forgot to mention the British developments, didn't I? But then you were busy, fastening your zipper.'

'It was a cheap shot, asshole!'

'But with a purpose,' insisted Powell. 'What Ann tried with Beth last night wasn't a good try, either. An even cheaper shot. So listen up, Harry, because neither of you listened well enough yesterday. You tell Ann – tell her so that she fully understands – that as long as Beth has to live in that apartment she treats her like she should: like a daughter, difficult though that seems for Ann. Beth's sacrosanct: untouchable, in every way. I'm going to speak to Beth every day and if I so much as suspect she's getting a hard time I'll go ahead with the civil suit against you, personally, as well as filing an internal complaint. I'll get you fired and I'll enjoy doing it and you and Ann can live happily ever after on Welfare. You tell her that with my love.'

*　　　*　　　*

Barry Westmore, head of the forensic team, was waiting when Powell got back to the incident room. Hair and bone samples from the exhumed skeleton in the grave of Myron Nolan had produced an identical DNA for each American crime scene, as well as those in England.

Chapter Twenty-three

The investigation was suddenly moving at remarkable speed but still not fast enough now that their time limit to prevent more killing was measured in hours. And there were immediate operational difficulties because of its expansion.

With the discovery of the Gatwick flight it was obvious that Townsend and Basildon should split up, keeping London as the central control point but with Basildon supervising the airport ambush from a separate incident room at Crawley. The problem arose from the initial refusal of a third Chief Constable to accept the intrusion of a chief superintendent from one force and Rapid Response units from London, relegating his officers to subsidiary back-up. It was settled only by the personal intervention of the British Home Secretary, who in turn had had a personal Sunday night telephone conversation with the American Attorney-General during which mutual co-operation and jurisdiction between America and the United Kingdom had been made clear. The Home Secretary spoke to all three police controllers, insisting on no territorial jealousies, and making it his decision that the arrest would be organized as originally proposed. While resolving the practicality of command and hoped-for execution, it meant that

Henry Basildon and Christopher Pennington confronted a solid wall of resentment when they finally got to Crawley, which worsened with the arrival of the three Rapid Response units.

Four o'clock in the morning is the quietest time at Gatwick, the time Basildon chose personally to go there with Pennington, the unit commander Roger Cooke and a Crawley chief superintendent, George Preston. Even before they studied the maps and plans of the airport complex Cooke, a superintendent, chose passport control for the seizure. The plan was to put men around the Hertz receiving desk, for the first alert of Taylor's return and to position others in plain clothes as apparent passengers who would gradually close in upon the man as he moved through the airport, totally to enclose him at passport control. Their return to the police head-quarters coincided with Jeri Lobonski getting there, and more resentment.

Several hours earlier Hertz had frustratingly confirmed the rental by a Harold Taylor from London airport of a blue Ford Escort not fitted with the Hertz automatic electronic tracking facility. It had, however, been hired on the Visa credit card and Visa's London processing centre confirmed its use also to buy eight gallons of petrol at a Richmond garage on the day of Samuel Hargreaves's death: the attendant had even written the Escort's number on the credit card receipt, as an extra payment insurance. A watch was established on the number but the department manager warned there was sometimes up to a week's delay in their receiving the confirming transaction docket after the computer-recorded purchase, which only got queried if the card had been cancelled for non-payment or reported stolen. By coincidence it was a confidence-flushed William

Rodgers, who'd earlier found the Gatwick flight reservation, who spoke to the Visa authorities. At no time did he make it clear that the Visa was issued by an American bank, from which payment authorization would come direct, initially bypassing London, wrongly assuming the American source would have been obvious to the man to whom he was talking. The mistake caused a four-hour delay in getting any closer to Harold Taylor.

The only national car number recognition computer operates from the vehicle registration centre in Wales – and is accessed by police only if a car is involved in a reportable incident – but Townsend logged an 'advise-on-sight' alert, covering every possibility, no matter how remote.

And promptly at nine o'clock on the Monday morning he personally telephoned the Ministry of Defence, the previous day's war museum search having proved fruitless, to be told by the first official he spoke to that the man didn't have the slightest idea even where personnel records from 1949 of men seconded to the Four Power Control Commission were stored. Knowing from the Home Secretary's earlier intervention that the investigation now had diplomatic and political muscle, Townsend gave the man thirty minutes to call him back with the guarantee that he'd found out and that a search was being made for the whereabouts of Major Walter Hibbs before he'd ensure that the Minister himself would be asked to do it.

'You want confirmation of that in writing from the Prime Minister's Office or the Home Secretary? Your choice,' he exaggerated.

'I wasn't being serious,' protested the man.

'I am,' said Townsend.

And in the house in the hamlet known only locally as

Lower Norwood Janet said: 'This is going to be a special day, isn't it darling? Mummy coming home, getting better.'

'Very special,' Taylor agreed. 'That's why I bought the champagne, to welcome her back.'

'What about to celebrate us?'

'That too.' He was happy, excited at what was to come.

Janet had the gardener cut a lot of flowers, to brighten the drawing room with two homecoming arrangements and there were sufficient over to put in her mother's bedroom. Taylor waited impatiently for Vera Potter to finish his room before carrying in his satchel, into which he crammed his intended binding cord and gagging tape. He only left two jackets and three pairs of trousers in the wardrobe, against the unlikely event of Janet coming into the room. All his other clothing – shirts, underwear, socks and shoes – he packed in readiness to leave quickly, after tonight's ritual. As he did so he could hear Janet humming, happily, from her mother's bedroom at the other end of the linking corridor. This time – this watering with blood – was going to be the best of any return. What, he wondered, was love like: the sort of feeling Janet claimed to have? Physical, like an erection or an orgasm? Or something completely different, an emotional experience that was beyond him? He would have liked to know. He didn't like to admit failure of any kind – he *never* failed – but he remembered the shaman's warning, so very long ago, that part of his sacrifice for the never-ending life was never to understand what ordinary mortals called love, for want – such a desperate want – of a better description.

Taylor was uncomfortable about leaving his satchel

in the house. He knew Janet well enough by now to be sure she would not look inside, even if she came into the room – which there was no reason for her to do, because they'd never share the same unconsummated bed again – but always before he'd kept the satchel with him at times like this and he felt unsettled not doing it.

There was a key in his bedroom door, so he locked it before hunching over his current memorabilia. The eyes of Samuel Hargreaves and the hooker – and the cats – appeared to be losing their colour. A chemical reaction of the formaldehyde becoming overheated inside the trunk, from the sun, he guessed. He hefted the killing needle in his hand, like a practising juggler, lightly – so very lightly – touching the cutting edge of his scalpels. Could he do it? Just this once could he not kill first, to limit the blood flow, but start the dismemberment when Janet was still alive, so she'd feel it? He became excited again, erect, at the thought. He'd try. Just this once because of how different it had all been: extend the experience.

He carefully repacked the specimen jars and his instruments – at the last moment remembering his souvenir letter from Hibbs to his wife – and put the satchel inside the wardrobe where the jackets and trousers remained. It had never been a consideration before, but why hadn't he bought a small padlock to lock the satchel? They'd had them, all sizes and designs, in the gas station where he'd got the petrol and bought the cord and the tape. Stupid oversight. Too late now. Not important.

They ate early, veal escalopes in a hot vinaigrette sauce with just new potatoes and *al dente* string beans that crunched when he ate them, and at the end of the meal Janet looked demandingly at him and he didn't know what he was expected to say.

Choosing safety he said, 'That was excellent!'

'I was trying to impress you.'

Stupid whore! 'You don't have to try.'

'So I've passed the kitchen test!' she said.

'You've passed every test. I'm not sure I can pass yours.' Did ordinary people really talk shit like this? It was unbelievable!

'You already have, my darling. Many, many times.'

It was on his insistence that they left far too early; impatient now to get the old woman back to the house, where he'd have them both, whenever and however he chose. They were forty-five minutes ahead of schedule but Edith Hibbs was ready, as impatient as he was, sitting in her wheelchair, her few emergency belongings already packed up on her bed. Taylor demanded that he push the wheelchair, savouring the control. Nothing could save her now. She was his. Both were. Cat and mice, cat and mice: stupid mice, clever cat.

There was a brief hiatus at the car, when he realized the old woman expected to be lifted into the vehicle and that he would have to come into physical contact with her to do it. He hated the feel of her bird-thin arm around his neck and having his arm beneath her sharp-boned legs to get her into the back seat, although she was very light, bird-like again and it wasn't difficult.

He didn't have to bother much with conversation on the way back to the house. Janet and her mother kept up the bird analogy, chattering and chirping with inconsequential twittering he longed to silence. He had to lift her back into her wheelchair at the house and he did so glad that it was the last time he'd need to touch either of them other than on his terms, doing what he wanted to do.

Edith Hibbs was delighted with the flowers and

269

giggled in expectation when he appeared with the tray and the already arranged bottle and glasses.

'Here's to your recovery . . .' toasted Taylor, first raising his glass towards the old woman. He turned the gesture sideways, to encompass her daughter: '. . . and to Janet and me.'

'May the two of you never know misfortune,' said the widow. In his excitement the slur the stroke had left in her voice was more obvious to him.

'Trust me that we never will,' said Taylor.

In the FBI incident room in Pennsylvania Avenue Powell replaced the telephone from his third direct conversation with Townsend, getting up to go to Amy but seeing her crossing the room towards his side office. They met halfway.

'He's using the Visa card!' he announced, triumphantly. 'A place named Richmond, like in Virginia. We could get a trail.'

'I know,' said Amy. 'That's what I was coming to tell you.' She led him back to her computer banks, pointing to two of her screens. 'Here's Richmond on his payment statement. What about Midhurst?'

'What about Midhurst?' echoed Powell.

Amy held her finger to the previous day's charge logged against the Visa number. 'Yesterday he used it at another gas station at a place named Midhurst.'

Powell was asked to hold, because Townsend was on the other line, so he disconnected to call Lobonski direct. Basildon had already found five Hibbses, none with military rank, in the telephone book, and was asembling squads to check each one when Townsend came through.

'You don't need to check them all,' said Townsend. 'It was the Ministry of Defence I was talking to.'

*   *   *

He forced a second glass of champagne upon a protesting Edith Hibbs and topped up his and Janet's glasses, feeling as he always did in the last few moments, very calm, very relaxed. He'd make it a game to the very end. Janet was stupid – trusting – enough. And there was nothing the infirm old bitch could do to stop him. Done before she realized anything was wrong. Then play some more.

'Back in a moment,' he said. 'Just going to get something.'

In the bedroom he cut off two lengths of cord and fashioned a noose at one end of each, tightening both several times around his own wrist to ensure they closed smoothly. Satisfied, he coiled both lengths carefully just inside the very top of his satchel, looped to avoid either snagging on anything else when he pulled them out. He whistled tunelessly as he went back down the stairs, wanting them to know he was coming. They were both looking towards the door when he entered, Janet smiling curiously at the satchel.

'A surprise!' he declared.

'This has got to stop,' said Janet, imagining another gift.

'It's going to,' he said. 'Stand up and put your glass down.'

Janet did as she was told. Her mother was smiling at them both.

'Close your eyes and put your hands out, palms together!' he commanded, reaching into the bag for the first length of cord.

He actually had the noose open and held out as her arms came forward, snapping it closed and wrapping three more strands around her wrists before she jerked her eyes open, mouth wide in astonishment. He secured the binding by pulling the cord between the strands, needing only to immobilize her, before Janet said, 'Darling . . . what—?'

Without replying he kicked her, viciously, in the backs of her knees. She began to buckle and he forced her down further, behind her, looping the second noose around her ankles but this time running the cord up around her neck so that she was in a kneeling position with her head pulled up.

'Stop it! What are you doing!' she said, becoming frightened at last but not screaming.

Her mother did, though: not really a scream, although she meant it to be. It came out as a small mewing sound, as she struggled to get up. He only half rose to shove her back but he did it so hard the chair teetered at the very edge of tipping over before righting itself.

Janet was twisting her wrists, back and forth, trying to dislodge the cord but Taylor was in front of her again, wrapping more and more rope on top of what already held her, this time knotting it properly, as he did the further twine he wrapped around her ankles.

Edith Hibbs was trying again to rise when he got to her and simply encircled her arms and chair back. Desperately she kicked out, catching his shin. He moved to back-hand her across the face but stopped himself. Instead he overcame her weak struggle and tethered her legs to those of the chair.

Rigid with control the kneeling Janet said, 'I don't know what's going on but I want it to stop. Please let us go.'

'I can't do that,' said Taylor, flushed and smiling. 'But you are going to know what's going on. I'm going to tell you: tell you all of it.'

* * *

Although there was no outright panic everything was organized at great speed and there were mistakes and oversights, as there had been with the credit card. Townsend and Basildon agreed the strongest likelihood was that the family of Major Hibbs and anyone else who might have been in the house were already dead and that therefore the airport preparations had to remain in place although Basildon no longer needed to be there. Believing Harold Taylor was still likely to be in the village – and wanting to avoid warning him – they held back from flooding it with a police swoop from Midhurst. The larger force was moved into position to seal the area completely. Into the village itself went only the local policeman from the adjoining hamlet of Upper Norwood, although not in uniform, to look for the identifying blue Ford Escort. He was not to approach anyone in the vehicle, if he found it. Or go to the Hibbs house.

It was only when they were on their way, their route being cleared by siren-blaring motorcycles, and followed by one of the Rapid Response units, that Henry Basildon realized their flawed reasoning.

'We're relying too much on suppposition,' he declared. 'We could be making a terrible mistake.'

'How?' demanded Jeri Lobonski.

'Assuming they're dead,' said the other man. 'If he hasn't hit whoever's there and they're still alive we've got to warn them.'

Basildon let the car phone ring a long time before disconnecting. 'No,' he said. 'We didn't guess wrong.'

Taylor had stopped talking at the telephone's ring, sniggering at the startled look of hope on both their faces. 'What a shame! No-one to answer it. An empty house, no-one at home. Another booking lost.'

'This has gone on long enough! Let me up!' said Janet.

'Defiance! I like that. I can't stand it when they start to whimper and plead. Piss themselves.'

'What's going on? Why are you doing this?'

'Listen!' he said. 'Listen and don't interrupt.' He took the long-ago letter from the satchel, turning more towards the old woman. *'It is insufficient for me to know that this inhuman monster is being removed from any civilized society for the rest of his unnecessary life,'* he read, looking up. 'Recognize the words?'

Edith Hibbs, speechless with terror, gave a vague head shake.

'Your husband's letter, when he was in Berlin. The one you kept upstairs in your boxes, with all that other crap.'

'What have you done?' demanded Janet, incredulous.

Instead of replying Taylor proudly said, 'That was me he was talking about! I'm the inhuman monster. He didn't know how inhuman, but you're going to.'

'This doesn't make any sense!' said Janet. 'Please let me up so we can talk about whatever's wrong.'

'Watch!' he said, leaning closer to her. 'This is the me you know . . .' He transmogrified, moving his head back and forth between them: '. . . and this is the man your father – your husband – sat in judgement on in Berlin in 1949 . . .'

Both women screamed, Janet much louder than her mother. Her eyes rolled up into her head, too, and she would have fainted if he hadn't grabbed her. When she became aware of his touch she tried to pull away but couldn't. He saw, disgusted, that Edith Hibbs had been sick.

If he took Janet's tits off from behind, as he always

274

took off the heads, the blood spurt would be away from him: probably wouldn't get splashed at all. He undressed unhurriedly, folding everything neatly, edge to edge, on a chair by the door. His erection was enormous.

As he walked back to them he said to Janet, 'See what you missed.'

Edith Hibbs said, 'No! Don't defile her. Don't touch her!'

'Wait until you see what your daughter does!' he said. 'She's really very good.' To Janet he said, 'And I know just what you're thinking . . .' He took the ice pick from the satchel. 'But I'll have this an inch from your eye, all the time you are doing it. And the moment you bite I'll blind you. So forget it.'

'If I do it, will you let us go?'

'Still brave enough to bargain!' he said. 'You really are remarkable!'

'Will you?'

He made a rocking motion with his free hand. 'Maybe I will. But then again, maybe I won't.'

'If you let us go I won't tell anyone. About anything. I promise. Just get dressed and untie me and you can go away and we'll forget anything ever happened.'

'*Don't patronize me!*' he roared and they both shuddered, recoiling as far as they could.

'I'm sorry. I'm really very sorry,' blurted Janet.

He suddenly realized that if he was going to keep them alive he'd have to cut their clothes off: wouldn't be able to fold everything up neatly, as he always did. The thought upset him. Should he bother? Just this once, he decided; see what it was like just this once.

He slid the scalpel blade steadily along the left arm seam of her blouse, with Janet transfixed, horrified as it came towards her throat.

275

'Isn't it fun, so many games?' he said.

There was a near-collision between Basildon's lead car and that following as the cavalcade braked almost too late to turn off the main road at Halfway Bridge. As the driver regained control Preston grabbed the ringing telephone. Holding it slightly away, but staying linked to the control room, he said, 'The local man thinks he can partially see behind the Hibbses house from the church-yard. And that there's a blue car there, although it's too far away to make out the number.'

'Shit!' said Basildon. 'Move the Midhurst people in but not *through* the village: around it to seal off every road. Lanes too, down as narrow as a footpath.'

'What about the local constable?' asked Preston, after relaying the message.

'No-one answered the phone,' reminded Basildon. 'It's too late for him to go in single-handed. We don't know how many people are dead inside that house but they're going to be the last the bastard kills.'

Almost at once the driver said, 'Here's the road block.'

He managed to get all Janet's clothes off intact, apart from the blouse and the flimsy pants which he gently pulled away from her crotch to snip apart, relieved they weren't stained. It reminded him he hadn't taken a pair from the drawer upstairs, as an extra souvenir. Janet hadn't made anything awkward, still hoping she could bargain. Even though they were cut he succeeded in neatly folding the pants with everything else to go on a chair next to his.

When Janet saw him moving towards her mother, she said: 'No! Oh dear God no! Please!'

'There isn't a God. And I'm the one with the power of

life or death,' he said, beginning to cut the arms of the old woman's thick coat.

Edith Hibbs looked up at him and said, 'You'll rot in hell. Suffer eternal damnation.'

'You haven't understood, have you? Neither of you.' He grimaced, as her bony, skin-sagged body began to appear.

At that moment, at the top of the hill overlooking the village, the local constable finished explaining what George and Vera Potter had told him and said, 'This is Vera's key. She cleans. The gossip is that Janet and him have hit it off.'

'Jesus Christ!' said Lobonski.

'You going to show your mother what a clever girl you are?'

'Are you going to let us go?'

'Do as you're told.'

'Please!'

'Do as you're told.'

'You filthy, obscene pig!' said Edith Hibbs.

'Never did this with Walter, did you?'

'Don't do it, Janet! He's going to kill us. He's mad. Totally insane.'

Taylor turned away from the kneeling, tight-lipped girl, towards the old woman. 'You're going to be sorry for that. I'm not going to tell you how, not yet. But guess what? You're going to do it for me, not Janet. You're going to do something you've never done in your life before. Which face do you want, this one or that, this one or that . . . ?' He'd fucked whores unprotected. Could he put his cock into a vomit-stinking mouth? He didn't think so. But it was a wonderful way to terrify Janet, make her beg even more.

'NO!' screamed Janet, realizing what he intended making her mother do.

The village had only two street lamps, neither close to the Hibbses house, and it was very dark. It was totally deserted, too, although there was distant sound from the pub whose windows gave no outside light. There was closer noise, though, hurrying overhead birds and flying things, insects scavenging, the rustle of small hunters and the hunted in the black hedges and unseen undergrowth.

The special squad were eerily froglike in their night goggles, able to move quietly, but without such help Basildon, Lobonski and Preston literally followed in their footsteps close to the straggled hedge to hide from the house any movement until the very last minute.

And then there was Janet's scream.

The unit moved at once, without any apparent command from Roger Cooke, sprinting the last few yards careless of being seen, using the key because it was quicker and quieter than trying to batter down the door but Janet heard them and screamed again, 'Here! In here!'

'Stay as you are!' yelled Cooke, crouched, legs splayed, the Smith and Wesson extended before him, left hand steadying his right. 'You move, I'll shoot.'

Two of his men circled towards Taylor, keeping out of their controller's line of fire, their own weapons trained upon the man. When one was alongside Edith Hibbs's chair, the commander said, 'Now back off. Back off from both of them. Come towards me.'

Taylor did.

'On the floor now! Drop the knife. Face down on the floor, arms and legs splayed.'

One of the men who'd approached Taylor was already

cutting Janet free, his companion still concentrating on the naked man.

Taylor remained kneeling, smiling at the entry of the three detectives.

'I said face down! Down!'

Taylor's smile became an open laugh, not hysterical but genuine amusement. 'This is better! This is how I'm going to do it! Cause the sensation!'

'Mummy!' wailed Janet. 'Oh, Mummy!'

Everyone looked at her except the pistol-holding policeman.

Janet said, 'She's dead.'

It was Lobonski who went to Janet, with his coat to cover her nakedness.

Janet said, 'Mummy first. Cover my mother.'

Chapter Twenty-four

The legal co-operation between Britain and America was at breaking point from the very outset because of Clarence Gale's absolute determination to re-establish public confidence in the FBI – as well as to gain personal public recognition for himself – which totally alienated the unaware Wesley Powell from the British. It was more than a week before he realized what had happened.

Alerted by Lobonski within minutes of the seizure, the Bureau issued a media release almost three hours before any British confirmation. By the time that came Gale was already appearing, with Powell beside him, at a press conference that coincided with the main evening news of America's three major TV channels. Gale remained strictly within the truth, but only by a hair's breadth, by inference reducing British participation to little more than a formality, acting throughout to Washington's instructions. He planted the seeds of what very quickly developed into an international sensation by talking of factors in the investigation defying scientific or rational explanation and disclosed the connection between the serial killing and Myron Nolan, 'which is also, at the moment, totally inexplicable'. He made Powell's public identification as the task force leader appear a taunting, even life-risking, bait and called upon the media that had criticized Powell in their ignorance to put the record straight now that reasons were being given for the Bureau allowing Powell to be pilloried.

'Wesley Powell is a brilliant agent who from the beginning has conducted an extraordinary investigation into an extraordinary case. I have today attached an official commendation to his record.'

Powell, embarrassed for several reasons by the exaggeration – particularly regretting that Amy Halliday was not being recognized in the praise – hedged the persistent demands about the science-defying factors, although, in trying to respond to three questions at the same time, he inadvertently used the phrase 'previous existence', which was instantly seized upon.

It was an irritated Malcolm Townsend, anxious to retrieve the promotionally useful publicity he feared being diverted, who more knowingly used the expression 'back from the dead' when he and Basildon appeared side by side at the British press conference. They also issued the Pittsburgh freeze frame of Myron Nolan, which within twenty-four hours was being published alongside faded but still visibly identical archive photographs of Nolan at the time of his 1949 trial. Words like 'supernatural' and 'ghosts' and 'ghouls' began to appear in headlines. Ironically, so did Walter Hibbs's 'inhuman monster' description alongside lengthy extracts from the tribunal evidence of the children's deaths and maiming.

Amy insisted she understood why she, technically still a researcher, could not have been included on the podium with the Director but Powell didn't believe her. He urged her, that first day, officially to apply for a transfer and spent two hours on his own memorandum of support, itemizing every contribution she had made and stressing that had it not been for her Harold Taylor would have killed two more people and still been free to kill others.

The Director insisted Powell co-operate with the now eulogizing television, radio and newspaper requests that flooded in, for personal interviews. Powell doggedly refused to talk about anything he considered prejudicial to eventual trials, in whichever country they might be held, but confronted with the pictorial evidence he was forced openly to agree that with no other logical explanation it appeared that Myron Nolan, murdered forty-eight years before, had five weeks earlier been walking the streets outside the apartment of the murdered Marcus Carr, president of the military court that jailed the man for life. One of the possibly prejudicial facts he was withholding, along with Townsend, was that matching fingerprints which were, he knew, going to send the sensation into a fresh spiral.

'No!' he insisted to one question. 'I do not believe in ghosts, the supernatural or the paranormal.'

'No,' he replied, equally emphatically to another. 'I cannot explain it, any more than anyone else.'

For the first full day following the arrest and for several days afterwards, Powell tried to contact Townsend and Basildon, always to be told they were unavailable. From London Jeri Lobonski complained they were refusing his calls too, and finally Powell wrote as diplomatic a memorandum as possible to the Director, suggesting an approach be made at the earlier established political level to restore a relationship. He received a curt written reply from the Director that the matter was being resolved. The British detectives continued to refuse to take his calls.

Powell was at least able to devote some of the time forced upon him to his private life. He rigidly kept his promise to Beth – and by so doing maintained the threat to Ann and Beddows – to telephone her every day, relieved there was no suggestion of any pressure from Ann. The lawyer Powell engaged was sure that upon the facts there would be no difficulty getting custody – particularly if Ann didn't oppose the transference – but that until a court hearing varying the conditions of the existing order Powell had to comply strictly with those that currently existed, which meant Beth had to continue living with her mother. He was to limit his contact with Ann and Beddows to the absolute minimum, make no threats nor get into any dispute with either or both of them.

It was when Powell was explaining to Beth the need for her to continue living at Arlington instead of moving at once to Crystal City on the first Friday – promising to talk more fully about it the following day – that Beth reminded him of another promise: to invite Amy to spend the Saturday with them.

A reason to do that came within thirty minutes of his replacing the telephone.

They were still using the incident room, not knowing what, if any, trial submission documents might have to be prepared for Britain, although the manning had been greatly reduced. John Price and Matt Hirst had already re-based and the extra support staff had been reassigned. Powell hadn't been aware of Amy leaving that Friday but he was of her returning: hurrying across the main room towards the side office, she was smiling, visibly flushed.

'I got the transfer! Just been told personally by the Director, who's also given me a commendation for what I've done here. I automatically go up two grades with the appointment.'

283

'You deserve every bit of it.'

More soberly she said, 'Gale also told me what you wrote to him.'

'Not a word of exaggeration in anything I said.'

'Impressed the hell out of him.'

'You impressed the hell out of me.'

'Not a bad team.'

'Very professional.'

'That was the understanding, wasn't it?' she reminded him.

Seizing the opening, Powell said, 'We didn't rule out celebrating success. And now you've got a double reason.'

'No, we didn't rule it out. And I'm glad we didn't.'

He chose the Four Seasons, because it really was a celebration, and let her excitement fuel the conversation, patiently enjoying and responding to all her gabbled questions. She wanted to know every detail about her training at Quantico and if there'd be resentment at how she'd become an agent and what to do about it if there was and if he'd mind her calling him if something came up she needed guidance about.

'I guess I'm asking for an unfair advantage but that's never held me back up to now,' she said, with her customary ingenuous honesty.

'That might complicate things,' he said, seeing the further chance and deciding to take it. The investigation couldn't be complicated so there was no reason why he shouldn't. The only problem could be the embarrassment of rejection.

The lightness went at once from her face. 'I'm sorry. I didn't mean to . . .'

'It would be keeping things vaguely on a professional level,' he interrupted, not allowing the misunderstand-

284

ing. 'And we banned personal intrusions into professional situations, didn't we?'

Her smile came back. 'I seem to remember we did.'

'I was kind of hoping the ban might be lifted with the end of the case.'

She didn't speak.

Quickly he tried to anticipate her dismissal and at least save the evening. 'Now you say I'm out of order and that you're sorry but it was great working together.'

'Or that I'd begun to give up hope that you'd ever ask. And that I'm glad you did.'

'So am I,' said Powell.

They came together very relaxed, as if they were long-time lovers each knowing the pleasures of the other, neither failing the other, and they climaxed together and when they did she cried out in her excitement. He made love to her again and she was ready for him and it was as good as before and she screamed again, laughing in the darkness at their becoming professionals in something else.

In the darkness he said, 'You're going to think I've conned you but I haven't. I wanted this to happen but I think the sequence is wrong and now I'm nervous.'

'I don't know what you're saying.'

He told her at last about applying for custody of Beth and for the child to live with him, which would need a bigger apartment or maybe a house, and perhaps a housekeeper when the job took him away.

'I *think* I see where you're coming from, as far as I am concerned, but maybe you'd better spell it out for me,' said Amy.

'Beth wants you to share Saturday with us. I said I'd ask you. But I don't want you believing you're being enmeshed or railroaded into any surrogate mother nonsense. You're not, no way. My solemn word.'

'I'll need to go home to change in the morning,' said Amy. 'Guess it might be an idea to bring the laptop back with me.'

Which is what she did. She also arrived loaded with grocery sacks, having planned the day with Powell before she'd left, neither knowing that this Saturday Beth's homework would include home economics. The moment they'd kissed, Beth asked if Amy knew she was coming to live with her father and Amy agreed it would be terrific. Computer theory was again a homework subject and Powell sat back, relaxed and forgotten with one of the previous week's Coors while Amy played computer games until Beth became thoroughly comfortable with the keyboard and command keys. Then Amy took the child practically through the set course. Beth finished, declaring, 'I understand it! I didn't but now I do!'

The homework finished, the two disappeared into the kitchen to make lunch and afterwards they all drove to the river and hired a boat and sailed almost as far as Alexandria before turning back. Beth giggled, delighted, when Powell was recognized at the marina and asked for his autograph and said she wanted one too, for her best friend at school. Amy and Beth were ahead of Powell leaving the marina. Amy walked with her arm around Beth's shoulders and Beth managed to get her arm somewhere close to Amy's waist.

When Powell returned to the apartment from taking Beth home Amy said, 'You didn't tell me Ann was with Harry Beddows.'

'But Beth did?'

'Shouldn't she have done?'

Powell completed the story and said, 'You want to laugh at the original, see-nothing Mr Magoo go right on ahead.'

'Hurt pride?'

'Battered and bruised.' Powell regarded Amy very gravely, caught by a sudden awareness. 'I don't know where you and I are going to lead to, but what's happened between us makes you vulnerable, more so maybe than me. Let's keep a lid on it.'

'You serious?' queried Amy, surprised.

'As serious as it's possible to be,' said Powell. 'They tried to use Beth as a weapon. Beddows is in a better position to hurt you. And he would if he knew it would hurt me.'

The post-mortem finding was that Edith Hibbs, already suffering vascular deterioration, died of a heart attack. Virtually the entire population of Lower Norwood attended the funeral, after which she was laid in the family vault. Janet was upset by the number of press and television cameramen and grateful that Chief Superintendent Preston had anticipated it and drafted in sufficient police to prevent the service being disrupted. She didn't expect Townsend or Basildon to attend and thanked them for doing so. She hadn't been into the house since the night it happened and had already instructed estate agents to sell but she had to open it for the after-funeral reception. Vera Potter organized the catering and stayed behind afterwards to clear up and lock the house. Some of the journalists stayed on in the village, too, and bought drinks for Vera and George, who'd grown to enjoy their names and photographs appearing in newspapers.

'She was very keen on Mr Barkworth, you know,' confided Vera. 'I'm sure she was in love.'

'No,' said the journalist who'd bought the last round of drinks. 'I didn't know.'

Clarence Gale's summons came halfway through the second week. Harry Beddows was already in the Director's office, stiff faced, when Powell entered, the first time they'd physically been in the same room since the earlier corridor confrontation. Powell got the impression Beddows had been with the Director for some time: there were sheets he recognized from the case files at his feet and an empty coffee cup.

'Time to resolve things with the British,' Gale announced. 'Although it actually looks, odd though it may seem, that Taylor's done it for us.'

'How?' asked Powell.

'Tell him, Harry.'

Beddows's features stiffened further and he didn't look at Powell when he spoke. 'Taylor has refused to make a statement – say anything – unless you're personally there.'

'Harry's been trying to smooth out the misunderstanding, as you know,' said the Director, coming as close as he intended to admitting he'd caused the rift by calling his immediate press conference.

'No,' said Powell, at once. 'I didn't know.'

'We've exchanged memoranda,' said Beddows. 'The Director has had copies of your replies.'

The warning bell sounded in Powell's mind like the klaxon of an oncoming express train. 'My understanding was that they were queries on the investigation: nothing to do with the British problem.'

Gale frowned curiously between the two of them.

288

'Something going on I don't know about?'

'I'm not sure,' said Powell. 'Is there, Harry?'

'No,' said Beddows, replying to Gale. 'You asked me to bring things with the British back on track. That's what I've been doing.'

'OK,' said Gale, doubt still in his voice. Briskly he picked up: 'Don't know what it means, Taylor wanting it to be you, Wes. But it makes sense, your being the case officer. There'll probably be some evidential difficulties: uncertainty about what can be produced about crimes committed in the jurisdiction of other countries.'

'I'm at a difficult stage with the extradition,' argued Beddows. 'It's complicated. I think I should continue with it.'

The warning sounded even louder in Powell's head. He had to tiptoe on eggshells, he realized. What was there safely to work on: try to understand? No question that Beddows would have been screwing him. No way, either, to find out how, this soon. What *could* he be certain about? That Beddows was desperate to get to London.

'Wes can do that, too.'

Beddows began to colour. Still keeping his attention rigidly on Clarence Gale, he said, 'Your instructions were to restore a working relationship. That's what I've been attempting to do. I feel – and I can't stress this too strongly – that I need to be the person to go there, to cement things positively. That and to ensure we get Taylor back for trial here.'

'But Taylor will only talk to me!' Powell seized his chance. It was bizarre, he conceded. He didn't know why the mad bastard was insisting – probably never would – but if he hadn't, Beddows would probably have succeeded in screwing him.

'No!' decided the Director. 'Wes can do it.'

Powell wondered how difficult it would be to find out what Beddows had been up to.

Powell's lawyer assured him there would be no difficulty getting the hearing rescheduled but added: 'It'll remind the judge how liable you are to be sent away at a moment's notice.'

'Ann doesn't even want Beth.'

'You were arguing when Ann said what she did: a remark in the heat of the moment. Maybe you shouldn't have made the threats you did.'

And maybe, thought Powell, he wouldn't need to implement them for personal reasons. It was far too soon to be sure but he suspected that in his desperation Beddows had done something officially culpable.

Chapter Twenty-five

Jeri Lobonski, a fair-haired, mournful-faced man with the high Slavic cheekbones of his Polish ancestry, made the customary resident's courtesy trip to meet him at the airport. Determinedly alert to everything – the faintest sound of breaking eggshells – Powell at once noted the total absence of the equally customary resentment of headquarters intrusion. Harry Beddows was a division head, someone who could call each and every shot. Lobonski wouldn't even have known he was being embroiled in a survival intrigue.

Lobonski said, 'We're playing catch-up here. And you're jetlagged. You sure you still want to meet them right away?'

Was there any hidden meaning there: an order the man was carrying out? 'Absolutely,' insisted Powell. 'It's taken long enough to get this far: too long.'

'They were truly pissed off, you going public so quickly. Blamed me absolutely. Townsend openly told me to go fuck myself the day after. Called specially. It was the last time we spoke.'

Their car joined the morning rush hour crawl on to the motorway. It all sounded convincing enough, thought Powell. He could risk the question, if it were sufficiently vague. 'Harry Beddows been going through you?'

Lobonski frowned across the car. 'What's Beddows got to do with it?'

'He hasn't worked through you?'

'No.'

'You had any contact with Townsend or Basildon?'

'I only got past the switchboard to Townsend's office now when I said it was about your arrival. And then I still had to speak to Chris Pennington.'

He had to accept that, Powell supposed. 'More catch-up than you might imagine.'

'Do I get to know what's going on?'

'You've been caught up in a situation that doesn't concern you,' said Powell, guardedly. 'Wrong place at the wrong time. It's too complicated to explain but I'll make you a promise. However it hits the fan, you won't get covered by the spray.'

'If I was supposed to be reassured by that, I'm not.'

'Trust me,' said Powell. 'Who contacted you about Taylor insisting he'd only talk if I was there?'

'Wes!' protested the other man. 'I haven't understood a word you said since you got off that goddamned aircraft. You *are* jetlagged. Why don't we put it back, until this afternoon at least?'

'You don't know about Taylor's insistence, either.'

'The first I knew was when I got your call last night, telling me to set up a meeting. I thought you'd been talking direct to them. What else can I tell you!'

'You're doing well enough,' said Powell. 'Taylor's refused to talk to anyone – agree a lawyer, even – unless I'm here. Otherwise it would have been Harry Beddows. The Director gave him the job of straightening things out.'

'It's getting a little clearer,' said Lobonski, astutely.

'Not much but a little. You want me to say it again, I will. Harry didn't come through me.'

'You want *me* to say it again, I will. You won't get hurt in the fallout.'

'I would have thought this was difficult enough, without making it more so ourselves,' said the man.

'It is,' agreed Powell. 'My problem is I don't know precisely what additional difficulties have been created.'

Lobonski had tried to beat the traffic by taking the Embankment detour and failed. As he finally turned up towards Victoria and New Scotland Yard he said, 'It's not going to take long to find out. We're here.'

The atmosphere in Townsend's office was glacial, the impression of ice splintering, not eggshells. There were no handshakes or insistences upon first names. Both Townsend and Basildon wore waistcoats with their immaculate single-breasted suits, Townsend's complete with a looped gold watch chain. The support officers were hopeful clones, although the cloth and tailoring was just slightly inferior. Powell judged all four to be state-of-the-art cops able to discern a main chance through a thick fog, even blindfolded. That was hopeful.

His approach determined in the first few seconds from that assessment, Powell said, 'Each of us knows the personal advantages of this case.'

'You certainly did,' said Townsend.

'You've every reason to be pissed off. So have I.' It caught them, which he'd hoped it would.

Basildon said, 'What else could you have expected but suspension?'

It was like the opening of giant doors, with floodlights beyond. 'Who told you I was suspended?' demanded Powell. For the first time there was what could have

293

been a stir of uncertainty among the four hostile men. Lobonski was doing well to hide his total confusion.

Basildon said, 'That's what we understood.'

'From Harry?' pressed Powell. He wanted Lobonski to hear the confirmation.

It was Townsend whose patience gave. He said, 'I am pissed off. And getting more so. This is all total, unnecessary bloody nonsense! It *is* a good case. You put it at risk.'

Powell said, 'I want to get our problems out of the way as much as you do: more so, perhaps. So let's stop fucking about. Rushing in front of the cameras and into print ahead of you wasn't a mistake or a misjudgement. It was a calculated, positive decision – not by me but by the FBI Director himself – because of the shit the Bureau had been getting, up until then. And because my Director is a media maniac. I didn't like it – still don't like it – but it was expedient, politically, in America. It shouldn't have been done like that but it was. And for that reason.'

The surprise was obvious from all four Britons, although only Pennington openly showed it, quickly clearing his expression. Townsend said, 'That's another version of the same event.'

'What's the one Beddows gave you?'

'That you were told to inform us but that you didn't, wanting the credit all for yourself,' said Basildon.

'Told by the Director?' pressed Powell, wanting it all.

'Yes,' said Townsend.

'In front of Beddows?'

'Presumably,' said Basildon.

What more was there! 'Has there been a written explanation: an apology?'

'To my Commissioner,' said Townsend.

'And to my Chief Constable,' added Basildon.

He was on the point of winning, decided Powell. He'd expected to feel something – anything – but there was nothing: no feeling of triumph or satisfaction. It actually seemed unimportant. 'From the FBI Director, Clarence Gale?'

'In his name, by Harry Beddows,' said Townsend.

'You've seen it?'

'My guv'nor sent me a copy, as a matter of courtesy,' said Townsend.

'You think you could further extend that courtesy: let me have a copy?'

'Not until I know what this is all about,' said Townsend. 'And I mean all.'

'There's been a lot of internal expediency, as well as external,' said Powell. 'Believe me, I'm sorrier than you are that you got caught up in it. You've been openly lied to: so's your Commissioner and your Chief Constable.'

The surprise was even greater, more obvious, this time. Townsend said: 'You sure you know what you're saying?'

'I'm positive about what I'm saying: professionally I wish I weren't. I will do my best to see that you get another apology: a correct one from the Director himself. I'm certainly prepared to give you one now, in writing, if it helps get this whole business out of our way, so that we can start working again properly and not waste any more time on this.'

'I'd certainly like to stop wasting time,' said Townsend. He very quickly found what he was looking for in the file on the desk in front of him. 'This is what we got from someone called Harry Beddows.'

'One more thing,' said Powell, accepting the letter. 'What problem is there with extradition?'

'Texas would have right of trial, for the Gene Johnson

murder?' queried Townsend. 'And Texas has the death penalty, right?'

'Right,' agreed Powell.

'We don't,' said the detective. 'The United Kingdom won't extradite to a country that exercises the death penalty.'

'Never?' pressed Powell.

'Only if there is agreement that it won't be imposed, even if there's a finding of guilt . . .' He shrugged, impatiently. 'I'm not sure why we're having this conversation. I know it's all been explained already by our Home Office, to your Attorney-General's department.'

Powell sighed, deeply. 'There've been a lot of crossed wires. Now there aren't.'

The initial reaction of both Powell and Lobonski was shock, although not at Harold Taylor himself. In an American jail they would have been separated from an accused multiple murderer by reinforced glass, communicating through microphones, with Taylor's wrist and ankle manacles even then tethered to a waist chain, immobilizing the man far more effectively than he'd immobilized Edith and Janet Hibbs.

There was no protective separation between them and the man was not restrained in any way. He was sitting at a central table to one side of which recording apparatus was installed. Until their arrival Taylor had been guarded by just one, unarmed prison warder.

The moment Taylor saw Powell he said, 'The gang's all here, including the FBI's Superman himself! Not as impressive as you looked on CNN.'

There was nothing immediately outstanding, special, about the man but at the same time Powell wasn't unimpressive, conceded Taylor, studying the man intently. There was a confidence, as if he were sufficiently self-assured not to need to draw attention to himself with any outward effort. Someone to treat with caution, perhaps. Or was he? Maybe it was time for another game, involving all of them. He'd become bored, so long by himself.

Performance time, Powell recognized, studying the killer just as intently. Maybe a mistake, too, for them all to have come together: pandering to the man's need always for superior control. Why not? If they got a statement – anything that helped – it was justified. From the scientific analysis of the freeze frame photographs he knew everything about Harold Taylor's size and build but it still didn't look right. Too slim, bland face, totally unremarkable: mousy hair, mousy figured, mousy man. But what should murderers – mass murderers – look like? Pointy toothed, slavering, talons for fingers?

Taylor said, 'I'm innocent, until proven guilty. Get all the papers, have a television in my cell. I've seen all your public appearances.'

'I've seen the result of a lot of yours,' said Powell.

'It was a challenge, your being personally identified, wasn't it,' said Taylor. 'You really think you could have got me to respond?'

'You're arrogant enough.'

'But too clever. Far cleverer than you.' The man was quick though, noted Taylor. Picked up on the game: picked it up but didn't properly know how to play it.

'And you're in a cell, charged with murder, manslaughter and kidnapping and before I go today I'm going formally to charge you with four more killings,' said Powell. 'I'd say that makes me – all of us here – cleverer than you, wouldn't you?' Not quite unremarkable, thought Powell, correcting his earlier impression.

There was about Taylor a demeanour Powell had never before encountered, a tightly wound attitude that at any minute might snap or uncoil, an unsteady spring.

He was good, Taylor conceded. Not good enough, of course, but adequate to make it interesting. He said, 'You really think you've won?'

'It looks like it to me.'

'Silly man! You don't know – understand – anything yet.'

'So tell us,' said Powell.

Instead of answering, Taylor smirked at the two British police chiefs alongside the American. 'So it really is true, what they say on television and in the papers? He's in charge – does all the talking – and you carry the bags?'

'We take it in turns,' said Henry Basildon, refusing to be goaded.

'Tweedledum and Tweedledee,' mocked Taylor. 'You don't deserve to be made famous by me.'

'We'll recognize when you get too frightened,' said Townsend, seeking to mock in return.

The eyes momentarily flicked. 'I'll remember that: remember to ask some time who ended up more frightened.'

'I'm not frightened, I'm flattered that you wouldn't start without me,' prodded Powell.

'That's most important,' said Taylor, abruptly – surprisingly – serious. 'I always need to know who my enemies are, for when I come back.' He looked steadily at each of the men grouped around him. 'And now I do. I've got you all marked.'

A stir of uncertainty came from the two support officers and Basildon couldn't prevent a slight shift.

'See!' demanded Taylor, triumphantly. 'I've won!'

'I hope I haven't wasted my time coming all this way for a vaudeville act,' jeered Powell. 'I thought you had something to tell me.'

'I want to know where I am going to be tried – here in England? Or in America?'

'Here, in England,' said Townsend.

'I elect to be tried in the United States,' the man declared.

Why? wondered Powell. He said, 'You don't have the choice.'

Fuck! thought Taylor. He hadn't wanted that. He wouldn't ask – make himself the supplicant any further – but he didn't think television was permitted in English courts as it was for American trials, which was what he wanted: the biggest possible audience, global village fame. 'You absolutely sure about that?'

'Choose a lawyer and ask him,' said Basildon.

Taylor remained silent for several moments. 'So the British get the glory?' Time to recover: taunt.

Worried about formalities, Christopher Pennington filled the convenient silence by informing Taylor of his right to be questioned in the presence of a lawyer, which Taylor waived, and then pedantically recited the official caution of any statement being used in court if considered relevant.

'You'll want to use it,' insisted Taylor. 'This is going to be the biggest case of your careers. You're going to be famous for the rest of your lives.'

Would the arrogance crack if the man realized the evidence there already was against him? wondered Powell. 'We know about Myron Nolan. The fingerprints. His handwriting—'

'Don't forget the Pittsburgh photograph,' Taylor cut him off, triumphantly. 'But how do you explain it!

299

That's the mystery, isn't it? What the media are so hysterical about.'

'Why don't you put us out of our misery?' sneered Basildon.

'Only too pleased,' said the man, brightly. 'I am the reincarnation of Myron Nolan. Who was the reincarnation of Patrick Arnold. Who was the reincarnation of Maurice Barkworth – until now his was the best of my returns – who in turn was the reincarnation of Luke Thomas. As whom I was born again from having originally been Paul Noakes . . .'

He laughed, even louder, at the expressions on all their faces. 'Isn't that the most incredible thing you've ever heard! Now listen very carefully. No-one will believe it – just as you don't believe it at the moment – unless it's proven, so I'm going to give all the details of every previous life, so you can find the facts to support all I'm going to tell you. We don't want to get it wrong, do we?'

There'd been no conversation in the cars coming from the prison and there was a reluctance to begin back in Townsend's office. Unasked, the man poured whisky for all of them and all of them accepted.

At last Powell said, 'The absurd thing is, it makes it all perfectly logical.' It was embarrassing to say.

Basildon and Townsend exchanged looks.

'A lot of people believe in reincarnation,' offered Bennett, hopefully.

'I don't,' stated Townsend. 'He's a bleeding nutter.'

'Non-stop, for three hours!' recalled Basildon. 'The detail was incredible.'

Only now, as the adrenalin began to seep away, did Powell begin to feel the pull of fatigue. He said, 'And

300

we've got to check out every single thing he told us.' He might, he supposed, have to recall some of the support staff to help Amy. At least they'd know where to look now: Taylor had supplied dates – often times – and even numbers of streets for every claim he'd made about his supposed American existences.

'If it all checks out . . .' started Bennett, slowly.

'. . . he's the world's first reincarnation,' picked up Townsend. 'But I'll give ten-to-one that I'm right.'

Jeri Lobonski accepted Powell's division of labour without comment, going at once to a side office with a secretary to transcribe each of Harold Taylor's three full tapes for the detail Washington was going to need.

There had been no incoming messages waiting for them but when Powell reached Amy she said Beddows had come three times into the incident room, asking about contact from London. There had been no familiarity or curiosity to indicate that the man had any suspicion about them. She listened silently to Powell's précis of the interview with Harold Taylor, together with his permission to reactivate the incident room with as many extra staff as she needed to check every detail that would be faxed as soon as possible.

When he finished she said, 'I seem to remember saying something about it being creepy as a joke, a long time ago.'

'No-one's laughing here.'

'You believe it?'

'I'm trying hard not to. I won't find it easy unless you can disprove it, from what we're going to send you.'

'It *is* scary, Wes.'

'I remember you saying that some time ago, too.'

'What do I say to Harry Beddows if he comes back?'

'Tell him what I've told you. Show him the statement.'

'What about the other business?'

'There's nothing to worry about.'

'You going to tell me about it?'

'Just trust me. What you don't know about you can't inadvertently make a mistake about.'

Clarence Gale listened without interruption, too, not immediately speaking when Powell finished. Then he said, 'You are aware of the implications of what you're saying?'

'Yes.'

'Do you wish to make it official?'

'As official as I possibly can. It's not only a personal attack upon me. It affects you, personally, and the Bureau.' There was a risk, he supposed, of Gale himself being identified as the cause of the initial problem.

'You've a copy of the letter, to the Police Commissioner?'

'Yes.'

'I want it included tonight in the diplomatic bag from the embassy, addressed personally to me. Have you spoken to Beddows?'

'No.'

'Don't, not even if he tries to make contact with you. Refer him to me. Everything now's the subject of an official inquiry.'

Powell was lucky to reach the custody lawyer on his first attempt and was glad he'd made the effort, because he'd almost acted upon impulse.

'No!' The man refused at once. 'Leave it to what he appears to have done professionally. If you include the personal stuff in your application for Beth it looks malicious: maybe as if you created an entrapment for him, instead of his attempt to create one for you. It'll make a bigger impression on our judge if I can show you had the integrity *not* to use it.'

Chapter Twenty-six

Even though her evidence formed no part of any American case Wesley Powell wanted to meet Janet Hibbs, but the previous day's bewildering encounter gave added importance to the interview. He was hopeful of the one that was to follow, with the prosecuting lawyer, too. He seemed to be achieving a lot very quickly.

Townsend and Basildon – as well as Lobonski – went with him, leaving their support officers to check as much of the statement as possible. The woman remained the chief British prosecution witness and after the media frenzy about a suggested romance she'd been moved from her London flat into a safe house. It was in Basildon's division, in Barnes, overlooking the river but like all protected witness locations Powell had ever visited it was sterile and unlived-in, fully furnished and equipped but lacking even the artificial homeliness of an hotel.

Janet's sweater was stained and missing a button on the shoulder and she hadn't bothered with make-up or even, he suspected, to brush her hair. Despite the carelessness and the black hollows pouching her eyes she was clearly an attractive woman, although even more clearly one who had given up, on herself and everything else.

She smiled in sad recognition at Jeri Lobonski and said, 'You're the one who gave me your coat. I never thanked you. You were the first to be kind.'

'How are you?' he said, smiling in return.

'How do I look?' she came back at once, bitterly. After being introduced to Powell she said in weary resignation, 'What more do you want?'

'To know everything I possibly can about the man you knew as Maurice Barkworth but whose real name, as far as we're aware, is Harold Taylor,' said Powell. He outlined the killings in America, despite her insistence that she'd already read about them, and said it still might be possible to arraign the man there on charges he wouldn't face in England.

Responding to her obvious need, Powell said, 'If he is extradited to the United States the trial will be in Texas. Which has the death penalty.'

There was no resignation in Janet's smile now. Leaning intently forward she said, 'To see killed the bastard who killed my mother and did what he did to me I'll tell you whatever it is you want to know.'

She did in far greater detail than in the police statement she had already made, unembarrassed even at describing her fellatio when sex hadn't been possible. She had trusted Taylor, she told Powell, and sincerely believed herself to be in love. At Powell's urging she recounted as much as she could of the precise words he'd used when he'd finally attacked her and her mother.

'He actually told you it was because of what your father had done to *him*?' pressed Powell. 'Not to someone named Myron Nolan?'

She nodded. 'It excited him, to talk about it. He described everything: the courtroom, what the weather was like, what it was like to be in Berlin in those days. It was as if he'd really been there.'

'Did he mention anyone named Myron Nolan?'

'No. I've read the name in the papers since, of course.'

'You called it excitement,' said Townsend. 'Was that all it was? Could it have been more than that? Madness?'

'Of course I thought he was mad, suddenly turning on us like he did. But only then, at the last minute.'

'What about in the days leading up to it?' asked Basildon.

'Totally gentle, totally calm,' replied Janet. 'I'm not trying to invest the time with things that weren't there but having thought about it as much as I obviously have, I've come particularly to remember the calmness. Even when he attacked us he was always aware of himself, watching himself. The only exception was when I tried to reason with him. He screamed that I was patronizing him.'

'So his demeanour was a conscious act?' said Lobonski.

'It had to be, didn't it?' she said, bitterly again. 'All a great big fucking act!'

'Anything else you've thought about, since?' asked Powell.

Janet gave the question time. 'He was fanatically neat. And clean . . .' She laughed bitterly. 'Can you believe it attracted me to him! Wiped his restaurant cutlery on his napkin, before using it. Rubbed his hands together sometimes, as if he was washing them. Did it a lot at the end, when he was telling us how he was going to kill us.'

Basildon said, 'That night, when we burst into the house? You told me he changed his face. I didn't include it in your statement, then or later. I thought you were hysterical. You had every reason to be.'

Janet shuddered but said indignantly, 'He did! Several

306

times. It was horrible. Everything was horrible! But when he became someone else was the worst. That's what killed Mother!'

'Do you mean he physically distorted his face: twisted it out of shape, to look like someone else?' pressed Basildon.

'No, nothing like that,' she insisted impatiently. 'He had the young face – the face I knew – and then he made it change into a totally different man, whom I didn't know. It was the older man in the photographs I've seen.' She paused, looking between the four men. 'You don't believe me, do you? No-one will. I'm not just going to be humiliated by what I've got to say publicly, in court. They're going to think I'm mad, as well. Laugh at me.'

'I don't think so,' said Powell.

She looked curiously at them, waiting. It was Townsend who recounted their previous day's interview. He began embarrassed, warning her she wasn't going to believe it, and as he talked her face twisted into disgust.

'I don't want to believe it!' she babbled, her words colliding. 'People don't come back from the dead . . . They can't . . . that's . . . I don't know what it is!' She stopped. 'How much more unreal is this all going to get . . . ?' She forced herself to stop, a physical effort. 'That's what he *did* say, when he read out part of a letter my father had written, from Berlin! About an inhuman monster. He gloated and said that it was him my father had been talking about. It was the first time he changed his face . . .' She stared imploringly at Powell. 'Tell me what's happening . . . what it's all about . . .'

Powell looked at the other men, then at Janet, knowing he had to say it at last. 'I think it's true. I don't want to – I've been refusing to – but the only explanation I have is that Harold Taylor *is* a reincarnation . . .'

He waited for the sniggers. There weren't any. No-one spoke, either. Then Janet said, 'Are you going to tell the court that?'

'That's what's in Taylor's statement,' Townsend reminded her. 'It'll be produced as evidence.'

To Powell she said, 'So they won't think I'm mad, will they? I'll be humiliated but no-one will think I'm mad.'

'They'll probably think we're all mad,' said Powell.

'It's no part of any prosecution case to humiliate you,' said Townsend.

Janet shrugged, not reassured. '*Will* he be tried in America?'

'I don't know, not yet,' admitted Powell. 'We're going to try to find a way.'

'If he is – and is sentenced to death – I want to see him die. I want you to promise me you'll arrange that for me.'

'I promise,' said Powell, meaning it.

Hector McLeash QC, the lead counsel for *the Crown* V. *Harold Taylor,* was a flamboyant Scot who affected bow ties and overly long hair and had a connoisseur's taste in whisky. He had taken the prosecution brief for its publicity potential but was worried after reading Harold Taylor's statement that astonished sensation might too easily spill over into ridicule. It was a measure of his concern that he'd abandoned the normal procedure of leaving the preliminary official meetings to his instructing solicitor to come personally to New Scotland Yard to discuss it with the investigating officers, both English and American.

The solicitor, Dennis Riley, was a necessary balance

to McLeash's frequent theatricality. A professionally emotionless pinstriped man, he took constant notes and enjoyed the reputation of isolating the one incongruity that proved a client's guilt or innocence.

The barrister waited until Riley finished reading, wanting the other man's opinion. Riley pursed his lips, doubtfully and said, 'No court's going to like this. I can see an argument about admissibility.'

Turning at once to the two British detectives, McLeash said, 'Did he have legal representation when he said it all?'

'It was taken strictly according to the book,' said Basildon defensively. 'All the warnings and cautions are on tape.'

Riley carefully put his copy of the statement on Townsend's desk and said, 'Reads like the ramblings of a madman.'

'We'll anticipate the judge and try for psychiatric reports,' decided McLeash. 'That been suggested to him?'

'We wanted to get your views first,' said Townsend.

'Defence will insist,' predicted the lawyer. 'Insanity is the obvious plea.' To Riley he said: 'I'll want three separate assessments, to be on the safe side. Best psychiatrists you can find.'

'*Unfit* to plead,' queried Townsend. None of the sensation – and therefore none of the benefit – would come out if the court ruled that.

'I'd try it, with the proper reports, if I was defending,' admitted McLeash. 'Does he look, seem, obviously insane?'

'Totally rational,' said Townsend.

'A lot of completely insane people do,' said Riley, unimpressed.

'What about this woman, Hibbs? And funny faces?' demanded McLeash. 'I'm not happy with that.'

'Neither's she,' said Townsend, irritated at the other man's dismissal. 'She's frightened of being humiliated and laughed at.'

'So am I,' said McLeash. 'I'll want to go very carefully through her evidence before we call her. We'll get as many women on the jury as we can, during selection. I want as much sympathy as I can get for Janet Hibbs.'

'I'm not sure we should introduce face changes,' warned Riley.

'Neither am I,' agreed McLeash. He tapped the statement. 'So what about all this? It been checked out?'

'Being done,' assured Basildon.

'And in America, too,' said Powell, seeing his opening.

'If it is a matter of public record, he could have researched the whole thing,' Riley said. 'Tailored everything to fit.'

'That wouldn't account for the forensic and scientific evidence,' Basildon pointed out. 'That couldn't be made to fit.'

'His account, absurd though it looks, is the only thing that does fit,' insisted Townsend.

'I'll need pre-trial conferences with all the forensic and scientific experts,' McLeash told Riley. 'That's the evidence that's going to get the headlines. I don't want to be caught out on anything there.'

Riley made a note. 'We'll need experts on reincarnation, too.'

'Right,' agreed McLeash. 'Line up theologians: professors of religious philosophy, if there are such people.' He looked at Powell. 'A person would have had to be living in Outer Mongolia not to know something about the cases already, but I've got to be careful against prejudicing a British jury with any reference to your killings in the United States. But they're so inextricably linked I don't see how I can avoid something arising. And there are too many loose ends to allow any more. I'm going to need you here, throughout the trial. Maybe with some of your scientific and technical people, too. I'll make the formal request, of course, but I thought you'd like to warn your Director and legal officials, in advance.'

'When will the trial begin?' asked Powell, at once.

'Depends on the defence. A month, I'd say. Is there a problem?'

He didn't have the slightest doubt he'd have custody of Beth by then; be responsible for looking after her. How was he going to manage that, from three and a half thousand miles away? 'None at all,' he said.

He should have given priority to the Director's call-back demand when he returned to the embassy but instead Powell spoke first to Amy. She hadn't seen or heard from Beddows so far that day. Because it was so long in the past none of what Harold Taylor had insisted to be facts were computerized. The most obvious – possibly the only – sources were newspaper archives and she'd circulated the material to the appropriate Bureau offices.

'What's he like?' she demanded.

'Not at all like a ghost,' said Powell.

When he was connected to the Director, Gale said, 'Anything outstanding you can't leave to Lobonski?'

'No,' said Powell.

'The internal inquiry is scheduled for the day after tomorrow,' said the man. 'Come back.'

Chapter Twenty-seven

It was held in a seventh-floor conference room, with a sign on the door forbidding unauthorized entry. There was the ambience of a court, a Bureau counsel presenting the accusation of gross misconduct to a panel of two deputy directors, with Clarence Gale as the chairman/judge, and Harry Beddows allowed a lawyer from outside the Bureau to defend him.

Throughout, Beddows stared stonily ahead, never once looking across the room towards Powell, his accuser. Powell looked steadily at the other man, still finding it difficult to imagine everything Beddows – and Ann – had been prepared to do or tried to do. It went beyond deceit or cuckolding. They must, somehow, have come to hate him, which was absurd because he'd done nothing to either of them to earn or justify that hate.

The realization worried him. This wasn't the sequence he'd intended. He'd wanted to get the custody hearing over first, get Beth safely with him. Agonizingly he'd arrived back from London to a positive date – just three days from now – but that was still three days too long, too unpredictable, for her to go on living with them. The worst agony of all was having to accept there was nothing he could do about it.

There was a legal argument about the admissibility

of Powell's claim that Bureau funds had been mis-appropriated to relocate him to Washington when the purpose had been to reunite Beddows with his mistress but it achieved the objective of bringing the cause of Powell's marriage break-up before the tribunal.

There couldn't be any argument about the fact that Beddows had written unauthorized correspondence in the Director's name but the claim that Beddows had withheld from the Director information about the extradition procedure was disputed until a written memorandum was produced from the Attorney-General's office dated four days before Powell had flown to London, when Beddows had insisted to the Director there were still complications to be resolved to get Harold Taylor back to US jurisdiction.

Amy tried hard that night to reassure him that the postponement of the tribunal's decision prevented Beddows or Ann from taking their spite out against Beth. 'He won't do anything to make things worse. At the moment, officially, he's only suspended: still got a job.'

Beth didn't sound happy when he spoke to her by telephone, but when he posed a series of questions for yes or no answers she indicated that they weren't being too unpleasant. When Powell openly asked if they'd hit her – 'or anything like that' – Beth very positively said 'No.'

It would have helped if there had been more activity to fill the intervening days. Amy Halliday had been right about old newspapers being the primary source to support Harold Taylor's story. The accounts were reasearched from all over America by outside FBI offices and assembled and exchanged between Washington and London by Amy, leaving Powell with little to do but read them.

There were rare exceptions to newspapers. In the archives of the ship insurers Lloyd's of London was discovered the passenger manifest of the *Discovery*, a Harwich-registered brigantine. This proved that Paul Noakes, accompanied by his father George and mother Violet, sailed from Tilbury to Boston in June 1756. In London, over a period of a year before that, the *General Evening Post* and *Rayner's Penny Morning Advertiser* extensively reported six ritual murders of women, all around the St James's area and all of whose dismembered bodies had been displayed identically to those in the current investigation. Also reported was the mob sacking of a secret 'Devil's Disciples' temple in St James's and the killing, by burning to death, of 'an unnamed mystic Priest from the East'.

Rayner's talked of 'atrocities deeply foull' and described day and night church services at which the Reverend Jeremiah Norton-Smithie, 'a Priest of the Parish of St James's most anxiously exhorted a Populace much alarmed that protection could be found against the Devil unquestionably at large by praying most devoutly three times a day and by displaying the Cross of Christ most prominently in every room of their Dwellings. To omit a room, even the privy, risked leaving a door open to Evil.'

In the year following the *Discovery*'s arrival in America there were five matching ritual killings in Boston. In 1805, two years after the United States took possession of St Louis, the vigilante hanging was reported in the town's first news-sheet of Luke Thomas, for the killing of the ten-year-old daughter of an ostler at one of the three brothels Thomas owned. Bigger coverage had been devoted to eight unsolved ceremonial murders.

Maurice Barkworth's graduation, with honours, was recorded in the early annals of the San Francisco Medical College in 1824 and so was the enrolment of 'Maurice Barkworth, American' in the London College of Surgeons four years later. The archive of the London college also still contained a number of critically acclaimed papers written by Barkworth. Most were on his ophthalmic research into the possibility of retinal retention of their killers by victims of violent attack.

The Flanders field court-martial in 1916 of Patrick Arnold, for shooting in the back an officer who had ordered a frontal daylight attack upon German machine-gun emplacements, had survived more completely than those of Myron Nolan in Berlin, thirty-three years later.

On the day of the custody hearing Powell was at the court an hour earlier. Amy was with him.

As they waited Amy said, 'I know you've got a cast-iron case but it would still help if you were married, don't you think?'

He looked sideways at her, initially startled, then smiling. 'Is that a proposal?'

'I thought I should,' Amy smiled back. 'It was taking you far too long to get around to it.'

He said, 'I'd be honoured to accept', and they both burst out laughing, only stopping just before Ann and Beddows arrived with Beth.

Beth looked subdued, even when she saw them. Powell was immediately aware of the contrast between the svelte sophistication of Amy and Ann's thrown-together dowdiness. Harry Beddows refused to meet his look.

It was a closed child's court, the judge a plump-featured, grey-haired woman who ordered that Beth wait in an ante-room with a female court official.

315

Powell sat with a feeling of *déjà vu*, caught by the similarities with the FBI hearing, and wondered if Beddows was reminded too. Powell's counsel supported the application for the custody variation on the grounds of fitness by alleging that Ann was not interested in the child – quoting the mistake and abortion remark, her refusal as a qualified teacher to help with Beth's school work – and said she had conspired with her lover, Powell's work superior, to move from one side of the country to the other to continue an adulterous relationship unknown to the court at the time of the original order.

Ann's counsel attacked Powell's single-parent inability properly to care for a thirteen-year-old, with a job taking him not just all over America but all over the world, and Powell replied looking directly at Amy that he was shortly to be married, enjoying the effect upon Ann and Beddows.

It was the judge's decision, at the end of the hearing, to call Beth into court. The child entered nervously, looking to Powell for guidance, not Ann.

The judge had Beth sit beside her and said, 'You know what this is all about, don't you?'

'Yes. Who I'm going to live with.'

'Who would you like that to be?' asked the woman.

'Dad and Amy,' said Beth, at once.

The order granted Powell total custody, with an additional order for Ann's visitation to be decided by the court after the submission of specialist reports, in view of the woman's animosity evidenced during the hearing.

Hector McLeash formally asked the FBI for Wesley Powell, Barry Westmore, Geoffrey Sloane and Amy Halliday to travel to England for the trial, which was scheduled to start in the last week of the month. Powell arranged for Beth to go to summer camp.

Having a positive starting date allowed an entire fortnight of normality for Powell, Amy and Beth; and an oasis of delighted discovery that Powell and Amy were compatible in virtually everything, not just in bed. The French café in Georgetown became their favourite. They enjoyed the same music, spanning light opera and modern jazz, and took Beth to a concert featuring both at the Kennedy Center. The following weekend, the last full one they had, they overnighted in New York to see a Broadway production of a Cameron Mackintosh musical, which Amy declared to be their celebration at becoming a new family.

Powell didn't like violent crime movies and discovered Amy didn't, either. She wasn't offended when he accused her of getting on a popular bandwagon by claiming Hemingway to be overrated and he conceded that Steinbeck sometimes intellectually took too far his recurring theme of original sin. After Beth's overenthusiasm at their first meeting came a calmness, and the bond between Amy and the girl developed as easily and naturally as Amy's relationship had with him, neither of them pushing or trying too hard, just letting it happen. Homework help and shared kitchen duties were a standard part of life in the Crystal City apartment. Amy made Beth's first period ('welcome to womanhood!') something to be excited, not frightened about.

Two days before they flew to England Powell was summoned to the Director's office to meet Ross Kirkpatrick, the American government lawyer assigned to the already briefed English QC, Cedric Solomon, to make the formal extradition application after the British murder trial. It was a getting-to-know-each-other formality but Clarence Gale held him back after Kirk-patrick's departure. Abruptly the Director said, 'We found against Beddows.'

Powell waited.

'This case is going to cause a sensation. God knows how much.'

Powell still couldn't think of a response.

'Publicly to announce Beddows's dismissal would fuel it further. Risk embarrassing the Bureau. He's being allowed to resign, on health grounds.'

And keep his pension as a pay-off. Had Clarence Gale privately condoned the lie that Powell had been suspended? He'd never know, Powell accepted.

'It creates, of course, a division head vacancy,' said Gale. 'I'm offering it to you.'

His pay-off, Powell acknowledged. He said, 'Thank you, Mr Director. I am delighted to accept.'

Harold Taylor didn't want a defence as such, although he decided formally to engage a lawyer, determined against any court obstruction. What he needed was someone who was qualified but incapable, a puppet to his ventriloquism. He met – and rejected – four provably able QCs before he found Jonathan Fry, an obviously bumbling, ineffectual man who clearly sought the brief out of desperation and whom Taylor at once dominated.

'You should not have made that unfortunate state-ment without legal advice,' complained Fry, who constantly sifted through his disarrayed bundles of paper and never seemed to be able to find what he was looking for in them. 'It hasn't made my task any easier.'

'That's what I told him,' complained the instructing solicitor. Michael Joliffe stuttered, which made it diffi-cult for him to pronounce the Latin with which he

318

frequently interspersed his sentences to prove his legal ability, which was limited and was why Taylor had accepted him, too.

'It's my defence,' said Taylor.

'What is?' frowned Fry.

'The evidence is that Myron Nolan is the killer?'

'Yes,' said the barrister, doubtfully.

'And the evidence also is that Myron Nolan's dead. And dead men can't kill. I'm Harold Taylor, twenty-five years old. Not Myron Nolan, who'd be about eighty-three now. The police have got the wrong man.'

'But this reincarnation—'

'No-one's going to believe in reincarnation. It's ridiculous.'

'The Hibbses . . .'

'A sex game that the police burst in upon, between me and my fiancée.'

'But the old woman—'

'Kinky old bitch. You'll have to question Janet closely about that.'

'There is an alternative . . .'

'I do not have any mental illness,' blocked Taylor, almost impatiently. 'All the psychiatrists agree. You have to accept my instructions, don't you?'

'Yes,' agreed Fry.

'You've just had them. It's a not-guilty plea.'

My time to become the most famous person in the world, Taylor thought.

Chapter Twenty-eight

Hector McLeash stood but waited until the first stir of impatience from the judge before beginning: 'Some of the incontrovertible facts to be brought before you, ladies and gentlemen of the jury, may be bewildering in all but one respect – they prove beyond doubt that the man before you in the dock committed terrible murder.' Harold Taylor, at whom everyone looked, smiled back at them, lounged in his chair, the most relaxed man in the court.

Never in his wildest dreams could he have imagined everything working out so completely – so superbly – as this. Sensation after sensation and ever more to come, with him in total control, the ringmaster of his own spectacular circus with all the animals waiting to perform whatever tricks he chose. And he'd choose a lot.

More performing animals outside, too. The media's frenzied anticipation had approached such a crescendo in the days leading up to the trial that before McLeash had got to his feet the judge, Sir Alec Lockyer, had publicly warned newspapers, radio and television against contempt and forbidden the jury to read, listen to or watch any account of the trial until its end.

People would read, though. In detail greater – more staggering – than anything to emerge in evidence they were about to hear. He'd been amazed by the clamour from publishers not just from England and America but from France and Germany, too. Another opportunity. America would probably do it best and the offers from the five publishers there were all better than any from Europe. Six million dollars was the top so far but it would go much higher by the end of the trial. Double, maybe. He'd need a lot of money – as much as he could get – to set himself up as he had in Alabama in whatever new American penitentiary he was finally sent to. If indeed he bothered, with so much else available.

An American trial to follow this was another unexpected but fantastic bonus: after both – and the book – he really would be the most famous figure in the global village.

Already there were a lot of other letters apart from those from publishers. 'Messiah' was the most commonly used word. America again would be the place to form a cult – a religion – that would be the biggest personal joke of all: so many stupid people, eager to part with their money. And not just to be his disciples. There were more outright pleas from people desperate for the secret of reincarnation, offering whatever he demanded to be able to live for ever. He'd do it all, Taylor decided. Not just the most famous figure in the world; possibly its richest, as well. Literally its God. Fooling – and laughing at – everyone.

He began concentrating on his surroundings, wanting to remember it all, relish it all. Pity about there being no camera. The only disappointment. The English court would have looked good, a proper setting. The judge, a cadaverous, bespectacled man, bewigged and bird-plumed in scarlet and nested high upon an ornately carved bench covered by a crested canopy. Black-gowned, white-wigged counsel were before him, ravens to the judge's cock robin: Jonathan Fry, scrabbling as always for missing documents, McLeash, at that moment apologizing for the murder scene photographs being shown to the jury. That jury, all wide eyed with horror at the portfolios through which they were being led, eight women to four men who would be even more horrified when he performed his own trick. Powell, whom it had been so important to identify, was to the left of the chamber, obviously, from their whispered exchanges, with other Americans connected with the investigation there, three men and a woman, the woman very attractive, nice tits, full mouth, looking at him unafraid, curiously. Could fuck a woman like that, just as he could have fucked Janet Hibbs if she hadn't cheated him. Couldn't see Janet. Be outside somewhere, waiting to be called, with all the other witnesses. There were three artists by the press bench, sketching furiously. Get my good side, guys. The best way there would be to capture the scene inside the court, without a camera. Have to remember to clip the impressions from the newspapers. Read the accounts. Most of the reporters were taking notes as fast as the artists were drawing but some just stared at him. Word artists, he guessed . . . 'an ordinary, nondescript man . . . difficult to believe such horror, such atrocities . . . unbelievable stories of previous lives . . . returning from the dead . . . occult . . .' Wait for it, fellas: you ain't seen nuthin' yet.

'The scientific evidence I have outlined is precisely that, ladies and gentlemen of the jury,' McLeash was saying. 'Provable, unarguable, undeniable science. Nothing to do with fantasy, with ghosts or spirits or someone returning from a previous life. Yet those scientific facts provide the only explanation for the story you are about to hear. But Harold Taylor is not on trial

322

for returning from the dead. He is on trial for murder. And those same scientific facts conclusively prove that he is guilty of that terrible crime . . .' McLeash paused, theatrically. 'And now, ladies and gentlemen of the jury, I wish to read to you parts of a statement that the accused made, under caution, after his arrest for the further charge of kidnapping . . .'

None of them could possibly conceive the sensation this was going to cause, thought Powell, listening intently, gazing around the totally silent court. He thought already he could see the fear, the horror. They'd flown from Washington four days before the trial, using the time recovering from jetlag for daily legal discussions on the admissibility of FBI evidence into an England court not competent to try American crimes. In the evenings there'd been the predictable hospitality from Malcolm Townsend and Henry Basildon, as well as a cocktail reception given by the Metropolitan Police Commissioner and Surrey's Chief Constable. Powell had seen no reason why he and Amy shouldn't share a room and she'd seemed to expect it. Nor did either feel it necessary to explain to Westmore, Sloane or Jeri Lobonski. None of them appeared to want an explanation, anyway.

At the lunchtime adjournment that first day Amy announced: 'He doesn't frighten me. I expected that he would, when I saw him in the flesh for the first time, but he didn't, not even when he looks directly at me.'

'You're in the minority,' said Powell. 'Every woman on the jury is terrified. Two won't even look at him.'

'One thing I've never understood – although I'm glad for all sorts of reasons – is why Taylor would only talk when you were with Townsend and Basildon.'

'The simplest thing of all to understand,' intruded Sloane. 'He's the supreme control freak. What more absolute control could he exercise than getting someone to come three and half thousand miles when he demanded it?'

The drama ebbed and flowed over the succeeding early days but there was always more than sufficient to drive virtually every other event, in England or abroad, from news pages and airwaves. The insistence of a parade of photographic experts – the first incontrovertible scientific evidence – that the freeze frame faces, one unquestionably Taylor, were on the same body caused uproar both inside and outside the court, compounded by Fry's confused and failed cross-examination to get them to agree the opposite. That was overtaken the following day by the unarguable forensic matching of the dead Myron Nolan's fingerprints with those found at both current murder scenes, although Fry was more successful in getting the technicians, all of whom dismissed reincarnation as a possibility, to agree they didn't understand how it could be possible. The biggest headlines came on the Friday with DNA evidence, which McLeash produced as three samples labelled A, B and C. Four British scientists each swore that all were identical and could only have come from the same person.

'I seek the court's indulgence on an unusual request,' announced McLeash, as the last British forensic expert left the witness box. 'I do so to assist the court, for continuity, to try to keep as clear as possible in the jury's mind facts I have much earlier referred to as bewildering. And with the full agreement of my learned friend for the defence, I seek to call Wesley Powell, head of the FBI's

Violent Crime section, to testify upon just one point at this stage but on an understanding that I may recall him subsequently.'

'Mr Fry?'

Taylor's hapless lawyer was quickly on his feet, anxious for the first evidence he regarded as potentially useful. 'I support this application, My Lord, and will not oppose Mr Powell's recall at any time in the future.'

Powell had given evidence scores of times in scores of courts but had never felt as disorientated as he did mounting the steps to the unaccustomedly elevated witness box or taking the oath with which he was unfamiliar, although neither was the cause of his discomfort. When he looked across to the dock, which was at the same level as himself, he saw Taylor leaning intently forward, elbows on his knees, watching him. The man smiled and Powell only just avoided smiling back, burning with annoyance at the near stupidity. Perhaps, he thought, the disquiet he felt was because of the care he had to take to avoid influencing this trial by any direct mention of the American killings, preposterous though that caution seemed.

He agreed to McLeash's lead that he was familiar with the circumstances of a military tribunal in Berlin in August 1949, which had led to the jailing for life in America of Myron Nolan. Powell was aware of Taylor smiling fixedly at him, throughout.

'Where was Myron Nolan sent to serve his sentence?' asked the barrister.

'Florence, Alabama,' replied Powell.

'How much of that life sentence did Myron Nolan serve?'

'A little short of two years.'

'Why so short?'

'He was murdered in April 1951.'

'Are you aware of an exhumation of the grave of Myron Nolan in Florence, Alabama, on 30 May this year?'

'I am.'

'What was the purpose?'

'Scientifically to obtain hair and bone samples, to extract DNA.'

'Which was done?'

'Yes.'

'Did you subsequently make available to police here in Britain copies of the DNA string that was obtained, marked on the outer edge of the envelope for later identification with your FBI personnel number?'

'I did.'

Half turning to the jury – playing to the gallery and the assured headlines – McLeash said, 'I am now having handed to Mr Powell the DNA exhibit labelled C, previously identified as being the same as that found at the two murder scenes which are the subject of this trial . . .' Coming back to Powell, he said, 'Can you identify that envelope?'

'It's the DNA sample from the grave in Florence, Alabama, of Myron Nolan.'

Two small screams, maybe three, were audible over the general gasp that went around the court.

Fry was eagerly on his feet again, unusually prepared. Although he had no scientific expertise, qualified Powell at once, he understood it to be impossible by a calculation of several million to one for two people to carry completely matching DNA, unless they were identical twins. He further understood, however, that there could be similarities sufficient to prove family relationships.

'You have exhaustively investigated Myron Nolan, as far as you are able?'

'As far as the FBI was able,' expanded Powell.

'Was he married?'

'No.'

'Did you discover any evidence whatsoever of his having had children?'

'No.'

'But you don't know, for sure, that he did not have issue, do you?'

'No,' admitted Powell.

'Tell me!' demanded Fry, momentarily fulfilling his proper role, the papers before him undisturbed. 'How then do you explain the presence of Myron Nolan's DNA and Myron Nolan's fingerprints at the scenes where Beryl Simpkins and Samuel Hargreaves were murdered?'

It had to come, accepted Powell. 'I believe Harold Taylor to be the reincarnation of Myron Nolan.'

Once again astonishment silenced the court.

'You *believe*!' managed Fry.

'The evidence has convinced me,' admitted Powell. Taylor was smiling more openly than ever.

Fry was granted permission to recall the four forensic experts, all of whom confirmed the uniqueness of DNA and all of whom sceptically dismissed the concept of reincarnation but it was Powell's admission – and photograph – that dominated that day's coverage.

At their regular court cell conference later Fry nodded enthusiastically and said, 'We'd have to make it available to the prosecution, of course. Advise them in advance we're doing it.'

'Of course,' agreed Taylor. 'Totally wreck all their clever scientific stuff though, wouldn't it?'

327

Much later still, as they lay side by side exhausted by love, Powell said to Amy, 'Did I embarrass you?'

'Of course you didn't. I believe he's a reincarnation, too, although I don't want to. Are you embarrassed?'

'I was, by the television and evening papers. And probably will be when I see the coverage tomorrow.' He paused, uncomfortable with an admission. Then he said: 'You know what happened to me today?' He was glad of the darkness.

'What?'

'I think I was truly terrified, for the first time in my life.'

That weekend Powell and Amy played tourists. They went to Hampton Court by river and when Amy got off the boat she stumbled and went up to her ankles in the water, laughing that it would have never happened to Henry VIII, and walked with her sandals in her hand until they dried. He was recognized several times, as he had been that day with Beth by the Potomac marina, and twice asked for his autograph, which he avoided by saying it wasn't legally permitted. Amy accused him of being stuffy. Powell bought Beth a sweatshirt with a picture of the palace printed on the front and they got back to London in time for Amy to buy the girl three sets of underwear, which Powell said were too brief, to which Amy replied it was girls' stuff and that when they got back to Washington she'd have to think about getting Beth a training bra, because some of Beth's friends were already wearing them.

They ate alone that night, in a chosen-by-chance restaurant in Soho which wasn't as good as their Georgetown favourite, and Amy solemnly said, 'I'm going to be the best stepmother in the world to Beth.'

'I know you are,' said Powell, aware of her seriousness.

She didn't speak for several moments. Then she said: 'But we will have a baby of our own, won't we? I mean you do want to, don't you?'

'Of course I do!' assured Powell, seeing her need. Trying to lighten her mood he said, 'The amount of times we make love we couldn't avoid it if we wanted to!'

She laughed and said, 'Not immediately, I don't mean. In a year or two maybe, when . . .'

'When you've become an FBI star!' he anticipated. 'And next weekend we'll shop for you.'

Amy frowned. 'What do I need?'

'Aren't fiancées supposed to have engagement rings?' said Powell.

Chapter Twenty-nine

To a buzz of expectation from the court, Janet Hibbs gradually became visible as she mounted the rear steps of the box, the main, personally involved prosecution witness, and Taylor smiled, expectantly himself, and thought what a cheating bitch she was. Trying to look good, the vestal virgin. Tailored suit, hair immaculate, make-up perfect. Wouldn't last. Be a bigger stir than was going around the court at the moment when she had to tell everyone what happened. The whore was actually confronting him, taking the oath, turning slightly away from the judge and jury to look straight at him; even curling her lip, as if she wasn't afraid. Smile back at her: let her know what was going to come when Jonathan Fry put the questions Taylor had so carefully coached the idiot lawyer to ask, writing them out, numbering the sequence. The only problem, employing Fry, was getting the right questions asked, even written down. Weak as cats' piss. Couldn't hold a thought in his head. Didn't like the chin-tilted way the bitch was looking at him. Wished he could cross-examine her himself. Wipe that supercilious look off her face soon enough then. Cock-sucking cow. No room to be arrogant. All an act. Bad act at that. Sketch artists would probably glamorize her. Hope today they'd catch a better likeness of him than they had so far.

'I know how traumatic this will be for you,' McLeash was saying. 'I apologize in advance for the distress it will cause you.'

'I've suffered all the distress I'm ever likely to,' responded Janet.

Sanctimonious cunt. Still looking at him. Defiant. Not for much longer. Be distraught, crying, soon now. Not at the moment, though. Keeping up the pretence quite well, following the lawyer's lead. Thinking she was impressing everybody, staring him out – trying to stare him out except he wouldn't look away – as she answered. Go on smiling at her, waiting. Cheap shot, calling him Jekyll and Hyde. Rehearsed that. Reading too many newspapers. Got a lot of reaction from where the media were. Bitch.

'Insane?' queried McLeash, picking up on a reply to one of his questions. 'You mean he was raving, making no sense?'

'He wasn't raving but he made no sense. He said he had to punish us, my mother and me, for what my father did to him, in 1949.'

'Did to *him*, not somebody else? A relative, perhaps?'

'To him,' insisted Janet. 'He called my father a bastard and said we had to suffer for what he'd done, at a military trial. He said our blood had to water – cultivate – his new life.'

Taylor broke away from Janet's gaze, nodding in satisfaction at the fresh gasps that went around the court. Hadn't stared him out. He had an audience to respond to. Important they understood about the sacrifices. Tell them again when his time came.

'Your blood had to water – cultivate – his new life?' echoed McLeash.

'Those were his words.'

'What did you think he meant by that?'

'That he was going to kill us. He had a knife with a very thin blade, almost like a needle. And a bag, a satchel thing. He had a medical knife in there, a scalpel.'

Good that she hadn't collapsed yet. Needed to be explained like this, as it had happened. Hadn't expected her to be able to sustain it. Probably got something, pills, from a doctor. Need a lot more help before this was over. She'd be a laughing stock. A joke. Gave a blowjob to a dead man. Not one dead man: five dead men.

'Which he used to cut some of your clothes off, when he rendered you naked?'

'Yes,' said Janet, her voice unwavering.

'Was he naked?'

'He undressed first, after he'd tied us up.'

This is it! Coming to the part he wanted. See how long she could last out: keep up the act. McLeash wasn't comfortable; he hesitated.

'He did something else, didn't he . . . ? Something to his appearance?'

'He made his face change completely, from one person to another.'

Not what he'd expected, but it didn't matter. This was just as good. Judge was having to shout for quiet. Everyone looking at him, not able to believe it. Should he do it now? Very good at it now. Not difficult to be Myron Nolan but he hadn't been able to go back to anyone else. He wanted very much to do it now but it was too soon. Had to get the timing exactly right, when everyone was only listening to *him*, only watching him. Good enough that McLeash was offering the freeze frames.

'Do you recognize the face, from these pictures?'

'He *became* the older person.'

The whore was doing brilliantly! So much noise now – he could actually hear shouts of 'no!', giggles of disbelief, nervous laughter – that the judge couldn't make himself heard. Being ignored anyway. Smile and nod, let her know how well she was doing. McLeash having to shout, to ask the next question.

'What did he say, when he did that?'

'He'd gone through my mother's private things, found some old letters of my father's. One he said was about him. My father had referred to an inhuman monster. He said that's what he was, an inhuman monster. That he was going to prove it by sacrificing us. Me first, while my mother watched.'

More noise, much more noise, uproar, the judge going berserk, hammering the bench. No control. Not like *he* had control. Nod to let everyone know that's exactly how it had been. Take the credit.

'Your mother died, didn't she?'

'Of a heart attack. But he killed her.'

Not as I should have done but it was good enough. Got him here. Making him famous. No! What the fuck was McLeash doing, thanking her, sitting down. What about the blowjob? What he was going to make the old lady do and how Janet had pleaded, wanting to do it herself! Taylor twitched, pulling up from his seat, but held himself back. Jonathan Fry was rising, shuffling through his papers, dropping some. The prompt sheet! He could see his prompt sheet. Get it right, asshole. All you've got to do is read the question. Train a monkey to do that.

'That wasn't how it was at all, was it, Miss Hibbs?'

Not what they'd rehearsed! Improvising. Not clever

enough for that. Go back to your script, asshole.

'That was exactly how it was.'

'You were in love with him, weren't you?'

Better!

'Yes.'

'Thought you were going to marry him?'

Reading from the questions: even managing the derisive intonation. OK now.

'Yes.'

'You considered yourself engaged?'

Exactly right. No hurry. Build up to the denouement.

'Yes I did.'

'Told your mother? Had champagne to celebrate, when you brought her home from the hospital?'

The whore had shuddered, remembering! The first sign. Face looked redder, too. Any minute now. Smile at her, make her aware he knew what was coming. Glad she was looking directly at him. Wanted to see her face when she broke down.

'Yes, we did.'

'You claim he tied you and your mother up against your will?'

Frowning now, not properly understanding. Perfect.

'That's what he did do.'

'You didn't agree to what he was doing? Your mother didn't agree?'

Incredulous. Open mouthed. Not so assured, not any more.

'Agree!! Don't be absurd. Why – how – would we possibly have agreed!'

'You're a fit woman. Why didn't you resist, tell him to stop?'

He hadn't had any cause to worry. Jonathan Fry had been the right choice.

334

'He tricked me.'

Almost there. He'd correctly anticipated every answer.

'Tricked you! How did he trick you?'

All she had to do was tell the truth, which he knew she would.

'Told me to close my eyes. Hold my arms out, palms together.'

She sounded so stupid! Confirming it!

'Hold your arms out, palms together! It was a game, wasn't it? A bondage sex game you were quite happy – eager – to play but which the police broke in, to interrupt . . . ?'

Of all the reactions so far, that caused the biggest pandemonium. It came from the public gallery and the media, and McLeash was on his feet, unnecessarily protesting because Lockyer was already shouting to be heard above the noise, not to quell it, but to Jonathan Fry. The only person, apart from Taylor, to remain quiet and unmoving was Janet Hibbs. She stood frozen, her face, which had begun to crumple, set firm again.

'Mr Fry!' the judge managed at last, still having to shout. 'Unless you can justify this line of questioning to my total satisfaction I am going to take a very serious view!'

'I believe I can, My Lord,' said Fry, although hesitantly. 'I would ask the court's forbearance for just a few more minutes.'

'Take care, Mr Fry,' warned the judge. 'Take the very greatest care not to fall into an abyss of your own making.'

'You had every reason to believe you were going to marry Mr Taylor, didn't you?' persisted Fry.

'I have already told you that.'

'So you'd slept together, hadn't you? Had sexual relations?'

Janet Hibbs laughed loudly, apparently genuinely, not once but several times, extending her arm to point across the court but crooking her index finger limply. 'We occupied the same bed, yes. But he couldn't do it! He's impotent! A sad, little impotent man . . .'

'*No!*' roared Taylor, on his feet, clutching the dock rail, pulling at it in his fury. 'Her fault! She blew—'

'Look!' jeered Janet, shouting over him, limp finger still extended. 'Poor little impotent. Two heads but no penis . . .'

Taylor had no awareness of trying to climb over the dock rail to get to her until he felt the hands upon him, pulling him back and because he was unbalanced he fell and the two warders came down with him, on top of him and then there were others in the dock, police, and one put handcuffs on him. He couldn't see the court any more, just a line of faces raptly gazing over the edge of the high public gallery – and then Fry at the dock rail – but he heard the judge, already hoarse, shouting, 'Take him down, take him down!' and realized the worst thing of all. She'd made him lose control: cheated him again.

As they filed from the hastily adjourned court Amy said, 'Nothing could compensate for what she went through. But as revenge that was pretty effective: certainly put the hot poker up his ass.'

'Her big fear was being humiliated,' remembered Powell.

'She wasn't. He was,' said Amy.

It was obvious from his strutted re-entry into the dock that Taylor still felt so, too. It was heightened by the judge's immediate warning that if there was a repetition of his outburst Taylor would be sent permanently to the cells and the case continued in his absence. That was just as quickly followed by the judge's refusal to allow Janet Hibbs to be recalled for further cross-examination after Fry – the jury removed for the legal argument – set out his intended line of questioning, which the judge instantly rejected as unnecessary and salacious prattle contributing nothing to Taylor's defence.

The hearing developed a familiar, murder trial pattern. Further to spare the embarrassment of an already relieved Janet Hibbs, McLeash tightly led Jeri Lobonski and the British squad through their evidence of arrest, extracting what was necessary for his case but nothing more. He rehearsed Amy about admissibility, which she studiously observed but there was still enough to show it was Amy who'd located Taylor from three and half thousand miles away and led police to him in time to prevent Janet Hibbs's murder. Amy dominated that day's coverage with huge photographs and headlines such as COMPUTER SUPERCOP and MISS MISSION IMPOSSIBLE. The next day Powell followed Basildon and Townsend into the witness box formally to produce, in full for the first time, Taylor's statement. It was carried, verbatim, in virtually every newspaper.

To each man McLeash put the same question: 'As far as you have been able to ascertain, are the facts and the details the accused gave you about the five men he claims once to have been all totally accurate?'

And Powell, Townsend and Basildon each replied, 'Yes.'

'Tomorrow,' promised McLeash at the conclusion of that day's hearing, 'I will be calling the first of my expert religious witnesses on the subject of reincarnation.'

337

And taking my place in all the legal textbooks of the English-speaking world, he thought.

In his remand cell Harold Taylor meticulously added to his already bulging newspaper files. One was devoted entirely to the names and identification of every person who had given evidence against him.

Chapter Thirty

The court was so satiated with surprise that Ian Conway's request to affirm rather than swear an oath upon the Bible caused scarcely a ripple. It took the professor of religious philosophy, a neatly bearded man in roll-necked sweater and jeans pressed with a centre leg crease, almost five minutes to recite qualifications that included English and American philosophy doctorates, both with distinction, two periods occupying visiting chairs at American universities and authorship of ten books, three acclaimed as definitive studies of religious mysticism.

All Hector McLeash's early doubts about taking the case had long ago been washed away on the tidal wave of publicity and in anticipation of this precise moment – presenting Conway's evidence as the *coup de grâce*, the first and best of the expert witnesses whom no-one yet knew were going to make the unbelievable believable, reality unreal. McLeash was actually shaking with expectation, fortunately only slightly, as he stood waiting for the religious philosopher to undertake to tell only the truth.

'You are acknowledged, are you not, Dr Conway, as England's foremost authority upon worldwide religion, both ancient and modern?'

'In Europe,' expanded the man, didactically. 'I am also called upon frequently for my opinion and knowledge in the United States.' He had a mellifluous voice tinged with just the slightest trace of an Irish accent and talked looking directly at Harold Taylor, although not defiantly like Janet Hibbs but as a scientist or anthropologist approaching a previously unknown species.

'Then the court is indeed fortunate to have the benefit of your vast experience,' the barrister flattered him. Prepared for the affirmation, McLeash said: 'You don't believe in God?'

'I believe in a Supremeness.'

McLeash supposed he had to go along with it but he didn't want to be sucked down into a swamp of esoteric philosophy. 'Could you explain what you mean by that?'

'Paradoxically though it may seem, placing the two concepts side by side, all religion developed from ancient paganism, which became the mysticism of shamen,' said Conway, with a coherence drawn from a hundred lectures. 'All religions, whatever their title, share common paths. One of those original, most vital, paths was introspection: finding oneself. A belief – a god, if you like – does not have a physical shape or image. It lives within each person, belonging individually to each person. Needing an object to look at and pray to – like believing Heaven is among the clouds in the sky and Hell in the furnace of the earth – brings everything full circle, back to paganism.'

The verbal treatise was understandable enough but McLeash decided that was prescisely what it was: enough. He had headlines to provide, not ideology. 'Do you believe in reincarnation?'

'There is persuasive evidence of it. For obvious reasons it is a basic tenet of every major religion in the world.'

'What's the persuasive evidence?'

'The overwhelming number of people, of every creed and culture, with recollections of previous existences, sometimes going back thousands of years: Egyptian times, ancient Rome. It's particularly convincing with claimants who undergo regressive hypnosis.'

Taylor was nodding, with approving condescension.

'The reason for the belief being held by major religions isn't obvious to me.'

Conway smiled. 'Believing it's possible to be reborn takes away the fear of death, doesn't it?'

The movement – today's revelation – in the court was at the sudden awareness that what until now had largely been presented as supernatural – which meant it couldn't be true or real and that no-one therefore needed really to be frightened – was being calmly discussed as an accepted fact by an academic holding every achievable philosophical credential and honour. And shouldn't be nervously laughed at as absurd after all.

Powell leaned close to Amy and said, 'Why have we all been too scared to admit it?'

'I wasn't,' she said. 'It was all you macho guys.'

'Still not scared of him yourself?'

'Not of him. I'm beginning to wonder where this is all going to end and I don't mean this or any other trial. I know now why he wanted to see you before he made a statement; what he meant by seeing your face.'

'Identify for the court the religions that believe in reincarnation of some sort or another,' McLeash was saying.

Conway's recitation was immediate and almost casual, another well-remembered tract from countless lectures. 'Everyone who believes has a religion, sometimes only their own. But all the major religions of the

341

world accept reincarnation – Hindu, Buddhist, Zen, Tao, Jewish Cabbalists, the early Christian Gnostics and Cathars, the Islamic Sufi. Members of an ancient Hindu religion sweep the ground in front of them as they walk, to prevent stepping on a reincarnation in the lowest insect. Both Buddhists and Hindus believe that karma is created around everyone by their actions in mortal life: cause and effect, if you like. For every good act, a person gets good fortune; misfortune for every bad act. The Hindu believes we repeatedly reincarnate into a human body the experience the karma built up in previous lives. The Druze Arabs of the Lebanon – a breakaway Muslim sect – unquestioningly accept the arrival of children, complete strangers, identifying themselves as reincarnations of dead relatives. Their present biological parents surrender them, sometimes to return to their previous environments.'

'You have been in court to listen to the evidence of this trial so far?'

'Yes.'

'And heard read out the statement made by the accused, claiming to have reincarnated at least five times?'

'Yes.'

'Do you find that preposterous, the raving of someone suffering mental delusions?'

'Not at all. My only surprise is the apparent total recall, of every existence. I have never before encountered or discovered any evidence of such perfect memory, not even under regressive hypnosis.'

'But you are not saying you consider it impossible?'

'No. Just that I've no previous knowledge of its manifestation.'

'In his statement the accused talked of being promised

342

eternal life by a teacher named Tzu. Does that have any significance to you?'

'It's a Chinese word, meaning "master". The founder of the Taoist religion was Lao-tzu, which means "Old Master". He was born in 604 BC and is known to have led a mortal life. He was the court librarian of the Chou state of China and a contemporary of the Buddha and Confucius. There is also accepted teaching within the Taoist faith of a great falling out between Lao-tzu and his foremost disciple, who it was claimed was using the teachings and rituals of their religion for evil, not good.'

'It sounds remarkably like the Western religious parables of the battle between God and Satan?' suggested McLeash.

'I think it is a parallel rather than a parable,' agreed Conway.

Taylor was smiling and nodding vigorously, gazing around the court as if something was being proved.

'Have you ever heard before of someone claiming to be reincarnated provably having the same fingerprints, handwriting, blood group, DNA or facial characteristics of someone they were in a previous existence?' *Were*, realized McLeash. He was accepting rebirth as a fact. He guessed a lot of others were, too. Or would, after today.

'Not altogether, in a single reincarnation.'

McLeash had been looking down at his notes, methodically working his way through his list of prepared questions. Abruptly he looked up. 'Was that a qualified answer, Dr Conway?'

'There have been suggestions of handwriting becoming the same in the case of possession. I know of no other occasions when it's been forensically possible to make DNA or fingerprint comparisons, as it has been here.'

The groundswell of incredulous noise was heaving again, bringing the judge's head up sharply, although he didn't call for quiet.

He'd never again have such high-profile exposure, McLeash recognized: already, on the strength of this case, he'd been offered four lucrative briefs. He had to risk the irritation of Mr Justice Lockyer – who at the moment didn't look irritated anyway – to milk this milch cow of every last drop. 'Possession?' he queried, seemingly unsure.

'The occupying of a person by the spirit of another,' supplied Conway, patiently. This was his most public exposure, too, and he wasn't in any hurry to leave the stage.

'How does orthodox, established religion regard possession, Dr Conway?' asked the barrister. 'Occult nonsense, to be derided? Or something to be taken as seriously as, from what you've already told us, re-incarnation is viewed?'

'The Christian church – Protestant as well as Catholic – believes it is possible for a person to become physically possessed by a spirit, good or evil,' said Conway. 'Both churches have prescribed religious ceremonies of exorcism in the case of evil possession. The Catholic Church actually has priests who specialize in exorcism.'

McLeash caught the first shift of impatience from the judge. Quickly going back to his prepared list, he said: 'In the recorded cases of reincarnation, have you ever before heard of or accept to have been proven a reincarnated person transmogrifying at will, to assume the features of the person they were in a previous existence?'

'No I have not.'

'Do you believe it to be possible?'

344

'Not unless I personally witnessed it. Or saw convincing photographic evidence.'

Yet again McLeash produced the freeze frames. 'Would you consider that convincing photographic evidence?'

'They would appear to be. I cannot explain them.'

'So your expert testimony, to this court, is that all major religions accept that reincarnation – rebirth after a previous death – is possible? Just as it is possible for a person to become possessed with evil?'

'Yes,' said Conway. 'That is the established position and teaching of many churches.'

The question came unprompted to McLeash and he was glad. 'What about one becoming confused by the other? Have you ever learned of a person believing themselves reincarnated who was, in fact, possessed? Or of someone who was possessed being reincarnated?'

'No,' admitted Conway. 'But if we accept – as established religions accept – that both manifestations are possible then I do not see why there should not be an interchange, one for the other.'

'Have you ever heard of such a thing?'

'No.'

'Would it surprise you, if you did?'

'No.'

'Do you believe in ghosts, Dr Conway?'

'Not those who wear bedsheets and go "whoo" in the night,' smiled the philosopher. 'I can accept the survival of a spirit, at the end of a mortal life.'

The two religious witnesses who followed were a bishop named William Stevenson recognizable from frequent television appearances and newspaper contributions on Church of England doctrine and Monsignor

Patrick Shere, the English authority on Roman Catholic dogma.

Both men confirmed the belief of their respective creeds in reincarnation and possession. Monsignor Shere graphically described attending a service of exorcism to free a devout priest, psychiatrically found to be suffering no mental illness, of a spirit under whose possession he'd attacked and physically injured fellow priests at a retreat. Bishop Stevenson almost indignantly insisted that evidence of reincarnation would neither be anti-religious nor would it contradict any Christian teaching.

'It would be proof of the existence of God,' he said.

The latter part of the week was occupied by the evidence of three psychiatrists, all of whom were adamant that Harold Taylor did not suffer delusion and showed no evidence, psychiatrically or clinically, of brain or mental abnormality. One, German-born Gerhard Pohl, had taken Taylor back through each of his five previous lives under the regressive hypnosis described by Ian Conway. Taylor had not deviated in any detail or fact from the accounts he had given in his statement.

'Do you believe he was each of these men, in a previous life?' asked McLeash.

'Yes,' said Pohl, at once.

Another psychiatrist, Robert Porter, said: 'He implicitly believes the need for sacrifice, the shedding of human blood, to be necessary for his repeated and continued existences. But he knows at all times what he's doing. He's responsible for his actions.'

Porter's evidence concluded the prosecution conveniently on the Friday afternoon. That evening Taylor released the tension created by holding himself back from interrupting the psychiatrists by concentrating upon his newspaper files, taking particular care to add the reports of the psychiatrists.

On the Saturday, Powell bought Amy her engagement ring, a diamond flanked by emeralds. That night they telephoned Beth, by arrangement, at the summer camp. She'd got hives from some poison ivy but was all right now and was hesitant when Powell said he didn't think they'd be in England as long as he'd first expected.

'That means I don't get to come to London.'

'Maybe we'll bring you back on our honeymoon,' said Powell.

On the Sunday the American group was introduced by Ross Kirkpatrick to Cedric Solomon, the English barrister who would make the extradition application. Solomon was a large, fleshy man who liked a quick profit from briefs for which he could command the highest fees, and the case of Harold Taylor qualified on all his criteria.

'Don't imagine the slightest problem,' he said, after reviewing the evidence. 'Practically a formality.'

'That makes a change,' said Powell.

Chapter Thirty-one

The excitement of anticipation was phenomenal. Orgasmic. Better than orgasmic: better than any killing, any woman. Every eye upon him, the absolute focus of every attention. Total silence. Everyone waiting. Watching. Listening. Could see the public gallery for the first time, from the witness box. Packed. People crushed together on the benches, standing shoulder to shoulder entirely along the furthest back wall. Not a single unoccupied seat in the court and more people standing there, too. No-one wanting to miss it. Miss anything. I was there! Saw him! Close enough to touch him, the man who'd died and was born again, died and was born again and again and again. Moment in history. Fantastic.

Taylor affirmed, playing their stupid rules. But he would tell the truth. The truth was what he wanted to tell. The whole truth and nothing but the truth. He'd rehearsed Jonathan Fry not just that morning but on the Sunday night to get it all right. Every question, every follow-up. It didn't, in fact, matter if Fry lost his place, dropped the questions list. He didn't need to answer any specific questions. Just follow their stupid rules, to get his place on the stage.

Here now, he thought. Everyone straining to look at

him. Say what he wanted, irrespective of Fry's groping, stumbling prompt. Rehearsal time for himself. Rehearsal for what was going to follow in America. Cameras on him then. His face – as many other faces as possible – constantly filling the screen. Nothing like it, before or since. World audience, already primed from today. Waiting.

He felt very confident. Everything clear in mind. Ready. Had done it twice that morning, after Fry had left the cell. Taylor to Nolan, Nolan to Taylor. Like a juggling act: now you see me, now you don't. Try very hard to go back further, for America. As far as he could. Have his disciples – his congregation – by then. Kneeling, praying, standing on their heads if he told them to. That would be amusing, seeing the totally absurd things he could make them do. Make them call him Tzu. Master of millions. Stand on your heads. Stand on one leg. Put your finger up your ass. Tongue up the ass of the person next to you. Only wear red on Wednesdays, blue on Thursdays, nothing on Fridays.

Important to concentrate on Jonathan Fry, who sincerely believed the remand cell briefings had been his idea, his preparation. Delighted to take the court back to the beginning, London of the 1750s. Very dirty. Lot of smells. Never liked the smells. Lot of people living in the streets, although he hadn't had to. Bedroom of his own. Shoes to wear. Extra pair for Sundays. Always church on Sundays, prayers in the morning, prayers in the afternoon, prayers in the evening. Thank you God, for Your generosity and goodness. Forgive those that trespass against us. Stupid to forgive people who did you harm. Hurt them worse. Tzu taught him that. Enjoyed hurting people. Seeing the fear. Seeing the blood. Tzu liked it too. Allowed him to. Lots of bunters to choose from. Lift their skirts, open their mouths. Traitors in the temple, though. Informed the militia, hue and cry, lucky not to be in the temple when the mob attacked, beating, burning. They'd have found him, in time: hanged him and burned his body if his parents hadn't got passage on the *Discovery*. To save themselves, though. They'd burned him to death in the locked shack when he'd started the killings, in Boston. Mary Murphy the first, a seventeen-year-old Irish whore. Jeremiah Bates, potboy at the Blue Anchor on Beacon Street. Jane O'Hare, daughter of the haberdashery store owner who'd befriended his father and given him a job, on her way home from the church where she'd planned her wedding. Killed his parents the same way when he'd come back, as Luke Thomas. After dismembering them – sacrificing them – he'd burned them in the draper shop they'd opened in Plymouth, Massachusetts, before setting off West.

Not a sound, not a movement, in the court. They were engrossed, worshipping. How long would it take for the book offers to double, treble? Wouldn't employ a lawyer or an agent, after what James Durham had done. Easy to handle everything himself. Promote himself. Give interviews in prison. Present the book as his Bible. Anyone who believed in him – wanted to learn from him – would have to buy the book. Save the biggest sensation for the book. Promise the worshippers that he, their Messiah, would never again be away for as long as it had until now taken him to reincarnate. He'd return at once from now on, possessing whomever he wanted, doing whatever he wanted. No-one could stop him. Never had been able to.

He heard Jonathan Fry, obedient to his script, refer to St Louis and picked up the continuity. Scout for the

wagon train, to give himself the freedom. Killed an entire
family one night, not part of the train but trying to travel
literally in its wake, for protection from marauding
Apache and Sioux. Killed three Iroquois – two women
and a child – in a village he'd come upon by accident.
Got the wagons attacked in revenge but they'd fought
them off. Killed four more during the raid. Like St Louis.
Set up his first brothel in a tent, two more within a year.
The fourth was the first in a proper building. Personally
tested each of the whores before they started, before they
became diseased. Hadn't meant to kill the ostler's child.
Hadn't intended sexually to touch her but she'd thought
he had and started to scream and he'd had to stop her.
His neck hadn't been broken by the lynching noose, so
he'd strangled to death. Killed everyone who'd been
involved, when he'd returned as Maurice Barkworth,
even the whore who'd discovered the child and led the
mob to him. By the time he'd found her she'd been
running a brothel of her own in San Francisco, where he
enrolled at the newly established medical college from
which it only took him three years to graduate.

Good to get back to London in 1829. Same year as
William Burke and William Hare were found guilty
in Edinburgh of suffocating to death fifteen people to
sell for medical dissection. Easy to get bodies for experimentation in those days. Resurrection Men robbed
graves, taking the corpses naked, which was only a
misdemeanour, not the felony it would have been to steal
the burial shroud as well. Killed some of his own, of
course. Trying to confirm the theory that the victims
of violent attack died with the image of their killer
imprinted on their retinae. Lionized for that opinion –
and for his ophthalmic ability – for a long time until the
ridicule of other eye surgeons drove him to suicide, too

impatient to wait for a natural death from which he could return and start all over again.

They'd all died when he came back as Patrick Arnold, at the beginning of the century. The police would never have got him but it was easy to disappear anyway, answering Kitchener's call that his country needed him. Time for legalized murder. Reconnaissance corporal, a scout again as he had been on the wagon train, this time working for various units all along the Western Front, from Nieuwpoort in Belgium to Ypres and Arras and Albert and Soissons in France. Sometimes put the German heads on the marker poles that designated the hard ground beneath the constant, sucking mud. Stupid lieutenant, all of 19, deserved the bullet Arnold put into his idiot back for ordering the charge into the certain death of the German machine-gun emplacements they wouldn't believe existed, despite his insistence that they did.

The Army was literally an escape for Myron Nolan – from an ever enclosing NYPD and Port Authority investigation into the Gambino family source of the most lucratively loaded delivery trucks leaving New York harbour – but he had joined in 1940 never intending it to be a lifelong career, just a place to hide. It was only when he got there that he recognized its incredible potential. By the time America entered the conflict – and Lucky Luciano imposed a Mafia clampdown on waterfront war supply pilfering in exchange for jail parole – he'd been a master sergeant and an even greater master in the art of black market manipulation of every saleable, bribable, usable and influence-peddling commodity in the US Army. He'd travelled and killed all the way across Europe with Patton's Third Army and found real gold at the rainbow's end in Berlin. With so many opportunities he'd arranged a permanent transfer to the military support staff of Berlin's post-war Four Power Control Commission and was a cash-rich dollar millionaire, with more than another million dollars' worth of gold, antiques and art carefully stored in New York safe deposit facilities, when he bought the contaminated penicillin and streptomycin from Samuel Hargreaves.

'He identified Myron Nolan to the military police within five minutes of being questioned,' testified Taylor. 'So he had to die, obviously.'

He easily followed Fry's lead, avoiding references to the American killings with which he hadn't been charged, although not to conform – not to surrender control to the court or to Fry – but because it was important to have something new for the American trial. Destroy James Durham there, too. Expose the unctuous asshole as the thief he'd always been. Although they'd been circumspect – the woman particularly – it was obvious from what Powell and Amy Halliday had told the court that Durham had co-operated: led them to him. Had to be punished for that. Always essential to punish those that trespass against him.

The highest book offer increased to $9 million as a result of that day's hearing and reached $11 million by the end of the second day. Prayer meetings had already started outside the remand prison. He could hear their day and night chants, from his cell. In a lot of churches, as many as a hundred according to some estimates, vicars and priests were conducting special weekday services, most supporting the doctrinal opinion of Bishop Stevenson and Monsignor Shere. A minority didn't, talking of heresy and the Devil and the occult. Taylor watched the jail perimeter prayer meetings and some of the church services on his television, and what wasn't

353

televised was extensively reported in newspapers. All the time he carefully cultivated the hysteria from the witness box, drip-feeding the impression of something awesome – miraculous – still to come.

On the third day Hector McLeash rose to cross-examine. My ultimate moment, thought the barrister. Harold Taylor was thinking exactly the same.

'You have no conventional faith?'

'No,' said Taylor. Useful question, for the following he intended to create in the future.

'Do you believe in the Devil?'

Even better. 'No.'

'In whom did your teacher, Tzu, believe?'

'Himself.'

'So you believe in him?'

This really was very good: he could scarcely have done better if he'd written the questions himself. 'Utterly.'

'And you believe in reincarnation?'

'Of course. I am proof of it.' Not yet. Too soon yet.

'And possession?'

'Yes.'

'Beliefs of established religions.' asserted McLeash.

Shit! The son-of-a-bitch had caught him there. 'I accept what happens to me. It's the rest of you who seem to have the problem, although after this trial you won't have.'

'Tell us what happened to you.'

'Tzu was my teacher.'

'Who was the disciple who fell out with the founder of Taoism, Lao-tzu, for perverting the rituals and the creed?'

'Yes.'

'Are you saying that a man born six centuries before

354

the birth of Christ was the man burned to death in the eighteenth century, in London?'

'Yes.'

'Why didn't he return yet again?'

'He was too tired. It was time for him to go.'

'He taught you how to return?'

'He is always there, when I leave my mortal body.'

'What happens?'

Taylor could *feel* the tension. 'He asks me.'

'What?'

' "Do you want to live again?" '

'Then?'

'I say yes.'

'Then?'

'There is the creed – *Water – cultivate – every existence with the blood of others.*'

'Is Tzu your God?'

'He has enlightened me.'

'Have you ever possessed anyone, instead of re-incarnating?'

He had to get more control of the questioning, lead it in the direction he wanted. 'Not yet.'

McLeash's head came up, at the reply. 'You mean you could!'

'Of course.' The next experiment, he decided. Impose himself: project himself. Occupy. He was sure he could do it. A will weaker than his own, that's all he needed, according to the teaching. But there was a danger in choice, which was why he'd so far avoided it: encounter a stronger will, fail, and he couldn't return again. But what risk? Whose will – determination was stronger than his?

'Who do you believe yourself to be at the moment? Harold Taylor? Or Myron Nolan?'

The clever bastard had guessed! Use it then. Make this the moment. 'I have the physical body of Harold Taylor.'

McLeash nodded. 'But revenging the ills and injuries committed against Myron Nolan?'

'Yes.'

'So the body of Harold Taylor is merely the vehicle for a dead man's reincarnation? As Myron Nolan was for Patrick Arnold?'

'Absolutely. I'm glad you understand.'

'Who then is responsible for the murder of Beryl Simpkins and Samuel Hargreaves?'

'Myron Nolan.'

'Why Beryl Simpkins? She didn't harm Myron Nolan.'

Wouldn't say that apart from killing he could only get satisfaction from a dirty whore. 'I needed a woman. Fun. She died seeing something no-one else ever had before: a man change his face as she watched.'

McLeash didn't pick up on the remark. Instead he said, 'Myron Nolan is dead. That's why you've pleaded not guilty, isn't it? You want the court – the jury – to find that a dead man cannot commit a crime!'

'What other conclusion can they come to?' Almost there! Just seconds away.

'That Harold Taylor, the man standing before them and who has admitted the murders, is the man who committed them.'

'*Who* is standing before this court?' questioned Taylor. And then he did it. At last. With every eye breathlessly upon him he transmogrified, to become Myron Nolan. And stood there, a dead man.

The first scream came from the gallery, a screech of terror that was picked up, once, twice, three times. There was a deeper groan, a lot of voices, sounds, of disbelief: of people not wanting to believe, not wanting to be confused. A black woman juror in the front, then another in the second row, slumped forward in a faint. The most visible reaction throughout the court, seeming to spread out from the barristers and their juniors through their instructing solicitors and reaching up to the judge and his court officials, was physical recoil: everyone wanting to get away, put space between themselves and him.

He said, 'I'm the person who killed them. And I'm Myron Nolan, not Harold Taylor.' The American accent – the Bronx accent, hard, nasal – was very pronounced.

Uproar – panic and chaos – instantly followed. It was worse in the public gallery. The screaming hysteria caught, like fire in a wind, and there was a rush for the single, inadequate door which blocked at once. People fell and were trodden upon, crushed uncaringly by those behind fighting and clawing to get out. Police and court officials trying to get to the upstairs brawl became embroiled in stampeding media, neither deferring to the other, and there were more falls, more trampling. The judge hammered and shouted for calm and was ignored, although he managed to tell his clerk to tell McLeash and Fry and anyone else who could hear that the court was adjourned and that there would be a pre-trial conference the following day.

The American group didn't move – couldn't have moved if they'd tried – trapped just to the side of the witness box where the man with the face and head of Myron Nolan stood gazing down with total, smiling satisfaction – orgasmic again – at the bedlam he had caused.

'That isn't the proof of any religion,' said Amy,

broken voiced. 'That's total, obscene evil. He *is* a monster.'

'But we've stopped him,' said Powell, equally close to being overcome. 'He can't do any more harm.'

Ross Kirkpatrick, the American lawyer entrusted with gaining Taylor's extradition, said, 'He can. More people are going to flock to him than to any of the deities we've been lectured about. And his creed demands blood sacrifice.' He shuddered. 'We've opened Pandora's Box and released every evil that was waiting to be set free.'

'Hope remained,' said Amy, remembering the Greek legend.

'Not here it doesn't,' insisted the American laywer. 'I wanted to be part of this but I don't any more. I'm scared. Scared to hell.' He paused. 'Which is where all this is coming from.'

They worked late into the night at the embassy, relaying to Washington the verbatim evidence and each speaking literally for hours on end to their respective chiefs, Powell to Clarence Gale, Kirkpatrick to the US Attorney-General, giving their personal feelings and impressions.

'We'll bring him home by FBI plane,' decided the FBI Director, towards the end of his conversation with Powell. 'Give the media every access.'

'You sure that's a good idea, displaying him as some kind of Almighty of evil?' queried Powell.

'He's a real live Frankenstein's monster,' said Gale. 'And he's ours! The FBI got him and we're going to show everybody how goddamned good we are. And no-one's going to be allowed to forget it, ever again.'

Chapter Thirty-two

It had gone even better than Harold Taylor had anticipated; than he could have hoped. He'd awoken at dawn for the very beginning of television transmission, flicking from channel to channel to savour all that he'd caused. Three people in the public gallery had died – two men from heart attacks, a woman from fracturing an unnaturally thin skull after being knocked down and trampled in the rush to get out – and there had been at least thirty crush injuries, eighteen serious enough for hospital admission. Mr Justice Lockyer had ordered the public gallery closed for the last day of the trial.

The television also showed the prison surrounded by a crowd police estimated at three thousand and by the time Taylor left in a window-shuttered van the entire route to the court was thronged. He travelled all the way there to the sound of people calling his name – all his names – and screaming and chanting; sometimes he even heard a strange moaning he thought were mantras, although he couldn't recognize them. There were far more people around the court than at the prison and police had to form a shoulder to shoulder corridor to get the van through. Even so there was a lot of hammering on the side of the vehicle – the sound of missiles hitting it, too – and demands for him to show himself. Throughout Taylor sat smiling, satisfied, unsure at that moment how to continue the delirium, only knowing that he wanted to and would find a way.

His two prison warder escorts, both well over six feet tall, heavily built and clearly chosen for their size, sat directly opposite, unspeaking, not able to hide their apprehension. They'd stood well back from him when he entered the van and didn't come near him when he stood to get out. He chose the moment, grabbing out as the larger of the two climbed after him. The man jerked back, frantically, catching his legs against the van steps and falling prostrate in the yard. It was crowded, with other watching warders and police. None came forward to subdue him or help the man up.

Taylor said 'Just having fun' and walked, virtually unescorted, into the court basement at cell level.

Jonathan Fry, flushed and sweating in his usual haphazard uncertainty, was waiting in the cell complex, after the pre-resumption hearing with the judge in chambers. So was the instructing solicitor, Michael Joliffe. Both positioned themselves close to the cell door, as overwhelmed by nervousness as they were by inability. Idly Taylor wondered how many other people, attracted by the inevitable notoriety, he had doomed to inadequate representation by these two men.

'The judge is not just excluding the public,' the barrister announced. 'No-one who hasn't a proper purpose is being allowed in the court, either.'

'What about the media?' He could afford to relax – look forward – but there were essentials to ensure. He still hadn't decided upon his curtain call outrage. Was tempted, even to make his announcement about possession.

360

'They've a right to be there,' said Joliffe. 'They represent the public.'

'You get any steer from the judge, about the Myron Nolan defence?' Taylor demanded. It could influence – guide – how he orchestrated things in America.

'It wouldn't have been proper for His Lordship to have given any indication,' rejected Fry, formality overriding ambiguity. 'But I didn't get the impression he was sympathetic.'

Your Lord, not mine, thought Taylor. An idea began to germinate. 'What the hell *did* he say?'

'That he didn't want his court turned into a theatre.'

Taylor smiled, his decision made. It would be brilliant, like everything else he'd so far achieved. If he hadn't already decided upon possession next time it would have been difficult imagining it getting any better in the everlasting future. He was already thinking of England as a provincial run, finessing the major production for the bigger, better stage awaiting the live – how many lives? – performance on worldwide television. He was impatient to spring his final surprise. 'How long will extradition take?'

'If you're still sure you don't want to oppose the American application it's little more than a formality,' said Joliffe.

'No opposition whatsoever,' instructed Taylor. 'There's thousands of people out there in the streets. How many of them do you think believe I'm a god?'

Both men shifted with their customary indecision, neither wanting to reply. Eventually Fry said, 'I don't know.'

Taylor, the bully, said, 'What do you two think I am?'

361

Joliffe moved towards the door. Fry said, 'It's time for us to go upstairs.'

It was all remarkably quick. Straightforward. In his final address to the jury Hector McLeash contended that not just upon irrefutable scientific evidence but upon his own admission Harold Taylor, the man in the dock, had murdered Beryl Simpkins and Samuel Hargreaves and was guilty as charged.

Jonathan Fry's defence submission was that the scientific evidence upon which the prosecution relied proved the contrary: that Myron Nolan was the killer and that therefore Harold Taylor, his physical vehicle for the crimes, could not be found guilty.

'All of you believe in a God,' insisted Fry. 'I established that during jury selection. You have heard – and you must believe, because they were bound by Christian oaths – the evidence of learned churchmen and acknowledged experts on world deities that the doctrine of each and every one of you accepts the fact and the occurrence of reincarnation and possession. If that is your Church's teaching then you must find that the accused committed the terrible crimes he did, not of his own volition but at the command of a previous existence over which he had no control and could not resist.'

Mr Justice Lockyer's final guidance to the jury was more measured, every word and phrase the antithesis of the sensation they had sat through for the previous two and a half weeks.

He reviewed, point by point, all the scientific and forensic evidence, acknowledging each time that every DNA, blood group, fingerprint and handwriting sample that matched those of Myron Nolan were equally those of Harold Taylor, the accused before them in the dock.

The judge also took them, point by point, through the uncontested statement that Harold Taylor had made, admitting the killing of Beryl Simpkins and Samuel Hargreaves and what was, legally, the kidnapping of Janet and Edith Hibbs, resulting in the old lady's death.

'You have, ladies and gentlemen of the jury, witnessed in this court events unprecedented in British legal history or experience,' said Lockyer. 'I cannot – nor do I seek to – explain them. You have heard evidence from ecclesiastical and religious authorities, which I hope goes some way towards assisting you there, far more than I can. My function is to guide you on the law . . .'

He hesitated, turning briefly away from the jury to look at the barristers and then Harold Taylor. 'In this court, yesterday, we saw the inexplicable: the apparent existence of two men within a single body . . . A defence has been offered, upon that manifestation.' He hesitated again, consulting the notes before him. 'The law of this country is quite clear and quite explicit upon the guilt of murder. If there are two men at the scene of a crime and one makes no attempt or effort to prevent or dissuade the other from committing that crime, that act of murder, then each is equally guilty. If Harold Taylor is Myron Nolan and Myron Nolan is Harold Taylor – and by his own admission Harold Taylor brutally and horrifically killed two people – then the single man before you in the dock, Harold Taylor, is guilty as charged.'

It only took the jury an hour to agree.

Taylor stood, as instructed, and when asked by the judge if he had anything to say before sentence prepared himself for his final English drama.

Harold Taylor became Myron Nolan and Myron Nolan said to the jury: 'Never forget that I always

363

avenge myself upon people who harm me. And you've harmed me. You'll never know when it's going to happen but it will, I promise. I can't be sentenced to death, not here in England. But that's the sentence you've just imposed upon yourselves.'

This time four women fainted and on her way to hospital the black girl of the previous day died of a terror-induced heart attack.

It had been Cedric Solomon's intention to make the application for an extradition hearing immediately but Mr Justice Lockyer was again forced to suspend the court after imposing a mandatory life sentence because of the need for medical treatment and the scenes that followed Taylor's threat, although by comparison the mayhem was less than the previous day.

Instead, wishing to be seen to earn his brief, Solomon convened a pointless conference of the subdued, unsure Americans. It was Amy who voiced the unspoken thought of every one of them.

'We'll be marked as having harmed him, too, won't we?'

'He could live for another forty years in a Texas jail,' insisted Kirkpatrick, hopefully. 'And in all the cases we know about he hadn't started killing in his next reincarnation until he's around twenty years old.'

'So if I've died by then it'll be Beth or her kids he comes back to kill,' said Powell.

'In court he said he could possess people,' remembered Amy. 'If he did that he'd be reborn immediately.'

'Forty years at least before he dies,' repeated Kirkpatrick.

* * *

'He's a federal prisoner and it'll be an FBI plane,' declared Clarence Gale. 'So we're certainly not flying him straight to Texas, for them to get the glory for something they did damn all to achieve.'

'No,' said Mark Lipton, not sure to what he was agreeing.

'We'll bring him here, to Washington. And give the world their first chance to see him in the flesh.'

The Public Affairs director's face cleared, in understanding. 'At Dulles airport?'

'Every facility,' ordered Gale. 'Television and camera positions, the lot.' He paused. 'Obviously we can't set him up for a press conference but I think I might give one. It *was* the Bureau that got the bastard. I'm not going to let anyone forget or overlook that.'

Chapter Thirty-three

The unopposed extradition hearing *was* a formality, a rigidly structured legal quadrille with everyone dancing to a muted tune. The application was considered in camera, to prevent the reported evidence influencing any subsequent American trial, and the emptiness of the court added to the overwhelming and pervading sense of foreboding. No-one spoke without reason and those who did, did so in whispers. The judge, Sir Roger Black, was a fat, over-indulged man who normally dominated his court with a voice and personality matching his size. Now he hunched over his note ledger studiously avoiding eye contact or discussion with anyone but most of all with Taylor, who lounged even more than usual in the dock, content with – and enjoying – the effect his mere presence was creating. Without an audience he was actually uninterested in the proceedings, regarding them more than anyone else as an irritating, delaying necessity to get him to where he wanted to be next.

Cedric Solomon, with Ross Kirkpatrick acting as his junior, consciously lowered his usual sonorous tone as he outlined the facts of the American murders, in advance of calling Powell, Amy Halliday and forensic expert Barry Westmore for their supporting evidence. For little other reason than to relieve his boredom Taylor amused himself silently engendering the palpable fear, particularly during testimony, staring with fixed, unbroken intensity at every witness until finally, always despite themselves, they looked back into his blank, expressionless eyes to realize they were being put on to a vengeance register for the future. Taylor achieved his greatest disconcerting effect upon Westmore, whose scientifically tramlined mind couldn't accept what he'd seen and who, being examined himself with microscopic intensity, stumbled so badly through a lot of his forensic presentation that Ross Kirkpatrick thought some of it might have been devalued by concentrated cross-examination, which Jonathan Fry didn't attempt at all. Powell, by complete comparison, openly challenged by staring back and didn't stall, which got him put on the top of Taylor's mental list. Amy's faltering wasn't so bad – she even tried, futilely, to outstare him at first – but he undermined her in the end, watching her colour grow, from embarrassment and anger or maybe both, at the mistakes for which she had to apologize and then had to correct.

What he was never to know – but would have been delighted about if he had – was that the courtroom pressure he created caused the first ever argument between Powell and Amy.

It was at the end of the initial day, with Powell midway through his evidence, which Amy was to follow. No-one was speaking very much outside the court, either, but Amy had lapsed into complete silence during an uneaten dinner and unthinkingly, preoccupied himself, Powell asked what was bothering her.

'Jesus Christ, Wes! What the fuck do you think's bothering me!'

'It was a stupid question. I'm sorry. But it doesn't help.'

367

'What the fuck will? Tell me because I'd really like to know!' demanded Amy, attacking the only available target.

'Talking to each other,' he tried, desperately.

'Harold Taylor or Myron Nolan or whoever the hell he is isn't on trial!' she persisted. 'He never has been and never will be. Ever. It's us. You and me and everyone else. We're going to die. Whenever he chooses. And if it's not us it's going to be Beth and any other kids we have . . .' She gulped to a stop, full awareness settling. 'You know what that means! That means for us to have any kids will be like doing it knowing we're passing on some gene or medical condition that's one day going to kill them. So we shouldn't. Have kids, I mean. Can you believe that: honestly fucking well believe that! The bastard's ruined our life together, before we've even started!'

Powell hadn't considered it in those terms. Badly – stupidly again – he said, 'He won't. We won't let him.'

'Good,' she said, scornfully. 'I knew you'd work it out. So how are you going to stop him?'

'If there's a way I'll find it, I promise. Nothing's going to ruin us.'

Spacing her words, leaning towards him as intensely as Taylor had that day from the dock, Amy said: *'He can't be stopped!'* She was red faced, hardly in control.

He didn't have an argument against her but he didn't want to concede she was right, either. 'It's all happened too fast. No-one's had time properly to think. We've got to talk to psychologists and religious experts for ourselves. Try to understand it all better.'

'What's to understand! He dies, he comes back to life,

368

he kills everyone he thinks screwed him in the past. End of story. End of us.'

'Amy, give me a break! You think you're telling me anything I don't already know? Am not already terrified of? It'll end here in England soon. Just days. Then we'll all get back to America. Get Taylor back to America, where he can be locked up for the rest of his life and not do any more harm to anyone.'

'And we just wait!' she challenged. 'We move house, we going to send him change-of-address cards, make it easy for him?'

'No!' said Powell, temper finally gone. 'But if it takes something like that, we'll do it. We'll go into the Witness Protection Program. Change our names, location, Social Security, everything. We know from Durham that he has to find his victims, when he returns. We'll make it so he can't find us or our kids. Ever.'

Amy's anger stemmed, faltered. She looked at him curiously, head to one side. 'Could that work?' she asked, hopefully.

'The Bureau's keeping hundreds of people alive like that,' exaggerated Powell. 'And for us it would be easier than most. The greatest difficulty is for an already established family totally to change everything. But we're hardly established yet. We're not even married and Beth hasn't moved in with us. And she's only seen me on Saturdays and some holidays for the past three years. We were all three of us going to have to learn new lives anyway.'

Amy's face softened at last, as the idea took hold. 'It would be a way, wouldn't it?'

'I promised I'd find one. And that's only my first shot.'

'What about you and the Bureau, if that's what we've got to do?'

'What about you and the Bureau?' he asked back.

'I don't know,' she said, wearily. At once she added: 'I mean I do know, of course I do, if it comes down to the Bureau or us. About staying alive. But we can't think everything through this quickly. Whatever we do has got to be right, first time.'

'It will be,' promised Powell.

Solomon's submission that sufficient evidence had been produced for extradition to be granted took five minutes and Jonathan Fry's response, that the application was uncontested, even less. Mr Justice Black still didn't look directly at Taylor when he declared the extradition granted and hurried from the court.

Malcolm Townsend hosted the farewell party, although both the Police Commissioner and the Chief Constable made brief token appearances. There were toasts to a brilliant investigation even more brilliantly concluded from men made famous who knew their careers and promotions were assured, and promises of reunion at the Texas trial, which both Townsend and Basildon, together with their support officers, were flying to America to attend as potential witnesses. But the bonhomie was forced, like the drinking, and at one stage Basildon said quietly to Powell, 'Thank Christ he's going to end up with you. I'd be frightened to be in the same country as the bastard.'

The FBI plane was not scheduled to depart until the following afternoon. Powell had intended seeing Janet Hibbs in the morning but unexpectedly she'd accepted Townsend's invitation to the party.

Powell said, 'We had to cut a deal. The only way we

could get him back to America was on the undertaking he wouldn't be executed.'

'So I don't get to see him die,' accepted the woman. She'd maintained her recovery, looking even better than she had in court.

'There's still going to be a trial.'

Janet snorted a laugh, shaking her head. 'I've been through one of those already. There's only one thing I wanted to see happen. Now it won't. The bastard won!'

There was silence between them for several moments. Amy was across the room with Lobonski. She smiled but didn't come to join them.

Powell said, 'You're looking great.'

Janet smiled, genuinely this time. 'I got almost half a million for the house: fifty thousand more than the agents estimated. Notoriety value. Isn't that sick?'

'God knows how much sicker it's going to get before . . .'

'No,' she agreed, picking up from his pause. 'It's not going to get any better, is it?'

He took out a card and offered it to her. 'Keep in touch. Amy and I have been talking about it. Maybe we'll think of something.' She'd been a chief witness. She qualified for protection.

'I've been offered a huge amount of money, more than a million, to write a book,' Janet said. ' "I was going to marry a reincarnated monster", that sort of thing.'

'Are you going to do it?'

'Be a revenge of sorts.'

'You want revenge that much?'

'Yes,' she said, shortly, positively. There was another moment of silence. 'You frightened?'

371

'Yes. You?'

'I've got more reason than anyone to be. I've seen him in action.'

Although it was an FBI plane and the transfer between legal jurisdictions was under Bureau control it was the US Marshal's Service which officially took Harold Taylor into American custody aboard the aircraft in the private section of Heathrow airport. It was done totally unannounced, without any of the court journey hysteria. Taylor was smuggled from the still besieged prison in a closed, unmarked van initially without police escort; and when it slotted into place it was discreet, the two cars again unmarked and the solitary motorcyclist using neither siren nor flashing lights.

There were six marshals and because they were armed they did not physically disembark on to British soil. While their commander signed official acceptance of the prisoner, two more immediately hand- and ankle-cuffed Taylor, although not with the complete manacle chains which were laid out in readiness.

The aircraft was a Boeing 737, but without the conventional interior. There was a central conference area, with side desks equipped with telephones. Two held television sets. There were also five easy chairs, set against the bulkhead. The next cabin was given over to a communications centre, manned by an operator. There was a secure area at the very rear, with airline-style seats but with arm and leg mountings to which Taylor's hand- and leg-cuffs were attached. Taylor docilely allowed himself to be tethered, at once pressing the armrest button to recline his seat back as far as possible and closing his eyes: there was no useful performance to give here. Beyond the conference room and its adjoining galley and bar, to the front of the plane, were two executive office suites, also with telephones, and a final area, just before the flight deck, with three made-up bunks on each side of the bulkhead.

The rest of the Americans boarded half an hour after Taylor and his now departed English police and prison warder escort. As the agent now in official charge Powell went at once to the rear, to check upon his prisoner. Taylor kept his eyes shut, although he was obviously not asleep. The chief marshal, a former Green beret, said, 'Can't see what all the fuss is about.'

Powell said, 'I hope you don't.'

The group had spread themselves around the conference section, the largest area available, by the time Powell returned along the aircraft. The pilot came back immediately after take-off. His name was Al Jones, he was a Texan and he said at once there was a lot of bad feeling in the state that Taylor couldn't face the death penalty.

'People know about the deal before, the governor would never have got re-elected.'

'You're going to get your trial and your excitement,' promised Powell.

'He really do that stuff with his face?'

'He's a hell of an act,' said Geoffrey Sloane. Bitterly he added: 'I wasn't called. So it was a waste of time my being dragged into it.'

Everyone except the pilot knew the protest was at being identified by Taylor. The Texan promised that the bar was stocked and there were food boxes, cold meats, salad and fruit, for them to help themselves, and said, 'Think I might take a look-see in the back. You think he might do it during the flight?'

'Al,' said Sloane, the irritation obvious in his voice. 'You know what happens if he gets to know you? Thinks you're an enemy? He kills you, cuts you up, in his next life. You get to die.'

Jones smiled, although uncertainly. 'You mean it's true? You believe him?'

'We believe him,' said Powell. 'We wish we didn't.'

'Maybe I won't go back,' said the man.

'Best you don't,' said Powell. It was difficult to believe how very recently he would have been embarrassed at a conversation like this.

The forensic expert volunteered to be bar steward, serving himself a large Scotch first. The rest of the men took beer. There was hardly any conversation. Westmore kept drinking but the specially recalled Lobonski and Sloane stopped after one beer. Both settled in easy chairs, closing their eyes but not sleeping. No-one considered using the bunks. The pilot came back from time to time with flight details.

'We're going to get quite a reception,' he said, on the third visit. 'I thought we'd go into Andrews Air Force base, for security, but it's to be Dulles, for everyone to see.'

'I've been told,' said Powell.

'Director's going to be there himself.'

'I heard that, too.'

Clarence Gale was patched through when they were an hour out of Washington. Powell took the call on one of the side desk telephones.

'How's it going?' demanded the man.

Powell closed his eyes at the inanity of the question. 'How it should.'

'What's he doing?'

'Pretending to sleep, in the secure area.'

'He manacled?'

'Hand- and ankle-cuffs.'

'I want him fully manacled when he arrives.'

Powell sighed. 'OK.'

'There's going to be a press conference. I want you beside me.'

'OK,' said Powell again, careless if the contempt sounded in his voice.

'Everyone's to stay in the plane until I come aboard. Understood?'

'Understood,' said Powell. As he made his way to the rear of the aircraft Powell wondered, cynically, if Clarence Gale had allowed himself to be photographed holding the pointless conversation. When he told the marshal in command about the manacles the man said they'd intended to do it anyway.

Taylor wasn't pretending to sleep any more. He said, 'You and Amy together?'

Powell was glad he was half turned away from the man, hoping his reaction didn't show. 'No.'

'Lot of body language between you, in court.'

Powell turned to confront the man. 'All in your mind . . . whichever one you're using.'

'I'm never wrong.'

He had to turn the conversation! 'Then how come you're in chains, on your way back to life in a penitentiary? I got to keep reminding you of that?'

There was just the slightest familiar tightening around the eyes. 'You and Amy got me, didn't you? You and her, working together.'

'Which is what we do. And did. Worked together to catch you. Which was easy.'

'It won't be, next time.' Should he tell the arrogant bastard?

375

'Think about it!' demanded Powell. 'You committed suicide, as Maurice Barkworth—'

'To get back quicker,' interrupted Taylor. He would! He'd terrify the motherfucker.

'You're a failure. Always caught!'

'It doesn't *matter*! I can always come back!'

'You're twenty-five. I'm going to see to it that you're wrapped in velvet for the next forty years at least. Solitary confinement, so another Jethro Morrison can't get to you. Food tested. Doctors' checks, all the time. You're going to be the most cosseted man in the world. And when you die, years from now, it's going to be about a decade before you reincarnate. And by then I'll have seen to it that everyone you want to harm will have disappeared.'

'We'll see.'

'Forty years in a federal prison? Hell of a long time.'

'Not if I do commit suicide. And then possess next time, not wait to reincarnate. I can, you know. Possess someone. That would screw your timetable, wouldn't it?'

'Packed in velvet. Watched every minute of every day, like the freak you are.'

'Good act, Wes.'

Powell ached to get away but was determined not to give Taylor the satisfaction. 'You think I'm frightened of you?'

'I *know* you're frightened of me. You've every reason to be. You know why I wouldn't make a statement without you? Wanted to see who you were; what you were like. Always necessary for me to know the targets. I expect a lot of people who got in my way this time – people like you and Amy, everyone on this plane who

376

know I'll punish them – will go insane. Lose their minds before they lose their lives. What about that, Wes? You think you and Amy will go mad?'

'No,' said Powell, as strongly as he could. 'You're not going to send me mad.'

The pilot's landing announcement broke the confrontation. As Powell turned to leave Taylor said, 'But I do frighten you, don't I?'

Powell turned, at the door. 'You don't frighten me. It's what you are that frightens me.'

'Good!' mocked the other man. 'That was the truth. Denying you and Amy are together wasn't. It wouldn't have saved her, even if it had been.'

At the pilot's invitation Powell went on to the flight deck for the Dulles landing, astonished at the scene he could see through the window. From their approach height it appeared they were coming into the only cleared space amid a seething, ant-like mass stretching out from the perimeter, engulfing the car parks and the approach roads, a solid mass of people. There was an odd impression at the touchdown, a surge of movement – people raising their arms, beseeching, praying, kneeling, weeping – but no immediate sound above the whining engines as the aircraft taxied to where it was directed. Only when the engines were turned off could the noise of so many people be heard; it was even greater when Jones opened his flight deck window. The comparison came at once to Powell, who'd taken Ann to Niagara Falls during their honeymoon. But that was scarcely an analogy. This was a much greater, continuous sound, thousands upon thousands of voices making up a deafening, numbing roar. The entire perimeter of their parking area was ringed by three solid lines of arm-linked soldiers and

377

National Guardsmen and police and when the aircraft finally stopped those lines bulged inwards from every side as the crowd attempted to surge forward.

Powell was aware of Jones demanding permission to take off and of the control tower's reply that so many people had inundated the airport that it had already been closed to all commercial traffic and that there was insufficient runway length left for him to leave.

Incredibly the three-strand line held. A limousine, followed by two television vans, appeared along the narrow lane kept open to the terminals and control tower buildings and a set of old-fashioned, platformed disembarkation steps, not the normal Dulles elevated passenger carrier, was manoeuvred into place. The co-pilot and flight engineer swung the door inwards and the noise became even louder.

Harold Taylor appeared from the rear of the aircraft, shuffling in his ankle restraints now linked by chains to those tightly locking his hands, in turn tethered to his thick, leather and chained waistband. A marshal was attached, either side, by a further linking chain.

Too late Powell realized that Amy was sitting in the seat next to the door to the rear security area. She hurried up when Taylor emerged but stopped as the man spoke and Powell saw her already pale face blanch.

Powell pushed by the man and his guards, physically reaching out to Amy. 'What did he say?'

'That next time he's going to possess someone already living . . . that we won't escape.'

Powell couldn't think of anything to say, and before he could any words were impossible above the roar from

378

outside that filled the aircraft when the doors were opened. The space was abruptly filled by the urgent figure of Clarence Gale, swathed in the odd, almost heavenly light of the television strobe lights behind. His normally stick-thin body was bulged by a protective bulletproof vest.

The Director thrust out his hand to Powell, who automatically responded, and then gestured to the rest of the FBI personnel. He looked finally to the chain-encased Taylor, who smirked and said 'Boo!'

'You've got nothing to laugh about,' said Gale, beckoning Powell to the chained group's other side for them to emerge on the step's platform at the same time. Powell obediently slotted himself into place. He smiled ruefully at Amy, who grimaced back.

The noise reached an even more deafening crescendo as they emerged. It was impossible for them to see, because of the lights glaring up at them. They halted at Gale's arm wave, posing there. Powell wondered how five of them, three chained together, were going to be able to descend the steps without looking ridiculous.

The shots were never heard.

Powell was aware of the marshals thrusting back into him and of suddenly losing any feeling in his left arm and of the splattered wetness of Taylor's blood. One of the marshals was also hit, swinging the group around towards Powell who was suddenly confronted by Taylor's body – but that was all: most of the head upon which two faces had once appeared had gone. As he fell backwards, towards the plane, Powell saw Amy, screaming soundlessly, and she was covered with blood, too. He reached out, but couldn't get to her. He realized it wasn't an aimless scream – her mouth was forming the same word, over and over again, and then he knew what it was.

Amy was saying 'Who?' and what she was asking was who would Harold Taylor choose immediately to possess, not giving them any time, any place, to hide.

THE END

A MIND TO KILL
by Andrea Hart

She killed her husband with a knife

She was seen by sixteen people

She claims she is innocent

Jennifer adored her husband, Gerald. But one day she took a kitchen knife, went to his office and, in full view of the entire office staff, stabbed him savagely and repeatedly to death. It seems an open and shut case. Nevertheless, Jennifer insists that she is innocent of the crime – that the killing was carried out by Jane, Gerald's first wife, who died six years before.

Jennifer's bizarre defence is that at the time of the murder she was possessed by the spirit of Jane, bent on revenge. As the police and the lawyers question her, the interrogation turns into a frightening three-cornered contest – between Jennifer, her questioners, and Jane, whose turbulent presence within Jennifer's consciousness threatens her very sanity.

'The best novel on the subject of possession since *The Exorcist* . . . Frighteningly real'
The New Writer

'Brilliantly executed and quite scarey'
U Magazine

0 552 14622 6

THE COLD CALLING
by Will Kingdom

Life isn't easy for Detective Inspector Bobby Maiden. Death is even harder.

When Maiden is revived in hospital after dying in a hit and run incident, his memories are not the familiar ones of bright lights and angel voices, only of a cold, dark place he has no wish to revisit . . . ever.

But his experience means that Bobby Maiden may be the only person who can reach The Green Man, a serial murderer the police don't even know exists . . . a predator who returns to stone circles, burial mounds and ancient churches in the belief that he is defending Britain's sacred heritage.

Meanwhile, New Age journalist Grayle Underhill arrives from New York to search for her sister who's become obsessed with the arcane mysteries of the Stone Age.

The bloody trail leads to a remote village on the Welsh Border . . . and to people who know that *there are more crimes in heaven and earth* . . .

0 552 14584 X

THE SLEEPER
by Gillian White

'Peace on earth and mercy mild . . .' But there's no mercy here. There is no telling how long the body has been down in the cellar, rising as the water level rises . . .

In a wintry seaside resort an old woman goes missing from her residential hotel for the elderly, the inappropriately named Happy Haven. And in a remote farmhouse not far away, the Moon family gathers for Christmas. Clover Moon, the farmer's wife, looks forward to the forthcoming festivities with quiet desperation and dread.

What terrible secrets from the past are coming back to haunt them? As gales and blizzards cut off the power and maroon the Christmas gathering, where did the body come from which is swept into the farmhouse cellar by the rising flood water? In Gillian White's dark and disturbing world, where nothing is quite as it seems, a mystery from the past becomes a terrifying ordeal in the present, and a traditional family Christmas turns into nightmare.

'A dark, disturbing tale'
Sunday Telegraph

'A first-rate psychological thriller – perceptive, witty and full of suspense'
Good Housekeeping

0 552 14561 0

A SELECTED LIST OF FINE WRITING
AVAILABLE FROM CORGI BOOKS

14242 5	THE LEGACY	Evelyn Anthony	£5.99
14496 7	SILENCER	Campbell Armstrong	£5.99
14645 5	KINGDOM OF THE BLIND	Alan Blackwood	£5.99
09156 1	THE EXORCIST	William Peter Blatty	£5.99
14586 6	SHADOW DANCER	Tom Bradby	£5.99
13232 2	WYCLIFFE AND THE BEALES	W. J. Burley	£4.99
14264 6	WYCLIFFE AND THE DEAD FLAUTIST	W. J. Burley	£4.99
14578 5	THE MIRACLE STRAIN	Michael Cordy	£5.99
14654 4	THE HORSE WHISPERER	Nicholas Evans	£5.99
14512 2	WITHOUT CONSENT	Frances Fyfield	£5.99
14525 4	BLIND DATE	Frances Fyfield	£5.99
14225 5	BEYOND RECALL	Robert Goddard	£5.99
14597 1	CAUGHT IN THE LIGHT	Robert Goddard	£5.99
14537 8	APPLE BLOSSOM TIME	Kathryn Haig	£5.99
14622 6	A MIND TO KILL	Andrea Hart	£5.99
14686 2	CITY OF GEMS	Caroline Harvey	£5.99
14220 4	CAPEL BELLS	Joan Hessayon	£4.99
14543 2	THE COLOUR OF SIN	Janet Inglis	£5.99
14584 X	THE COLD CALLING	Will Kingdom	£5.99
14333 2	SOME OLD LOVER'S GHOST	Judith Lennox	£5.99
14599 8	FOOTPRINTS IN THE SAND	Judith Lennox	£5.99
14492 4	THE CREW	Margaret Mayhew	£5.99
14499 1	THESE FOOLISH THINGS	Imogen Parker	£5.99
08930 3	STORY OF O	Pauline Réage	£5.99
14391 X	A SIMPLE PLAN	Scott Smith	£5.99
14561 0	THE SLEEPER	Gillian White	£5.99
14563 7	UNHALLOWED GROUND	Gillian White	£5.99
14555 6	A TOUCH OF FROST	R. D. Wingfield	£5.99
14409 6	HARD FROST	R. D. Wingfield	£5.99